ANN GOERING

One Desire

MOTHERS OF GLENDALE

ISBN: 978-1-965499-37-5 - Ebook
ISBN: 978-1-965499-09-2 - Paperback
ISBN: 978-1-965499-38-2 - Audiobook

Library of Congress Control Number: 2024926296

www.coveredporchpublishing.com
www.anngoering.com

Requests for information should be addressed to:
Covered Porch Publishing, Ann Goering, PO Box 464, Branson MO 65615

Scripture quotations are taken from the New King James Version Bible. Public domain of United States of America.

Printed in the United States of America

29 28 27 26 25 A 8 7 6 5 4 3 2

*This book is dedicated to my Father, the
Giver of all good gifts and dreams;*

*My husband, who believes in me even when
I don't believe in myself;*

*And to my grandma – thank you for being my
"sign from God."*

FREE GLENDALE SERIES DISCUSSION GUIDE

There's a lot going on in these books, and we know how helpful it is to dig in a bit deeper and process them with someone.

If you're in a book club (or want to start one), the discussion guide can be used to facilitate conversation about the books.

OR--if you just want to go a bit deeper on your own, the discussion guide can help you process through what you're reading, what you can take from it, and how it applies to your own life.

Designed to feel like you're reading with a friend, the discussion guide utilizes questions, commentary, and Scripture to provide company and prompts to help you experience these stories in a deeper way.

To get your free discussion guide today, visit:

https://anngoering.com/discussion_guide_glendale_series

One

L ife had changed. Again. Her heart felt heavy, her eyes stung. She walked through the quiet rooms of her house and felt their emptiness acutely. She paused at the refrigerator and looked at the drawings that covered it, studied the photographs that lined the top. She smiled fondly at the precious faces smiling back at her. Closing her eyes, Jari Cordel let herself imagine her house full of precious little giggles and loud shrieks of laughter, just as it had been merely last week. She imagined it full of life, full of love, full of friendship . . . and mostly just full. Now, the large house felt empty.

She moved her eyes to the most recent photograph on her fridge, and a smile tugged the corners of her lips up. No matter how lonely she felt, Joe and Jessica's wedding day brought happy memories and the peace that comes from seeing the promises of God fulfilled in a loved one's life. The picture was not one of the many professional photos from the wedding that Jari had hung in the family room just the day before but a candid snapshot Joe's mother, Hannah, had shared.

After the wedding, with the setting sun behind them and the sand under their feet, Joe, in his suit, had dipped Jessi, wedding dress and all, over his knee and kissed her soundly. Their twin girls, Kelsi and Kamryn, were watching the moment transpire and were both giggling. Jari ran her fingertips over the

1

photograph impulsively, her heart swelling, then sinking, as it had so many times in the week since Joe and Jessi returned from their honeymoon to pick up the girls and move to their new home in Minnesota.

She turned swiftly, determined that she wouldn't cry again, but a sigh escaped before she could stop it. She began to move restlessly through the kitchen once more, unsure of what to do with her time.

She had never before struggled with feelings of depression as she now was. Her life could be categorized in three distinct segments—childhood, her wild years, and Jessi.

She sat down at the kitchen table and let her forehead rest against her arms, her mind racing back across the years.

Growing up in a small town in Kansas now felt as far away as an old dream; the kind you wake up from and can feel more than you can remember. In her teen years, her life had seemed almost perfect—perfectly boring, perfectly predictable, and perfectly perfect in her eyes.

Her dad owned the tire shop in town, and if you needed an oil change, new tires, new brakes, or your current tires balanced and rotated, you would undoubtedly end up at Skip's Tire Repair. Not only did he do the best work in town, he'd also owned the only tire shop within forty miles.

As a young girl, she'd spent many afternoons and Saturdays at the shop. She'd learned to love the smell of old oil and new rubber—smells that still took her back to the small garage on second street, just eight blocks away from their home on Elm. For years, she did her homework perched on a stack of new tires, watching her dad and his employees work as she tapped her forehead with her eraser in thought. She'd learned multiplication to the sudden ruckus of air compressors (which she had ceased to be startled by years earlier), the clatter of crow bars hitting the cement floor, and the high-pitched whine of an impact gun.

As she grew older, she was sent from her father's garage to her mother's flower shop. Instead of being surrounded by vehicles, tires, and loud noises, she was enveloped in the world of roses, gardenias, daisies, orchids and baby's breath every afternoon and on Saturdays from nine to five. With guidance from her mom, she was soon the fastest at wrapping a boutonniere and learned the delicate strategies of arranging a perfectly balanced bouquet of flowers. She'd helped her mother prepare the arrangements and then decorate for countless weddings. She'd taken orders and delivered bouquets for neighbors and fellow townspeople who were in love, in grieving, or in trouble.

In a small town, a flower shop was more than just a business. Sure, there were bills to be paid, but at her mother's store, a funeral was not seen simply as an opportunity to make a profit. Tears went into every arrangement as she'd watched her mother grieve for the friend who had passed away. Wedding orders didn't end the moment the last flower was delivered to the church. After the bouquets were handed out, Jari and her mom had changed into their dresses and attended the joyous event. Arrangements delivered to the hospital often resulted in a half-hour long chat with the patient and several phone calls once back at the shop to report on how they were doing. As she'd settled into her teen years, Jari thought that a small-town flower shop was exactly where she wanted to spend the rest of her life.

She'd played volleyball and cheered for the basketball team her sophomore year of high school, made straight A's, and was fully planning to marry the boy who had been asking her to be his girlfriend since the third grade. And then it happened.

She'd started hearing a whispering of rumors. Then the rumors grew. Every time someone approached her, wondering if her dad really was having an affair with Betty Wyndsor, the woman who cut his hair, she'd responded the same way—absolutely not. It was out of the question. Her father would never do that. Once, she had been so angry and tired of hearing the same ridiculous rumor, she'd struck her friend when she'd mentioned it. She had punched her right in the face. It was the only time Jari ever got sent to the principal's office.

She didn't understand why someone had started such a vicious lie about her dad—a man who had never been anything but committed to his family, a respected businessman in the community, and a good father. It didn't make any sense, and yet the rumors continued and grew even more widespread. A daddy's girl through and through, she'd rejected them vehemently, choosing to believe it was just the way of rumors—they grew and spread because of gossiping people, not because there was any truth to them. Soon, she'd thought, they would die down, and her life would go back to normal.

Still, family life grew tense, and things were strained at home. Her mother grew quiet and no longer laughed. Dark circles formed under her eyes, and they were regularly red and puffy when Jari arrived at the flower shop after school. Slowly, like a painful thorn in her skin that kept burrowing deeper and refused to be ignored, she'd began to consider the unthinkable.

She'd started to entertain the possibility that the rumors were true. Why else had her mother changed as she had? Why else had family dinners become tense and silent? Why else had her father's work seemed to suddenly double, keeping him at the shop until late at night? And yet, she'd been unable to bring herself to admit, or even truly consider, that the man she loved, admired, respected, and idolized could be doing something so horrible, so vile, so shameful. She couldn't believe that her dad would betray her mom—betray their family—like that. It didn't make any sense with who she'd known him to be. So, for a while longer, she'd closed her eyes and her ears and tried to pretend that everything was okay.

Finally, she couldn't pretend any longer. She had to know. One night, during the summer between her junior and senior year of high school, she'd snuck out of the house around ten o'clock and walked to her dad's tire shop. The lights were on inside, and she'd breathed a sigh of relief. He really was working as he had told her he was on the phone earlier. Still, she'd quietly turned her key in the lock, more certain by the moment that she was going to prove him innocent rather than guilty. She'd crept into the office, her excitement building, knowing she was going to fling open the door and find him changing a tire or perhaps under the hood of a vehicle, checking the oil. He would be surprised to see her, of course, but she would explain that she had brought his dinner down to him. Finally, her heart and mind would be at peace, knowing the rumors were just that and her father was the family man she had always known him to be.

She'd flung open the door between his office and the garage, her heart singing, and a moment later, found herself running from the shop, her hopes dashed, her heart broken, and her stomach churning. She'd stopped to throw up in some bushes and then, after spending several minutes crouched down trying to deal with what she had just seen, continued home at a slow walk, her feet dragging and her world crumbling. In that moment, she'd known that no matter what had happened in her first seventeen years of life or what happened in the next, she would never forget the look on Skip Braxon's face when she opened that door. There was no shame, no regret, no sadness. No, the expression she'd seen on her father's face spoke of only one emotion—relief.

In the days that followed, when there was no longer a secret to be kept, he'd become more brazen in his affair with Betty. When Jari got home from school one day the following week and went to the kitchen for a glass of milk, she'd noticed his favorite mug was missing from the cupboard. Running upstairs and pulling open the door to her mom and dad's closet, her worst fear was confirmed. His stuff was gone. He had packed up and moved in with Betty.

Her mother had openly begged him, weeping, to end the affair and come home to them. He'd answered with divorce papers. Her mother had yelled and wept. Though disillusioned and heartsick, Jari found herself torn between her parents. She'd begged her dad to leave Betty behind and work things out with her mom, but her pleading had been to no avail. He hadn't been interested in saving their marriage. In her grief, her mom became bitter and angry. She had nothing nice to say about the man Jari had grown up adoring, and while Jari had understood it, each bitter word felt like a knife in her heart.

As Jari had watched everything going on around her, the rage built within her until she simply couldn't do it anymore. The hometown she had always loved was suddenly too small. A month after her visit to the tire shop, she had withdrawn her life savings, left a note for her mom, and skipped town. She drove across the country to New York City, where she moved in with her cousin Nicole.

Everything she had grown up believing about her dad and her family—the very things that had always felt solid and sure—had crumbled. With her world in shambles, she'd began to question everything. As she did, she'd adjusted to city life. Breaking free of the rules, spoken or unspoken, of her family, her town, and the Midwest lifestyle she had been accustomed to, everything became permissible. She'd began modeling and lived by the philosophy that nothing was off-limits. The gigs paid well, and she had studied hard to get her GED. She'd partied her way through college, choosing pre-law as her course of study.

In a life where boys, booze, and fun never ran out, she had occasionally been taken off guard by moments of homesickness. In the midst of the chaos her life had become, sometimes she'd longed for her quiet family, the simplicity of the flower shop, the close-knit feel of her community, and the love of her parents. In those moments, she'd told herself that when things got bad enough, her dad would come to his senses, go home to her mom, and come for her. He would tell her how badly he had messed up, how sorry he was, and how they wanted her to come home so they could be a family again. Her next several years were fueled by that belief; but Skip Braxon never came.

She'd dropped out of college halfway through her junior year, deciding her time would be better spent modeling than in a classroom. Though she'd enjoyed the attention and glamour of her new profession, it quickly tarnished, and she'd soon realized she was bored. She'd always been a straight A student, and she'd needed a career that provided an intellectual challenge. When the man she had been living with announced he was getting transferred to Washington, D.C., she had been happy to move with him, ready for a change. Deciding to go back to school to finish her degree, she'd left modeling behind and sought work that would look better on her applications for law school. Her boyfriend knew someone who knew someone, and she'd found herself hired by the office of Senator William Cordel.

For as long as she lived, she would never forget the moment she met Bill Cordel, the senator from Virginia. He'd been handsome and distinguished, self-assured and commanding. He was a man who held a lot of power, and she'd felt the enormity of it as he studied her the first morning she had been sent into his office with a stack of folders to deliver. His gaze had been approving, and although he'd said nothing to her as he was on the telephone, he'd smiled and nodded his thanks.

Despite the fact that he was nearly twice her age, she became infatuated with her influential and charismatic boss. When he walked into the room, people paid attention. When he spoke, people listened. He was charming and a smooth-talker, and she found herself frequently pleading silently for him to glance her way, just waiting for him to speak to her.

She'd started leaving another button on her blouse undone and wearing bright high heels that drew the eye down her long legs. She had known he was married, but she had been convinced he was unhappy in his marriage and told herself she would be the heroine that came to his rescue. Knowing she was beautiful and having learned enough during her modeling career to know how to dress to please the eye, she'd played to her strengths to get him to notice her.

As it turned out, attracting the attention of Bill Cordel had been even easier than she expected, and it quickly escalated to a full-blown affair. Those early days were filled with passion, and he had been consumed by his desire for her. She'd known at the time that he was cheating on his wife to be with her while she, in fact, was still living with her boyfriend, who had known nothing of Bill. But none of that had mattered.

The first time Bill lied to his wife and stole Jari away for a romantic weekend in Paris, she had felt a sense of power she had never known. As she watched Bill sleeping beside her in their luxurious French hotel, she'd realized that even if she and her mother had not been enough to keep Skip Braxon from abandoning them to move in with his hairdresser, she had bewitched Bill Cordel heart and soul. After feeling positively helpless as a teen as she watched her family crumble, she'd reveled in how powerful she felt when she realized Bill Cordel would do anything she asked. She was in control, and that gave her a sense of security. After all those years, she had proof that she was indeed loveable, worth fighting for, and enough. Bill was a hundred times more important than Skip Braxon would ever be, and she had enjoyed having him wrapped around her finger. Still, for a reason she could not fully comprehend, her tears wet the pillow that morning.

By the time she finally agreed, Bill had been asking her for weeks to move in with him. She'd hesitated only because it felt good to be the one being begged. It felt good to be wanted so intensely. When he'd kicked his family out of his Washington, D.C. home, and she'd told her stunned boyfriend there was someone else and she was leaving, she'd felt a sense of accomplishment. In some way, she'd felt vindicated. Though she had been the victim, now she was finally the one who was winning.

Overnight, she'd gone from working to put herself through school while living in a mediocre apartment and eating ramen, to living in a gorgeous house in McLean with a swimming pool in the backyard, house staff, and credit cards without limits.

Bill had come from old money, which had helped him land his role as a senator to begin with, and what he'd called his paltry congressional compensation was merely a bonus. With more income rolling in from what he'd made off interest each year than his salary, his work as a senator hadn't been about the money; it had been about prestige and power. His lifestyle reflected his bank account, and Jari hadn't complained. For weeks and even several months, she'd reveled in her luxurious accommodations, the ease and glamour of her new life, and the affection of the man who was as infatuated with her as she was with him.

Of course, the media was ruthless during that time, exposing the affair, criticizing Bill, and bringing all her skeletons out of the closet. Photos taken during her modeling career were posted everywhere, and there were rumors that Bill could be removed from office. It made for some dark moments, but overall, they had been too happy together to be worried much by the media.

As is often the case, the talk about them eventually quieted down, and they became old news. Bill maintained his office, and she'd enjoyed days at the spa, shopping sprees, and being the object of a powerful man's devout affection.

Seven months after their affair had started, and five months after she had moved in with him, Bill asked her to marry him. She'd felt like the luckiest girl in the world. Though she had known his request was motivated partly by the fact that marriage looked better and steadier to constituents than their current arrangement, she'd also known he was in love with her and was determined to make her his for the long haul. He was worried she would tire of him and move on to someone who wasn't nearly two decades older; marriage was his attempt to make things permanent. Little did he know, he needn't have worried.

He was handsome, rich, esteemed, and powerful, and she had become thoroughly enamored. Her life in their D.C. mansion had been a far cry from her childhood in Kansas, and she had never felt prouder of how far she'd come. She'd been only twenty-five, yet she'd managed to escape Kansas, her blue-collar roots, and her broken family, and now lived the kind of life she'd only seen in the movies growing up. She had left a voicemail for her mom, letting her know she was getting married, but hadn't bothered to tell her dad. She hadn't talked to him or gone back home since she left town and walked out of her parents' lives such a long time ago, nor did she plan to.

Then, she'd met a Jewish man who changed her life completely.

In the most random of meetings, a petite elderly woman approached Jari in an upscale department store and had spoken to her about secret thoughts and events that Jari had never shared with another human being, let alone this woman she had never met. Stunned, embarrassed, and confused, Jari pulled her from the main aisle and asked how she had known about the things she spoke of. The woman responded that Jesus knew everything and sometimes, to get someone's attention, He shared some of those things with someone who knew Him.

She asked Jari to have a cup of coffee with her. Worried the woman would leak the secret she had used to get her attention—the secret Jari didn't even want to remember, much less have all over the news—she had agreed. She had been curious to know more about how the woman had known what she did, and over a latte, the woman with kind blue eyes and more wrinkles than Jari could count, shared Jesus with her. She'd told her of His holiness and how He desires holiness in His followers. She'd told Jari that God cannot be in the same place as sin and how that separated mankind, the object of his holy affection, from Him. She'd shared how He had sent His only son, Jesus, to die on the cross to pay the debt for all mankind. She'd said imperfect people could be reconciled to a perfect God because Jesus took on the burden of sin and death, then rose from the dead three days later, defeating Satan and evil once and for all. She'd told Jari of how Jesus ascended into heaven to sit at the right hand of the Father, where He intercedes for, and acts as, the Defender of His people when they're accused by the enemy, reminding the Father of His sacrifice that makes a way for every person to draw near, should they confess their sin and believe that He is the Christ.

The lady's testimony had been simple, yet the message was so compelling that Jari had found herself wanting to believe, wanting to be able to count herself among this Man's followers. Unexplainably, it stirred her heart like nothing else had. Yet she'd known deep down that it didn't matter if she wanted to be or not, she could never be a follower of Jesus. The woman had told her how God detests sin and desires holiness, and underneath all the fun she'd had and pride she felt, she'd known the lifestyle she had been living was very wrong. She'd known it all along. Even the wild and unprincipled life she had lived after leaving Kansas did not compare to what she had done with Bill. She had seduced him, then convinced him to cheat on his wife and leave his family for her. While she had embraced the power, pleasure, and victory, that day, hearing the woman tell her about the holiness of God, she had come face to face with her own sin. In the most painfully honest moment of her life, she'd realized she had fallen even lower than her father.

Yet the elderly woman across from her spoke of forgiveness, of what could be hers if she just said yes to Jesus. Jari stopped her, shaking her head. "You don't know who I am or what I've done. I don't think His offer extends to me."

The old woman's eyes had twinkled, and she'd reached across and grasped Jari's hand with surprising force. "I know exactly who you are and what you've done. I do watch the news every now and again. And honey, His offer of forgiveness was made just for you. He knows the worst of what you've done, thought, and said, and He looks at you and says, 'I have chosen her out of the crowd, and I want her. I choose her.'" Again, Jari shook her head. She'd known it couldn't be true. Why would God choose her? It made no sense. She was a small town nobody who had been living a big lie for years.

Still, that woman had not given up. After going home and being persistently pursued by the memory of that conversation and the longing it had created in her heart, Jari phoned the woman, Ruth, and had her come over to tell her more about what she'd called the Good News. After several more cups of coffee over which Ruth would tell her more about Jesus, read the Word with her, and answer her questions, Jari had accepted Jesus. Despite how shameful, selfish, and wrong she had been, she'd offered that if He wanted her, she would live her life for Him.

That same day, she'd told Bill that either they needed to speed up their engagement and get married, or she was moving out. Though he'd scoffed at her new faith and tried to get her to reconsider, he hadn't called her bluff. He had shared the news of their engagement with his daughter, and Jari had pulled together a quick wedding and honeymoon.

Getting married had fixed the uncomfortable conflict between her new faith and their living situation, but Jari had still been plagued by sorrow over what she had done. Even in her immaturity in the faith, and all of her weakness, brokenness, and confusion about how to move forward, she'd pleaded with her new God to fix the family she had broken, to undo the harm she had done. That was her first glimpse of how quickly God sometimes answers prayers.

By early summer, Jari and Bill's relationship began cooling down, and his career had reassumed the position of his highest priority. With a ring on her finger, the thrill of the chase was over, and the weekend trips to Paris, Ireland, or San Francisco were happening less and less frequently. He slowly began to speak to her as he did others. A bite crept into his voice more often than it had in the beginning, and the belittling began. She had seen him treat others in the same manner but hadn't thought much of it, as he had never taken that tone with her. With that changing, it became a daily battle to keep her own tongue under control.

What was worse than anything she experienced within their own relationship, though, was the way Bill treated his ex-wife and even his daughter, Jessica. He had been rude, intimidating and controlling, and Jari found herself worrying that one day he might treat her as he did them. Before the wedding, he had always stepped out of the room to call his family. As time went on, he stopped making an effort to call in private, and Jari had heard the way he talked to them. However, despite his tone and sometimes belittling words, Jari knew he still loved her and she loved him. While she had enjoyed the intrigue, power, and money, it was the man she had fallen in love with. She really had married him for him. Though he had some rough edges, she was certain they would be able to work things out.

When he'd decided Jessica should come live with them in D.C., which was met with considerable resistance from the teenager, Jari had found herself in over her head. Oftentimes, she'd wanted to leave and to get far away from the conflict, the fights, the stress. Instead, she'd pored over the Word of God, searching for answers and right reactions in the words found in the thick book Ruth had given her. Her new friend came over weekly, listened to Jari vent and gently taught, corrected, and encouraged her.

On the first day of July, Bill and Jari picked Jessica up from the airport. The teen had been furious with them, but what had hurt Jari the most was the dull, lifeless look in Jessica's eyes.

Realizing how very much alike she and Jessi really were—and knowing she was at least partly to blame for her pain—Jari had reached out to her, drawing on her own very similar experience in an attempt to help the teen. Despite all odds, a friendship began to grow, and Jari had found herself frequently caught in the crossfire between Bill and his daughter. Knowing how to stand up for Jessi and for what was right without disrespecting or dishonoring her husband had been a battle that nearly defeated her. She'd found herself driven to the Word and daily time with Jesus more and more, needing it desperately just to keep her head above water.

When Jessica had announced she was pregnant, everything grew more intense. Jari's relationship with Jessi strengthened as Jari drew alongside her to celebrate life and encourage Jessi not to do the very thing Jari regretted most in her entire life. It was the one thing she had never told another human being about, not even Jessi, but that the old woman in the department store had known. It became her single-minded mission to keep Jessi from having an abortion.

She'd known the pain and emptiness that one act had brought her, pain that still often gripped her heart in the secret place of three in the morning. Knowing the guilt that still filled her, she'd wanted to spare her stepdaughter from the same heartache.

With Jessica's announcement of her pregnancy, the fighting between Bill and Jessi had escalated. His arrows became more direct, constant, and painful. During that same season, Jari humbly had the honor of leading Jessica to Jesus, and they'd explored their new faith together. Still, the war going on within their house had continued to escalate until one fateful night when Bill drove home from work in a rainstorm and an accident ensued, which had taken the life of a young mother-to-be.

In that one night, everything in their home had changed. Bill had come to know the LORD and remarkable peace followed. Still, the media stayed like bulldogs after the accident. It had been a dark time for the whole family, brightened only by the birth of Jessica's twin girls, Kelsi and Kamryn.

Finally, healing began to come for all of them and that season passed too. For the next several years, Bill had wrestled with a lot of things in his work that the changes in his personal life brought up—priorities and convictions, morals and standards, and knowing how to move forward. All of his wrestling resulted in some big adjustments in his career. Jari had stayed with him every step of the way, proud of his transformation and the things he now stood for. Meanwhile, she'd spent her days with Jessi and the girls, helping however she could.

She'd watched the girls while Jessica attended college, then while she began her career. Jari had the girls for weeks, sometimes even a month at a time, when Jessica was sent to one disaster scene or another with her job, and Jari had enjoyed every moment of it. She'd loved filling the bottles, changing the diapers, watching the girls learn to crawl, walk, and run, loved the afternoon trips to the park, the spring visits to the capitol building to walk through the cherry blossoms, the magical feel of Christmas with little ones. While she knew they weren't, in so many ways, the girls had come to feel like they were hers.

And as much as she loved them, they were not the only ones she had grown attached to. Over the years, she easily came to think of Jessica as her best friend. Only nine years apart in age, Jessica had begun to feel like the little sister Jari never had. They shopped, went out for dinner, saw movies, went to the ballet, learned to cook, and spent their days—all together. They'd talked on the phone and texted many times throughout the day whenever they were apart, shared in each other's joys and sorrows, and thoroughly lived life together. She had helped Jessi through her heartbreak when she first came back to D.C., watched Joe's college football games right alongside her, and rooted for the young couple every step of the way as they fell in love all over again over the past six months. She had always been Team Joe and was relieved when they had finally pushed past all the challenges to get married. It's what Jari had wanted and prayed for, for years.

But now Jessica and the girls were gone. Jari sighed again, tears stinging her eyes.

Jari never once wished things had gone or ended differently. Joe and Jessi were made for each other. They needed to get married. They loved each other in a way that was beautiful and deep. The girls needed their father. And Jessi and the girls needed to be where Joe was. So, Jari had helped Jessica plan her wedding, pack her apartment, and prepare to move to Minnesota.

She was so happy for them all—she really, truly was—but what Jari didn't know and couldn't understand was where did all of it leave her?

Two

"You'll be home for dinner tonight, right, Bill?" Jari squeezed her eyes shut and chided herself for the pleading way she had asked the question. She knew Bill would be home for dinner if he could be. She knew it was a busy time for him at work. They had been through election years before, and they would get through this one. The only difference was that last time Jari had other people to spend her extra time with. In the past, whenever Bill was busy at work and Jari was feeling lonely, she could always hang out with Jessi, Kelsi, and Kamryn. But not this year. And the loneliness was becoming overwhelming.

It was quiet on the other end of the line for a heartbeat too long, and she knew he knew it hadn't been a good day.

"What would you say about me taking you out to dinner tonight? It's been a long day on the Senate floor, and I have some things I really need to get ironed out with Ryan. But if you want to meet me for dinner somewhere close by, I'll come back and finish later." He was trying, and that fact alone made Jari thankful. Unfortunately, an evening alone was no more appealing than eating dinner alone. She contemplated her options for a few seconds and decided she would take advantage of time with her husband, no matter how it came.

"That sounds nice. I'll come to your office around six, and we can grab a quick bite to eat together. Does that sound okay?" She could hear a commotion in the background.

"I'll expect you then. I have to go, honey. See you soon." There was a click, and Bill was gone. She hung up the phone, and the silence settled again.

Alone with her thoughts, her mind drifted back to her mother. Was this how she felt after Jari left? Before the affair, Mary Braxon had a full house and a happy life with her husband and daughter. Her days were busy at the flower shop, and her afternoons and evenings had been full of Jari's activities, dinner with her family, and normal family tasks like laundry, restocking the refrigerator, and keeping the cookie jar full. After everything had happened, she was left alone in a house that held so many memories. To Jari's knowledge, she still lived there.

She had not been back to Kansas, nor had she seen either of her parents since she left town. She talked to her mom on the phone for five minutes once every few years but had always politely declined her requests to come see her. Going back home simply felt too hard. Now Jari wondered if her mom still lived in her childhood home or if she had moved. She had never mentioned moving, but then again, they didn't talk frequently or for any great length of time. If her mom had moved, Jari wouldn't blame her. From personal experience, she knew that having an empty house that was once full felt worse than having one that had always been empty.

Jari headed upstairs to change and get ready to meet Bill for dinner, but as she did, she couldn't stop thinking about her mom. Was it still hard for her to be alone? Did it get any easier over the years? Had she gotten used to it? As lonely as Jari felt, she still had a husband that came home at the end of each day—more than her mother had been left with. She could not imagine being completely and utterly alone.

A thought that had been coming to mind off and on for the last several years came again. She needed to go home. She needed to face her past and her parents. Yet so many years had gone by, and so much had happened. After all the water under the bridge, she didn't know how she could.

She had shut her parents out of her life. Her dad, she reasoned, had deserved it, but what had her mom ever done to warrant being cut off from her only daughter? The affair hadn't been her fault or her decision. Yet, to Jari's seventeen-year-old mind, the emotions had been so big and so strong that it felt easier to simply reject them altogether. She could cope if she could simply ignore it had ever happened. Talking to her mom—or anyone from home—brought it all back up to the surface. She hadn't wanted to wade through the pain, so she had simply avoided the issue—and all those who reminded her of it. Later on, she wished she hadn't. She wished she had a relationship with her mom and the close-knit extended family she'd grown up with. But after being gone for so long, how did one make amends?

Thoughts of going back to Kansas and feeling reluctant to do so always brought up guilt. She had worked so tirelessly for reconciliation in the Cordel family, yet she had not pursued reconciliation in her own. It made no sense, yet she continued to stay away.

At first, the feelings were too deep, too painful to go back. To help someone else heal seemed much easier than going through the healing process herself. And then, even when there was healing in her heart, it just felt like too much time had passed. Things were so different. Where would she even start? She hadn't been home for nearly fifteen years. The thought of going home and facing her parents—even just her mom—seemed too big, too overwhelming.

So she told herself she would figure out how to go home later, maybe next fall, winter, spring or summer, once Jessi was out of college, the girls started preschool, Jessi's wedding was over, or—most recently—once the election was over. And in the meantime, she continued to let year after year slip away. With the passing of time, it never felt easier. Instead, her guilt grew, and she became fearful that something might happen to one of them and she would never be able to make things right. Yet, she continued to tell herself she would go home . . . later.

She changed her clothes and went in to touch up her makeup, momentarily distracted as her excitement grew at the thought of the mid-week date with her husband. She leaned forward toward the mirror to pat powder over her face, and she noticed a gray hair in the swoop of her bangs.

"Not today," she moaned, leaning forward to inspect it more closely. It was certainly there, and it was certainly gray. She made a face as she leaned back, tempted to pull it out, but knowing she couldn't do that every time she found a gray. There were surely only going to be more of them in the coming years. Instead, she pinned her bangs back in a way that not only looked trendy but also hid the silver strand.

Ruefully, she wondered if she would soon need to start dying her hair if she wanted to stay blonde. The very thought made her sad. She had always been proud of her naturally blonde hair, taking great joy in the fact that her golden-white tresses were real instead of fake. When she was little, her mom used to say her hair was the color of pure, Kansas corn silk. She had always liked that. "All things must come to an end," she told herself sadly, picking up her eyeliner.

As she finished applying her makeup, she thought grudgingly that she was far too young for gray hair. At least she felt too young. At thirty-two, it was to be expected that a few would begin to pop up once in a while in other people's hair, but she couldn't come to terms with the fact that it was happening to her.

Thirty-two. She remembered thinking anyone over thirty was old. She remembered her own mother's thirtieth birthday, and all the over-the-hill jokes the birthday guests had made. And here she was: thirty-two.

The worst part of thinking about her age was remembering that her reproductive clock was ticking. She didn't have many years left to have children before having a healthy pregnancy became a real concern. Not that it mattered, anyway. Bill already had a daughter—a grown daughter and granddaughters too. Though they had never discussed the subject in earnest, she knew he didn't want more children.

Determined to kick the melancholy mood, Jari pulled out her favorite pair of black heels and slipped them on with her dark jeans. Maybe her beloved heels would elicit happy feelings. She added silver hoop earrings and slipped a silver bracelet around her slender wrist before heading downstairs.

In the garage, she paused. She looked from the SUV that Bill had gotten to be her daily driver to the little red sports car he had bought her before they were married. She didn't drive it often, but it always made her happy whenever she did. She changed course, deciding to take it instead.

Driving down the streets of Washington, D.C. with her windows down and the radio on, she began to find the peace she had become accustomed to over the past few years, despite the traffic. She reminded herself that this season of loneliness would pass, and a new door of opportunity would open. She found relief in the fact that there was a plan for her entire life, and her purpose had not been exhausted by the time she was thirty-two. There was more still ahead, and perhaps the best was yet to come. She reminded herself of truth in faith, as she knew it to be true, even if she could not yet see it.

It was just going to take time.

She had started working in Bill's office shortly after arriving in D.C. Between work, college classes, and her boyfriend, she hadn't had much time for anything else. Then, once she added Bill into the mix, she had been busier than ever. After their affair was out in the open and she moved in with him, Bill thought it best to separate work and their personal life, so she had quit her job. No longer seeing the need for a college degree, she had embraced her new lifestyle, and spent her days shopping, redecorating, going to the spa, and visiting the country club. She made friends and had a buzzing social life. Seven months later, she became a Christian, and the glamorous life of pleasure that she was living began to chafe. She needed a change—a purpose for living.

It was around that time that Jessi came, and Jari had thrown herself wholeheartedly into helping the teen. Preoccupied with homeschooling and doctor's appointments, she no longer had much time for her friends—and part of her was glad, because they no longer had much in common. Once the girls came, helping with their care kept her even busier, and she began to find her purpose in them. She still occasionally went out for coffee, spent a day at the spa, or played tennis at the country club, but most of her time was spent with Jessi and the girls. Now that they were gone, she was rattling. And while she knew it wouldn't last, she also knew she was going to have to figure out who she was without them.

Finding a parking place outside the Russell Building where Bill's office was proved to be a challenge, despite the fact that it was after five o'clock. Bill wasn't the only person holding an office that was in the election year crunch, and he certainly wasn't the only one working late. With over thirty senators and several committees based out of the prestigious building that sat adjacent to the capitol, Supreme Court, and Library of Congress, the place was still humming with activity.

Though she had seen it countless times, Jari still took a moment to admire the Vermont marble columns as well as the ornate ceiling adorned with classical motifs and highlighted with gold leaf as she entered the building and crossed through the rotunda. Though not as large or elaborate as the capitol building or the Library of Congress, it was still a beautiful space, and she never tired of the beaux arts-style architecture.

When she stepped off the elevator and made her way to Bill's office suite, she found that the place was buzzing with activity as employees finished their work for the day and prepped for Bill's morning in the senate. Jari knew a few of them were likely still working on the details for the big campaign tour she and Bill would embark upon to Richmond and Norfolk in just a few days. The receptionist glanced up to see who had entered and smiled at Jari. "He's expecting you, Mrs. Cordel. You can go on back to his office, or you can have a seat, and I'll let him know you're here."

"I'll just go back," Jari told her, pausing to ask about her grandchildren before making her way back to Bill's office.

After the changes in their lives following Bill's accident, Bill had decided that as a way to honor Jari and protect their marriage, he would choose the women who were employed in his office more carefully and with different priorities in mind. He had honored his word, and Jari appreciated that he was careful not to jeopardize their relationship by carelessly entertaining temptation. He had also found that hiring secretaries based on their capabilities alone had brought wisdom, experience, and a sense of calm to his office. That had proved invaluable, and Jari was intentional to stay connected with and show her appreciation to not only them, but everyone who worked on her husband's team—both in D.C., and in his Richmond office. She knew firsthand that he was not a one-man team. He needed help. He couldn't do what he did alone. And she was grateful for those who served at his side and supported him in his mission.

After waving at Bill's right-hand man, Ryan, Jari gave a quiet knock as she entered Bill's office. He glanced up for just a moment before turning his attention back to the laptop in front of him. "Hi, honey. Give me just a minute to finish this."

She nodded and moved quietly around the room, looking at the awards and photographs that hung on his walls, as well as studying the paintings she had helped pick out. They had hired an interior decorator just the year before, giving his unwelcoming space a makeover, as he frequently held meetings in his office. Jari was pleased with the results. The furniture was plush and comfortable, while still being professional. His desk and bookcases were a rich mahogany; the marble fireplace was a stunning focal point, and the rug on the floor was warm and rich. In all, the office gave testament to the importance and position of its occupant, while keeping it simple—a motto Bill was attempting to incorporate into his life and career.

"Okay, sorry about that, Jari. Are you ready for dinner? Did you have any thoughts about where you want to eat?"

She turned to face him, receiving his light kiss. "It's beautiful out. Let's walk somewhere."

He nodded. "I know just the place." She fell into step beside him as they left his office.

"How was your day?" he asked as they watched the floors change at the top of the elevator.

"It was fine. A little difficult, but it's still just a process of adjusting," she answered truthfully, while keeping her tone light. He reached for her hand as they left the building.

"It will come, Jari. Jessica's move has been a big change for us all. It will take a while to get used to it." His voice was gentle, and she appreciated that he had left his work at his office and was focusing on their personal life—on her.

"I know. It's just hard, Bill. When you're at work, I'm home all by myself. There's no one to do things with anymore or spend my time with. There's no one to take care of."

"You can take care of me," he offered with a smile.

She hit his arm gently. "You aren't five."

"I know you miss the girls. Their move has left a hole. But honey, you have lots of friends," he pointed out as they waited for a stoplight to turn so they could cross the street. "I'm sure any one of them would love to spend a day with you."

She nodded. "I know, Bill. I do have a lot of friends. I should be thankful . . . they're just . . ." Jari let her sentence dangle.

"They're not Jessica?"

Jari nodded, yet knew the loneliness she felt went deeper than missing her stepdaughter. "It just doesn't feel like there's anything to look forward to anymore," she told him honestly, watching his face for his reaction. He took her comment in stride and reached down for her hand.

"What if we go on a trip once the election is over? We can go anywhere you want—just you and me. It would be a chance to get away from the cold, the pressure, and the busyness. I think by then we will both need a vacation. Jessica said they're going to Glendale for Thanksgiving, so we can go over the holiday. What do you say?"

Her face brightened with a smile at the idea. "We could go to the Caribbean and relax on the white sand beaches," she agreed, feeling her hopes lift. Their visit to Aruba for Jessi's wedding hadn't felt nearly long enough, and she would relish a chance to go back to the island just the two of them. "Or we could go to Europe and go on that castle tour I was telling you about the other night."

Bill gave a quick nod. "Wherever you want to go is fine with me. You plan the vacation and after the election is over, I'll whisk you away. We'll do whatever you have scheduled."

He opened the door to a Thai restaurant, and she was met by the welcome aroma of one of her favorite kinds of food. A mix of hot pepper and peanut scents filled the air. She sent her husband a bright smile, appreciating his thoughtfulness. He moved his hand to the small of her back, lightly pushing her toward the counter, encouraging her to order first. Once they ordered, they sat at a table outside and watched people milling around the downtown area.

They talked about the Senate calendar, proposed legislation, the upcoming election, and went over their schedule for the campaign tour. Bill updated her on the latest happenings in the political world, and they discussed the stance he should take on a dozen bills he would soon face. They talked about his work and how much longer he would have to stay at the office.

Finished with her dinner, Jari set her chin on her fist, her elbow on the table, and listened to her husband talk, interjecting when needed. She was genuinely interested in his career and the potential political changes that could affect the people of America, yet her mind felt divided. Half of her focus was on what he was saying, the rest on juggling troubling thoughts that refused to be pushed aside.

Bill took a break, scooping the rest of his dinner onto his fork, then chewing quietly as if lost in thought. Unable to keep her feelings to herself any longer, Jari opened her mouth to speak. As she did, unaware of her struggle, Bill checked his watch and stood. "If I'm going to make it home by ten, I'd better get back to the office."

Jari shut her mouth quickly, deciding it wasn't the time to share, and stood as well. Sending a silent prayer of thanks up to heaven for keeping her from talking to Bill about such an important subject at the wrong moment, she followed him out of the patio area and fell into step beside him on the sidewalk. Looking up into his handsome face, she could tell he was already focused on what he still had to do at the office. Feeling alone once again, she slipped her hand into his, wanting to hold on to him for just a little bit longer. They walked in silence, both lost in their own thoughts.

Jari turned her attention to the people walking around them on the busy D.C. sidewalks. The temperature was perfect, having left behind the slight chill of spring but not yet yielding to the oppressive heat of summer. The sky was fading to a dusty blue, a sure sign that dusk would be upon them shortly. Still, the sidewalks were full and busy. Jari smiled. She enjoyed living in the city.

Arriving back at his office building, Bill turned toward her fully and smiled at her, drawing her gently into his arms. "Thank you for coming to have dinner with me."

She wrapped her arms around him and hugged him softly, thankful for the chance to hold him and be held by him. "You're welcome. I enjoyed the chance to actually have dinner with my husband."

He chuckled at her gentle tease and pushed a piece of blonde hair behind her ear. "This hectic schedule will pass. It won't be long, and I'll be home for dinner every night again."

"When did that happen? I don't seem to remember a time when you were home for dinner every night."

He pinched her softly in the ribs, making her jump. "You know what I mean. I'll at least be home for dinner more often than not," he said with an amused smile.

She tipped her head back, looking up into Bill's blue eyes. "I look forward to that day."

He gave her a light kiss and pushed her toward her car. "I'd better get back up there so I can come home at a decent hour. Have a good evening, honey. I'll be home as soon as I can."

Knowing he was right, Jari gave a little wave as she climbed into her red car and then watched him round the corner to the building's front door. On the thirty-minute drive home, she reflected on the words she had almost spoken to him at dinner and was ashamed. This was not the time to talk to her husband about the longings that consumed her thoughts. It was a busy time in his career, and he had no extra time or energy to think about something that would change their entire lives. If something had to be put on hold, it had to be the dream that had taken root in her heart.

Three

J ari stood beside Bill, smiling out at the large crowd as he delivered his speech in Richmond. She watched the reactions on the faces of his supporters, watched as their expressions changed from understanding to agreement to hope to admiration. She felt a surge of pride in her husband, as she was once again impressed by his simple eloquence, fierce conviction, and unyielding commitment to stand for truth. It had not always been that way, and she was thankful she could be proud of what he now stood for. "He's a good man," she told herself, the supportive smile never leaving her face as she stood a step behind him.

In the audience, a movement caught her eye. A young mother was holding a sleeping infant as she sat listening to Bill's speech. The baby shifted positions in his sleep, and the mother settled him in her arms, bouncing him softly to soothe him. Jari could see the little one's face as he slept and felt warmth spreading through her as peace settled over his features. She studied the tiny nose, the chubby cheeks, and the dark eyelashes visible even from her place on the stage. She watched how he nestled into his mother in his sleep and how the mother cradled him gently; her hold speaking of the great love she felt for the infant.

As Bill's passion and volume rose as he approached the climax of his speech, several supporters broke into spontaneous applause, and the baby woke. He began to fuss as he buried his face into his mother's chest, and the father turned to help the mother cover herself and the child with a blanket. The little one fell silent as he nursed.

With the baby covered and Jari refocusing her attention on Bill, a great longing swept over her. Before she could stop them, tears stung her eyes. Blinking them back, her smile still instinctively in place, she took a deep, calming breath. "Jesus," she whispered softly, knowing He knew every word she didn't dare express.

Taking a deep breath and pulling her shoulders back, she pushed the thoughts and feelings away. She focused back in on what Bill was saying and was careful to keep her mind on his speech until the very last word. The audience erupted into applause, and he nodded his head to them and raised his hand in silent recognition of their approval. As the leader of the rally stepped forward to introduce the next speaker, Bill took Jari by the elbow and helped her down the stairs of the stage to their seats. The applause followed them. The next speaker made a wisecrack about not being excited to follow a speech like Bill's. Jari was sympathetic—her husband was an excellent public speaker. She wouldn't want to deliver a speech after him, either.

Once they were seated, Jari leaned lightly against Bill's shoulder and smiled up at him. "You were great!" she whispered. He shot her a grateful smile and a nod in response. She knew that after all his years in politics, he was confident in his public speaking skills, but, even still, encouragement was always appreciated. She looped her arm through his and sat comfortably, listening to the motivating speeches that followed.

After the rally was over, she stood at Bill's side, used to the routine, and shook hands, greeted supporters, made small talk, and answered questions. They mingled through the crowd, and she stayed right with him, joyfully playing the role of supportive wife.

Her heart jumped as she saw the young couple headed their way, the husband intentionally making a path through the crowd for his wife and baby.

Jari didn't hide the joy she felt when the husband gave her a respectful nod and approached Bill, while the wife stopped in front of her. "I saw this little one from the stage," Jari told the mother, holding out her finger for the baby to grasp. "What a handsome little man." The young mother beamed with pride.

"Our sitter had something come up at the last minute, and when we had to bring him, I honestly didn't know how he would do. I think he did okay, though. I hope he didn't distract you."

"Not at all. He was absolutely perfect," Jari told her with an assuring smile. "What's his name? How old is he?"

"Gracin—Gracin Matthew, after his daddy. And he was three months old last week."

"Gracin? What a neat name. Well, Gracin, you were certainly a very good boy today." Jari smiled down at the infant and then up at his mother, contemplating how to steer the conversation since the men were still deep in one of their own. Before she could say anything, though, a smile brightened the face of the woman in front of her as she glanced at Bill.

"Matthew is probably one of your husband's biggest fans. I think he feels like they have a lot in common. When he was majoring in political science, his priorities were quite different than they are now. After he graduated, we met, got married, and started a family. After that, well, he came to realize what was truly important in life—your family, your faith, your convictions. He's a city administrator right now, but I think he longs to be in D.C. someday."

"What about you? Is that your dream, too?" Jari asked gently, sensing hesitancy in the woman's statement.

"Yes. Well, what I want is to be wherever Matthew is. My place is with him, so his dreams are my dreams. But sometimes I wonder . . . do you ever feel forgotten? I want him to accomplish everything he dreams of, but I also want a husband who's present. I want Gracin to know his father." The woman shook her head. "I'm sorry if that's not a fair question."

"No, it's perfectly alright. And that's a very realistic concern. To answer your question, yes, sometimes it's lonely, especially during an election year. There are a lot of long hours between the office, the Senate, and the campaign trail. I have to fill my time with other things and other people. However, there are also times that he is home for dinner almost every night, and he has days off so we can spend quality time together. You have to keep perspective and remember that there are seasons to life . . . otherwise, the schedule could be too much."

The woman nodded and held out her hand with a bright smile. "I'm Jenna."

Jari shook her hand warmly. "It's a pleasure to meet you, Jenna. I'm Jari. Listen, if you end up in Washington, D.C., let me know. Maybe I can help with the transition."

Jenna smiled. "I'll do that. Thank you."

Beside them, the men were saying goodbye and shaking hands. Jari softly squeezed little Gracin's fingers and smiled at Jenna before they moved on. "It was nice to meet you."

~~~~~

"I saw you talking to that woman with the baby tonight."

The hotel room was dark, and Jari startled at Bill's quiet comment. She had thought he was asleep. She was now glad the darkness kept him from seeing the tears that wet her pillow. "Jenna. They seem like a nice young couple. It sounds like her husband is interested in getting into national politics. She said she thinks he dreams of being in Washington," Jari answered, her voice smooth and quiet, without a trace of her tears.

"I saw the way you looked at their baby." She could tell Bill was attempting to be gentle, but if there was one thing her husband was, it was blunt.

She bit her lip, trying to decide how to answer. Finally, she took a deep breath, knowing what she would say. She had told herself she wouldn't – not yet, not until the election was over—but he had walked right into it.

"I want children, Bill." Silence settled over the room for several long moments.

Finally, Bill cleared his throat, and she could hear him rubbing his hand back and forth over his chin as he often did when uncomfortable. His answer was simple, his tone flat. "I know."

She waited for him to say more. When he didn't, she prompted him as gently as she could. "Penny for your thoughts?"

"I'll be fifty-two next March, Jari."

"I know that."

"At the youngest, I would be seventy when our child was eighteen. Seventy!"

"Yes."

"I have grandchildren that would be older than my own child."

"It's true, it would be an unusual situation in some respects," Jari conceded slowly, trying to keep the desperation out of her voice as she continued. "But Bill, I didn't already have a family. I want to have children of my own! I want to have children together—with you. Sometimes, I feel like a late addition to your life . . . and I get it, I do, but I don't want it to be like that forever. I want to build a life *together*. I want to be like a normal couple. I want to see both of us in our child's face. I know you already had a baby and have watched her grow up, get married, and have children of her own, but I haven't, and I want that. I've spent years telling myself that it's okay; that it was just a childhood dream and that I don't really need children of my own. And maybe I don't; but Bill, I *want* them. I want them so much that it hurts."

"Honey," he breathed, his sigh deep. She chose to assume his sigh was not out of annoyance but out of deep turmoil, no matter how it may have sounded. She continued to convince herself of that while she waited for him to continue. "I know you want that. I've known for a while." Silence stretched for several moments. "And I'm sorry." She waited for him to say more, but he didn't.

"So, that's it? The case is closed? Your veto is final? You're sorry?" Jari asked, fighting to keep bitterness out of her voice and heart. How could he so easily dismiss a longing that seemed to consume her? There was another deep sigh from the darkness beside her.

"We never talked about it. I always thought we were on the same page. Lately I've realized we aren't, but . . . " his voice trailed off.

"But what?" she asked, trying to stay calm.

"I want to run for president one day. Not very long from now. In another six years it will be a presidential election year, and Jari, it sure feels like it might be the right time. This country needs leadership, and I don't know if I would even make it past primaries, but I want to try."

"I've wondered," she admitted quietly. She had often thought he may be thinking of such things, but he had never vocalized it before. She found herself wondering what they had spent their last six years of marriage talking about since they clearly hadn't talked about having children or Bill's vocational goals.

When he didn't go on, she pushed. "That means we can't have children? Lots of presidents have children, Bill."

"I'm going to be very busy. At this point, I don't think either of us even knows the meaning of the word yet. We would be traveling a lot. You know the strain of work and the campaign trail now . . . then think of that on a national level. That's hardly the place for a small child."

"I could stay home with the children," she offered quickly.

"I'll need you beside me." Jari pushed down her desire to scream at him, her frustration continuing to build. She wanted to ask if there was room for her dreams, too, alongside all of his, but she kept her mouth shut, knowing doing so could escalate the conversation to a disagreement and that would get them nowhere. "Besides, Jari, if I'm successful in my pursuit, do you know what children become when you're the president of the country?"

"What?" she challenged, already bristling at whatever he was about to say.

"Pawns. Bargaining chips. I couldn't live with myself if I put my own child in that kind of danger."

"There have been a lot of presidents, and I've not heard of their children being taken from them. Maybe there have been attempts, I'm not sure, but I don't recall hearing of any that were successful."

"There would be secret service around all the time. What kind of a life is that for a child, Jari?"

"Bill, becoming the president of the United States is a dream—it's not even a reality yet. It's not even something that we seriously have to consider. Being the president is a maybe six years down the road. Having a baby could be a reality right now!"

"It's my vocational dream, Jari—what the last thirty-plus years of my life have been leading up to. I will go after it." Bill's voice was hard, his mind made up, clearly frustrated with her.

"What of my dream, Bill?" Jari demanded, raising her voice, unable to keep the question in. "Why can you have yours, but I must deny mine?"

Again, silence stretched, and Jari wanted to reach over and shake her husband, forcing him to answer.

"I had a vasectomy. Fifteen years ago. Jessi was a little girl, and Carla and I decided we were absolutely done. We only ever wanted one child but gave ourselves time should we change our minds. We didn't. So, I went in and had the procedure to make sure we wouldn't have a surprise. Don't you see, Jari? It's not even that I don't want to give you what you want," Bill's voice, which had been so hard and final just a moment before, now shook and was full of emotion. "It's that I can't."

The hopes and dreams Jari had allowed herself to entertain more and more in the past few weeks were crushed in an instant. She didn't know what to say or do. Her chest seemed incapable of allowing any air into her lungs. She felt like her husband had just thrown her to the ground, knocking the wind out of her. Tears stung her eyes and rolled down the sides of her face to rewet her pillow.

"Jari?" Bill asked, his voice unsure and full of questions.

"I wish I'd never said anything," she admitted dully, her heart hammering, the shock immobilizing. "It was better to hope and dream than to know . . . to know you made a decision fifteen years ago that would affect our entire lives and that you made that choice with another woman."

"I'm sorry." He sounded utterly broken, and for the first time in years, her strong husband began to cry.

Compassion edged out bitterness and anger. "I know," she said softly, turning to him and wrapping him in her arms. Holding one another, their tears mixed and together, they wept.

Four

For the next several days, Jari plastered a happy smile on her face and listened to speeches, shook hands, and made small talk. She talked politics, campaign strategy and speech details with Bill. She talked to Jessi on the phone and read a book she had brought along. And yet, inside, she felt dull, lifeless, and alone. The hope of one day having a child of her own had sustained her when her home seemed vast and empty, and her husband seemed absent even when he was sitting right next to her.

"God, why?" she whispered into the quiet emptiness within her. "Why does it have to be like this?" There was no answer. It felt as if everyone, even her God, who had been an ever-constant companion over the past several years, was far from her. She glanced at Bill, who was riding in the back seat beside her. He was reading something on his laptop, seemingly not even aware that she was in the car with him. She felt completely and utterly alone. It was almost too much to bear, and she pressed her hand to her chest, pushing back against the ache.

"I will never leave you nor forsake you," she whispered to herself, reminding her heart of Truth. She knew faith was believing in what you did not see or feel, and she would cling to faith. With a new determination to hold fast to what she knew was true and right, she pulled out her sleek, worn Bible and opened it to familiar pages.

She let the words wash over her heart and mind and sink into her aching brokenness.

"Make my desires Your desires, Father. Make me long for the things You long for. Let me be about Your business," she prayed, feeling a familiar hope spread through her. The despair might come back in an hour; but for now, she believed in a greater plan, a greater Planner, and His perfect ways. And if the despair did return in an hour, she would come back to the Word, reminding herself once again.

Hour by hour, day by day, she did just that for the next two weeks. Feeling nothing, she pressed on, confident that whether she felt anything or not, this would be where hope was restored. An overwhelming sense of loneliness was broken by little moments of peace, and she clung fiercely to those moments. Despite how aimless she felt with her season shifting, she forced herself to rest in the knowledge that God still had something purposeful for her in the days ahead.

~~~~~

Bill folded his newspaper and laid it aside. He took a bite of his English muffin and then finished his yogurt before taking a drink of orange juice. Setting his glass down, he broke the comfortable silence that had settled over their breakfast table.

Outside, the sun was shining brightly, and the water sparkled as a gentle breeze created little ripples over the surface of the swimming pool. Jari planned to spend an hour sun tanning and reading after breakfast.

"I'm going to the doctor this afternoon," Bill announced.

Jari looked at him, startled by his firm announcement. He had just gone in for his yearly check-up no more than two months before. "Are you feeling okay?" she questioned, concerned.

Bill cleared his throat and set his forearms on the table. "I've been doing some research, Jari."

"On what?"

"Men who have had a vasectomy can have another operation to reverse it. It's certainly not a guarantee. There's a good chance that we'll still never be able to have a child," he paused and rubbed his chin.

Stunned, Jari stared at him. "But there's a chance?" Hope sprung into her heart.

"I'm not saying that I want to have a baby," he warned. "At my age, I'm better suited to be a grandfather." Her hope dissipated into confusion, not understanding what he was saying or where he was going with the conversation. He plowed ahead before she could ask questions. "But I figure that if I reverse it, then we'll just leave it up to the wisdom of God. Like I said, there's still a good likelihood that you'll never get pregnant; but maybe, if it's the will of God, maybe you will. We'll deal with that possibility if it happens," He finished, finally looking less firm and more unsure. "What do you think?"

Jari came out of her seat like a Jack-in-the-box and ran around the table to her husband, throwing her arms around his neck. "Bill! I love that idea." She drew back to look into his face. "Thank you!"

"Remember that it's not a sure thing," he warned, even as his handsome face softened into a warm smile. He drew her down onto his lap and held her for several long moments, resting his head against hers. "But even if it amounts to nothing, I'm going to enjoy this hope and excitement I see in your face. I've missed my vibrant wife. You've been listless since Jessica's wedding."

"I know. I'm sorry," she answered, knowing what he said was true.

"Don't be sorry! You gave up so much for them . . . invested so much. It's understandable that it's taking some time to adjust. If anyone should be sorry, it's me . . . for expecting so much and giving so little. You poured everything into helping my daughter. So now, if you want children of your own, even if I'm not so sure about it . . . well, I'd do just about anything to replace the hope that has faded in your eyes."

His loving words were like a balm to her tattered heart. For him to recognize her effort with Jessi and the girls, to validate her current struggle, and to put her desires above his own, meant so much to her. She leaned in and kissed him softly. "Thank you, Bill. Truly. Thank you for that . . . for all of it."

He kissed her again and then held her for several moments longer. As they sat there, her thoughts whirled, wondering about the research, the process, and the timeline. Finally, needing answers, she drew back slightly and looked at him. "So, you're going to talk to your doctor today, find out more, and maybe schedule the surgery? What kind of questions do you have for him?"

"The surgery is scheduled. I'm having it tomorrow at one in the afternoon. I'm going to the doctor today to have bloodwork drawn."

"Tomorrow?" Jari echoed, shocked. "When did you start planning this?"

"I called and made the initial appointment the day after we got home from our campaign trip," he answered gruffly. "They had an opening for tomorrow, and we're staying in the city for the next two weeks, so it's the perfect time. Besides, having surgery on a Friday allows me the weekend to heal before having to get back into the office. I would like it if you would come with me tomorrow."

"Absolutely," she quickly agreed, overjoyed at the thought of having Bill home from Friday until Monday. She was bursting with excitement at what this surgery meant, both for the possibility of having a child and for the chance to have a whole weekend of quality time with her husband in the midst of a very demanding campaign year.

"Good." He kissed her lightly on the lips, then checked the time. "I have to get into the office. I'm not sure when I'll be home. I will likely need to stay late."

Jari nodded as she stood. "That's fine. Stay as long as you need to. I'll wait up for you."

He left the table, and she followed him into the connecting great room where he picked up his briefcase. He gave her another kiss and walked out the door to get in the car that was waiting for him outside. She leaned against the open front door, watching him make his way down the walk. "Bill?" He turned to look at her before sliding into the car. "I love you," she told him, biting her lip and feeling the sting of tears in her eyes. "And thank you."

"I love you, too, honey. I really do," he answered. When she gave him a small smile and waved, he slid into the backseat of the car with his briefcase. Jari turned back into the house, her heart singing.

Regardless of whether or not they had a baby, her husband was putting her hopes and dreams above his own insecurities and preferences and was willing to try. She was more thankful for that than she could express and felt deeply loved by him. Hurrying back to the kitchen, she grabbed her phone and searched the internet for information about vasectomy reversals. She researched the risks, success rates, and recovery times. Finally, when she had her basic questions answered, she grabbed her book and a towel and headed outside, humming a joyful tune. Walking out into the warm sunshine, she stopped for a long moment to let the heat soak into her skin as she tipped her face up to the sun.

"LORD, You know how much I want a child of my own, but I want what you want more. Thank You for moving Bill's heart to even be open to the possibility. We both want Your will in our lives, so whatever that is, we will trust You. Either way, my soul will be satisfied in You and You alone, Father," she said into the hot mid-June air.

Jari crossed the stone patio to her favorite lounge chair and drug it to face the sun before kicking off her sandals and sitting down. Her mind raced over their breakfast conversation, about what it meant for Bill, about what it meant for her, about the possibilities it held. She made a plan for the weekend and a quick list on her phone of things she needed to pick up. Then she opened her book and started to read while letting the sun bronze her skin and the warmth soak into her bones.

~~~~~

"Are you ready for this?" Jari asked, standing beside Bill's hospital bed. Even though it was for a good cause and optional rather than necessary, seeing her strong, commanding husband lying on a hospital bed dressed in a gown, awaiting surgery and completely at the mercy of the doctors, was frightening.

He reached for her hand and wove his fingers between hers. His gaze was intense. "Since the moment I met you, you have supported me in my career, doing whatever you could to help me succeed. You do the same for everyone around you. It's who you are, Jari. You do whatever you can to help people achieve their dreams. Well, I want you to have your dreams, too, honey. At least a chance at them."

His words were like a blanket of love that settled over her. "Thank you," she whispered, squeezing his hand.

"It's time, Mr. Cordel," the nurse at his shoulder said, having completed her preparations. She stood poised to wheel him away to surgery.

Jari shifted her eyes back to Bill's face and squeezed his hand again. "I'm going to be in the waiting room. I'll be in to see you as soon as you get out of surgery." He nodded. His eyes were locked on her face, as if trying to memorize everything about her, and she bent down to press a kiss against his lips, feeling a surge of fear shoot through her. She pushed aside the what ifs for the time being, determined to hide her fear. "I love you."

"I love you, too," he answered, his voice gruff.

Jari watched as the nurse wheeled him out of the room. When he was out of sight, she made her way to the sitting area where she had been instructed to wait. Taking a seat in a section where she could be by herself, she fought the fear that was rapidly spreading through her. Her hands began to feel clammy. Sometimes even routine surgeries went terribly wrong. And what if things were different? Their age difference of nineteen years had never been an issue before, at least not in her eyes. But she allowed herself to imagine, just for a moment, what it would be like to be sitting in the waiting room if the reason were different. It was not unheard of for men his age to have serious health complications.

She was still in her prime and that all seemed distant, but at fifty-one, Bill was well into middle age. What if he was in the hospital for a serious condition, rather than the hope of having children?

But he wasn't. She reminded herself that it was simply an outpatient, elective surgery, and that there was no reason to worry. With more empathy, she glanced around at others sitting around the tense, quiet waiting area. There were small clusters of people sprinkled throughout the room who talked quietly amongst themselves, and Jari assumed they were families waiting for a loved one. Just five chairs to her right was a lone lady whose white hair and lined face suggested she was easily approaching eighty. Slow, quiet tears were slipping down her wrinkled cheeks unchecked.

Jari stood, taking her purse, and crossed the distance between them. "Is this seat taken?" she asked. The woman glanced at the chair next to her and shook her head. "Would you mind if I sat down? I noticed you're here by yourself, too, and . . . well, sometimes it's nice not to wait alone."

A glimmer of a smile crossed the woman's lips, and she nodded. "Please."

As Jari sat down, she was struck by how much the lady beside her reminded her of the dear woman who had led her to Christ and mentored her through her early years of being a Christian. Ruth had gone home to be with the LORD nearly two years earlier, and Jari still missed her. She felt the familiar longing for her friend and mentor rise up in her heart, and she remembered sitting at her funeral, tears of sorrow, grief, and loss running off her cheeks. Even as she had cried, though, her heart had constantly reminded her that Ruth was home at last, and that she had been both ready and eager to go—to meet the Man she had loved so greatly, face to face.

The sweet memories fading, Jari turned to the woman beside her. "I'm Jari. I'm waiting for my husband Bill to get out of surgery."

Another flicker of a smile. "I know who you are. I recognized you the moment you walked into the room. I saw your husband speak at a charity event a few months back. You were there too." Jari dipped her head, humbled once again that someone she had never met knew who she was. "I'm Agnes. I'm waiting for my husband, Rodney."

"How long have you been married?" Jari asked gently.

"Just three years," Agnes said faintly, and Jari tried to cover her surprise. "Oh, I know. At my age, you were expecting me to say sixty years or something of the sort, weren't you?"

"Marriage can be a beautiful thing, no matter if it's been long or short," Jari offered.

Agnes nodded. "My first husband, Tom, and I were married for forty-seven years. When he died of lung cancer twelve years ago, I thought I would never remarry—that I could never love again. But then, there was Rodney. I was living in an active seniors' community and had my group of girlfriends—other widows like me—that I had learned to enjoy life with; but there was this man who insisted on scraping my windshield when it snowed and came over every Tuesday to carry my trash out for me. He fixed things in my home when they needed fixing, brought me my favorite coffee, and delivered meals when I was feeling poorly.

"As guilty as it makes me feel to say this, in many ways, he spoils me more than Tom ever did. He is a charmer through and through. When he asked me to marry him, I found myself saying yes before I had time to talk myself out of it. We have enjoyed three wonderful years of companionship, traveling, and sharing in each other's lives. He's good with my children and grandchildren, and I adore his only son and his family."

Agnes blinked back tears and continued. Jari let her, having no desire to interrupt. The woman's story was a welcome distraction. "Rodney is addicted to adventure and loves to travel . . . even in his old age," Agnes added with a watery wink. "I'd never left the state before I married him, but his enthusiasm and insatiable thirst to go to new places turned me into quite the world traveler too," Agnes declared proudly. "The first year we were married, we spent a month in Greece. The next year was six weeks in Spain. Last year, we spent a month traveling through Europe by train. We got to see most of the cities you hear about over there—Amsterdam, London, Dublin, Vienna, Frankfurt, Paris, Zurich . . ." Agnes trailed off, obviously enjoying the memories each town brought up.

"Where are you off to this year?" Jari asked gently.

"We just returned from Africa last week. We went on a safari. We saw lions, elephants, and giraffes, all in their natural habit. One night, we slept in a native hut, complete with a straw roof, hammocks, and mosquito nets. We watched native dancers and listened to the music they played on their drums. We shopped in outdoor markets and saw women carry pots of water on their heads. It makes you think twice about taking a long shower, that's for sure . . . and it gave me a new appreciation for going to the sink and filling up an entire glass with clean water that I could selfishly drink myself," Agnes rattled on. Jari noticed the woman's hands were trembling, and she couldn't blame her. Waiting was hard.

"It sounds like quite a trip," Jari responded with a smile.

"It was. It was the trip of a lifetime," Agnes agreed softly. "We did things I never imagined I could do . . . or would want to do, but I did, and it was remarkable. Rodney was so excited to go. He said that was the one trip he wanted to take before he died . . . and now..." A tear slipped down Agnes' cheek, and she lifted her weathered hands off her lap, then let them fall, a sorrowful acknowledgement of what her husband might be facing.

"What's he here for?" Jari asked, reaching out to hold Agnes' weathered hand in her smooth one.

"I came home from water aerobics this morning and found him on the ground in our living room, writhing in pain. He was able to let me know that it was abdominal and that it was extreme. Other than that, I don't know what's wrong with him. I tried to get him up and couldn't, so I called the ambulance. Once we got here, he was rushed back, and I've been sitting here, waiting for some kind of word, ever since." Agnes' lips trembled. "His son lives in Florida but caught a flight up as soon as I called him. He should be here in a couple of hours. Hopefully, I'll have something more to tell him by then."

"Well, we'll wait together," Jari told her firmly, keeping a tight hold of the older woman's hand. She knew what it felt like to be all alone.

"I know you have a reputation for being something of a praying lady," Agnes said, her blue eyes bright. "If that's one of those rumors that is actually true, Rodney and I would sure appreciate your prayers today."

"Oh, trust me, the LORD has already been hearing about Rodney from me," Jari answered firmly, squeezing Agnes' hand warmly.

Together, they waited for news of their husbands, hoping and praying that, when it came, the news would be good.

~~~~~

Not more than two hours after Bill was taken into surgery, the doctor approached Jari and let her know that the surgery had gone well, and Bill was in recovery. Faced with the dilemma of whether to go to Bill as she had promised or stay and wait with her new friend, Jari asked if Bill was awake. When the doctor said he wasn't yet, but should be waking up within the next twenty minutes, she decided to stay just a little longer.

Agnes had heard from her stepson a few minutes earlier. He had landed at the airport in D.C. and would catch a cab as soon as he could find his way out of the airport. He should be at the hospital within the hour. Jari wanted to stay with the woman until she heard news of her husband or until family arrived to wait with her.

When a doctor in scrubs, with his face mask pulled down around his neck, approached the nurse's desk to ask the whereabouts of a waiting family member, the nurse gestured to Agnes and Jari. Jari heard her new friend inhale sharply. Her knobby knuckles went white from grasping Jari's hand as the doctor made his way across the room to them.

Jari tried to decipher the look on his face, but could not read him at all. His young face was hard, but she wasn't sure if it was because he was the bearer of bad news or if he was simply a hard, firm, fast-paced man.

"Mrs. Tundril?" he asked, directing his question at Agnes.

She nodded and rose with quiet dignity, releasing Jari's hand to do so. Agnes' clasped her hands in front of her and straightened her back, seemingly prepared to take whatever news the doctor was about to tell her. Jari stood as well, bracing for the worst, wishing Rodney's son had already arrived from the airport to hear the news with Agnes. She knew that the woman beside her was wishing for that as well. She laid her hand on Agnes' arm to let her know she was there for support.

"Mrs. Tundril, has your husband been out of the country recently?" the doctor asked, his face still unreadable.

"Why yes, we just returned from Africa last week," Agnes answered, obviously caught off guard by the question.

"That makes more sense, then. I wish we had asked you that two hours ago."

"Is my husband alive?" Agnes asked, her voice trembling.

"He's a very sick man, but yes, he's alive. We've been a bit perplexed. We thought he had an intestinal blockage and were ready to operate, but we could not find the site of the blockage.

We've since discovered that your husband has a very bad case of intestinal parasites that have been wreaking havoc on his digestive system. He likely picked them up from consuming food prepared in unsanitary conditions during your travels. We have him on medication, and as long as we can get rid of the parasites before they deplete your husband of all his strength, he should make it."

Agnes sank down in her chair, clearly overwhelmed with relief. "So, he's going to be okay?" she asked as if she could hardly believe it.

"I'm not making any promises, but if his body responds well to the medication and he works hard to regain his health, I don't see any reason why Mr. Tundril won't make a full recovery."

"Thank the Lord," Agnes breathed, her hand flying to her heart.

"However, I want you to listen to me, Mrs. Tundril. You say you were traveling with your husband?" He waited for her nod. "I would strongly recommend that you get into your doctor and get checked for parasites as well. If you have any, you want to get them stopped before they can do the damage to you that they've done to your husband." Agnes nodded again, absentmindedly. It was clear that she wasn't in a place mentally to worry about her own well-being. "We're moving your husband to recovery. I can have a nurse take you to him."

"Yes, please," Agnes said, standing again. As an afterthought, she turned back to Jari and caught her hand. "Thank you for waiting with me!"

"You are very welcome. I'm so happy it was good news, Agnes!" Jari told her, beaming.

There was a new light in Agnes' eyes. "Me too, dear. Me too."

"Go see your husband," Jari said with a big smile and a gentle push. Agnes looked at her for a moment longer, then nodded and hurried away to join the nurse who would take her to Rodney.

After watching Agnes hurry down the hallway to her husband, Jari collected her purse, and made her way down a different hall to Bill's room. Knocking softly, Jari entered the quiet hospital room she had been directed to. He was awake but blinking heavily, the effects of the anesthesia still evident.

"Hey there, handsome," Jari said softly, grateful that the surgery had gone well, and that her sturdy, commanding husband was still strong and healthy.

"Hey," he answered, his speech thick. "Have you talked to the doctor?"

"Yes. He said the surgery went very well." Jari perched on the side of Bill's bed and took his hand in both of hers. Bill nodded. "I think we're here a little longer while you recover, and then, as long as you're doing well, I can take you home."

Bill nodded again. "Home would be good."

A wave of tenderness swept over her as she realized once again that he had endured all this—gone through surgery—just for her. Jari leaned down and kissed him gently on the lips, then on the cheek. "I love you, William Cordel."

"Love you," he answered, his words slurring and his eyelids growing heavy.

Drawing back, Jari ran her fingertips down the side of his face. "Sleep now, love. We'll talk more when you wake up."

Five

J ari woke to find sunlight streaming through the windows, casting rectangles of golden light across the carpet of her bedroom. She turned her head and found that Bill was still lying beside her. Panic flooded her, thinking he had overslept. Even on Saturdays, he was always up and on his stationary bike well before the sun shone into their bedroom windows. Calm returned, though, as she remembered his surgery from the day before. He was home for the day. They would be spending the entire weekend together. No catching up on things at the office, golf, events, or social activities for him this weekend. She couldn't remember the last time that had happened.

"Good morning," she told him, noticing that he was awake.

"Good morning," he answered. Turning over, she snuggled up to him and put her arm across his chest.

"How are you feeling?"

"Sore," he answered with a wince.

"That's understandable." There were several moments of silence.

"If we do have a baby someday, would you want a boy or a girl?" Bill asked, surprising her with his thoughtful question. "Mind you, I'm not saying I want one or that we should seriously try. I'm just asking if we had one, what would you want?"

Jari felt okay with what he'd said. He still had reservations, and she could understand that. She appreciated, in the midst of them, his willingness to be open to whatever the LORD had for them. "It doesn't matter to me. I would be happy with either."

"Well, I think . . . if it ever did happen, I think it would be nice to have a boy. I've never had a son."

Jari smiled, her heart warming. "I think a boy would be nice too."

"Do you think he would get made fun of for having such an old dad?" Bill sounded worried and unsure, and it surprised her. He rarely was either. She took a while to collect her thoughts and formulate an answer.

"I think he will love you and be proud to have you as his father. He will grow up with a truthful, faithful, deeply convicted dad who is committed to change and to doing the right thing, and that's more important than how many candles there are on your birthday cake. I think he will know that too."

Bill put his arm around her, hugging her in silent thanks. He stayed quiet, and when she glanced up to check his expression, found that he looked lost in thought.

"Do you think I screwed up with Jessica?" he finally asked.

Again, Jari took several moments to answer. "I think God's grace is very great, and I think Jessi is a wonderful young woman with a great dad whom she's proud of. I think you can be proud of that and proud of her."

"I am proud of her. Very proud. Sometimes I wonder, though, if Carla and I hadn't been such a mess, how things would have been different for her. I wonder if she wouldn't have had to suffer so much."

"God works all things to the good of those who love Him," Jari reminded gently, and Bill grunted.

"I've wondered how it would affect her if we had a baby," Bill admitted after a minute. "Would she be jealous? Grossed out? Offended? Would she feel replaced, or like she wasn't enough? I've hurt her so much already. I don't want to continue to do so."

"I've wondered how she would react too," Jari admitted. "But Jessi is a mature young woman who loves us both. I think she knows that I want children, and I'd like to think she might even want that for me. I think at first it will be a little strange, and it will definitely be an adjustment, but I think in time she'll be happy for us."

Bill nodded. "So do I. I wonder what the girls would think."

"They love babies, so I don't think they would object in the least."

Bill chuckled. "You're probably right."

"We'll just have to be very intentional about being there for the three of them, even from afar. And you'll have to continue being intentional about being a good dad to Jessi and grandpa to Kelsi and Kamryn, even while having a little one of your own. It could be difficult sometimes to be daddy and grandpa, but I think if you're aware and intentional, all parties involved will feel loved and important."

"Jari . . . I wasn't a good dad when Jessi was young. What if I'm not again? What if I'm just not any good at it?" He sounded scared.

Jari mulled over his question. "You're not the same man that you were then."

He grunted his agreement. "I still work a lot. I'm still not great at sharing what I'm feeling, or being empathetic, and you know as well as I do that patience is not one of my strengths."

"Hey, you're working on all that, and you've come a long way," she argued, sticking up for him. "And you are a wonderful grandpa to Kelsi and Kamryn. They adore you! I have no doubt our child would as well."

"That's because I sneak them candy when you aren't looking."

She smiled. "Oh, I see it. You're not pulling anything over on me."

Bill smiled and was quiet for a long while. "We're talking as if we were actually going to have a baby," he finally observed. "We need to remember that there's only a chance, not a guarantee."

Jari's smile was bright. "But a better chance than there was yesterday."

He smiled faintly, and they were both quiet for several more minutes, lost in thought. Finally, Bill sat up. "I think I'm ready for some of those waffles you promised me last night."

Jari smiled. "Me, too. Come on, I'll make you some."

Bill sat on the couch, propped up with pillows, reading the morning paper, while Jari nearly danced around the kitchen, mixing up waffle batter and thinking about what it would be like to have a son or daughter. When breakfast was ready, Jari sat with Bill in the great room to eat.

Once finished, Bill leaned out to set his empty plate on the coffee table. Jari noticed that his efforts elicited a sharp intake of breath and a wince of pain. After he settled back into the couch, he nodded at her with a smile. "That was a good breakfast. Thank you. It hit the spot."

"You're welcome," she answered, finishing her own waffle and setting her plate carefully in her lap. "What would you like to do next?"

Bill leaned his head back on his pillows and turned to look at her. "Did you have something in mind?"

He knew her well. "You could finish reading your papers out by the pool," she answered, her face hopeful. "It's beautiful out, and you might enjoy the chance to spend a few hours in the sun."

"I don't know about hours," Bill answered with a wry smile. "You forget that I wear a suit and tie every day. I'd rather not add a sunburn to my other ailments. But sitting in the sun for a little while sounds nice."

"Alright. Fair enough. I'll take our dishes out to the kitchen and then come back to help you up."

Coming back into the room, Jari watched him collect the three different newspapers he had spread out on the couch beside him and sent him an amused smile. "You know, most people read the news on their devices these days, honey. It's not the 1900s anymore. It would be a lot simpler—for you—if you made the switch."

"I like the feel of holding a physical copy in my hands, you know that," he said, wincing as he stood. "Besides, I thought you were supposed to be convincing me that I'm young this weekend, not reminding me that I'm old," he told her, tipping a rueful smile up at her.

She laughed. "My apologies."

Jari walked slowly with him out the patio doors to the far side of the pool. She brought a lawn chair and positioned it to face the sun, helping him sit down as gently as possible. Still, after he sat and swung his legs up, he let out a long sigh as he settled back, finally relaxing his jaw.

"Still sore?" she questioned, knowing the answer. Bill grunted. "Would you like some ice?"

The look he shot her suggested he wasn't amused by her offer. "I'll pass," he responded dryly. Jari laughed and handed him his newspapers, freeing her hands to help him pull his white t-shirt over his head. She dropped it by his chair and turned.

"I'm going to get my suit on, grab my book and some water, and I'll be back. Want me to get anything for you?"

"My sunglasses?"

She nodded and returned ten minutes later with the promised items. Settling in the chair beside her husband, she opened her book. An hour later, they made their way back into the house. She left Bill on the couch to rest while she showered and made lunch. After she brought their lunch in on a tray, she turned on the movie of his choosing, and they spent the afternoon watching movies together and relaxing.

Late in the afternoon, Jari glanced up and noticed Bill was napping. She spent several moments studying his face, and then snuggled up closer, being careful not to wake him. Having a relaxing Saturday with her husband was an unusual occurrence, and she wasn't complaining. Though she felt bad that he was in pain, she was thoroughly enjoying their uninterrupted time together. Her thoughts drifting, she started to wonder what it would be like if they were simply resting together while their baby was napping upstairs—or if she were pregnant. Glancing up to make sure he was still sleeping, she moved carefully to pull her shirt over the throw pillow she had been hugging against her. Gazing down at the bump it made under her clothes, she tried to imagine what it would be like to be pregnant.

Her thoughts returning to his questions from earlier, she wondered what it would be like to have a child together. Would it be a boy or a girl? Would it look like her or Bill? Would she be a good mom? She had learned a lot about taking care of babies when the girls were little, but that had been several years back, and she wondered if it would be different when it was her own. She wondered if Bill would be around to help with diapers, feedings, and sleeping. She was guessing he hadn't been when Jessi was little, nor had he helped with that sort of thing with the girls. But Jari wouldn't have the support that Jessica had, and she would need him to lend a hand. She wondered if he would be willing to do so.

Looking up at him again, she watched him sleep. Her husband was very good at rising to the occasion. He loved her. And he had been intentional about correcting past wrongs and being there for the people in his life over the past several years. She anticipated that she would see more of the same should they have a baby. He would have a second chance at fatherhood, and she didn't think her husband would miss the opportunity to do better. Pulling the pillow out from under her shirt, she smiled and set it aside. Feeling happy, she pressed a kiss against Bill's shoulder and snuggled in closer, thankful to be married to such a good—if still imperfect—man. She directed her attention back to the movie.

The next morning, they elected to stay home from church and watch the service online, rather than going and facing the questions that Bill's stiff movements would undoubtedly bring. The dream of having children was too precious to Jari and too uncertain to share with anyone just yet, even her church family. Bill was content with resting on the couch, knowing his crazy schedule was less than twenty-four hours away.

With bowls of cereal and cups of coffee, Bill and Jari sat side by side on the couch and watched the church service. Bill thumbed through his Bible to follow the pastor's sermon. Jari sat with her notebook open on her lap, taking notes and writing down key phrases she wanted to remember.

She thought of Jessica and wondered what church they had visited that morning. While they hadn't found a church they felt was a good fit for them yet, Jari knew both Joe and Jessica were eager to do so. Other than that, the newlyweds seemed blissfully happy, and Jari was delighted. Jessi seemed to be loving her time at home with the girls and said Joe was enjoying practicing with the team.

Her thoughts momentarily off-track, Jari thought of the date, and realized Joe would know in six to nine weeks whether he would play with the pro football team he had been practicing with since getting to Minnesota or if God had something else planned for them. Again, Jari prayed for God's will to be done; but if it was His will, she prayed He would secure Joe a spot on the team and let the young man's hard work over the spring and summer be worthwhile. Jari made a note at the top of her page to ask Jessi about church and if Joe had heard anything from the coaches when she talked to her on Monday.

After the church service was over, Jari made lunch, and they spent one more blessedly calm, quiet, relaxing day together reading, watching movies, enjoying the sunshine, and playing games. She couldn't remember the last time they had spent an entire two and a half days at home together, just resting. It was nice and had been exactly what she needed. That evening, when Bill suggested the idea, she served their dinner out on the back patio where they enjoyed a sweet, cooling breeze and the calm that settled with the evening sun.

Once their plates were empty, Jari took a long drink of iced tea and settled back in her chair, looking across the table at her graying husband. He, too, had settled back and seemed to be deep in thought as he looked out across the patio into the landscaping on the far side of the pool.

"Bill, thank you. Thank you for giving my dream of having children a chance and thank you for this weekend. I've needed this time with you, and it has been wonderful."

Turning his attention back to her, Bill smiled. "You're welcome. I've enjoyed it as well. We need to do this more often." He reached across the table to take her hand, and she simply nodded, appreciating his comment. She knew in his line of work, weekends like the one they had just shared didn't come often; and with his aspirations to one day be president, an increase in them wasn't likely. She appreciated his desire to spend more time with her, though. For the moment, that was enough.

"Thank you for not being on your phone all weekend," she told him sincerely. The next worst thing to being alone was being with Bill when he was glued to his phone. She knew he needed to stay up on what was happening in his home state, the District, the country, and the world; but between staying in the know and the emails that seemed to flood his inbox continually, his phone could keep him as absent while they were in the same room as he was when physically away. During the weekend, he had checked his phone a handful of times, but primarily kept it put away—a fact she appreciated immensely. He nodded.

"Sometimes, it's nice to just be the two of us . . . to feel like a normal couple," he offered. Jari couldn't agree more.

They watched the sunlight fade and twilight descend. They watched the stars come out, just a few at a time, until the sky was full of them. Despite the city lights, as the night grew darker, the stars dotted the expanse above them. Still, they sat quietly at the patio table, holding hands, clinging to their relaxing weekend together as long as they could. Finally, Bill stood with a quiet grunt.

"We'd better call it a night. The morning will come early." Circling the table, he pulled Jari to her feet, even as she gently protested. She knew he was right, but didn't want the day, or the weekend, to end. He helped her clear the table, and they headed inside, where they watched the news from their bed.

Lying curled up against Bill, Jari felt her anxiety rising in the darkness, knowing he was going back to work, back to a crazy schedule and long days at the office; knowing that she was going back to long days of being alone. Feeling herself fill with dread, she took a deep, calming breath and pushed away the unsettling thoughts. She thought instead about the weekend they had shared and the act of love her husband had so selflessly endured. Again, his willingness to entertain the possibility of children for her sake warmed her heart. When she finally fell asleep, long after Bill began snoring, she slept with a smile on her lips.

Six

During the next several weeks, Bill was busier than ever. Jari felt like she barely saw him amidst the buzz of the campaign, combined with his regular work in the Senate. Deciding to kick the melancholy mess she had been in all summer and knowing she needed to find a purpose outside of Bill and the possibility of children, she set about restructuring her life without Jessi and the girls. She reached out to friends and got intentional about building community, started attending a new Bible study at church, began serving at a local homeless shelter, and volunteered to help with a reading program at the library. Twice a week, she took Bill lunch at his office, deciding it was better to spend half an hour with him for lunch than to not see him at all.

It seemed as if he was home only long enough to sleep, shower, and leave, grabbing a couple of breakfast bars and his to-go mug of coffee on his way out the door. With August quickly approaching and the Senate preparing to recess, Jari knew the busy season was far from over. While Bill's days were currently full on the Senate floor as they wrapped things up before leaving for the month, in August he would be busy traveling through the state of Virginia, campaigning, connecting, attending events, and holding town halls to hear from his constituents. As the summer wore on, Jari learned to live for Sundays, thankful that she got to spend at least one day a week with her husband.

On a Sunday evening near the middle of July, Jari carried their steak dinner outside, and they ate on the patio, catching the last rays of sunshine and enjoying a few moments of calm. They had taken to eating outside nearly every Sunday evening, and Jari loved it. The fresh air and evening sun, combined with the slow pace and the company, made it her favorite time of the week.

They finished their dinner before the sun went down, but continued to sit there, enjoying the pleasant warmth that only a summer night could bring. Despite the fact that neither of them had spoken in over ten minutes, Jari appreciated the opportunity to simply be near her husband while his mind was on things other than business and his phone was inside on the coffee table.

"Do you ever wish I wasn't in politics?" Bill asked slowly, breaking the silence.

"Yes." Jari's answer was quick and instinctive. "Every day."

Bill nodded. "Sometimes I do too," he admitted. Jari tried to cover her surprise. She had never heard Bill talk of his career choice with regret. "Sometimes, when I realize I haven't seen you while you were awake for more days than I can count on one hand, or when I sit outside like we are tonight and think about how some people do this every night of their lives, or when I count up and find it's been two months since I've seen my daughter and granddaughters . . . and when I realize that if we have another child, I might see them once a week in some seasons of our lives as well, sometimes I regret the choices I've made."

"You love what you do, Bill," Jari said, measuring her words carefully, wondering at the window Bill was giving her to thoughts and feelings he had never shared before.

"Yes, I do. I love working for and representing the people. I love serving the state of Virginia. I love putting my time and effort into making this country a great place to live for those who call it home.

And I love the work, the buzz, the campaigning, the lobbying, the speech giving, the connecting with people, and everything the job encompasses, but sometimes I feel stuck, Jari—wrapped up by the red tape and trapped by the process. It's hard to make progress, and sometimes it feels like no matter how hard we work, we're just spinning our wheels. Sometimes, I feel the weight of every decision I make pressing down on me, and I feel old."

Jari lovingly searched her husband's face. She saw the gray hair around his temples, the new lines around his eyes, the frustrated set of his jaw. "Bill, you're exhausted. You've been working too many hours, and you're tired, love. That's all."

He shrugged his shoulders. "I am tired. I hope to God that's all it is. I feel ineffective, old, and boring. Sometimes, I wonder if I should give all of it a rest and let one of the younger men take over."

"This country needs the energy of youth, it's true, but it also needs the wisdom that's only brought by age," she answered, her voice firm.

"If only we were moving forward. I just don't see progress being made. I used to have the energy and determination to push things ahead. I used to feel unstoppable. Now, I just want evenings in my own backyard with you and a decaf coffee. And I can't help but wonder if I'm too old for this . . . too old to make a difference . . ."

Jari had never heard him so down. In the privacy of their own home, she did the only thing she could think of to snap her husband out of the rut he was slumping into. She stood and kicked off her shoes, dropped the skirt she still wore from church and discarded her shirt carelessly on her chair.

"What are you doing?" Bill asked, his worn-out expression replaced with a surprised smile.

"You are not old and boring. You have a lot of surprises left in you . . . a lot of fire still in your bones," she told him firmly, unbuttoning the few buttons on the golf shirt he was wearing before pulling it over his head. Bill looked up at her, his expression almost one of wonder. She turned and ran lightly to the still pool where she dove under the water. When she came up, she pushed the long blonde hair out of her eyes and motioned for him to join her. "Come on! The water's nice! Come swim with me!"

At her prodding, he finally stood and, after a few moments, did a cannonball into the pool beside her, causing the still water to explode in a series of ripples and waves. When he came up out of the water, gasping and shaking the water from his hair, he grabbed her and pulled her close, laughing. She listened to the sound of his laughter for a few moments, bottling up the precious sound in her memory to enjoy again later.

Jari put her hands on either side of Bill's face and looked him in the eyes. "You, William Cordel, are not old or ineffective or boring! See, you can even surprise yourself still, can't you?" He laughed and kissed her firmly.

Her mood turned serious. "I believe in you more than any other man alive. You have everything it takes. Don't even think about moving over and letting someone younger take your place. You were created for the position you hold right now. There is so much purpose in it. You have too much to offer, too much to give, too much wisdom, too much that America needs, to bow out now—now, when you finally stand for truth, justice, life, and righteousness! Democrat, Republican or Independent, you are the kind of man that America needs in government! You are the kind of man who needs to lead, set the course for, and guide this country. You are not done, Bill, not even close. You have so much more to do! So you tell those lies to get out of your head, and you remember that you are the right man in the right place at the right time, and that you have a job to do!"

Bill stared at her for a long moment, then planted another firm kiss on her lips. "I love you," he told her, his voice almost triumphant.

She grinned at him. "I love you too."

"You're good for me," he told her.

"You're right. I am," she agreed, and he chuckled, pulling a piece of long blonde hair that floated on the water.

Hours later, lying in bed while Bill slept beside her, Jari found herself asking God again if He would please give them a child, but this time for a new reason.

Hearing Bill laugh earlier had caught her off guard, and now she realized why: she hadn't heard him laugh since the middle of May; since Kamryn and Kelsi left for Minnesota. Having children in the house had filled them both with joy and kept them young. After long weeks at the office and carrying around the weight of the country on his shoulders, being with his granddaughters always helped Bill unwind and let go of all the stress he accumulated at work. With a start, Jari realized that Bill needed a child as much as she did. He was afraid he was too old to be a new father again, but what had become crystal clear to her was that a child would be what kept her husband young.

~~~~~

As a familiar ring erupted from the speakers, Jari kept her eyes on the traffic around her and hit the green button on her large display screen.

"Hello?"

"Jari, he got the job! I mean position! Whatever you call it. Joe's going to play pro ball this year!" Jessica was jubilant, her voice dripping with pride and joy.

Jari let out a delighted shriek and did a happy dance in her seat. Everything was working out. "Jessi! Yay! That's great news! I knew he was going to make the team."

"I know! Joe just called! The coach called him into his office, said he wouldn't start—obviously—but that they would keep him on as a third-string quarterback! He said Joe shows a lot of potential!" Jessica was breathless, and Jari could picture her best friend's shining eyes and excited smile.

"Of course he does! We know how talented he is. I'm glad they see it too," Jari answered. "Man, I can't wait to watch his season!"

"Me too," Jessi bubbled. "Okay, you can't say anything. They haven't made the official announcement yet. They're going to release their final roster tonight at practice."

"Oh bummer, I was planning to call all my football buddies once we hang up," Jari joked.

"I know, I know. I just wanted to make sure it didn't somehow get out. Jari, I'm so thankful this happened! I'm so glad this worked out . . . it serves as such a confirmation for Joe of everything that happened last spring."

Jari knew exactly what Jessi meant. Earlier in the spring, Joe gave up his lifelong ambition of being a pastor after having a dream in which he had a conversation with God about the course of his life. Making a bold move that was contrary to everything he had worked so hard for, he approached a coach who had wanted to draft him during his years of playing college ball and asked for a second chance. The coach hadn't been able to make him any promises but told him he could practice with the team during the summer and then see what happened at the start of the season.

Without anything concrete to count on, Joe finished his year of seminary and withdrew for the fall semester. He let his apartment go and sold nearly everything he had, following only a direction he believed was from God and for the best of his new family.

And it had paid off.

"Me too, Jess. Me too." Jari couldn't stop smiling.

"It really is such a picture of the kindness of God," Jessi said softly. Jari agreed. "We're going to start looking for a house; hopefully we'll find one within the next week. We want one that's decently close to the field, but in a nice neighborhood. And we need one that's big enough to hold our growing family."

Jari couldn't miss the smile she heard in Jessica's last sentence. "What do you mean?" Jari asked immediately, her eyes wide, excitement swelling inside of her. "Are you saying what I think you're saying?"

Jessi laughed. "Yes! I'm due next spring!"

"Jessica!" Jari squealed, knowing her voice rose several octaves. Jessi was still laughing.

"I know! We're so excited! And the girls . . . ! All they talk about is trying to decide if they want a little brother or sister."

Jari laughed, too. "I wonder if they know it's not up to them to decide?"

"I've tried to explain that, but they continue to weigh the pros and cons and discuss it as if it's their decision alone."

"How funny. How far along are you?"

"Around eight weeks. So, I'm not very far along yet, but I've been to the doctor, and she said everything looks good."

"Oooo. A honeymoon baby," Jari said, grinning.

"No! Not a honeymoon baby . . . We've been married three months, and I'm only eight weeks pregnant," Jessi protested.

"Well, you have to admit, you guys are efficient. That's all I'm saying," Jari teased, unable to help herself.

"Jari!" Jessi scolded.

"How have you been feeling?" Jari asked, switching directions with a grin.

"Sick, but not as sick as I was with the girls yet, so that's been nice. Of course it is still early . . ."

"Well, that's something, though! How long before you have to be out of the condo?"

"Next weekend."

"What will you do? You can't find and close on a house that fast!"

"Right. There's no way. We'll have to stay in a hotel for a few weeks until we can close on a house. We're going to start house hunting today—after Joe gets home. He's on his way now."

"How exciting, Jess! You're buying your first house!"

There was a sudden silence, then Jessi was back. "Hey, Jari, Kara's calling, and I want to tell her the news! Can I call you back?"

"Sure," Jari agreed quickly, and they hung up.

As quiet descended over the car, Jari's heart sang. Things were working out so wonderfully for Joe and Jessi. He was going to play in the pros, they were going to buy a house, they had two beautiful children and now another on the way. She was happy, so happy for them. She felt like breaking out in spontaneous song, yet, coexisting with that happiness was the same longing she had felt grow increasingly stronger as the summer went on. Someday, would it be her turn?

Seven

J ari woke up slowly, fighting to stay asleep and continue the dream she was having. Finally, she gave up. Opening her eyes, she looked groggily around her bedroom. It was flooded in September sunshine and she released a deep sigh.

She hadn't been back to Kansas in a decade and a half, so why did she still dream about it? How did she seem to smell the crab apple blossoms that used to bloom on the tree in their front yard, the tree she herself planted when she was in first grade? Why did her mother and father seem so real, their faces so clear and lifelike? Why did that dream, her family, her town, elicit so many happy memories and such a longing to go back—back to Kansas, back in time—when she had left in such a mess of hurt and anger?

But she hadn't dreamt of how things had been her last year in Kansas. No, in her dream, she was much younger, and the time was much happier. Her dad was around more, and her parents still shared lively conversations and held hands as they walked around the lake while she sat on the grassy banks to throw bread to the ducks.

"Go back." The quiet command that seemed to blow across her soul made her groan.

"I can't go back," she said aloud. And she knew she was right. She had been gone for a long, long time. She had run away. Sometimes, if a person was gone from somewhere long enough, it just became too long to ever return; and that's how it was with her and Kansas.

She hadn't seen either of her parents in over fifteen years. She hadn't seen grandparents, aunts, uncles, cousins, neighbors, friends, or community members for the same amount of time. After so long, how could she just show up back in town? Especially in a small community where everyone knew everyone. Broadcasting she was back from the top of the weathered water tower would be no more effective than the local grapevine.

She was sure she had been the talk of the town when she left without a word, and then again when the story about her affair with Bill hit the tabloids years later. Her return would likely create just as big of a buzz, and all the rumors, all the gossip that had hopefully been laid to rest after their affair had become old news, would resurface, take on a new form, and sweep across the little town like a grassfire on the prairie during a windy August drought.

Imagining how the gossipers' tongues must have wagged, pointing out 'like father, like daughter,' she cringed. Jari could picture them pitying her mom and blaming her dad. She was sure they had asked how she could have done it after what her dad had put their family through; and even after all these years, she had absolutely no answer or defense. How had she done what she did to the Cordel family after what she and her mom had gone through? She still didn't know. It was inexplainable and inexcusable.

And yet the small-town gossips weren't even the worst of it.

How could she show up on her mother's doorstep after so many years away? She'd been gone nearly as long as she'd lived at home. What would her mother say? Jari didn't even know how her mom had taken it when she left. Was she angry? Shocked? Sad? Did she somehow understand? They had only had half a dozen clipped phone calls since that always followed the same pattern:

"Jari, it's mom."

"Oh, hi."

"Hi." That was always followed by an awkward pause. "How are you?"

"I'm fine. How are you?" Jari's heart was always racing by now, wanting to tell her mom the truth and hear the truth in return—to dive below the surface and reestablish a relationship, but without the courage or know-how to do so.

"I'm okay," her mom would say. Another pause. "Are you staying busy?"

"Yes, things have been busy here. Are you?"

"Yes, I'm staying busy at the flower shop."

"Good. I'm glad."

"Are you healthy? Getting enough to eat? Do you have everything you need?"

"I'm good, mom," Jari would say. She always had tears in her eyes by this time.

"Good. How's your husband?" That question had been added on after Jari left a message on her mom's voicemail letting her know she was married. It was the only time Jari had called. Her mom hadn't answered. She didn't know if she had been busy or if she'd been too angry to talk to her. Jari had always imagined her mom had seen the tabloids, knew why she was calling, and couldn't bring herself to speak to her.

"He's good."

"Well, that's good. I'm glad to hear things are going well." Another awkward pause. "So . . . I have to get to the store, but I was just thinking about you and thought I would call and make sure you're still alive."

Jari would laugh through her tears of regret and thank her mom for calling before they both hung up.

Now, she wondered again what would happen if she finally found the courage to go home. Would her mom welcome her in? Where would their conversation begin? How would they reconnect after Jari had walked out of her mom's life fifteen years earlier and made no effort to be an active part of it since? Jari was afraid the only way to move forward would be to completely start from scratch. That would be horribly awkward and unnatural when the person she was getting to know was the woman who gave birth to her, raised her, nurtured her, and loved her. Jari wiped away tears of remorse just thinking about it. Her mom didn't deserve the way she had treated her. Jari had made a really big mistake but was too scared of rejection to try to fix it.

And while her mother was the one person in the entire world that she most wanted to reconnect with, the person who kept her away more than the rumors, the fear, the guilt, the awkwardness, or anything else that stood between her and returning home to reconcile, was her father.

When she had first left home, she hated him. Fiercely. Unyieldingly. Uncontrollably. He'd ruined their family. He had ruined her life. She'd trusted him, and he had stomped on her heart, her sense of security, her sense of being loved. With a series of bad decisions, he had left her feeling angry, alone, shaken, uncertain, insecure, and desperate to capture the affection and attention of a man. Any man.

For years, she did whatever she had to do to earn a man's attention, to secure and sustain his love. She believed the lie that she, in and of herself, was not worthy of love, and that she had to earn someone's love through performance and perfection. Even in the moments she was most certain she was earning 'love' well, she was terrified that it wouldn't be enough to hold on to her significant other. She bounced from one relationship to another, terrified of being abandoned and choosing instead to do the leaving herself, convinced that it would hurt less that way.

When she met Bill, she had felt an incredible sense of superiority that she had been enough to pull him away from his family. She enjoyed her power over him and relished the fact that he came to her beck and call. She knew as long as she held all the cards, he wouldn't leave. She used everything she had to keep him coming back for more until she had secured a spot in his fancy home and a large diamond ring for her finger.

Bill had seemed content not to ask questions. They didn't talk about their motivations, past, or even about the future outside of wanting to be together. She had been desperate to be chosen and wanted, and he had been power-hungry and greedy for assurance. While she felt accomplished and fulfilled by him choosing her above all else, she had made him feel virile and proud to have won the love of a beautiful young model.

While she had indeed loved Bill, she knew even at the time that her anger toward her father was playing a dark, strange role in her drive to have him for her very own. Even all those years after leaving Kansas, her hatred had not lessened—time had healed no wounds.

Within the first year of their relationship, though, those very feelings of hatred and anger toward Skip Braxon and the insecurities he had caused that had helped fuel her desire to be with Bill were taking a backseat to new feelings. As her eyes opened, and she honestly faced for the first time the kind of woman she had become, the two emotions which flooded every thought or memory of her father became guilt and shame.

How, when she had hated him so fiercely for what he had done to her and her mother—to their family—could she show up back in town having done no less? How could she potentially face a man she was so angry with, knowing he had committed no greater of a crime than she?

If she could be assured that she could go home and see her mother without running into him on the street or even seeing him across a crowded room, she might muster up the courage to buy a plane ticket and see if her mom would allow her back into her life, but as it was, there was no guarantee. She had no idea what it would be like to see him, face him, or talk to him. She had nothing to say to him and didn't want to hear anything he might have to say to her. She had no context to even begin to process how to reconcile with him. She didn't even know who should apologize first. They were both guilty parties. Unfortunately, just as he had told her when she was little, they were two peas in a pod.

With another groan, she threw the covers back and climbed out of her big four-poster bed, wiping her tears as she did. This was not the way she had wanted to start her day. Thoughts of Kansas belonged in a dusty box in the back corner of her memory, not at the forefront of her mind. Refocusing, she said good morning to the Lord and spent a few minutes praying for her mom, her dad, and for her own heart.

"Help me live out of a place of freedom," she prayed as she squirted a pea-sized amount of toothpaste onto the end of her toothbrush. As she began brushing, she found herself dropping her toothbrush in the sink and running to the toilet, where she promptly lost the contents of her empty stomach.

Pulling her hair back out of her face and returning to the sink, she winced. Was her past still so upsetting that it caused her to be physically ill? If so, it was probably time to seriously consider going back to counseling. Vomiting was a serious reaction to fifteen-year-old memories.

Washing her mouth out and putting her toothbrush away, she headed downstairs to make herself an English muffin for breakfast.

As she ate her breakfast and drank her orange juice, she opened her Bible and pored over the words she found. It was amazing to her that the entire concept of the God she served and the world He created was so beyond her limited understanding, so beyond anything she could even imagine. Yet it made sense, and deep within her, it felt right. She was always amazed at the sovereignty of God when she read His Word. She found herself laying down her life, her hopes, her dreams, and her will once again.

As she had done hundreds of times before, she pictured herself scooting her family unit to the foot of His throne and giving it over to Him again. She repented of the anger she still felt and asked Him to cleanse her heart and make her in right standing before Him. Still, she knew she needed to do more than pray. She needed to be obedient.

"If it's Your will that I go back to Kansas, I will, LORD," she whispered into the quiet of the house, every word difficult to say. "Please, just make it clear and help me. Give me courage, LORD, because I'm scared."

After breakfast, Jari quickly changed and headed to the homeless shelter where she was scheduled to serve lunch. On the drive to the shelter, she went over her schedule for the rest of the day—serve, home, shower, meet Bill at his office at five o'clock and be at a benefit dinner by six.

At the shelter, she was greeted by other volunteers who had become her friends. Jari pulled her hair back and tied an apron on over her clothes, then joined the volunteers stirring big pots on the large stove.

"What's on the menu for today?" she asked, grabbing a spoon and stirring a large pot of boiling carrots that the chef pointed her toward.

"Chicken sandwiches, pasta salad, cooked carrots and red-hot apples," Tony the chef answered, his tone as terse as it always was when he was in the middle of preparing a meal. Tony was a top chef at one of the restaurants in downtown D.C., but volunteered at the shelter twice a week. He had started volunteering after one of his childhood friends ended up on the streets.

"That sounds delicious," Jari answered, leaning over to inhale deeply over the carrots, then doing likewise over the red applesauce that was simmering in another pot. "It smells delicious too."

"It'll do," Tony grunted.

Jari knew that if there was one thing that frustrated their chef, it was the lack of ingredients and spices he had to work with. She could understand. For a man who was accustomed to being in a fully stocked kitchen with nearly everything he could want at his fingertips, the shelter's pantry must seem sorely lacking.

Jari stirred as Tony worked quickly around her, adding brown sugar and butter to the carrots, then pausing to add more salt to the pasta salad on his way back to the refrigerator.

"Carol, are you busy?" he asked a dark-haired woman who had just returned from putting silverware and napkins at the beginning of the serving line.

"Not too busy for you, Tony!" she answered cheerfully. "What do you need?"

"Will you chop the tomatoes for the pasta salad?"

"Absolutely." Carol headed for the cutting board that was on the counter beside Jari. As she took her place and waited for Tony to bring her the tomatoes he was collecting from the fridge, Jari smiled and greeted her.

"Have you heard from Brad?" she asked, hoping Carol's answer would be affirmative.

The dark-haired lady shook her head. "Not yet. Not since a few weeks ago."

Jari nodded. "Well, it will come. He'll call or email soon." Carol nodded her head in silent agreement.

Carol's youngest son, Brad, had joined the army a few years earlier and was currently deployed. With news networks reporting a fresh wave of insurgent attacks in the region his unit was patrolling, resulting in the deaths of several US soldiers, Carol was growing increasingly anxious.

"He's a good soldier, Carol. Definitely a son to be proud of." Jari's comment drew a smile from Carol.

"Yes, he certainly is. How has your week been? Have Joe and Jessica found a house?"

Jari appreciated that her new friend had taken the time to learn about her family, her life, and what was important to her. "They have a couple they like, but I still don't think they've decided on one."

"Well then, they haven't found it yet. When they look at the right house, they'll know it's the one," Carol assured her with a motherly smile.

"I suppose you're right," Jari agreed. She had never bought a house . . . or even picked one out. From her parents' home, she had moved in with her cousin, who already had an apartment in New York City. From there, she moved in with several different men, all of whom were already settled in apartments or condos. When she married Bill, she moved into his large, luxurious home, and relocating had never been an option. That was fine with her. She loved the house they were in. Choosing a house to rent or buy was simply a foreign concept to her. "I just hope they find one soon. They've been in the hotel for over a month already."

"It's a process. They'll get it figured out," Carol told her.

Their conversation moved on, and they chatted happily as Carol chopped and Jari stirred. Tony moved around them, adding a shake of this and a scoop of that to his creations. When the food was ready, they helped situate all the pots on the serving counter before manning their stations.

Jari was intentional about smiling warmly at each person who moved through the line, looking them in the eye, and greeting them as they stopped for a scoop of carrots. Many kept their eyes averted, but a number of the regulars returned her greeting, and some even smiled back.

Having not worked at the shelter long, she was still in the first phase of her long-term strategy to help make a difference. She wanted to spend a few months simply helping in the kitchen, serving lunch, offering a smile and a short greeting. As those who frequented the shelter grew accustomed to her, and she ceased to be new to them, she wanted to start venturing out to mingle with them. Eventually, she would build the trust needed to allow them to share their stories with her and vice versa. Once she learned more about their needs and challenges, she could take what she learned back to Bill and see what they could do to help on a bigger scale. And hopefully, someday, if the opportunity presented itself, she could share Jesus with them.

She longed to tell these she served a few times every week that there was One who had created them, loved them, and cared about them from the moment of their conception. She wanted to share the news that He didn't see them as others did. It had no impact on His love for them where they slept at night or what clothes they wore. He knew them, loved them, and desired to be close to them. The hope of one day sharing that message is what kept her coming back Monday, Wednesday, Friday after Monday, Wednesday, Friday.

As she served and smiled, she wondered again if her strategy was the correct one. Just a week after starting at the shelter, the urgency of the situation became all too real when a woman she had served roast beef to and smiled at one day was reported dead the next. Jari had not heard the details as she absorbed the weight of the news. She had been given the honor of rubbing shoulders with that woman for one day. If Jari had shared the gospel, would it have made a difference? At the very least, could the woman have perished knowing her Savior and having eternal life? But Jari hadn't shared the gospel. She had remained friendly but quiet. She spent the weekend rethinking her strategy of becoming a familiar face and building a relationship before sharing the Good News of Jesus.

Despite the gravity each day held, she ultimately wound up at the same conclusion she had come to before. While she knew that sometimes the opportunity came to share the gospel after having just met someone, and the LORD moved on the person's heart and brought about salvation, oftentimes, building a relationship and sharing out of that place of trust and credibility was how she saw Him move. If the opportunity presented itself sooner, she would share her faith, but unless it was blatant, she would put in the time and effort to get to know and genuinely care about those she came in contact with while waiting for the LORD to stir their hearts and give them ears to hear. She looked into a scruffy man's face, smiled, and dished him his scoopful of carrots.

After the meal was served, she helped carry serving pans and utensils back into the kitchen, then stationed herself at a sink where she set about washing what seemed like a never-ending stack of dirty pots and pans. She scrubbed down the countertops around her, washed out both sides of the sink, then rinsed out her sponge. She pulled off the long yellow gloves that stretched up to her elbows and laid them on the edge of the sink before washing and drying her hands. Looking around, she found other things to do until the clean-up was done for the day. Saying her goodbyes, she grabbed her purse and headed to her car.

As she stepped out into the late-September sunshine, she took in a deep breath of fresh air. The temperature was still warm enough that she would turn the air conditioner on once she got to her SUV, but she remembered the almost crisp quality of the air the evening before, when she had enjoyed a cup of tea out on the patio—a telltale sign that fall weather was indeed right around the corner. Pausing in the sunshine, she reminded herself to enjoy the heat for as long as summer held on, only giving way to the excitement of fall when the temperatures turned cooler and the leaves began to turn. Staying present kept her heart thankful.

Sliding behind the steering wheel of her SUV, she turned it toward home, rolling the windows down to let in the fresh air. Glancing in her rearview mirror, her eyes fell on the backseat. Readjusting her mirror to give her a view of the cars behind her rather than the empty bucket seats, she realized afresh how very bare it seemed.

For years, car seats for Kelsi and Kamryn had stayed permanently buckled into her SUV, but now she had taken them out. Even after a few months of not having them there, their absence made her sad, and she sent up another prayer that she would someday install another car seat into her car. She hoped that this time, it would be for her own child.

Her mind turned to thoughts of a baby. She thought about Bill's confession of his vasectomy, the surgery to reverse it, and the three months since. She wondered if she ever did, how long it would take to get pregnant. Would it be months? Years? She knew the success rate of a pregnancy after a reversal ranged from thirty to over ninety percent, and that felt like a very large and uncertain range. The doctor had warned that the length of time since Bill's vasectomy dramatically decreased the chances, but she didn't know by how much or what exactly the chance was to begin with.

Her thoughts turned into prayers, and she fervently beseeched the LORD to give them a baby. She wanted to be a mother. She wanted to build a family with Bill. She wanted to parent together. She wanted freckled faces and bright eyes to fill the back of her SUV again. She wanted a family—her own family. Guiltily, she tacked, "If it's Your will" onto the end of her prayer, only remembering at the end to leave the matter up to the sovereignty of God.

Letting out a deep sigh, she began to wrestle again with the desire for children that seemed to consume her. In all other areas of her life—with Jessi and then Carla, with Bill, with their marriage and her early fear that there would one day be another woman, with his career and future aspirations, with her own purpose, even with Kansas, she could trust it to the LORD and believe that He knew best. But with her dream of having a child, the longing that filled her was so intense that as the weeks wore on, she couldn't seem to leave it in God's hands.

She couldn't seem to hold it loosely enough to get the perspective to admit that His ways were better and to truly trust Him with the outcome. She was certain she wanted her own way. She was certain she wanted a child. Life would be better, more complete, more fulfilling, deeper, happier, and more meaningful once she had a baby. Now, if only she could get pregnant.

Once home, she grabbed an apple, marked a few things off her to-do list, and headed upstairs to get ready for the black-tie affair she would attend with Bill that night.

She teased her swooped bangs before pinning them back and pulling the rest of her light hair into an elegant, low side ponytail, which she curled. Stepping into her tea-length, black dress, she took the time to make sure each layer of netting that held out the full skirt was smoothed into place. She adjusted the sweetheart bust and squirmed just a little in the bodice to get it straight. After fastening black strappy heels on, she paused to clasp a delicate silver chain around her neck, positioning the sapphire pendant just below the dip in her collarbone. She quickly added matching sapphire stud earrings and a dainty sapphire and diamond bracelet. Spritzing herself with her favorite perfume, she grabbed her black clutch and hurried down the stairs where she paused for one last look in the mirror before going out to the car Bill had sent for her.

Once in the car, she texted Bill to let him know she was on her way—his cue to put away his work and change into the tuxedo he had taken with him that morning—and then called Jessi. When the car pulled up outside the Russell building, he came out the door and slid into the back seat beside her.

"You look lovely tonight," Bill told her, his face alight with admiration. Her smile was quick and bright.

"Thank you. You look very nice yourself. No one will guess you came straight from the office."

He chuckled and pulled at his collar. "I'm still not sure why they have these black-tie events when it's still so blamed hot out. They should wait a month or so, and it would be more bearable."

"They probably do it just to make you uncomfortable," Jari teased. "I'm sure that was their sole purpose in scheduling it tonight." He pulled on a blonde curl.

"I like your hair tonight."

"Thank you."

"And your dress. Is it new?"

She shook her head, enjoying his approving assessment. "Not new, but I've only worn it once, and not recently."

He nodded. "Well, I like it. A lot."

"Thank you," she answered with a smile, holding herself a little straighter and feeling a little prettier. Even after six years of marriage, a dress, heels, and her husband's appreciative approval could make her feel like the most beautiful woman in the world. She took a moment to enjoy the feeling.

On the long drive across town, made longer by rush hour traffic in the city, Jari told Bill about her day and asked about his. They discussed what legislation had come before the Senate, the upcoming trip they would take to do more campaigning, approval ratings, and how the election was shaping up in the polls. He read her a rough draft of a speech he had been working on with Ryan for their campaign trip, and she made comments and suggestions, some of which Bill scribbled down in the margins to work into the speech the next day. They talked about Jari's call with Jessi and how she was feeling now that she was officially in her second trimester.

As they finished the last fifteen minutes of their drive, Bill briefed her on the specifics of the dinner, the charity foundation, and their cause. They discussed who would be there, who they would sit with, and the implications tonight could have on both the campaign and their political life. Jari's final question was what was on the menu. She was absolutely starving.

When they pulled up to the front steps, the driver, Todd, opened the door for them. Bill stepped out first, then turned to help Jari. They stopped to speak to several news reporters, making pleasant small talk while Bill slipped in positive comments about the charitable organization, which he had carefully drafted with Ryan earlier in the day. Once inside the front doors, the reporters became scarce; but the foyer was teeming with politicians and celebrities alike, who stopped to greet them. With every minute that passed, the burning hunger in Jari's stomach grew more and more intense.

When they finally arrived at the large wooden doors that separated the foyer from the dining room, and a worker swung the door open to allow them entrance, the decadent smell of dinner hit her like a tidal wave. Though she was starving, Jari felt her stomach churn in immediate response to the aroma. After rapidly asking where the closest restroom was, she had to focus on swallowing as she quickly made her way through the crowd to the privacy of the bathroom, where she promptly lost the contents of her empty stomach.

Washing her mouth out at the sink, it occurred to her that she had thrown up three times in the last week. She dabbed at her lips carefully with a paper towel, not wanting to smudge her makeup, her motions slow as her mind worked. Surely she couldn't be . . . She couldn't even finish the thought.

It was too soon. There was no way anything could have happened so quickly . . . could it have? Bill's surgery had come with no guarantees, and they had been unsure if anything would ever come of it, much less so soon. Still, three times in one week was a surprising number, considering she hadn't thrown up in at least a couple of years.

Backing away from the sink, she threw her paper towel into the trash and went back out to find Bill. She did her best to crush her suspicions, determined not to even let herself hope or dream until she had some kind of conclusive evidence. Even still, a spark of hope jumped to life in her heart.

She found Bill still standing beside the large wooden doors leading into the dining room, and when his eyes met hers, she saw his concern. As she drew near, he stepped closer, placing his hand at the small of her back and bending down to her ear so his whisper could be heard.

"Are you feeling okay?" he asked, his eyes dark with worry.

She nodded. "I think I'm just hungry."

"Are you sure? We can go home if you don't feel well."

She appreciated his concern and squeezed his hand. "Thank you, but I'll be okay."

He met her eyes for another moment and then nodded, stepping back and motioning to the doorman. The door swung open again, the smell of food was released, and this time, Jari concentrated on taking deep breaths through her nose until the nausea passed. They made their way through the dining room that was quickly filling with people until they found their table. Bill reached out to offer friendly handshakes to those who were already seated, while Jari greeted them with a bright smile.

Bill held her chair for her, and she sat down. Taking a sip of water, she spent a few moments looking around the grandly decorated room. It was large, easily accommodating the hundred plus tables, while still providing room for a dance floor. A glitzy jazz band was providing music, and a podium was set up on the stage, where the foundation's president would later address the crowd. It was beautiful, but similar to dozens of others she had seen. Her attention waned.

Looking for something else to focus on, Jari watched the people milling around the room as Bill fell into easy conversation with the politician sitting next to him. She wished everyone would find their seats quickly so that dinner could be served. Her thoughts turned back to the questions that sprang up in her mind in the bathroom, and she came to the same conclusion—surely not.

Still, a voice of hope in her heart that would not be ignored kept questioning. What if she was?

Finally, suited waiters started pouring from a door on the left side of the grand dining room with towels draped over their arms and large silver platters held high above their heads. As they began serving salads, chatting stragglers hurried to take their seats. Jari waited in anticipation as a waiter approached their table and placed a salad in front of her. She tried not to stare at the rich greens, the mandarin oranges, the delicious-looking strawberries, or the crunchy toppings as she waited for the rest of the table to be served, but the smell of the vinaigrette that topped it all kept pulling her attention back to her plate. Finally, everyone had their salads, and they began to eat.

Seeming uncommonly attentive, Bill noticed her hunger and selected a French roll from the basket in the middle of the table, split it open, and buttered it before handing it to her. She shot him a grateful smile, and he nodded at her, almost looking amused. She wondered if her hunger was that obvious.

After a few minutes, she looked ruefully at her empty plate, and decided the salad had disappeared much too quickly. To her surprise and gratitude, Bill held out another buttered roll. She forced herself to eat it slowly as she made small talk with the woman beside her, finding it difficult to keep her mind focused on the conversation.

Like a lightbulb coming on, she realized that she wasn't pregnant; she had simply forgotten to have lunch. All she had eaten since breakfast was the apple she had grabbed before showering. That explained her insatiable hunger. Her heart fell, even as her mind reveled in the fact that it made sense. She gave herself a little shake and refocused on the woman beside her. Still, as she saw the waiters flood out of the kitchen again, she was increasingly eager for them to make their way to her table.

Later that night, after eating the wonderful four-course meal, listening to the speakers, mingling through the crowd, and taking to the dance floor with Bill for several numbers, Jari was laughing as she slid into the car. Bill slid in beside her, and Todd shut the door.

"I know you balked about the ticket price, but that was worth every penny you paid for them," she told him, her eyes shining. "The Chicken Florentine was the best I've ever had, and it was a fun evening."

He nodded. "It *was* fun. I'm glad we had an evening like that in the midst of all the busy."

"Me too."

Quiet settled over the car for a few seconds before Bill reached over and took her hand. "I think on our way home, we should stop and pick up a pregnancy test." His words were measured, his tone untelling.

Jari couldn't help a startled jolt. "What . . . ?"

Bill's solemn face broke into a wry smile. "I'm not home a lot, but when I have been, I've noticed you've been especially hungry, and you haven't felt well," he paused, and then continued carefully. "I've had a pregnant wife before and a pregnant daughter . . . I know the signs."

Jari shook her head. "It's too soon. There's no way I could be pregnant already."

Bill shrugged. "It's been three months. I can't imagine you would be yet either, but maybe you should take a test just in case."

Leaning up, Bill relayed the stop to Todd. When he turned into a drugstore and Jari moved to unbuckle, Bill placed his hand on hers to stop her. "I'll go. It's been a full night. You stay in here and rest."

By the time he climbed back into the car, her mind was whirling, and the hope she had been trying to crush all night was singing.

Since the day she left the abortion clinic, over a decade earlier, she had never once thought she could be pregnant. She had never once entertained the idea that she could be carrying a human life within her, but now, here she was with a pregnancy test in a bag on the seat beside her. It seemed preposterous to think about, considering that Bill only had his surgery just three short months ago; but still, he was right. The signs were all there. She thought back to the moments during the week that she was sick, and everything seemed to lead to the conclusion that yes, she was with child. She couldn't stop smiling.

Once inside the house, she hurried upstairs, leaving Bill to his nightly routine of locking doors and turning off lights. She was breathless and excited as she walked into their bedroom, the bag still clutched in her hand. Tossing it onto the bathroom counter, she hurried into the closet and quickly changed into a pair of pajamas. She had her dress hung up, her heels back in their spot, and her jewelry put away in record time. When she left the closet, Bill was sitting on the bed taking off his shoes.

"That was fast," he observed, an amused smile lifting his handsome face. She ignored his tease and went into the bathroom, picking up the test and opening it quickly. She couldn't wait to see the results.

"Now that I think about it, I should have gotten more than one. Since I didn't, make sure you read the directions, honey, so you get an accurate result," Bill told her, appearing in the doorway, his black bowtie undone and hanging around his neck.

"How hard can it be?" she asked, amused.

He shrugged and continued on to the closet, where he hung up his tuxedo jacket and pants, and laid the shirt aside to be sent out for dry cleaning. Heeding his advice, she pulled the directions out of the box and scanned them quickly. Her disappointment was acute.

"What is it?" Bill asked, considering her expression as he came into the bathroom in a t-shirt and boxers to brush his teeth.

"It recommends taking the test first thing in the morning to get the most accurate results," she told him, her heart sinking in disappointment. The morning seemed like such a long wait.

"You'll be awake in eight hours, sweetheart," Bill reminded her, rinsing his toothbrush under the running water.

"I know." He was right. It felt like a long time, but it really wasn't. Knowing there was nothing she could do to make the morning come faster, Jari washed her face and brushed her teeth before joining Bill in bed. After she folded the sheets back over the down comforter, creasing them as she did every night, Bill rolled over and put his arm around her.

"If it's supposed to happen, it will."

"I know. I just got so excited. You're right—I have been feeling sick and hungry, and I didn't even let myself consider the possibility, but tonight when even you noticed . . . I just want to take the test and see the results, whatever they are, so that I'll know one way or the other."

"Even me?" Bill asked, dryly. "Is it so hard to believe that I might actually be observant?"

"I've been waiting for this, wanting this, for so long. After thinking it's not even a possibility, to knowing it is now and that it might be happening . . ." Jari went on as if he hadn't spoken.

"You need to calm down, honey. Otherwise, you're not going to get any sleep tonight," Bill reminded her. She chose to believe his intentions were more sensitive than his tone.

"I just wish I already knew."

"You wouldn't get any sleep if you did," he told her, kissing her shoulder. "If you had already taken the test and it was positive, you would be too excited to sleep. If it was negative, you would be too disappointed. Think of it this way—by having to wait, you at least get a good night's rest out of the deal."

Jari shot her husband an amused smile through the cozy darkness. It was cute that he was trying, but he clearly didn't understand women. She had already passed the point of getting a good night's sleep long ago. The moment he suggested stopping for a test was the moment that went out the window. She was certain she was going to spend the midnight hours filling with hope and then trying to tamper it back down, just to repeat the cycle again five minutes later.

After all, Bill was right: the test could be negative. There was no guarantee that it would be positive. So she had been sick a few times over the last week; maybe it was just a stomach bug. She had been hungry, but every fall she found herself less interested in the salads and fruit she ate all summer and more ready for the soups, breads, and heavier foods that came along with winter.

"One thing's for sure—if you are pregnant, the baby's initials should be SDC," Bill said after a long silence, his voice sounding decidedly sleepy.

"SDC? Why SDC?" she asked, her mind humming.

"Skinny Dipping Cordel."

She jabbed him in the ribs with her elbow as a blush sprung to her cheeks. "That was way out of my comfort zone, and you know it! I was just trying to help."

He chuckled. "Oh, you did, honey, you did."

Eight

*T*he day was cold and the sky bleak. Jari stepped off the bus and was hit by a blast of icy air. She didn't think the winter wind could be as biting anywhere else as it was in upstate New York.

After pausing to zip her coat and pull the hood up over her hair, she started down the sidewalk, still having several blocks to walk until she reached her destination. Her face was numb when she finally arrived at the clinic she sought, and she questioned her sanity at deciding to go out on the coldest day of the year. Still, she knew she needed to carry out her plan before it was too late, and there was no time like the present.

Opening the front door, warmth flooded her, making her cheeks sting. The office was quiet, calm, and nicely decorated. Jari approached the receptionist and checked in. As she took a seat in the small waiting room, she thought again about her decision.

She had found out she was pregnant two weeks earlier. She only had a rough estimate of how far along she was, likely somewhere between ten and sixteen weeks. When she found out, she had been so shocked that her legs gave out and she had to sit down on the side of the bathtub. The tears came swiftly, and she'd wept, angry that it had happened to her, angry that the contraceptive hadn't done its job, angry that she had to deal with the entire situation.

One thing was as clear to her now, sitting in the waiting room, as it had been sitting in her bathroom that day. She was not ready for a *baby. Maybe in a different place and at a different time, she would be excited about the possibility, but not here. Not now.*

She had just landed her first big modeling job. It was a bigger gig than she'd ever had, and she would make enough money from it to give her plenty to live on for the next few months. If she did well, her agent predicted he could secure her a position at fashion week. That was a really big deal; she was finally making it professionally in ways that she never had before. How would she explain her bloated appearance to the director of photography? How would she convince him, or any boss for that matter, that her baby bump was an admirable quality for a model?

In addition to ruining her career, her personal life couldn't stand the strain of a baby. The beauty of her lifestyle was that she could go where she wanted when she wanted and with whom she wanted. It had only been a month since she left New York City to move up north to be with her boyfriend, Griffin. Already, the move and the commute were starting to wear, and their relationship was becoming strained. To be perfectly honest, he bored her. He was solely intellectual and lacked the charisma and pizzazz that could hold her interest. Was he someone she wanted to have a baby with? Not at all. And the baby likely wasn't even his

No, it just wasn't a convenient time in her life to have a baby. Her career, her personal life, and her appearance couldn't handle it. Something had to be done.

A nurse opened a door and called her name. Smoothing her shirt as she stood, she followed her into the back part of the office and entered the room the nurse ushered her into.

"Go ahead and change into this and the doctor will be in shortly," the nurse told her, handing her a paper-thin hospital-issued gown. Jari took it from her and noticed that even as certain as she was, her

hands were shaking. She looked at the gown in her hands, the hospital bed, and the sterile room. The nurse turned to leave.

Jari turned with her, doubt overshadowing her for just a moment. "The . . . I mean, it's not really a baby yet, right?"

"No. Not this early. Right now, it's a fetus and looks nothing like the babies you see around town."

"It won't feel anything, will it? Like, it won't know what's happening?" Jari asked, despising the questions, even as they came out. There was nothing wrong with what she was doing. As a woman, she had a choice. It was her body and her life. She didn't have the time or desire to have a baby, and it would complicate her life in ways she probably hadn't even begun to imagine.

"Like I said, it's not a baby yet. It can't feel anything, and of course it can't understand what's happening. It has no intellectual capabilities at this point. It's just a little clump of tissue."

Jari nodded. A clump of tissue. It was basically just like getting liposuction or having your gallbladder removed. Still, even with her mind satisfied, she hesitated. "Will it hurt?"

"Not much," the nurse assured. "Listen, Miss Cordel, babies are a really big responsibility. Are you at a place in your life where you want a baby?" Jari shook her head. "Are you at a place in your life where you could give a baby the care it needs? Are you ready to stay up nights with it? Feed it every two to three hours? Change dirty diapers? What about finding and paying for childcare while you're at work?" Jari nearly got dizzy shaking her head. "Then, for your sake and the fetus', you're doing the right thing. What kind of life would that be for a child . . . and for you? It's your choice. You get to make a decision that's best for you, best for the fetus, best for your partner . . . best for everyone involved. If having a baby isn't plausible for you right now, then you're doing the right thing; end it now before it goes any further."

"I'm doing the right thing," Jari repeated to herself. The nurse waited a moment to see if she had any more questions, and, when she didn't, left Jari alone to change.

But the nurse had lied. It did hurt–a lot. Once they were done, Jari knew that everything she had based her decision on had been a lie, because as she changed back into her clothes and left the clinic, she somehow was able to sense an absence. She felt more alone inside her body than she ever had before. In that moment, she had the heart-shocking realization that just a few hours earlier, there had truly been another living being inside of her. There had been two where there was now only one.

~~~~~

Jari woke up abruptly. She looked around the dark room and listened to the sound of Bill snoring beside her. She instinctively smoothed the crease of the sheets over the comforter, then raised her shaking hands to her face. Her cheeks were wet. She wiped her nose with the back of her hand and took several deep, calming breaths.

She hadn't dreamt about the day she had an abortion in several years, and certainly not in such detail. It had been over a decade ago, yet the pain and emptiness felt as fresh as if it were only yesterday.

She would never forget how empty she felt on her way home that day, or how she had laid in bed and cried the rest of the week. At the time, she had thought it was the right decision—her only option—yet she couldn't force herself to eat a bite of food, leave the house, or get out of bed.

She counted up how old her child would be, and her heart sank. Twelve. She would have had a twelve-year-old. In the years since her abortion, she had come to think of the baby as a girl. Now, the minutes ticked by on her bedside clock as she tried to imagine what the preteen would be like. She tried to picture her in her mind, wondered about her personality, and guessed at what she would enjoy. Sadness filled her, knowing she would never know.

What she had done that day was so permanent. There was no going back—no changing her mind. The child was gone.

Tears coursed down her cheeks and wet her pillow as she cried out to God. She knew she didn't deserve to ever have another baby. He had given her one, and she had discarded it like a piece of trash. She had played God and cut off a life that He had destined to live. Her heart wrestled with the consequences of her actions, and sorrow pooled within her like a painful lump. Even after all the times she had asked the Lord for a baby, even after all the years that had gone by, even with a test lying on the bathroom counter waiting for morning to come, she had a hard time believing that God, even in His great mercy, could give her another chance. Surely, He would not give her another baby. She didn't deserve one. Her throat tightened painfully until it was difficult to draw in a breath.

Her eyes fell on her husband, lying asleep in the bed beside her. Through the darkness, she could just make out the features of his handsome face. He was a good man. A man of principle and conviction. Though it hadn't always been that way, he had grown leaps and bounds in his character over the past five years. Though he looked the same, he was not the same man she had married. She loved who he had become and how they had grown together. Watching him sleep, her heart filled with dread. She hadn't ever told him about what she'd done, and though part of her wanted to be free of the painful secret she bore, she was terrified for him to know. What would he think of her? Would he still love her?

If she had only told him in the beginning, back when he wouldn't have cared. Back then, he wouldn't have thought twice about it. But now, he understood the sanctity of life. He fought for the rights of unborn babies. And she knew he would grieve over what she had done. In the deepest part of her, she was still afraid that his love for her would run out, that he could tire of her just as he had Carla. If he found out what she had done, if he knew the depths of her shame, would he reject her? Would his love for her fade? Would he still want to be married to her? The weight of her sin bearing down on her, keeping her trapped in her secret prison of regret and shame, her tears came faster.

Knowing they were on the verge of becoming sobs, she turned over and forced herself to take several deep breaths. She couldn't wake Bill. She couldn't face the questions that would come if she did. And she couldn't endure much more of the pain that felt like a physical weight pressing down on her chest. The emotions, the guilt, were too big and too consuming. So she closed off the painful memories of the abortion as she had so many times before and focused on tracing patterns in the texture on the walls until her eyelids grew heavy, and she finally fell back asleep.

The next morning, Bill woke her with a kiss. Covering a yawn with her hand, she pushed herself into a sitting position and leaned back against the headboard. She glanced at the clock and saw that her alarm was set to go off in five minutes.

"I'm ready to head downstairs to read the paper but don't want to go down until you take the test. I think we should read the results together."

In a rush, it all came back to her—the nausea, Bill's suggestion, stopping by the store, and reading that she should wait until morning. Her dream and midnight sorrow forgotten, her excitement spiked, and she jumped out of bed.

"Don't read the results without me," Bill called after her, chuckling, as she ran into the bathroom. Her heart warmed at his words. Whether or not he had wanted a baby, he cared enough to want to read the results together. She followed the directions, then set the test on the counter with the directions covering the results window while she brushed her teeth. She knew she needed to give it time to develop properly, but her excitement made the short wait feel excruciatingly long. Bill came to stand beside her as she finished.

"Are you ready?" he asked as she dried her mouth on the towel. Straightening, she took a deep breath and nodded, pressing her hands to her stomach, trying to calm the butterflies within and the shaking that had overtaken her.

Bill reached for the test and picked it up, leaving the directions on the counter. His expression didn't reveal anything as he looked at the results window.

"Well . . ." he paused and looked up at her face, his expression serious. Her heart pounded faster and faster until she felt as if it would burst from her chest. Suddenly, his face broke into a grin, and he turned the test so she could see it. "I hope you were serious about wanting a baby!"

She covered her mouth with both hands, stifling her sharp intake of breath. "We're going to have a baby?" she cried, barely able to believe it. Bill nodded, and she started jumping up and down in excitement. She bounced into his arms and held on tight, still bouncing. Tears ran down her cheeks as she laughed, and she released a happy shriek of delight.

The news only beginning to sink in, she drew back, studying Bill's face. His expression was absolutely beautiful to her. So many emotions filled his face—vulnerability, uncertainty, nervousness—but more than any other, joy ruled his expression.

"Are you happy?" she asked, putting her hand against his chest.

He reached out and pulled her close again, pressing his cheek against hers. "Very happy," he told her, kissing the side of her face and then pressing it against his once again. "I'm happy that you're happy, and . . . I'm happy that we're having a baby." He pulled back so he could see her face, his expression serious again. "I won't lie to you—I still have my concerns. I feel old. I feel scared. I feel ill-prepared for the task of having an infant, but because we left it up to the wisdom of God, I know it's right. And even if it's scary, I want to have children with you, Jari. You are the love of my life, and you are going to make a wonderful mother."

Tears collected in her eyes again, and she felt her face blossom in a loving smile. "I love you, Bill Cordel. Thank you. Thank you for being willing to go down this road—for even giving it a chance. Thank you for trusting the LORD."

Bill pressed a kiss to her temple and gathered her into his arms to hold her for another long moment before stepping back. "I'd better grab some breakfast and get to the office. I still don't know why they plan dinners like that on Thursdays—it feels like it should be Saturday today."

She released him begrudgingly, knowing he was right. He had stepped out on a limb, agreeing to start a family with her. She needed to allow him to do his job and focus on his career in the midst of it, even after the exciting news they had just discovered.

Jari walked with him through their bedroom and down the stairs. Leaving him to pick up his morning papers on the front step, she veered off into the kitchen to start the coffee. Standing with her hip against the counter, she thought of their options for breakfast. She looked at the toaster and considered the English muffins they had nearly every morning but decided against them. This was a day for celebrating.

Deciding to make something special, she opened a cupboard and pulled out a box of blueberry muffin mix. She hummed a joyful tune as she moved about the kitchen, measuring the water and mixing the batter.

She was pregnant! They were going to have a baby! She could hardly believe it.

Her steps light, her heart singing, she sprayed the muffin pan and spooned batter into the extra-large cups. Satisfied with the four giant muffins it would make, she sprinkled brown sugar and oats over the top. She poured Bill a cup of coffee and took it to him.

To her surprise, not one of the morning papers was out of its protective sleeve. They had all been tossed carelessly onto the table, and Bill was leaning back in his chair, one ankle propped up on the opposite knee, a troubled look on his face.

Jari's heart fell at the worry she saw etched into the lines that had gathered around his eyes and the hard slash of his lips. Was he having second thoughts about the baby? Had his doubts overshadowed his excitement? She set his coffee down carefully and touched his shoulder.

"Are you okay?" His only answer was a grunt. "Is it the baby?" she asked, her words careful and measured. He turned his head quickly to look at her, surprise replacing his worry.

"No! No, it's not the baby," he said, catching her hand and kissing the back of it. Releasing it, he sat quietly for a long moment. "Have you noticed any unfamiliar cars parked outside lately? Or parked farther down the street?"

His thoughtful questions filled her with unease, even as she felt joy that he wasn't having second thoughts about the new life growing within her. She closed her eyes, trying to remember.

"Not that I've noticed," she finally answered, and he nodded quietly, lost in thought. "Why?"

He took a long moment to answer, almost as if he wasn't going to. "When I went out to get the papers, there was a black SUV parked across the street. When I opened the door, he sped off, spinning his tires."

"Did you see who was driving?" Jari asked, trying not to jump to conclusions.

"No, the window tinting was too dark."

"Well, maybe it was a coincidence," she said slowly, attempting to be rational. Perhaps the driver had simply been looking up directions on their phone or texting, and just happened to leave as Bill opened the door.

Bill thought for a moment longer and then nodded. "Maybe it was. Just keep an eye out for the next couple of days, okay? Each time you walk by a window or door facing the street, just glance out and see if that same vehicle is anywhere around. And keep the doors locked, just in case."

Jari nodded firmly, praying for peace as she pushed away the fear that was trying to edge its way into her consciousness. "I will."

The lines of concern fading, Bill reached out and pulled Jari down onto his lap. He kissed her soundly and then rested his forehead against hers. "We're going to have a baby!" he said, his expression full of wonder.

Her heart soared at his reminder and tender affection. "I love celebrating this with you," she told him softly. "And I'm so excited to have your child and build a family together."

The oven beeped, letting her know it was preheated and ready for the muffins. She leaned in for one last kiss before jumping up and hurrying around the peninsula to put the muffins in the oven so she wouldn't make him late for work. Bill reached for the newspaper closest to him and pulled it out of the protective sleeve before flipping it open and giving it a hard shake to make it stand upright. Jari set the timer on the oven and poured herself a glass of orange juice.

As she waited for the muffins and sipped on her orange juice, her mind turned back to the news of the morning. She was pregnant! After wanting a baby for so very long, with the intensity of her longing building year after year, now that she was actually pregnant, it almost seemed surreal. "Thank You, Father," she whispered brokenly. "Thank You for giving me a gift I do not deserve."

The weight of knowing what she had done all those years ago and the magnitude of His mercy brought her close to tears, but she blinked them away. It was not a day for wallowing in the sins or sorrows of the past, but for celebrating. She didn't feel worthy of being given a second chance at being a mother. She didn't feel worthy of being the recipient of such loving-kindness. But the truth was, the LORD had shown her mercy. The truth was, she was pregnant, and there was a new life growing within her.

She spread her fingers over her abdomen and looked down at the place where her tiny little one grew within. "Things will be different this time," she promised. "You are wanted, you are rejoiced over, and you are loved. We are thrilled about you and cannot wait to meet you!"

She sliced an orange and arranged the slices decoratively on two plates. The timer on the oven went off, and she cracked the oven door to see if their breakfast was ready. The aroma caused her belly to growl and her mouth to water. The tops of the muffins were golden brown, and the streusel topping was crumbly. Perfect. Jari pulled the pan from the oven, placing a muffin on each plate with the orange slices, and carried them to the table.

As she set Bill's plate in front of him, he took a long sniff of the freshly baked aroma and smiled up at her appreciatively. "Now, that's a breakfast worth waiting for."

"Good," she told him, pausing to press a kiss against the top of his head, then reaching for his empty coffee cup. Hurrying back to the kitchen, determined not to let her muffin grow cold, she filled his coffee cup, grabbed her own glass of orange juice, and joined him at the table. He said a quick prayer, and they ate their breakfast, Jari savoring each bite, and Bill hurrying so he could leave for the office.

Still chewing, Bill scooted his chair back and stood, collecting the newspapers he hadn't yet opened and tucking them under his arm. He bent to kiss Jari goodbye. "Thanks for breakfast, honey." He held her eyes for a long moment. "I'm happy about the baby. I'll be thinking about it all day." Her answering smile was bright and warm, and he kissed her again. "I'll be home when I can. It might be a late one tonight. I have that committee meeting this afternoon."

She nodded, used to the routine. "Have a good day, Bill," she told him as he stood straight again and drained the rest of his coffee. "I love you."

"Love you too. See you tonight." He reached for his briefcase and headed for the door, which she heard shut behind him seconds later.

Not yet finished with her breakfast, she peeled a slice of orange and ate it slowly as she formulated a plan for the rest of her day. She was serving lunch at the homeless shelter again, but otherwise, the whole day spread out before her.

Reaching for her laptop, she slid it closer and opened the top, powering it on. First on her agenda was finding good prenatal vitamins. Then she would clean up breakfast, start some laundry, call and make an appointment with her doctor, and spend some time in the sun, finishing her book, before getting ready and heading into town. The warm days wouldn't last much longer, and she wanted to take advantage of them as long as she could. After serving at the shelter, she would go to the mall to buy Bill a new pair of gray dress slacks. She had noticed the week before that he had a small stain on the right pant leg of his current pair, and she knew he wore them often. Thinking of recent loads of laundry, she decided she would get him a few more pairs of black socks as well, as the dryer seemed to be eating them again.

Suddenly, the thought of folding little baby socks filled her mind and drew a tender smile. The knowledge that baby clothes and accessories were going to become part of her reality in the near future surprised her again. It was going to take a while to really comprehend what that positive test meant.

Smiling, she began her search for prenatal vitamins. Half an hour later, she left the table and went to grab her purse from where she had left it by the door the night before. Taking her wallet out, she left the purse where it had been and started back to the table, flipping through to find the credit card she would use to place her order.

As she passed through the great room, she glanced into Bill's home office. Something out the window on the far right of the room caught her attention. Through the sheer window treatment she had picked out specifically for its ability to allow visibility out but not in, she saw the front end of a black vehicle parked across the street.

Alarm coursed through her as she slowly made her way toward the window for a better look. Sure enough, a black SUV with darkly tinted windows sat across the street. She tried to identify whether or not there was a driver in the vehicle, but couldn't make anything out through the tinted glass. Her first instinct was to call the police, but when she glanced up from the SUV to the Randall's house, which was right up from the ominous vehicle, she saw their driveway was full of cars and vehicles lined their side of the street. Jari breathed a sigh of relief. The black SUV wasn't anything suspicious, just a guest at her neighbor's party. Likely, a guest had arrived early for the morning bridge parties Elizabeth Randall frequently hosted and simply got spooked when Bill came out on the front porch.

Feeling much more at ease, she left the window and made her way back to the table and her laptop, where the website was still waiting on her credit card information to complete her transaction.

Nine

I should tell my mom, Jari thought as she took the exit off the freeway that would take her home. She had just finished at the doctor's office and was on her way home to get ready to meet Bill for dinner. Except for Sunday, she had barely seen him in the six days since they found out she was pregnant, and she was ready for some quality time with her husband.

At her appointment, Dr. Corvich had shared in Jari's joy when she gave her the results of her official pregnancy test. She was, in fact, going to have a baby. Jari had watched Dr. Corvich offer exceptional care to Jessica years earlier as she walked with the teen through her pregnancy, and now, Jari couldn't think of anyone else she wanted walking with her through her own.

Together, they calculated that Jari was eight weeks and four days pregnant. Dr. Corvich showed her a replica of the size of her baby, and Jari was amazed that such a tiny thing would eventually grow into a child, and one day, an adult. Dr. Corvich laughed at Jari's amazement and responded by saying, "Just add food and water!"

They went over healthy nutrition and the dos and don'ts of pregnancy. They discussed the importance of exercise, but the need for Jari to keep her heart rate within a healthy range for the baby. Dr. Corvich suggested she avoid caffeine, sushi, blue cheese, and buffets, and encouraged her to make sure she was getting all her fruits, vegetables, and water. She explained the prenatal process and some of the things Jari could expect over the next eight months. Jari remembered some of the information from when Jessica was pregnant, but the reminder was helpful, as was hearing the latest pregnancy rules, which, according to Dr. Corvich, seemed to always be changing.

Now, as she drove home, the only thing she could think about was calling her mom and telling her the news. Mary Braxon should know that she was about to become a grandma, and Jari could think of nothing she wanted more in that moment than to tell her. Still, she never moved to pick up her cell phone.

After so many years away, with only an occasional phone call that was always more stilted and awkward than comfortable and deep, she didn't even know what her mother's reaction would be if she called to tell her. Nor would she understand the journey Jari had been on to get to this point or the joy that she felt. Her mom wouldn't understand how deep the emotions went or be able to share in the appreciation of the kindness and mercy of God that was being displayed. To call and tell her mom of the news and have the kind of superficial, impersonal response that would understandably come would be worse than not calling her at all. On the flip side, the thought of having a conversation which went into the deep things of Jari's past and heart in order to give her mom the understanding necessary to respond in a deep and meaningful way seemed too overwhelming and scary.

No, she wouldn't call and tell her mom. Not now. She would wait until the news sank in, and she had fully explored the depths of joy it brought. Maybe then she would be ready to tell people who would simply be excited with her about a new baby.

Oh, but if only the last fifteen years hadn't happened like they had, and she could call and cry happy tears with her mom, dream about the future, and make plans together for the pregnancy and birth. Her mom was the best at entering into other people's stories and feeling the highs and lows right alongside them. If only Jari hadn't shut her out—or had the courage to let her in. If only she could share the news and her mom could start making arrangements at the flower shop so she could stay with Jari for a week or two during her postpartum. If only her mom could be there for the birth of her first grandchild, and share Jari's joy as Dr. Corvich laid her child in her arms for the very first time. But that wasn't going to happen, and it was Jari's fault. She had walked out when she should have stayed. She had stayed away when she should have gone back. And now, too much time had passed. "Father, please heal my family," she prayed into the interior of her car. She didn't have the courage to go home yet, but she had the courage to pray and trust that He was working in her heart and in the hearts of her family in Kansas.

With calling her mom out of the question, the only other person Jari wanted to tell right away was Jessica. Too ashamed, she had never told her stepdaughter about her abortion. Jari had never even shared about her desire to have children of her own because of the complexities of Jessica being Bill's daughter, but even still, she felt that her best friend had known she wanted them. Now, she wanted to share her happy news with her. But she didn't call her either. Telling Jessica about the baby was more complicated than telling a best friend, even though that's exactly what she was. Jessica was Bill's daughter—his grown daughter—and the situation had to be handled carefully. Telling Jessica, not knowing how she would react to the news now and in the years to come, was what Bill was most nervous about. Jari wanted to proceed carefully, as a couple. Unfortunately, that left her with no one to call.

As Jari turned onto her street, her breath caught as she noticed a black SUV parked in front of her nicely manicured yard, positioned in such a way that it was hidden from the house by a large, sculpted bush. From its hiding place, Jari knew her front door was visible, as was the garage door. She glanced up the street to the Randalls', but this time, their wide circle drive was empty.

Uneasiness rose up within her, and she bit her lip, contemplating what to do. Though she wasn't close enough to make out the license plate, the chrome wheels were fancy and set it apart. She felt sure it was the same SUV that had been parked outside her neighbors' during their party last week and the same SUV she had noticed driving two cars behind her as she ran to the grocery store yesterday evening. Was it simply a new neighbor who happened to need groceries as well? The idea seemed unlikely given the SUV's current parking place.

Her mind flashed back to the scare they'd had at Jessica's apartment last spring. A man who was upset with Bill had broken into Jessi's apartment, ransacked the place, and left a threatening note. The perpetrator was arrested just twelve hours after the ransacked apartment was discovered, yet Jari remembered all too well the fear she had felt in those twelve hours, as well as in the weeks leading up to it when they had been receiving threats from the same man. It was comforting that the culprit had been caught, yet enemies were not uncommon in politics. Bill had made plenty of them. A shiver ran through her, and for the first time, she felt fear for their unborn child and acknowledged the ramifications of having a father who held a political office. And, if their future held the fulfillment of Bill's vocational aspirations, it would only get worse.

Rethinking her decision to go home and change before dinner, she made a right at the corner. The idea of walking into the house alone with the suspicious vehicle parked outside was frightening. She would tell Bill about it at dinner and wait to go home until he was with her. She checked the clock. She had two hours before she was supposed to meet him. Considering her change in plans, she needed something to do. Weighing her options, she headed to the mall, deciding it was best to spend the time in a public place rather than home alone in their large and spacious house.

Her heart began to race as she glanced up into her rearview mirror and spotted what she thought was the black SUV four or five cars behind her in traffic, though without being able to see the wheels, she couldn't be sure. She considered calling the police, but hesitated, not wanting to make a big deal out of nothing. If it truly was a coincidence—or a different SUV altogether—she didn't want to appear fearful and foolish. She decided if she could lose the vehicle, she would wait and tell Bill about it at dinner and let him decide the best course of action. If she couldn't, she would make the call. Thankful that she knew the area so well, she made a few sudden turns onto connecting streets before circling back around to continue on course. After glancing in her rearview mirror several more times, she breathed a sigh of relief, thankful that she seemed to have lost her tail.

Pulling into the mall parking lot, she circled for several minutes, looking for a parking place that was close to the doors and under a light post. The days were getting shorter, and she didn't want to take the chance of having to walk a long distance through a dark parking lot alone. Finally, finding a parking place she was satisfied with, she pulled in, grabbed her purse and cell phone and headed for the mall entrance.

The air held just a hint of coolness, and she caught the scent of fall on the breeze. The leaves on the trees were likely only a few weeks away from turning, and, her thoughts momentarily diverted from the alarming situation at home, her excitement began to build. She loved the East Coast in the autumn. The landscape exploded into a vibrant display of color, painting a picture capable of taking one's breath away. It was in the fall that she loved living in D.C. the most. No matter how many years she had lived there, she never tired of the radiant reds, vibrant oranges, and dramatic golds that graced the trees every autumn.

She thought again of her mom and wished she could come to D.C. in the fall to see the colors. Growing up, Jari had thought fall in Kansas was beautiful. And, in its own way, it was. The colors were decidedly understated when compared to the colors out East, but it held a charm and beauty of its own. Still, she knew her mom would enjoy the fall foliage as much as she did. Their love of fall was something they had shared.

She remembered as a child, hunting for leaves on chilly fall days with her mom. Once they found several types of leaves, they took them in the house, put a sheet of paper over them, and colored them with the long side of crayons so the ridges and designs of each unique leaf would stand out. They would sip hot apple cider while they colored, and her mom would make cookies, which she let Jari eat warm.

Smiling at the happy memory, Jari decided she would start the tradition with her own child in a few years. Giving the great outdoors one last glance, she swung open the door to the mall and went inside.

Turning toward her favorite department store, she found herself wishing Jessica was shopping with her. They had spent countless hours together in the store, looking through rack after rack of merchandise, searching for the perfect top, dress, pantsuit, or pair of jeans. It was the store they had always shopped for the girls' clothes in, and where they found the bridesmaid dress for Jessica's sister-in-law, Kara, to wear in Joe and Jessi's wedding. The department store held a lot of memories for Jari, and nearly all of them included Jessica.

Suppressing the loneliness that was rising up inside of her, Jari wandered through the different departments and found herself in the baby section. Excitement replacing the lonely feelings, she meandered through the section, oohing and ahhing over several outfits and blankets. Unable to resist a soft, gray and white striped sleeper with a green gator on the side, she picked up one for a newborn and tucked it under her arm.

In the baby girl section, she held up several adorable outfits but kept glancing back to one particular set that included a pink hat that was made to look like a strawberry, a onesie with a matching strawberry on the chest and little pink pants that had strawberry feet. Finally, she added the outfit to the gray and white sleeper under her arm. Whatever gender the baby was, she reasoned, she would have something for it. She simply couldn't help herself.

Before she could tear herself away from the baby section, she added a ridiculously soft white blanket with the words 'little miracle' stitched into the bottom right-hand corner, and a yellow-hooded duck towel to her small stash. Finally, forcing herself to move on, she considered her reflection in a mirror in the ladies' section.

The restaurant where she was meeting Bill wasn't terribly fancy, but her jeans, long-sleeved tee and ornamental silk scarf weren't going to cut it. Flipping through hangers on rack after rack, she found a lot of cute options, but nothing she was terribly excited about. Moving to a rack of casual dresses, she found a black one that was perfect.

The dress itself was plain enough, but the black sheer poncho that went over it was as long as the knee-length dress underneath and went down to her forearms. The wide band of black sequins that lined the hem of the poncho all the way around added class and style. She hurried to the dressing room and put it on, enjoying the feel of the fabric and the stylish look of the dress. She had seen a similar style in a magazine just the week before. The underdress was form-fitting, yet had a lot of give in the fabric. It would be perfect as she grew with the baby, as would the flowing and shapeless overdress. Keeping the dress on, she added the black heels she had been wearing with her jeans, collected her things, and headed to the check-out counter.

Laughing with the clerk about wearing her new purchase home from the store, she checked out, putting the clothes she had been wearing in the bag with the baby things. When the clerk commented on the sweet baby items, oohing and aahing over them just as Jari had, Jari smiled and agreed, but didn't tell the woman she was expecting. Eventually, the press and the public would know that Senator Cordel was expecting a baby with his second wife, but she didn't want it to get out before they told Jessica.

With her purchases nicely packaged in a bag, she headed to the ladies' room, where she touched up her makeup and added a spritz of hairspray to her long, blonde hair. Admiring her new black dress in the mirror once again, she was satisfied that she would be appropriately attired for her evening out with Bill. Checking her watch, she put on lip gloss, dumped her travel-sized cosmetic bag and hairspray back into her purse, and left the bathroom.

She expertly made her way through the department store and back into the mall. Starting to feel hungry and knowing she still had to make it through rush hour traffic to the restaurant, she picked up a fruit smoothie, which she drank on her way back to the entrance. Stepping out the door cautiously, she scanned the parking lot for the black SUV. Not seeing it, she quickly made her way to her car and got in, her keys positioned in her hand in such a way to allow her to ward off an attacker, should it be necessary. Once inside her car with the doors locked, she tossed her bag into the back seat and put her purse on the seat next to her.

Backing out of her parking place, she made her way through town, moving slowly in the rush hour traffic. She parked outside the restaurant five minutes early and headed inside to meet Bill. Giving the hostess her last name, she was escorted to the table that had been reserved for them. Her heart fell a little when she saw that Bill had not yet arrived. She took her seat, hoping he wouldn't be long.

After not being able to talk to anyone about her doctor's appointment, the outfits she had found, the black SUV, or the other happenings of her day, she realized just how much she was coming to depend on Bill to not only be her husband but also her friend.

When their relationship first started, it had been based on passion. As busy as he was, they had been focused on simply seizing any moments they could find to be together. Their first year as a couple had been a series of whirlwind trips and romantic weekends away. It had felt glamorous and exciting, thrilling and full of adventure. By the time Jari found herself needing companionship in addition to romance, Jessica had arrived, and she hadn't needed Bill to fill the role of her best friend—something he was fine with as he continued to be consumed with his career. Over the years, Jessica had filled that companion role for her as they discussed every part of their lives together, sharing feelings, thoughts, ideas, and plans on a daily basis. Now that Jessica was in Minnesota with a husband who filled that role in her life and a daily schedule and a life of her own, Jari was keenly feeling the hole her dear friend's absence had left. They could still be friends, *were* still friends—even very close friends—but it wasn't the same.

Now, Jari needed Bill to step up and fill that role of deep companion. She knew that girlfriends were important, and she had them, but she needed Bill to be the best friend he had never been—the one she felt comfortable sharing her heart, her dreams, her struggles, and her joys with. And she realized she needed to step up and be that to him as well.

When they first met, their relationship was based on chemistry rather than conversation, mutual likes, similarities, or friendship. As the initial wave of attraction passed and cooled, they thankfully found their way into a comfortable relationship that worked. She supported him in his career, and he gave her the time, money, and independence to do whatever she desired. She listened to him talk about work, and he listened to what was going on with Jessi and the girls. They tried to fit in dinner together at least three times a week and once in a while, when they weren't in an election year and she didn't have anything else going on, Jari joined him for a round of golf on the weekends. They had learned how to be man and woman and husband and wife, but looking back, she realized they had never learned how to be friends.

Over the past few months, that had slowly begun to change. She found herself hearing more of Bill's hopes and dreams for the future and sharing some of hers with him. Even in the midst of the busyness of an election year, they had spent more quality time together than ever before. They discovered some things they liked to do together, such as spending evenings on the patio and going on walks. Bill had begun texting her once or twice throughout the day, just to ask how she was doing and let her know he was thinking about her. She took more of an active interest in what was going on with him at the office and in what he thought about things. Now, she realized how much she was looking forward to this dinner with him, not only for the comfort of being with *someone*—anyone—but for the sake of being with *him*. She looked forward to hearing how his day had been and telling him about her own.

Glancing up as motion near the door caught her eye, she saw him coming toward her, and she smiled, standing to greet him. Reaching her, Bill took her elbows and pulled her close for a brief moment, pressing a sound kiss against her lips and smiling warmly at her. "You look beautiful."

Returning his warm smile, she accepted his compliment. "Thank you."

"I hope you weren't waiting long," he went on as he moved to hold her chair. When she was seated again, he took his own seat across from her.

"No, I've only been here about ten minutes," she answered.

"Good, good. Well, do you know what you're having tonight?" Bill asked, opening the menu. Her husband was strictly predictable. They would see to the business of ordering their dinner and then, and only then, would the conversation begin.

"No, I haven't even looked," she admitted, picking up her own menu and glancing through it.

Bill set his down. "I'm ready to order."

Wondering at how he always decided so quickly, she asked, "What are you having?"

The waiter came to take their drink order. Bill ordered iced tea, and Jari settled for a strawberry lemonade.

"I'm having the prime rib with a salad, red potatoes, and steamed vegetables," Bill answered once the waiter left. "What looks good to you?"

Glancing through the menu again before answering, she made a face. "Everything. That's the problem."

117

Bill chuckled. "I'll decide for you then. You'll have the sirloin with lobster, a salad, the red potatoes, and broccoli."

Jari's first instinct was to object, but she bit her tongue before she could. Bill was a man who was used to being in charge and was a classic fixer. If she struggled to decide on something, he tried to help by deciding for her. Knowing he was only trying to be helpful, she reminded herself of the independence she normally enjoyed and smiled. "That sounds good."

Tomorrow, she could decide for herself what she would eat; she could humor him tonight. Besides, his selection for her sounded delicious. If she objected, it would only be on principle. The waiter came back with their drinks, and Bill ordered for them both. As the waiter left, Bill turned toward her. She considered telling him about the SUV but held off, wanting a few minutes of normal conversation before they broached the subject.

"So, how was your day?" he asked, reaching across the table to take her hand.

"It was good," she answered honestly, thankful that the days had become much easier than they had been in early summer, when she had battled loneliness so intensely.

"What did the doctor say?" Bill asked, stirring a packet of sugar into his iced tea and then taking his first drink. For a brief moment, Jari wished that she, too, could enjoy a glass of tea with her dinner as usual. But Dr. Corvich had recommended avoiding caffeinated drinks altogether during her pregnancy, and the little one inside of her was certainly worth the sacrifice. Jari sipped her lemonade and relayed the details of her doctor's appointment to Bill. He nodded as she talked, asking a question here and there. She appreciated the way he was putting effort into being an active listener.

"How was your day?" she asked when she finished telling him about her doctor's appointment. Their salads were brought in the midst of him conveying the happenings of his day and the challenges he was facing, both in his office and in the campaign, and he continued talking between forkfuls of lettuce. It wasn't until the main course had been served that Jari knew she had to face the topic she had been dreading.

"Is your dress new?" Bill asked, cutting into his prime rib.

"Yes, it is."

"Well, I like it. It's very pretty."

Jari smiled, appreciating his compliment and the effort he continued to put forth. "Thank you. I'm glad you like it." She paused. "I was planning to go home and change after my appointment before coming to meet you for dinner, but that didn't end up working out. Instead, I went to the mall and found this to wear to dinner."

"Just felt like doing some shopping?" Bill asked, looking amused. "How many things did you pick up for the baby? I knew once you had your first appointment, the accumulation would begin."

Jari made a face at her husband. "I did end up getting a few things for the baby, but for your information, that's not why I went to the mall instead of going home."

He chuckled. "Do tell, why did you go to the mall if not to shop?"

Jari hesitated for just a moment, enjoying the lighthearted conversation, reluctant to see it end. "The black SUV was parked just up the street again, Bill. With a clear line of sight to the house."

Bill's amusement faded quickly. "You're sure it was the same one?"

"I'm sure."

"Was it parked outside the Randalls' again? Perhaps they have company from out of town staying with them."

Jari shook her head. "It was parked north of the house this time, behind that large shrub." Bill rubbed his chin, his mouth flattening into a thin line. "I turned at the corner instead of going home. I thought about calling the cops but was worried I was jumping to conclusions and that it would turn out to be nothing. So, I decided to go to the mall. I thought if something suspicious was going on, there would be safety in being in public."

Bill exhaled hard. "You should have called the cops and let them check it out. Or called me and let me handle it."

She shrugged. "I knew you had meetings this afternoon."

"Well, I'm glad you didn't go home at least. Staying in a public place was probably wise."

"When I left the neighborhood, I think they were tailing me. I lost them easily enough. If they do mean us some kind of harm, I don't believe they're professionals."

"Well, that's a relief," Bill shot back, the concern and frustration evident in the lines that had gathered on his forehead and in the sarcasm in his tone. He held up his hand as if needing a minute to think and get control of himself. "So, we spotted the black SUV six days ago, not since, and then they were back again today?"

"I saw it yesterday, too," Jari admitted.

"Where?" He didn't look happy.

"It was a few cars behind me when I went to the grocery store."

"Why didn't you tell me?"

"I'd hoped it was simply someone from the neighborhood—maybe guests at the Randalls', just as you suggested."

Bill shook his head. "You should have told me. Don't assume anything." He thought for a moment. "Did you get a look at the license plate?"

She shook her head. Sighing, he put his head in his hands and massaged his temples. Jari reached out and touched his hand. "What are we going to do?"

"Well, we're going to call the police and have someone meet us back at the house. We'll file a report and ask them to do frequent drive-bys."

"Will you hire Mr. Myers?" Bill had hired Joseph Myers less than a handful of times over the years when security became an issue, either by threatening means or simply family privacy. The former FBI agent and his small contingent of ex-agents were well-trained and very effective. Their presence had brought her comfort and a sense of security in the past, yet the inability to be alone in her own house, on her own property, or out in public grew old very fast. That was one of the issues she was most concerned about should Bill achieve his goal of one day becoming president. She knew it wouldn't take long before she felt smothered by the secret service.

"Yes," Bill said thoughtfully. "I think I will. Do you agree? Do you think I should?"

Jari was surprised that he had asked her opinion. Weighing the options against the present situation, she finally nodded. "Better to be safe than sorry."

Bill gave a decisive nod and pulled his cell phone out of his pocket. "Excuse me. I'm going to step outside and call Joseph."

Jari agreed, feeling better already, knowing the house would be checked out and patrolled by the time they arrived home. She would actually get to sleep—something she hadn't expected to do much of since seeing the SUV outside her house earlier.

In Bill's absence, Jari's mind moved on to other things, and she let it wander as she enjoyed each bite of her dinner. Within five minutes, Bill took his seat across from her again.

"Did you get in touch with him?" Jari asked.

Bill nodded. "Everything's taken care of."

"Good."

Bill was quiet as he ate, and Jari followed suit for several minutes. Finishing her meal, she settled back in her chair with a satisfied sigh. Bill gestured to the dessert menu. "You choose tonight."

Her face lighting up, Jari took the small, thick menu and turned the pages slowly, reading each description fully before moving on to the next item. Knowing what she would choose even before she opened the menu, she finally put it back.

"Strawberry cheesecake?" Bill asked, his smile returning for the first time since she had told him about spotting the black SUV.

Jari grinned sheepishly. "It's just so good here."

Finishing his last bite, Bill raised his hand and motioned to the waiter. The neatly attired man cleared their plates, and Bill asked for a single order of the strawberry cheesecake. The generous slices were plenty to share, and they enjoyed one of the restaurant's spectacular desserts each time they visited. He ordered two cups of coffee with their dessert, and Jari requested decaf.

When the waiter departed, Jari sat forward in her chair and reached across to take Bill's hand. Meeting his eyes, she smiled. "I want to tell Jessica about the baby."

"So soon?"

Jari nodded. "I need for her to know. I need to be able to talk with her about it."

Bill was quiet for several moments, and he rubbed his chin thoughtfully. "I can understand that," he finally said before pausing. "But I want to tell her in person."

"In person?" Jari hadn't considered the idea. She had assumed they would call Jessica together after discussing how to share their news.

"Yes. In person. This is a big deal . . . a big change. I want to tell her in person, to answer all of her questions, but most importantly, to see how she takes the news."

Jari could tell Bill's mind was made up, and there was no room for debate. Not that she wanted to argue. Telling Jessica in person would mean traveling to Minnesota—something Jari had wanted to do since Jessica and the girls moved. Her heart jumped at the idea of seeing Jessica, Joe, Kelsi, and Kamryn. Maybe, if they timed it correctly, they could even go to one of Joe's games and watch the team play live rather than on television. Yes, telling Jessica in person was a great idea.

"Is Joe's game home or away this week?"

"Home," Jari answered confidently. During their last call, Jessi had mentioned how excited she was to have Joe home for the week.

"You know, this actually could be perfect timing," Bill said slowly. "If we are able to get a flight out tomorrow evening, we could meet Joe and Jessica for breakfast on Saturday, spend the day with them and the girls, and maybe look at some of the houses they're considering. Then we could attend church with Jessica on Sunday and maybe, if we're lucky, snag tickets to the game. What do you say?"

Jari beamed across the table at her husband. "I like how you think."

"Perfect. We can go spend the weekend with Jessica and Joe, and that will give Joseph and his team time to watch for the SUV and see what they can find out." Bill nodded decisively. "This will work well. I'll text Ryan and have him book us a flight."

Jari nodded. "I'll call Jessica on the way home and tell her we're coming."

"Just tell her we miss them and got a free weekend," Bill instructed. "That's true too."

Their cheesecake and coffee came, and they ate their dessert and drank their coffee in comfortable silence, both thinking of the upcoming weekend. When the cheesecake was gone, Bill met Jari's eyes. "You ready?" She nodded, and he came around to hold her chair as she stood to join him. "You know, pretty soon you'll need help standing up," he told her with a light chuckle. Her smile was warm in response—she was already looking forward to that.

Ten

"So, how do you think we should tell Jess?" Jari asked, buckling her seatbelt. The arrangements for their weekend trip had all been made, she had spent the afternoon packing, and they were now in the car on their way to the airport.

"I'm not completely sure," Bill admitted. "How do you tell your grown daughter that you're going to have a baby?" Jari had never heard him sound so unsure.

"She'll handle it well, Bill, you'll see. Jessica is a mature young woman who loves us both and wants the best for us."

"Mature or not, she's still my daughter. She doesn't want to think of me . . . you know. Besides, being pregnant at the same time as your stepmom is probably going to seem weird, no matter who you are or how much you want the best for someone."

"That's all very true," Jari conceded. "It's certainly going to be an adjustment."

Bill was stroking his chin again. "I sent her an email from the office today, telling her we'd like to meet her and Joe alone for breakfast tomorrow, and asked if that would be possible."

Jari couldn't hide her disappointment. She was not only looking forward to seeing Jessi and Joe but also Kelsi and Kamryn. Having to wait until after breakfast to see, hold, and hug the girls seemed like a long time.

"I know you're excited to see them, but I don't want the girls there when we tell Jessica. She's going to need time to process without her own daughters being there to ask questions. Especially since she's pregnant and probably extra hormonal." He held up his hands in an act of surrender at the look Jari sent him. "I didn't mean that as a criticism, it's just a fact of life. She might need a little extra time to adjust. I think it's best if we tell Jessica and then, after giving her time to process, we can tell the girls."

"The girls will be excited," Jari assured him.

"Yes, I think they will be too; but it's more complex and complicated for Jessica, and I want to respect that."

Jari nodded, understanding. "Did you hear back from her?"

"Yes. She's arranged for them to spend the morning with a friend." Bill's serious demeanor broke as he smiled. "She sounds really excited about us coming, honey."

Jari's heart swelled, and the excitement that had been building within her since making the decision to fly to Minnesota the night before, jumped to new heights. She couldn't wait for morning.

"I talked to Joseph before we left," Bill told her, changing the subject. "His team hasn't spotted the SUV today. Did you see it at all?" Jari shook her head. "Hmm. Well, either the guy got spooked with the police coming by last night and Joseph setting up camp, or he's taking the day off. We'll see if he shows up tomorrow."

"Maybe it really was nothing. Maybe it was just someone in the neighborhood, and it was all a coincidence."

"Time will tell," Bill answered grimly, never one to be too optimistic.

Once they got to the airport and made it through security, they stopped for a quick dinner before continuing to their gate, where they sat and waited almost an hour due to a delay. To pass the time,

Bill opened his briefcase and sifted through paperwork, which to Jari seemed never-ending. She pulled out a book.

After boarding, they settled back in their seats and waited for take off. "I'll let you lead the conversation tomorrow," Jari said, taking Bill's hand in her own. He nodded. "It'll be okay. You'll see."

"It will be nice to spill the beans right off the bat, so we don't have to worry about it the rest of the weekend," he conceded.

Jari agreed. "I'm looking forward to spending time with the four of them."

"So am I. It's been too long since we last saw them," Bill answered, leaning back in his seat and looking more peaceful.

"May was a long time ago," Jari agreed sadly. There wasn't a day that had passed in the months since Joe and Jessi's wedding that she hadn't missed Jessi and the girls. After spending nearly six years with them day in and day out, their abrupt departure had been jolting. Phone calls and video chats were usually enough to ease the sting of their absence, but being with them in person would be exponentially better.

"You know, in a way, it's nice to have them out of the state and taken care of since it's an election year, and our schedules are pretty full with campaign activities." Bill held up a hand to silence the protests he saw on her face. "But I miss the interruptions, the little giggles, and all the shrieking in the house more than I ever thought I would. I miss Jessi being close by, needing help moving furniture, inviting us over for dinner, or calling me to come pick her up because she ran her car out of gas." Bill chuckled and so did Jari as she recalled how annoyed Jessica was with herself when she did the latter last spring. "I knew I would miss them when they left, but I didn't realize I would miss them this much."

Jari squeezed Bill's hand and rested her head against his shoulder. Her husband could be blunt and seemingly unfeeling at times, but in moments like these, she was reminded that he had a tender heart beneath the weathered and hard exterior. It was in these moments that she felt connected to him in a deep way—moments that seemed to be growing closer together and more frequent.

"I can only imagine how much you've missed them," Bill continued. "You were with them more than I ever was. You've helped raise the girls all these years."

"It has been hard," Jari confessed, holding his hand a little tighter. "As you know, there have been some really lonely days." It was quiet for several moments.

"I can see why you want to have children of our own. I know how much you care for Kelsi and Kammy, and I'm sure they've left . . . quite a void. I know they have for me."

Jari didn't know how to respond or even if a response was necessary. She got the feeling that Bill simply wanted her to know that he understood. She appreciated that. A lot.

Throughout their flight, they went back and forth between sitting in comfortable silence and sharing conversation. Bill worked on more paperwork, and they munched on pretzels and ginger ale. When the plane landed at the Minneapolis/St. Paul International Airport, they picked up their luggage and summoned a taxi.

On their way to the hotel, Jari called Jessica to let her know they had landed and were headed to their room to get some sleep. The excitement in Jessi's voice warmed her heart. They went over the details for breakfast the next morning, and then spent a few minutes chatting about their flight, Jessi's day, and their plans for the weekend. When they pulled up outside of the hotel, Jari ended the call with a promise to see her in less than twelve hours.

The next morning, Bill and Jari took a taxi to the restaurant Jessi had specified and arrived fifteen minutes early. Nervous and excited all at the same time, Jari sipped the cranberry juice she had ordered and watched Bill. He was pensive this morning. He rubbed his jaw and drank his coffee, glancing toward the door every twenty seconds. She knew he was worried about telling Jessi about the baby. His unease emanated from him.

Her own emotions went back and forth. She couldn't wait to see Joe and Jessica, and excitement bubbled up within her, even as her nerves served as a lid on that same excitement. She honestly wasn't sure how the conversation was going to go, and she so desperately wanted it to go well. She needed Jessica, her very dearest friend, to be excited with her. Even more than that, she knew that Bill needed his daughter's support on the one thing he was most nervous about.

Bill wasn't one who took risks. Everything he did was calculated, strategic, and planned. It was a necessary skill in his profession, but it was more than that—it was who he was. Their affair had been his one moment of uncalculated weakness, his one instance of doing something foolish that didn't make any sense. In the midst of his carefully strategized life, she tried to tell herself that her husband had been deeply in love with her—drawn to her—and even his calculated nature could not keep him from being with her. She needed to think of the beginning of their relationship like that, not as a foolish mistake on his part, caused by a midlife crisis. She wished their relationship and their marriage hadn't started on such shady terms, but there was no going back to change things. Now, all they could do was give it their best to move forward as a godly couple. Still, she knew their affair had been wrong, and it had gone against the very core of who Bill Cordel was. Not necessarily morally at that time in his life, but contrary to his strategic nature.

Knowing that, knowing the kind of person he was, she knew this baby was likely one of the most uncalculated, unplanned, and unconventional things he would ever do. And she knew that weighed heavily on him.

She was about to reach for his hand when he abruptly stood. Following his gaze to the front door, she saw the reason. Coming out of her seat, all of her concerns and apprehension forgotten, Jari nearly danced across the restaurant until she reached the beaming couple and threw her arms around them both at the same time, blubbering hellos and feeling moisture in the corners of her eyes. She squeezed Jessica for a long time, feeling all the months of missing her fall away in that instant.

Jessi laughed and returned the hug. "Oh, Jari, I've missed you!"

Finally stepping back, Jari swiped at her eyes. "I've missed you, too! So much! Come on, come say hello to your dad. He can't wait to see you!" Looping her arm through Jessi's, they crossed the restaurant together to the table where Joe and Bill were just shaking hands and Joe was taking a seat, his customary grin in place. Jari sat down while Bill and Jessi embraced, Bill holding on to his daughter a moment or two longer than Jari had ever seen before. She smiled as she realized he really had missed his only child. Her husband was becoming more tender than she had ever known him to be.

When everyone had taken their seats, Bill asked Joe about football, and Joe filled them in on his last game. "And tell them the good news!" Jessi prompted, squeezing her husband's hand, her crystal blue eyes full of excitement.

"I was able to get tickets for everyone to tomorrow's game," Joe said, grinning.

Jari beamed, barely able to contain her excitement. She'd been so hoping he would be able to. Jessi had said he was going to check to see if he could, but she hadn't been overly optimistic. The team they were playing was a known rival, and tickets were hard to come by, especially on such short notice. Jari couldn't wait to see their son-in-law play in-person. She had watched nearly every game he had ever played in college and had caught all his games so far in his rookie year in the pros. For years she had sat side by side with Jessi, holding her breath when he got sacked, cheering out loud when he made key connections, jumping up and down when he scored touchdowns. Because of Jessi, football had become a fall staple for her, and it had always included the young man sitting across from her husband. Seeing him play in person, feeling the energy of the crowd, experiencing a pro game with Jessi was going to be fun.

Bill nodded, looking pleased. "Glad to hear that. We'd love to watch you play on something other than our television."

"There's no guarantee I'll get playing time," Joe warned. Jari had always appreciated the young man's humility when it came to his football career.

"But you might, especially if Mike's shoulder is still giving him problems," Jessica interjected, looking hopeful.

Joe shifted his gaze from his wife to Bill and Jari. "Our starting quarterback went out early in the preseason with an injury, and the second-string quarterback has been having some problems with his throwing shoulder."

Since they had watched every game, the explanation wasn't necessary, but Jari appreciated Joe's effort to fill them in. "Well, it's a shame there have been so many injuries, but we're happy that you may have a chance to throw the ball. That doesn't always happen in your rookie year," Bill responded.

"Yeah, it's quite an honor . . . and a responsibility," Joe conceded, rubbing the back of his neck.

"He's doing a great job, though," Jessi bubbled, staring up at her husband with open admiration. "Don't you think? I know you've been watching!"

"Every game," Jari promised, not able to hold back a grin. "And yes, you've been having a great season, Joe."

Joe bobbed his head, obviously uncomfortable with the praise, and Jessi sat watching him, her eyes shining. Jari's heart warmed. From the first moment she saw Joe and Jessica together, back when they were both still in high school, she could see how much love and admiration the young couple had for one another. Now, more than half a decade later, it had clearly only grown with time. It made her heart sing and put her mind at ease about their move—and their future. Love like theirs was rare. She enjoyed seeing them together. Knowing Jessica and the girls were happy made dealing with their absence easier.

The waiter came to take Joe and Jessi's drink orders and Bill picked up his menu, gesturing for everyone else to do the same. Looking over the wide selection of breakfast items, Jari felt her mouth start to water. She had eaten a granola bar before she took her shower, finding that a little snack helped with the morning sickness, but even still, her stomach growled. She had never known hunger like she had in the past week.

"What's good here?" she asked, noticing that neither Joe nor Jessi were looking at a menu.

"They have a great breakfast buffet," Jessi told her, gesturing to a long serving bar near the back of the restaurant. Jari turned in her seat to look as Jessi continued. "They make omelets to order, as well as pancakes and waffles."

"They have crepes, bacon, sausage, fresh fruit, bagels, homemade biscuits and gravy, quiche . . . pretty much anything you can think of for breakfast," Joe added. "And it's all really, really good."

Jari snapped her menu shut and set it on the table in front of her. "I'll have that."

"I think I will, too," Bill agreed, setting his menu down as well.

"Great, then we can go up at any time," Jessi told them as she stood. "And I vote now, because I'm starving!"

"Me too!" Jari was only a step behind her. Reaching the buffet, Jari hoped no one heard how her stomach growled. The spread looked amazing. Sliced mangoes and strawberries sat among grapes, cantaloupe, watermelon, oranges, apples, bananas, and peaches. Beyond that, the hot foods began. More concerned with filling her plate than looking to see what the hot food section held, she started down the line and heard Bill chuckle behind her. She sent him a playful glance. "I told you I was hungry."

"So I see. Your plate looks like Jessi's. Wonder why," he teased quietly, poking her lightly in the ribs. Jumping, Jari batted his hand away. His expression was amused, and she enjoyed the knowing glance he sent her. It was nice to share a happy secret. Glancing across at Jessi going down the opposite side of the buffet line, she saw that Bill was right. Her plate looked an awful lot like his daughter's. She laughed and shrugged her shoulders, continuing down the line.

As they all took their seats again, she asked how Jessi had been feeling. "A lot better now," Jessi answered. "The very day I turned thirteen weeks, it's like I felt better overnight. It was crazy, but I'm very thankful. I don't remember being as sick with the girls as I have been this time."

Joe reached over and rubbed his wife's back as he finished his first piece of bacon. "It's true. She has been really sick. I've never seen anyone throw up so much."

Jessi nodded. "And it wasn't just in the morning, either. It seemed like I had morning sickness morning, noon, and night." Jari cringed inwardly, wondering if that was what she had to look forward to. "Did I have that with the girls and I'm just forgetting, or wasn't it that bad?"

Jari thought back for a few moments. "I don't remember you being that sick, but I may be forgetting too. It feels like a long time ago. I know you were sick, but I don't remember it being constant."

"Same here. Well, regardless, I'm glad it's over. Now, more than being nauseous, I'm just really hungry . . . all the time . . . but have a hard time thinking of what sounds good. I'm hoping that too will pass."

"Hopefully it will," Jari agreed.

"Yes, it certainly does look like you're struggling to find your appetite," Bill observed dryly, gesturing to his daughter's full plate. Joe laughed, and Jessi made a face at him.

"Dad, I meant when I try to think of something to make for dinner."

"Oh," Bill answered with a grin. "I see."

"My mom says she was a lot sicker when she was pregnant with me than she was with the girls," Joe paused, grinning. "Maybe that means we're having a boy."

"A son would be nice," Bill commented. "Someone to carry on the family name." Considering the thoughtful expression on his face, Jari wondered if he was thinking of Joe and Jessi or of their own little one. She smiled.

"Yeah, I think we would both be pretty happy with a boy," Jessi agreed, smiling up at Joe again, her eyes shining once more. He nodded in agreement, his face stretched in a big grin.

"But we'll be happy with either," he added.

When everyone's mouths were temporarily full, and the silence had lasted a handful of seconds, Bill cleared his throat, and Jari braced for what she knew was coming. "On the baby subject . . . " He waited until he had Joe and Jessi's attention. "Jari is expecting." As soon as the words left his mouth, the tension in his shoulders visibly eased, and the hard lines in his face smoothed out. Jari could see how relieved he felt, just to have the news out in the open.

The silence stretched. Joe and Jessi both looked completely stunned—and for good reason. Jessi's eyes darted from her dad to Jari. "Really?"

Jari nodded, smiling hopefully. "I'm not very far along yet . . . not quite nine weeks."

Jessi looked back at Bill, confusion the dominant emotion in her expression. "I thought . . . Wait, Dad, didn't you have a . . . ?" It was clear that she didn't want to finish her sentence.

Bill nodded. "I had it reversed." His words were so calm that Jari would not have guessed how nervous he was about the conversation had she not known.

"You had it reversed?" Jessi echoed. Bill nodded. "So, you were trying for a baby?" He nodded again. Jessi looked at Jari. "Wow. That's a lot to . . . You're really pregnant?"

"Yes." Jari sent up a silent prayer that joy would come in the wake of the shock. Thus far, Jessica had shown no emotion other than confusion and surprise. Jari knew the next few moments were crucial. Jessica's reaction was important to her but especially to Bill.

Like the sun bursting out from behind a heavy cloud, a grin filled Joe's face. He reached across the table and shook Bill's hand emphatically. "Congratulations!" Next, he reached for Jari's and gave it a tight squeeze. "How exciting!"

Jessi was recovering quickly from her shock, and she followed her husband's lead. "Wow! This is great! Are you guys excited?"

"Yes," Bill responded simply, his open smile an affirmation of his answer.

"Good." Jessica paused, clearly still trying to process. "Well, tell me how this happened," she continued, leaning forward in her seat, preparing for the story.

Joe chuckled. "Spare us the details. We're expecting, too . . . I think we know how this happened, Jess." His words elicited a girlish blush from his wife. Bill and Jari laughed while Jessica hit Joe's arm.

"You know what I mean. Tell me the story. I never expected this. I mean, I've wondered several times if you wanted kids, Jari, but I knew about . . . well, about Dad, and I never considered the possibility. I thought it was just a done deal, and I guess we never talked about it. Don't get me wrong, I'm happy for you guys," she paused and reached across to squeeze Jari's hand. "So happy! I just know there must be a story behind all of this, and I want to know how you got here."

Jari started by telling Joe and Jessica about the longing to have children that had been growing inside of her for the past several years. She explained how Kelsi and Kamryn had fueled that desire while also helping to satisfy it. For the first time, she was a hundred percent real with Jessica about how hard it had been over the summer, after they had moved. Bill conveyed the conversation they had on the campaign trail about Jari wanting a baby and about his doubts, concerns, and finally, his inability to do so.

"You didn't know before that?" Jessica asked Jari, clearly shocked that Bill had never told his wife about his surgery.

Jari shook her head. "I don't think we ever actually had a conversation about having children. I just assumed that your dad had you and didn't want any more kids, and I guess he assumed I felt the same . . . or that I already knew about his vasectomy." Jari glanced at Bill, and he nodded.

"Speaking of which, how did you know about that? About the fact that I couldn't have any more children?" Bill asked, his tone dry as he looked at his daughter.

"Mom." Jessica spoke the one word simply with a shrug of her shoulders. "There was a time when you two weren't on the best of terms. During that time, privacy wasn't a major concern."

Bill's expression clouded. "I should have known," he said grimly. "I always wondered what sort of—"

"Anyway, how did you go from that conversation to sitting here telling us Jari's pregnant?" Joe asked, his grin in place as he steered the conversation back on track.

After a brief pause to reset, Bill shared his decision to have the surgery reversed, his continued doubts, and his commitment to leave it up to God. Jari told them about the surgery weekend and how nice it was to have time together in the middle of such a busy season. Jessica nodded, fully understanding what a campaign year entailed. They skipped the skinny dipping and instead shared how they felt when the test was positive.

"Wow," Jessi finally said at the end of the story. "Well, it sounds like a miracle for sure! How crazy that it would all happen so soon."

"That's exactly how we felt. We never dreamed it would happen like this," Bill admitted. "I had resigned myself to adjusting to the possibility of this happening eventually . . . down the road. Even having children after a surgery like that isn't a guarantee, especially since it had been so long since my initial surgery. There was only a chance that it would ever result in having a baby—and then to have it happen so soon . . . I just wasn't sure I was ready." Bill paused, and Jari tried to keep herself from feeling disappointment at his words. She wondered if he was still more wary of having a baby than he had let on. "But when the test was positive . . . there are just no words. Just like when your mother and I found out about you, Jessica. No matter what kind of doubts or apprehensions you may have had even just a few minutes before, when that test is positive and you realize you're going to have a child . . . none of it matters anymore. In that moment, all you know is joy."

Bill's last words put Jari's mind at ease, and she wished he shared feelings like that more often. She was glad to hear him put words to his emotions and to have them be so positive. She wanted to give him a hug but settled for a warm smile and making a mental note to tell him later how much she appreciated the glimpse into his thoughts.

"I know the feeling," Joe agreed, his eyes shining with tenderness.

As Jari finished her quiche, the last of the food on her plate, Jessi pushed back her chair and stood. "We can continue this conversation in a minute. Right now, Jari and I have empty plates, and I know at least I'm still hungry! We'll be back."

Jessi looped her arm through Jari's and led her back to the buffet bar. "Did you try the breakfast casserole? It's absolutely amazing!"

"No, I haven't."

"Get some this time. You'll love it." Jessi handed Jari a plate but didn't let go right away. When Jari looked up at her, Jessi held her eyes for several moments. "Are you happy, Jari? About the baby?"

Tears instantly welled up in Jari's blue eyes. "I'm *so* happy, Jess. I am just overflowing with excitement, and . . . outside of salvation, I've never been the recipient of such a personal gift of God's mercy. I don't know how to explain the joy I feel over carrying this baby . . . or how it touches me that He gave me a second chance to do so." Jari fought to keep her voice from breaking.

Jessi smiled—a full, warm, sincerely joyful smile—and blinked back tears. "Then I am so happy, too. Truly."

To keep her tears at bay, Jari took her plate and started down the line, spooning more fruit onto her plate, then looking for the breakfast casserole Jessi recommended.

"Jari, what do you mean He gave you a second chance? Have you been pregnant before?" Jessi asked from behind her, curiosity lacing her tone. In that one moment, Jari felt cold inside.

She had not realized what she had said . . . or what she had revealed. Her abortion was one thing she had never shared with anyone, not even Jessi. She had wanted to a few times but had never found the courage to speak the words to her friend. She had never owned up to what she had done by telling someone about it. And she was afraid of what Jessi would think of her if she did. In some ways, not talking about it made it feel less real. Without speaking the words, she could almost convince herself that it had never happened. But it had.

She thought of telling Jessi the truth now, explaining what being pregnant really meant to her, but it felt too late and too shameful. Something inside of her seemed to taunt her, convincing her that if she shared her deepest, darkest secret, her stepdaughter would turn away from her. It would forever change how Jessi saw her. She wouldn't want to be friends with someone who was capable of taking the life of their own child.

Jari turned back to the buffet and lifted a piece of breakfast casserole onto her plate. "We weren't sure that we would ever be able to have children after the operation your dad had. Getting pregnant, and so soon, felt like a second chance," Jari answered carefully. That was true, too. Both were gracious gifts that were absolutely worth being thankful for.

"Yeah, that really is amazing!" Jessi agreed. "Well, Jari, I want you to know that I'm very excited for you guys. It's a lot to take in, that's for sure . . . I'm not going to lie—it's a little strange to hear your father announce he's going to be a dad again; but really, I can see how happy you *both* are, and I love you both so much. I'm really happy for you."

Jari was relieved and overjoyed at Jessi's words but felt a tinge of guilt that she hadn't told her stepdaughter the complete truth. "You should tell your dad that too. He was so nervous about telling you."

"That's why you came to Minnesota? To tell us in person?" Jessi asked, connecting the puzzle pieces.

Jari grinned. "No. That was how your dad justified coming to Minnesota in the middle of his campaign with elections just over a month away. We came because we miss you all terribly."

Jessica wrapped her arm around Jari's waist and gave her a little squeeze. "We've missed you guys too. A lot. Being here with Joe is so wonderful . . . finally our family is complete. But being away from you has been really hard. It's funny how our little immediate family can be complete, but it feels like the family we've known ever since the girls were born is missing. It's definitely . . . bittersweet."

"That makes sense, Jess. It really does. This is where you need to be—here with Joe, as a family. We'll just have to do a better job of coming to visit and see if we can fill in that part of your life as well."

"Do you think Dad would ever move away from D.C.?" Jessi asked, her face hopeful. Jari laughed, and Jessi's expression fell into a pout. "I know, I know. It just never hurts to dream." Their plates full for a second time, Jari and Jessi headed back to their table together, where Joe and Bill were lost in conversation about the upcoming election.

~~~~~

"Jari! Grandpa!" Kelsi and Kamryn raced down the sidewalk to where Bill and Jari were waiting beside Joe's SUV. Jessica followed at a more leisurely pace, still chatting with the lady who had been watching them. The girls had spent the morning playing with a friend from their new small group at church.

After breakfast, Jessi had insisted that Joe swing by Bill and Jari's hotel and that they pick up their suitcase and check out. All she would say was that they had found other arrangements for their lodging. Eager to pick up Kelsi and Kamryn, Jari had agreed, packing up quickly. Though she had been curious about their new accommodations at the time, she forgot all about it now with the twins racing toward them. Her heart swelled painfully, and tears stung her eyes. Oh, how she had missed them!

Upon reaching them, Kelsi jumped into Jari's arms, and Kamryn threw herself against Bill's legs, both girls clinging to them as if their lives depended on it. Laughing, Jari lifted Kelsi up, hugging her tightly, as Bill did the same to Kamryn. Reaching over, Jari gave Kamryn a hug and a kiss on the cheek, while Kelsi clung tightly to Bill's neck for several moments. For a full minute there was laughing, multiple greetings, and even a few tears. May had never seemed so distant as it did at that moment. The girls seemed to have grown a foot. They had changed a lot, looking more like little girls and even less like toddlers.

When things began to settle down, Joe slapped Bill on the shoulder. "What do you say we head home? We have a bit of a surprise for you guys, and then I need to get over to the field."

"Home? I'm surprised you can bring yourself to call a hotel home, though, you guys have been there long enough it's probably started feeling like it," Bill responded dryly. Jari shot him a look. She knew her husband wasn't happy his daughter and granddaughters had been living in a hotel since having to move out of their temporary condo the third weekend of August, but it wasn't like it was intentional, and she was sure Joe had found them a nice place. As Jari had told him before, it wasn't like they were homeless; the young man was making plenty of money. They were simply taking their time, making sure they found the right house. Bill held his hands up, getting her warning. "But that sounds like a plan."

Joe just grinned good-naturedly.

"A surprise?" Jari asked the girls, shifting her attention back to them, and they nodded, their smiles big. "What is it?"

"We can't tell you, silly," Kamryn giggled.

"No? You won't tell us?" Jari feigned hurt feelings, but both girls stood their ground and shook their heads.

"We can't! Mommy made us promise," Kelsi explained.

"Oh, okay. Well, if you promised, then I won't ask you anymore."

Joe opened the car door for the girls, and they crawled into the third row before buckling themselves into their car seats, leaving the second row for her and Bill. She noticed that both girls, and Joe and Jessi, were all smiles and she felt her suspicion rising. Whatever the surprise was, all four Colbys were definitely excited about it.

On their way back to Joe and Jessica's hotel, the girls told them about their morning, including everything they played with and had to eat. Jari relished their happy chatter, remembering how the girls had told her about a hundred other days in the same detailed manner. She loved it.

When Joe parked the SUV, the surprise was obvious. "I thought you were staying in a hotel until you found a house. What are we doing here?" Bill asked, peering out the window.

Jari had thought the same thing, but judging by the four grinning faces, it was clear that the house they were parked in front of was the surprise. "What?" she cried in excitement. "Did you buy a house?"

"Surprise!" Kelsi and Kamryn cried from the backseat. All four Colbys started talking at once.

"I was going to tell you, but we were holding off until we got through all the red tape and were certain it was going to go through. And then we felt sure you would be coming to visit sometime soon and thought it would be such fun to surprise you whenever you did! I'm sorry I didn't tell you! We really did live in a hotel for a few weeks," Jessi explained, laughing.

"Do you like it, Jari? Do you like it, Grandpa? Do you? Do you?" Kelsi demanded.

"We have our own rooms and so will the baby!" Kamryn announced.

"It's in a great school district, not far from the stadium, and in a really safe neighborhood," Joe offered.

"How long have you had it?" Jari asked, ecstatic, trying to make sense of all the different things they were saying at once. Recalling all the conversations with Jessi about how they hadn't found the right place yet, she made a face at her friend. "I can't believe you lied to me!"

She did understand, though. Jessi really had no choice but to lie or spoil the surprise—Jari asked her about the house hunt every time they spoke on the phone. In fact, she had wondered a few times if Jessi was becoming discouraged with trying to find the right place or if she simply wasn't that eager to do so, as she only talked about it whenever Jari asked and only in passing. Now, Jari knew why.

"I know!" Jessi groaned. "I didn't really lie, I just didn't tell the complete truth, which," she looked pointedly at the girls, "is only okay if you're planning a happy surprise like this or like a birthday party or something. Otherwise, we tell the complete truth all the time." She directed her attention back to Jari. "We were able to negotiate a quick closing for the first week of September. So, we spent a few weeks at a hotel, in between when we had to be out of our apartment and when we closed on this, but moved in about two and a half weeks ago," Jessi told them. "It's the perfect house, you guys! We love it!"

Joe started the car moving again, and they pulled around the house and into a garage that was positioned on the side, rather than the front, to make it more aesthetically pleasing from the street.

"Well, let's see it!" Bill said, opening his door as Joe turned off the engine. As Joe and Jessi led them on a tour of their new house with the girls skipping alongside, offering their own comments on every room, Jari took in the sprawling ranch-style home.

The house seemed to be quite new, likely built within the last five years. The floor plan was spacious, the design beautiful. A large kitchen spilled into a dining room, which adjoined a bright family room with French doors out onto a big deck. A beautiful yard spread out just beyond the deck, with mature trees so thick around the boundaries of the property that the wooden fence was nearly hidden from view. A large playset was set up near the back, and the whole yard was park-like.

The family room opened up to the den on one side and the front sitting room on the other, which spilled back into the kitchen. A large, stone, double-sided fireplace separated the family room from the sitting room with a walkway on either side. All the windows were big and beautiful, allowing light to spill into every room, making the house bright and cheerful. To the right of the entry were the bedrooms. Kelsi and Kamryn each had their own room, just as Kammy had announced. Another bedroom sat vacant, a room clearly designated as the nursery. At the end of the house was the sprawling primary suite. Joe and Jessi were all smiles as they showed off their corner of the home, which was beautiful enough to make Jari consider remodeling her own.

At the other end of the house, off the dining area and family room, was a staircase that went down to the walk-out basement. Joe and Jessi explained that the basement wasn't finished, but took them down to show them around the large, open space. Joe described their plans for the future to put in another bedroom, a home gym, sauna, and another family room, complete with a wet bar and a pool table for when he had his teammates over. A second deck, just inches above the ground, stretched out from the basement's sliding glass doors. A hot tub had been set down into it. Jessi explained that not only would the hot tub be a fun place to retreat to in the middle of the cold Minnesota winters, it was also a great place for Joe to relax after a hard game or practice.

Back upstairs, there were two bedrooms on the other side of the staircase, each with their own attached bath. Both rooms were comfortably furnished and designated as the guest rooms. "You can choose which room you want to sleep in!" Kelsi offered. "I like the other one because there's lots of yellow in the decorations and I think it feels cheerful," she said, motioning to the room across the short hall.

"I like this one because it feels relaxing," Kamryn interjected.

Jari looked at Bill, and he smiled. "Maybe we'll stay in here this time and next door when we come to visit again," he told the girls, making them both happy.

"This is huge, you guys, and really nice," Jari said, looking around again appreciatively.

"We wanted a nice place to settle down and raise our family in. I really like the coaches here, and we're hoping they'll keep me around for a good long time. We want at least one or two more kids after the baby . . . maybe more . . ." Jessi made a face at Joe's words, and he grinned at her. "Maybe. So, we wanted a place we could put down roots."

"Well, you found a great place. This is beautiful. And it looks amazing considering you just moved in," Jari answered, in awe of how decorated and homey the new house already looked.

"Well, I've had two and a half weeks, and you can't believe how much I can get done being home all day."

"How much shopping she can get done," Joe said with a wink at Bill. Jessi hit his arm, and he grinned.

"Unpacking is more like it. Our moving truck got here the day we closed, so I've had lots of time to settle in. And after all the transition, it was really important to me to get it looking like home right away. There's still that corner full of boxes downstairs, but I'll get to it in time. The main thing is that it feels like home up here, everyone has a bed, and the kitchen has been unpacked so we can eat."

"Well, that sounds like a big accomplishment in two and a half weeks," Jari said. "You've done amazing." Bill agreed, and Jari watched the happy smile fill Jessi's face. Since Jessi was seventeen, Jari had always been on hand to help her with whatever she needed help with. She knew her stepdaughter had struggled with anxiety over moving so far away from her, and Jari had suspected Jessi was at least a little worried about whether or not she could do things on her own without her there to help. Now that she had, Jari could see how pleased Jessi was with their praise.

With the tour finished, Joe left for practice, and Bill and Jari had the rest of the afternoon with Jessi and the girls. They all went outside and watched the girls play on their playset, where Bill pushed them on the swings. Later, Jari colored with them at the kitchen table, hearing all about the girls' kindergarten, while Jessi showed Bill around the large backyard.

After walking the fence line of their acre and a half lot, Bill and Jessi ended up sitting down at the patio table for a cup of herbal tea while they continued their conversation. When they finally came back inside, Bill looked younger and more refreshed than Jari had seen him look in months. Her smile was warm as she met his eyes. His daughter was good for him.

Later that afternoon, they told the girls their news, and when the twins heard there would be another baby in the family, they cheered. Joe got home in time for dinner, and they ate together in the dining room before settling down with popcorn and a movie. After the girls went to bed, the adults stayed up and talked until late, when they split to their different ends of the house to get some sleep before the big game.

Eleven

Sunday was bright but crisp. The smell of autumn was thick in the air, and a cold front had moved in overnight, making a coat necessary to ward off the chill. Snow had not yet fallen in the Twin Cities, but many were predicting that it wasn't far off. If the temperature was any indication, Jari had to agree.

Bill and Jari went to church and caught a quick bite to eat with Jessi and the girls before heading to the stadium. The place was humming, the rivalry between the two teams evident in the number of fans that turned out for the big game. Finding a place to park took twenty minutes, and then the long walk to the stadium gates began. Both girls started out walking, but their little legs tired quickly. Bill carried Kelsi for a few minutes, then switched her out for Kamryn. Putting Kamryn down and telling Kelsi to wait a while longer before her next turn at being carried, he shot Jari a sideways grimace.

"I need to make time in my schedule to get into the gym more."

She laughed. "You're not used to carrying them anymore, are you?"

"My muscles aren't," he agreed, chagrined.

"It's not just you. They're getting heavy! I don't carry them anymore, that's for sure!" Jessi offered, ruffling Kelsi's hair.

"That's good," Jari told her. "You shouldn't be lifting them when you're pregnant." She shifted her attention to the five-year-olds, her face brightening in a grin. "You girls are definitely growing big and strong! It's probably because you're in kindergarten now." The girls both mustered up a smile, but Kelsi followed it by tugging on Jessi's hand.

"My legs hurt, Mommy."

"We're almost to the stadium. You'll make it. Your legs are younger than any of ours."

"But they're shorter," Kelsi whined. "I have to take so many more steps than you."

Jessica gave the dainty brunette an amused smile. "You'll live."

Once inside the gates, they made their way through the inner corridors of the stadium until they found their entrance. Bill led the way to their seats, and they filed into the row, the girls promptly sitting down with dramatic sighs.

"Right on the fifty-yard line. Nice," Bill commented, his tone full of appreciation for their perches above the field. "It's amazing he could come up with these seats at the last minute."

"He has a lot of favor," Jessi answered, getting settled in her seat.

"Think he'll play today?" Jari asked.

"I hope so," Jessi paused. "Sometimes, I think he hopes he won't."

"Why's that?" Bill asked, leaning out around his wife to see his daughter.

"I think he just feels a lot of pressure. Playing in the pros isn't like playing in college. On one hand, I think he's constantly itching to get in the game. Every week, I watch him study the play, the line-up, the result—the whole game. He's constantly analyzing. You can almost feel how much he wants to be put in just in how intensely he follows the game. But on the other hand, when he's in, he feels responsible for the outcome, no matter how many minutes . . . or seconds . . . he plays. He feels responsible for every loss—it's

149

personal. And, I think he feels a lot of pressure to prove himself to the coaches."

"That makes sense. I'm sure there is a lot more pressure now than there was in college, and he was out of it all for a while," Jari sympathized.

"The pressure will make him a stronger player," Bill assured firmly, following on the heels of his wife's empathetic response.

"You're right. It will. He says the same thing," Jessi told her dad.

Before kick-off, Bill scooted by them all to go on his first snack run. He came back fifteen minutes later with drinks for everyone and candy for the girls. Jari took out a hat and pulled it down over her ears just as Minnesota kicked off. She looked over at the twin girls beside her and saw that their mittens were sticky from their candy, but still on their little hands. Let them get sticky, she thought; at least they were warm. There was still a decided chill in the air, even inside the enclosed stadium.

Both teams came out playing well, feeling the energy of the crowd and the rivalry. It was tied at seven going into the second quarter. The defenses seemed evenly matched and equally as reluctant to give up points. The scoreboard didn't change throughout the second quarter, and they went into halftime still tied.

During halftime, Jari stayed to watch their seats and belongings, while Bill went to purchase more drinks and hotdogs for everyone. Jessi took the girls to the bathroom. Munching on a piece of candy Kamryn had shared with her, Jari sat in the stands by herself and watched the fans. The northern accents were thick in the conversations going on around her, and she enjoyed listening to them. Letting her mind wander, she soon found herself thinking of baby names. If the baby was a girl, she had always liked the names Olivia and Amber. If it was a boy, she liked Judah and Adam. Still, she wasn't set on any of them. She was excited to discuss it with Bill in the coming months and decide on a name together.

Bill got back first, and she helped him carefully set down the drinks and hotdogs. She was hungry and ate hers before it got cold, as did Bill. Jessi and the girls got back just after the start of the second half, Jessi looking frazzled and frustrated. "You would not believe how long the line for the women's restroom was," she told Jari as she sat down.

Jari handed her the snacks Bill had brought them. "I can imagine."

"Thanks for the soda and hotdog, Dad." Jessi raised her hotdog to Bill, and he nodded, his mouth full.

Just a few minutes into the second half, there was a sack that made the Minnesota fans hold their breath. A lineman missed his block, leaving the quarterback wide-open and defenseless. The quarterback tried to escape the tackle, but there was no way to get out of the pocket fast enough. He landed hard on his throwing shoulder—the shoulder he had already been having problems with. After the whistle was blown, the quarterback stayed down, writhing in pain and holding his throwing arm. The trainers ran onto the field. The crowd was quiet. Jessica whispered to the girls, explaining what was going on, and they sat on their knees to get a better view.

When the trainers helped the quarterback to his feet and he walked off the field with them, the crowd erupted into respectful applause, fans of both teams applauding alike. As bad as she felt for the injured player, Jari squeezed Jessi's hand in excitement. "Here we go!"

"LORD, please watch over him and protect him while he's out on the field and give him wisdom. Let him play well and feel good about his game, whether it leads to a win or a loss, and let him bring You glory," Jessi murmured aloud.

"Amen!" Jari agreed heartily, watching Joe jog onto the field and huddle with his teammates.

"Daddy's in!" Kamryn cried, seeing Joe on the big screen, and clapping her hands wildly.

"Woohoo!" Kelsi crowed, jumping out of her seat and doing a little dance before climbing back up to sit down again.

As the huddle broke and the team ran to the line of scrimmage, Jari found herself holding her breath. The ball was snapped, and Joe threw it, landing the football smoothly in the hands of a wide receiver for a gain of six yards. On third and five, Joe connected again, this time with the tight end, to pick up the first down. Jari and Jessica cheered as if he had just scored the winning touchdown.

On the next set of downs though, they went four and out, after a tipped pass, a failed run, and a sack. Jari had never been so thankful to see a quarterback pop up from the bottom of a pile. As Joe ran off the field while the special teams ran on, she released a sigh of relief. She loved to see him get playing time but was thankful when he was safe on the sidelines. Glancing at Jessica, Jari could tell she felt the same way.

An injury now could change Joe and Jessi's entire future. It would be a shame to see his professional football career end, just as it was starting. Jari had no doubt that Joe was going to wind up as some team's starting quarterback in the years to come, and with the way Jessi loved their new house, she hoped it would be Minnesota's. Wherever it was, though, Jari was sure the promotion was coming. The kid had been too good in college and had too much drive and ambition to stay in the background for long. Jari was confident it wouldn't be too many seasons before coaches began to take notice, and Joe Colby would rise to the position of starting quarterback—as long as he could avoid injuries.

The minutes seemed to tick off like seconds during the rest of the game. Joe and his offense played well, despite the constant battering from the opposing defense. Joe was sacked two more times, his offensive line obviously growing weary. During the remainder of the third quarter and the entire fourth, they were only able to put up three more points on the scoreboard. However, when their opponents went four and out as the final seconds of the game ran out, the field goal proved to be enough, and Minnesota claimed the victory.

Jari was up dancing and shouting with the girls, while Jessi, more poised, clapped and cheered wildly. Bill shared in the celebration as well, giving a long burst of hearty applause and hugging first Jari, then Jessi and each of the girls, congratulating them on the victory.

As much as Bill and Jari wanted to personally congratulate Joe on the win, they didn't have time to stay until he got out of the locker room. With how long it would take to simply get out of the stadium, then out of the parking lot and the general area in the midst of so many fans, they had no time to spare if they wanted to catch their flight. Anticipating their tight timeframe, they had told Joe goodbye before he left for the game that morning and planned to call him from the airport to congratulate him.

Gathering their trash, their belongings, and their coats, they made their way up the stadium stairs toward the exit. "If he ever gets traded to Miami, one benefit would be that we wouldn't have to lug these to all the games," Jessi commented, lifting one of the coats that filled her arms.

"Very true," Bill chuckled, dumping all the trash in a garbage can as they passed. With his hands free, he took the coats Jessi and Jari carried, leaving their hands free to hold on to the railings and the girls.

Finally making their way through the stadium, they paused to put on all their gear and started the long trek to Jessi's vehicle. The cold walk drew even more complaints from the girls than it had on the way in. It had been long early in the afternoon, but now, with the temperature continuing to fall and the fading excitement of the game leaving them all feeling a little drained, it felt like a marathon. Finally reaching the vehicle, Jessica started it, turning the heater on full blast, while Bill and Jari waited for the girls to climb into the back.

"Welcome to Minnesota," Jessi told them with a grin as Jari rubbed her hands together and held them in front of the heater vent.

"And it's only going to get worse. You're not even in winter proper yet," Jari reminded. Jessi grimaced in reply.

"I'm glad you and the girls can just stay home where you're warm and safe this winter, instead of having to get out on icy roads," Bill added.

"Me too. It's nice to be a stay-at-home mom. Especially when the baby comes, it will be nice not to have to think about going back to work and finding daycare and everything."

"And I like that you're home with us, Mommy, and don't have to go on any more long trips," Kamryn added from the backseat.

"Me too!" Kelsi agreed.

As the heater did its job and chased the bite out of the air inside the SUV, Jari turned to Jessi. "If only we were flying home tomorrow morning, this would be the perfect night to try out your new hot tub!"

Jessi laughed, agreeing heartily. "It absolutely would be!"

"Except neither of you can. Hello, pregnant ladies. Even I know that," Bill told them. Jari laughed. They could always count on him to be realistic.

"Listen, Dad, we can dream."

The easy conversation continued as they sat in line, waiting to get out of the parking lot, and then made their way to the airport. Jari was reluctant to see the miles pass, not at all looking forward to leaving Jessi and the girls. She had a feeling her house was going to seem very big and very lonely again and that she was going to miss them all the more from having just seen them.

At the airport, Jessi pulled up in the unloading zone and sent Jari a sad look. "This weekend went too fast. I wish it wasn't over already."

"Me too." Jari felt moisture in her eyes and blamed her changing hormones.

"It did go too fast," Bill agreed, reaching up and putting his hand on Jessi's shoulder for a quick squeeze.

"Grandpa, do you and Jari *have* to leave?" Kelsi asked from the backseat, her voice on the verge of pleading.

"Yes. We have a plane we have to catch, and I have to go to work in the morning," Bill explained, turning to the girls.

"Awww, sad."

Bill chuckled at Kelsi's response, echoed by Kamryn. "We'll come visit again soon. I promise."

"Sooner than last time? We haven't seen you in a very long time," Kelsi pointed out.

"Sooner than last time," Bill promised. Reaching over, he kissed each of the girls on the forehead and squeezed their hands, struggling to know how to give them hugs while they were buckled into their car seats.

The three adults got out of the warm vehicle. Jessica and Bill embraced and said their goodbyes, while Jari told the girls goodbye. She wiped at her tears as she shut the door and turned to hug Jessi. This goodbye felt even harder than when Jessi and Joe had left D.C. for Minnesota. The weekend had seemed so short. She held on to her stepdaughter for a long time, and Jessica returned the embrace. Finally, Jari straightened her shoulders and stepped back with a shaky smile.

"Like your dad said, we'll be back soon."

Jessi laughed a little as she drew her fingertips under her eyes. "You'd better be! You made a promise to sleep in the other spare room."

Bill chuckled. "So we did."

"Really, guys, thank you for coming," Jessi said, taking a deep breath and smiling. "It meant so much to all of us. We've been missing you like crazy. And congratulations on the baby! We're so excited for you! I mean it. And it will be so fun for the babies to have each other to grow up with. I think they'll be good friends! And I'm glad you came to tell me in person. It was great to hear the news while seeing your smiling faces."

Jari beamed, and Bill nodded respectfully. "Well, you take care, Jessica and . . . good luck with your little project too."

"Her project?" Jari asked, turning to look at her husband in disbelief. "That's what growing a baby inside of you is? A project?"

Bill shrugged, and Jessi laughed. "Thanks, Dad."

"We have to go. It was great to see you, honey. Drive carefully going home." Bill squeezed Jessi's shoulder.

She nodded. "I will."

"Don't forget to stop for gas. We don't want you three sitting on the side of the road . . . again."

Jessi groaned and rolled her eyes. "Dad. Seriously? That happened once." He chuckled and she turned her attention to Jari. "Love you guys."

"Love you too," Jari answered, giving Jessi one last hug and waving to the girls through the car window. They waved back.

Putting his hand on her back, Bill directed Jari toward the door. They made their way into the airport, checked their suitcase, went through security, and found their gate. Checking on the status of their flight and seeing it was delayed, they wandered over to a small eatery to have some dinner before boarding.

The flight was uneventful, and they took a taxi home once landing. When it pulled up along the curb outside their home, Bill sent Jari into the house with her purse and the suitcase, while he went to talk to members of Joseph's team.

Jari waited anxiously for him and the news he would bring as she pulled the suitcase up the stairs and into their room to get ready for bed. During their weekend in Minnesota, she had barely even thought about the black SUV or the semi-threatening situation that awaited them at home, all but forgetting there were two motives for their weekend away. Now, back home and alone in the large, dark house, she was eager to find out if there had been any suspicious activity over the weekend or any sightings of the darkly tinted car.

Finishing brushing her teeth, Jari found herself rubbing her lower stomach. A tightening that wasn't quite painful, but decidedly uncomfortable, had begun in the area as she pulled the suitcase up the stairs. Contemplating that, Jari shook her head. The suitcase was full, but it hadn't felt heavy. She hadn't considered that it could possibly strain her. She regularly did more lifting than that in the home gym. The pain went away as suddenly as it had come, and perplexed, she moved on, getting a washcloth out of the cupboard to wash her face.

The alarm system alerted her to the fact that a door had been opened. Listening carefully, she reminded herself that it was probably Bill and tried not to give room to fear. Soon, she heard his familiar footsteps on the stairs and relaxed. She finished washing her face and crawled into bed, sitting propped up against the headboard, forcing herself to wait patiently as he changed for bed in the closet. When he came back into the room, the lack of worry on his face instantly reassured her.

"Everything was quiet over the weekend?"

"Yes. There was no activity whatsoever. They didn't see the black SUV or any other vehicle hanging around, and there was nothing else they categorized as suspicious. I'm going to have them continue watching for the next couple of weeks, but I think either it was just a random coincidence, or he wasn't ready for the big leagues and decided to make himself scarce. Either way, I don't think there's anything to be worried about." Bill stooped over and kissed Jari's forehead. "You can rest easy tonight, my dear."

A tender smile filling her face, she nodded. "I'm glad to hear that."

"I still need to get ready for bed, but I thought you might be worried out here and wanted to let you know there's no need. The threat seems to be long gone, and Joseph's men are stationed outside, keeping an eye out just in case," Bill assured, heading into the bathroom to brush his teeth.

When he came back and crawled under the covers beside her, getting his pillow adjusted just right, he let out a long sigh. "We'll have to visit Joe and Jessica again soon."

"It was fun, wasn't it?"

"It was. She's a good girl, isn't she?"

"Jessi?"

"Mmmhmm."

"Yes, she is," Jari agreed warmly.

"I'm really proud of her."

"You should be."

"She took the news well, don't you think?"

"She did. And I'm so glad. She made me feel excited about having a baby . . . even more excited than I already was. She didn't make me feel weird or like it was something to be ashamed of," Jari said softly.

Bill rolled over and wrapped his arm around her. "It isn't weird or anything to be ashamed of."

"I know. I just . . . I wondered, just like you, how she was going to take the news. She'll have three children older than her brother or sister. I really needed her to be excited for us. She's your daughter, but she's also my best friend."

Bill kissed the side of Jari's face and then laid back, quiet for several moments. Suddenly, he chuckled.

"What?"

"When we were outside talking on Saturday, she asked if we could call them cousins."

"Who?"

"The kids. All the kids. She asked if the girls and their baby can call our baby their cousin rather than calling them their aunt or uncle. And she asked if our baby could call her their aunt instead of their sister. I told her I thought that would be okay."

Jari laughed, happy that the awkward situation of what to call everyone had been addressed. She hadn't been quite sure what titles to give everyone either, as she, too, thought it would be weird for their baby to have nieces and possibly a nephew older than himself. "I think that sounds like a great plan."

"I thought you would. With both of us being only children, it might be nice for our kids to have an aunt and uncle. And Jessica is the closest thing you've ever had to a sister."

"So, now we're having kids? Multiple kids?" Jari teased, picking up on what she assumed was a slip-up.

Bill was quiet for a few moments. "If there's one thing I could do over, I wouldn't make Jessica grow up as an only child. When she was little, and I was young and immature, I thought being an only child would be best for her because she wouldn't have to share our attention. I reasoned we would be able to give her so many more opportunities if we didn't have to ration out our resources. It also just seemed easier. While that still may be the best decision for some families, as I get older, sometimes I think about how nice it would be to have a brother or a sister—some sort of family left now that my parents have both passed away. It would be nice to have someone who shares my family memories—my memories of childhood—someone to reminisce with and see during the holidays. As I get older, I often wish I had given that to Jessica. I know we are now, but it's different. They won't have the same childhood or the same memories." Bill paused. "I don't want to make the same mistake twice."

"I understand," Jari offered simply. And she did. As she got older, she often wished for the same thing. Even as a teenager, when everything happened with her dad and she felt so alone, she wished she had a sister or a brother to process the situation with. She rubbed Bill's arm that was draped over her stomach. Inside, her thick-skinned, blunt, hard-headed husband was actually tender and thoughtful. And he wanted to have more than one child with her. Her heart sang.

Bill yawned. "I'm starting to lose it."

"It's been a big weekend," Jari agreed, covering a yawn of her own with the back of her hand.

Turning over, he reached out and turned off the lamp on his bedside table, letting darkness settle over the room. He turned back and put his arm snuggly around her again. "Don't worry about getting up with me in the morning. I'll probably just grab something fast for breakfast and head to the office early. You should sleep in."

Jari considered his offer. She liked getting up with Bill in the mornings before he left for work. Sometimes, that was the most time she had with him all day. It also got her mornings started earlier, and it somehow always felt better to get up with someone rather than getting up alone in an empty house. Still, she was exhausted. The weekend had been fun, but tiring. The baby probably needed her to sleep, she rationalized. "I think I will."

"Good. Goodnight," Bill murmured sleepily.

"Goodnight," she answered. "I love you, Bill Cordel." There was no answer other than a subtle shift in his breathing, indicating he was asleep.

Twelve

J ari woke up slowly, going back and forth between being awake and asleep for almost half an hour. Finally, she forced herself to wake up for good. Turning her head to glance at the clock on her nightstand, she was shocked to see the numbers showing nine after ten. She couldn't remember the last time she had slept past eight o'clock, even on the weekends.

Feeling guilty, she flipped back the covers and jumped out of bed. That one quick action sent a sharp pain shooting through her lower abdomen. Catching her breath, she froze until the pain subsided.

Once it finally disappeared completely, she turned back toward her bed, moving carefully now, her eyebrows drawn together in worry. As she made her bed, she thought back to when Jessica was pregnant. She had been further along, but Jari remembered her talking about having pains shoot through her abdomen every now and again. Dr. Corvich had explained that the ligaments were stretching as the babies grew. As Jari set the decorative pillows into place, she wrote the odd pain off as a similar occurrence. She smiled as she realized her baby was growing.

Considering the late hour, she decided to shower and do her makeup before breakfast and headed into her bathroom. Once ready, she hurried downstairs to start the day. Glancing out the windows around the house as she walked, she spotted two security personnel situated around the property. Their presence made her feel at ease, and she wandered through the house to the den where she stood at the window and looked up and down the street. There was no black SUV, or any other parked cars for that matter, in sight. Breathing another sigh of relief, she continued to the kitchen, where she poured herself a glass of orange juice and a bowl of cereal. Carrying it to the table, she sat down and pulled the newspaper Bill had left her closer.

She opened the paper and scanned the stories as she ate, getting caught up on all that had happened in D.C. while they were away, as well as what was happening in the rest of the world.

After finishing her breakfast, she went upstairs to get her Bible and journal and curled up in her favorite armchair, where the sunshine streamed through her bedroom window. She spent time with the LORD, and when she was done, she felt refreshed and capable of handling whatever the day brought. Standing, she left the sunshine.

As she went back downstairs, she formulated a plan for her day. She had taken the day off from helping at the shelter, as she had anticipated it being a tiring weekend. Now she was glad she had. Even after sleeping in, she still felt tired. Determined to do something productive before resting, she grabbed a rag and went back into Bill's den. When she looked out the window earlier, she had noticed the thick layer of dust on the dark wood furniture. Knowing the lady who cleaned for them weekly wouldn't be in until Friday, she had determined to correct that before the day was done.

Straightening the few things on the desktop, she sprayed the citrus-scented furniture polish and wiped it. Finishing, she turned to the bookcase. As she began to dust each shelf and the objects it held, slow, dull pains began to ebb and flow through her lower abdomen. They were quiet and not uncomfortable enough to stop her, entirely different from what she had felt earlier as she jumped out of bed, and even different from what had happened the night before as she pulled the suitcase up the stairs.

Feeling slightly uneasy about the odd pains, she hurried to finish dusting the den, then put the rag and spray away. She had originally planned to dust the rest of the lower level as well, just to get it done, but decided instead to leave it until Friday. Thinking again of Dr. Corvich's explanation of stretching ligaments, Jari grabbed the remote and stretched out on the couch, flipping through the television channels until she found reruns of a show she had grown up watching. The familiar theme music drifted over her, and the characters she had spent half an hour with every day as a young girl filled the screen. She found herself relaxing into the couch, the pains gone, and the troubling thoughts forgotten.

Although she had originally planned to watch just one episode, simply to stretch out and rest a little bit, she didn't end up turning the television off until she had spent three hours on the couch. She had forgotten what a good show it was and liked how it took her back to happy times at home. She remembered sitting in a recliner with her mom watching the show after school, munching on a chocolate chip cookie still warm from the oven.

Smiling, Jari stood and went about her day, taking it easy for the most part as she marked a few things off her to-do list. The odd pains came and went throughout the rest of the afternoon and evening. They were dull and only slightly uncomfortable, but definitely there. Jari decided that if she woke up with them in the morning, she would call her doctor.

Jari had dinner and watched one of her favorite movies before going upstairs to read in bed. Bill worked late, catching up after being gone all weekend and hashing out details with Ryan for the campaign trip they would take later in the week. He got home just after ten and looked exhausted. They talked only long enough for him to tell her about his day and give her a heads-up on what their weekend trip would be like before he fell asleep. Turning out the light, Jari turned onto her side and held her husband as he slept.

The next morning, Jari got up with Bill and made breakfast for him while he showered and got ready for the day. When he came downstairs, she had his newspapers laid out, a cup of coffee, and a plate full of fruit, scrambled eggs and an English muffin arranged at his place at the table. Nodding in appreciation, he kissed her cheek before sitting down to eat.

She sat down with him, and he prayed before lifting his English muffin. "I'll probably work late again tonight."

"I figured you probably would."

Bill shot her a contemplative look, then nodded, seeing that she was only being realistic. "It's hard to be gone for a weekend with elections coming up, especially when we're leaving the day after tomorrow."

"I understand. What kind of things will you work on today?"

"Ryan and I are working on speeches, and I'm reading through his briefs on the communities we'll visit in the Shenandoah Valley at the end of the week, as well as all the things going on in the Senate today. There's just a lot right now."

"You sound so thrilled."

"It's just another day at the office," Bill replied, quirking a smile at her over his half-eaten English muffin.

"At a job you love," Jari reminded.

"Ninety percent of the time, yes."

Jari considered her aristocratically handsome husband. "What's bothering you?"

Bill didn't answer for several seconds, but continued eating. Finally, he took a drink of coffee and cleared his throat. "It would just be nice if D.C. were closer to Minnesota."

Understanding came like a switch being flipped. "You're missing Jessi and the girls?"

"And Joe," Bill added. He paused and then sighed. "They're our only family. The girls are changing so fast. Jessi needs you right now as much as you need her. And with the baby . . . it just feels like an inopportune time to be dealing with the demands of the state, the Senate, committees, and reelection."

"The election will be over before you know it," Jari reminded softly, gently squeezing Bill's forearm. He just grunted and resumed eating.

As he finished his last swallow of coffee, he stood. "Thanks for breakfast, Jari. It was good."

"You're welcome."

He grabbed the newspapers and his briefcase. "I'd better go. Have a good day."

"You too." He gave her a kiss and left her sitting at the kitchen table alone. She heard the front door open and shut as she fell back to eating her breakfast, contemplating what Bill had said.

He had always been so independent and confident, sometimes almost aloof. She had heard him talk more about family in the past forty-eight hours than she had accumulatively in the years since meeting him. Perhaps Jessi moving and then seeing her in her new home reminded him of his own lack of family. Perhaps he was missing his parents. Perhaps he was missing the fact that they didn't have family close by anymore.

When Jessi and the girls were around, as strange as it was, Maybelle, Carla and Tim had been part of their family. They could all count on holidays together, as well as Jessi and the girls' birthdays, and usually at least one Sunday dinner a month. It was important to all of them that Jessi and the girls' lives were complete and unfragmented. Now, without that common tie, the small group they had come to know as their family, however strangely connected, had fallen apart. Jari hadn't seen Maybelle or Carla since Jessi's wedding in Aruba. It wasn't that they disliked each other or had a falling out, there just wasn't the push or the reason to get together like there had been.

Family. The word ran through Jari's mind over and over. She might be an only child, but Jari had family. She had two parents who, to the best of her knowledge, were still living. She had aunts, uncles, and cousins galore. She had godparents, grandparents, and second cousins twice removed . . . and she had known them all well.

In that moment, a thought came that had never crossed her mind before. By cutting off communication and relationship with her family, was she denying Bill an opportunity he was yearning for deep inside? Was she depriving him of his opportunity to have in-laws? With his parents having already passed on years ago, in-laws were the closest thing he could have to fill that void. He hadn't been close to his parents, nor had he made much of an effort with Carla's from what Jari could gather, but now, with so many things changing, did he find himself longing for that? If he had a choice, would he want to go to Kansas and connect with her family—the only family they had other than Jessi and the girls?

They had only talked about her family a few times over the years. When he had first asked about them, just after their relationship started, she had simply told him she wasn't close to them. He hadn't pressed, seemingly content to leave the subject alone. The couple of times he had asked since, she had shared that they lost touch after she left for the city. He had assumed she disliked life in the country, always dreamt of living in a big city, skipped town after graduation, and had simply drifted apart from her parents as a result. She hadn't corrected him. It was easier than digging into the details of her past, and back then, she hadn't thought it mattered. He had seemed content with his career, daughter, granddaughters and her, so she hadn't considered the ramifications her choices had on him. Now, with him sharing his thoughts on family, she began to wonder if she was keeping something from Bill that he was longing for. The thought was unsettling and made her feel so utterly selfish.

Feeling uneasy about the direction her thoughts had taken, Jari got up from the table to use the restroom before finishing her breakfast. She was trying to drink more water since finding out she was pregnant, and it had resulted in more trips to the bathroom than she had ever made before. Still distracted by her thoughts of family, she suddenly felt her heart jump into her throat.

There was bright blood on the tissue.

~~~~~

Jari's hands shook as she dialed the number of her doctor. Why was there blood? There shouldn't be any blood. Not now. Not when she was just over nine weeks pregnant. The receptionist answered, and Jari asked to talk to Dr. Corvich. The doctor was out of the office for the morning, but the receptionist put Jari through to her nurse. The nurse asked a few questions before telling Jari that a little spotting was very common during early pregnancy. She said that if it got worse or if Jari began to experience painful cramping, to let them know.

When Jari hung up, she took a deep breath and tried to relax. Spotting was common. It didn't mean anything was wrong. It didn't mean something had happened to the baby. Forcing herself to take one deep breath after another, she carried her breakfast to the couch along with her water bottle, and sat down to rest, taking the nurse's advice to heart.

Stay hydrated, the nurse had said. Jari drank half her water bottle—sixteen ounces of water—without taking a breath. Rest, the nurse had said. Jari put her feet up on the couch, reclining back until she was barely upright enough to finish her breakfast.

Stabbing a piece of fruit with her fork, she put it in her mouth and chewed slowly as she flipped through the channels, checking to see what was on television. Finding the same old show she had watched the day before, she settled into the couch and finished her breakfast. The episode was familiar.

She remembered sitting crisscross on the floor in the middle of her parents' living room, watching the episode as she ate a peanut butter and jelly sandwich her mom had made for her after school. When her dad walked through the front door, getting home from work, she had jumped up and ran to him, giving him a hug and a kiss on the cheek before returning to her spot on the floor in front of the television. He came in to watch a few minutes with her before going in to shower and clean up for dinner.

The happy memory was shattered when a piercing pain rolled through her abdomen.

~~~~~

Jari wanted to cry, but couldn't. The rolling cramps were too painful to even speak through, her heart too heavy for tears. "God, please! Please stop this and save my baby!" she cried out into the quiet of her empty house. "You control life and death. You are the Author and Sustainer of life. You have complete control. Please, stop what is happening, and let my baby live! Please!" Her urgent pleas seemed to fill every space within her as her heart and spirit cried out to heaven to be heard.

It all hit so suddenly. The pain came on with an intensity she hadn't known in years. All she could do was lie on the couch and toss and turn as each wave of cramping came, trying to find some relief.

With shaking hands, she called the doctor's office again. The nurse had been kind and sympathetic, explaining that there was a chance Jari was miscarrying, but with her being so early, said there was nothing they could do to stop it. She would simply have to wait and see what transpired in the coming hours. The nurse had recommended continuing to drink water and rest. She had told her the signs to watch for that would mean she needed medical attention and reminded her that there was still hope.

After hanging up, feeling helpless and in despair, Jari reminded herself of that over and over again: There was still hope. There had been no great loss of blood; the baby hadn't passed. It was still inside. It could still live. God could still intervene and save her baby. He could still change the trajectory of her story.

She thought about calling Bill, but looking at the time, realized he was on the Senate floor. Besides, what would she say? That she *might* be miscarrying? She didn't want to say it. She didn't want it to be true. She wanted to cling to hope.

So she laid and prayed while fighting through the anguish, hoping, praying that the cramps would subside, and she would come out the other side, still pregnant with a living, growing, developing little one within her. As the minutes ticked by and the pains kept coming, feeling like a hot, searing knife was slicing through her lower abdomen, she continued praying. However, with each passing wave, doubt began to creep in—doubt and a little bit of anger.

"Why?" she demanded as her muscles tightened and pain shot through her. "Why is this happening? You could stop this!"

Nothing stopped. "You could save my baby right now if You wanted to!" Nothing changed. "Why?" she asked again, tears pricking her eyes. "Is it because of what I've done? Is this punishment for the life I've led . . . the choices I've made? Are you doing this to punish me?"

Just a few months ago, she thought her dream of having children would never come to fruition. She thought it was completely out of the question. That was even before she talked to Bill, before she found out it wasn't just logically out of the question; it was physically impossible. After she found out about his vasectomy, she realized that any hope she had clung to had to be extinguished. In the following days, she experienced the grief of a deep loss.

She knew the LORD had moved on her husband's heart when he came to her and told her of his decision to have the surgery reversed. She could not believe what he was saying—what he was signifying. She knew it could only be a work of God that could convince him to put her desire for children above his own physical comfort, reservations, and plans for their future. Still, the chances of conceiving were slim, and she understood that if she ever did get pregnant, it would be a gift from the LORD—His intervention in their lives.

When she became pregnant so soon after Bill's surgery, her surprise had gone deep. But not deeper than her joy and her peace. She felt peace knowing the baby was from the LORD, that He was showing His kindness to her, and that it was His will for them to have a child. She found peace in the knowledge that He had forgiven her for what she had done, that He was a God of second chances, and that He was showing her the greatness of His mercy. She had felt absolutely certain that everything would go well with the pregnancy.

After all, if He had orchestrated things so perfectly and so miraculously to give them a child, why was there any reason to doubt the baby would be born? Why was there any reason to doubt He would finish what He had started? No, this baby was clearly a gift from Him, ordained by Him, and a part of His will for their lives. She never considered that complications could arise, or that the pregnancy could end in miscarriage. Miscarriages didn't happen in situations like this. It didn't fit with the rest of the story. It wasn't how the story was supposed to end.

Pain ripped through her again, and she moaned. Feeling the need to use the bathroom, she climbed the stairs to her bedroom, every move she made feeling like it drove the knife in deeper. With every step, she was in greater agony, both physically and mentally, as she grew in certainty of what she would find when she made it to her bathroom. With every passing moment, doubt made its way further into her heart.

By the time she made it to her primary bath, she wondered why, if it had so clearly been His plan, His will, His hand that had set everything up, was it now falling apart? If His plan was falling apart and He wasn't stopping it, then was He really as good and kind and powerful as she'd always thought?

In that moment, as she made it to the bathroom and found that blood had soaked through her clothes, she wondered if everything she had believed in for the last six years was a lie. In one of the darkest moments of her entire existence, as life physically left her body, she wondered if the One who she believed in so wholeheartedly, if He Himself had been a lie. In that moment, she felt cold, dark, empty, and lifeless within.

Sitting in her bathroom, she shook as blood poured from her body, taking with it the hopes and dreams that had filled her heart with so much joy and made her future look so bright. In every way, she started feeling cold and numb. She began to shiver; the chill making her increasingly uncomfortable until she was so cold that her discomfort turned to misery. She started to feel nauseous, and the room started to spin a little. Belatedly, she realized the amount of blood she was losing could not possibly be normal. She looked around for her phone, knowing it was past time to call the doctor, but realized in her anguish, she'd left her phone downstairs.

Knowing she had to find a way to get back downstairs to it, she did what she could to clean herself up and pushed herself to her feet. As she did, she felt lightheaded, and she had to reach out and stabilize herself against the wall. She took one shaky step and then another. As she took a third step, her vision started to go dim around the edges and the room started to spin until she couldn't make out which way was up. Her knees buckled, and she felt the chill of the tile as she crumpled down onto it. She wanted to call out, but there was no one home to hear her. In that moment, from the deepest part of her heart, she cried out to the One who only a short time earlier, she questioned if she even believed in at all.

"Jesus, please help me!" she cried, her weak voice echoing in the large, tiled bathroom. The words had barely left her lips when suddenly she stopped shaking, the coldness eased, and the spinning room blurred into black.

~~~~~

Sometime later, Jari woke up slowly, feeling groggy. She didn't know how much time had passed, but as she slowly pushed herself up off the floor to a sitting position with shaky arms, she found that she had the strength to do so. She felt exhausted and weak, and found she was lying in a puddle of blood, but she was alive.

She looked around her bathroom blankly, her brain feeling foggy and confused. Her eyes fell on the tiny bundle she had wrapped in tissue. With painful clarity, it all came rushing back. It hadn't been a bad dream. Just like that, it was done. Just like that, her baby was gone. Just like that, she wasn't pregnant anymore. Just like that, she was alone in her body once again. It all felt so familiar. From a different place and a different time, she knew this feeling well.

She sat perfectly still, perfectly quiet for a long time, staring at the tiny bundle. Her hands still trembled, whether from loss of blood, the aftereffects of the horrible cramping, or the knowledge that her baby, her little gift from God, was dead, she wasn't sure. Nor did she care.

It all felt like a horrible dream. That morning, she had woken up pregnant, with new life growing within her. She had been dreaming of what it would be like to have a little one in the house and was counting down the weeks until her ultrasound. She was thinking of different ways to decorate the nursery. She was brainstorming names. She was thinking of her and Bill in the context of family—their own family—him, her, and the baby. And now it was all over. It was all lost. How could something so devastating happen so fast?

Jari knew she should call the doctor, but didn't feel physically strong enough to get up, much less walk downstairs to retrieve her phone. She knew she should call Bill, but didn't have the emotional or physical strength to do so. Even if she could, what would she say? How would she tell him? How could she possibly bring herself to explain what had happened? How was she supposed to speak the words that seemed like they would rip her very heart out if she spoke them aloud? How was she supposed to tell him she had lost his baby? She had been solely responsible for keeping the baby safe, healthy, and growing and somehow, for whatever reason, she hadn't been able to do it.

The grief was like a heavy weight sitting on her shoulders, numbing her mind and even her emotions, but the guilt . . . the guilt felt like something tightening around her, growing tighter and tighter around her rib cage, making it harder and harder for her to breathe. The combination of the two was overwhelming. She wanted to run and hide, but she knew there was no hiding from the emptiness within.

So she continued to sit on the bathroom floor, staring at the bloody bundle, wondering how it had come to that. She wondered what she had done wrong, and if things would ever be okay.

Instantly, she was walking out of the abortion clinic again. She had all the same emotions, all the same realities, all the same knowledge. All she could think about was that this baby, too, would never be born, never have a chance to grow up, never have the chance to live. Even if it hadn't been by choice this time, it was still her fault. It had to be.

Maybe she hadn't drunk enough water. Maybe she shouldn't have flown. Maybe she shouldn't have walked so far at the football game. Maybe she shouldn't have carried the suitcase up the stairs. Maybe she shouldn't have let herself worry about the black SUV. Maybe she shouldn't have dusted. Maybe she shouldn't have eaten at a buffet, even if it was only breakfast. The list was never ending. It was her fault. If for no other reason, maybe she wasn't deemed worthy to carry a child because of what she had done. Maybe it was payback . . . retribution.

Either way, her baby was dead . . . again.

She sat on the floor, unmoving, for the rest of the day. She knew she should get up, but she couldn't find the strength or motivation. She knew she should call Bill, but she didn't. She knew she should call Jessi, but downstairs felt so far away. Finally, after darkness had fallen over her bathroom, she finally moved onto her hands and knees, her body stiff and achy, and crawled around the bathroom floor, cleaning up the mess as best she could. She crawled into the closet, not trusting her legs to stand, and found an empty shoe box. Laying the small bundle inside, she put the lid on. Very, very carefully, she pushed herself to her feet. After waiting several moments to make sure her legs would hold her this time, she inched her way through her room and down the hall to what would have been the nursery. Doing the only thing that made any sense to her in that moment, she put the box inside the room, and quietly closed the door behind her as if the baby were only sleeping.

Keeping her hand on the wall for support as she made her way back into the bathroom, she turned on the shower to get the water hot. Once it was, she stood under the stream of water for a long time without moving, resting her back against the shower wall for support. She wanted to wash away all the remnants of what had happened. She wanted the warmth of the water to soak into her—soak into her very soul—and warm up what felt like nothing but ice . . . but the warmth never made it past her skin.

Finally, when her legs started to shake again, and she knew her strength was almost gone, she washed, turned off the shower, and stepped out, drying herself with a towel before pulling on clean clothes. As her legs began to weaken, Jari dropped to her hands and knees, knowing she needed to get to bed before she collapsed on the floor again. Seeing her soiled clothes still lying on the floor, she gathered them up and threw them in the wastebasket, knowing she would never be able to get the stains out, anyway. Without turning on a light, brushing her teeth, or even brushing her hair, she crawled through her room and up onto her bed, slipping between the sheets. She was still lying there awake, unmoving, when Bill entered the room hours later.

Pretending to be asleep when she heard him climbing the stairs, he came in and seemingly fell for it. She could tell he was purposefully being quiet as he moved around the room, trying not to wake her. When he sat on her side of the bed, it startled her, but she kept her eyes closed, feeling too weak to open them and face him. He turned on her lamp and gently shook her shoulder.

"Jari?" Reluctantly, she opened her eyes, but couldn't bring herself to look up into his face. She was surprised he woke her. She had assumed he would think she was tired and let her sleep. Her gaze fell to his hands, where he was holding the clothes she had thrown in the trash. She cringed, wishing she had found the strength to hide the waste basket before making her way to bed. He raised the clothes slightly. "What happened?" His voice sounded strained. She couldn't find any words.

When the silence stretched, Bill dropped the clothes on the floor and got down on his knees beside the bed, forcing her to look him in the face. His color was ashen, lines of concern etched clearly across his face. "Honey?" When she still didn't answer, he reached out to touch the side of her face. She flinched. Pain showed in his eyes. "Honey, did you lose the baby today?" His voice caught, and for the first time since it had happened, tears welled in Jari's eyes.

"I'm sorry," she whispered brokenly.

Bill's eyes closed, and he inhaled slowly. "Oh, Jari." She couldn't watch. She closed her eyes again, wishing she could close her heart to the pain as well. Feeling tears slipping out of her closed eyes, she pressed her fists to them. Bill reached out and pulled her hands away. "Jari." As soon as he let go, she covered her face with her hands. He pulled them away again, his grip feeling like iron as she fought to keep her face covered. Her cheeks were aflame. She felt overwhelmed with shame.

"I'm sorry," she told him again.

His face crumpled, and he reached out, gathering her up in his arms and pulling her to a sitting position as he crawled up onto the bed beside her. He gently drew her onto his lap, cradling her against his chest. "Don't be sorry! This isn't your fault!"

She knew it was, but didn't say so.

"Honey, why didn't you call me?"

"I left my phone downstairs. I couldn't get to it."

She felt him shudder. "When did it happen?"

"It started this morning, not long after you left. I'm not sure when it ended," she admitted, her voice dull.

Bill pressed his face against the side of her head. "I wish I had known so I could have come home to be with you. That must have been so scary for you to go through all alone." It was quiet for several long moments. "Are you okay? Are you ... sick?" His voice sounded fearful.

Jari wanted to snap out of it. She wanted to comfort her husband. She wanted to hold him and tell him everything he wanted to know. She wanted to process what had happened and grieve together. But she couldn't shake the numbness. She couldn't think of anything to say. She couldn't get past the hurt or the shame, or the fact that it was her fault. She couldn't get past the grief that threatened to consume her. She couldn't think of any words to describe how alone she felt inside ... how empty she was.

"I don't know," she finally said, knowing he was waiting for an answer.

He pulled back a little, his face lined with worry. "Can I take you to your doctor? To the hospital?"

She shook her head. "I don't want to go anywhere."

Bill sat and looked at her for a long time. "Can I do anything?" Jari shook her head. "Can I get you anything?" She shook her head again. "What can I do to fix this?" Bill finally pleaded, his voice breaking and tears welling in his blue eyes.

With his last question, she turned, feeling stunned, and met his eyes for the first time. What could he do to fix it? Could it be fixed? Was there anything either of them could do to fix what had happened? Was there any way they could take the baby wrapped in tissue lying in a box in its room, and put it back inside of her and make it grow, develop, and live again?

"It's gone! The baby's gone," she wailed. Still holding her, Bill laid back against the pillows, wrapping her tightly in his arms. Tears rolled down the sides of his face as he tried in vain to comfort her. Jari wept uncontrollably, her body shaking, the sound of her grief filling the room. Eventually, she fell asleep in his arms, her exhaustion overcoming her.

Thirteen

Waking up to see the first light of the morning starting to lift from the east, Bill carefully slid his arms out from under Jari and stood. The confusion that sometimes comes with the haze of just waking up dissipated as he stepped on damp fabric and looked down to find his wife's bloody clothes. It all came back in a rush, and he had to steady himself on the nightstand for a few moments before his head felt clear enough to stand on his own.

Crossing the room to the dresser where he had left his cell phone the night before, he did something he hadn't done in a long, long time. He texted Ryan and let him know he wouldn't be coming into the office, taking any phone calls, or answering any emails. With that done, he slipped his cell phone into the top dresser drawer. He might be a senator, and in the middle of a reelection campaign, but his wife needed him.

Seeing her Bible beside the armchair under the window, he sat down and opened it, thumbing through the pages mindlessly. Suddenly, his eyes filled with tears, and he scrunched them shut, pressing his lips into a thin line.

"Why?" he screamed in his mind. "Why God?" There was no answer. "Why, when we weren't even expecting it, would you let her get pregnant only to have it end in miscarriage? Why?" His demands went unanswered. Drawing the back of his hand across his eyes, he sniffed and looked over at his wife. "We left it up to

You—up to Your wisdom. It was such a journey just to get to the point where I was okay with the idea. It was such a deep dream in her heart. Why would You give something that brought about so much excitement and joy, only to take it away? It doesn't make any sense! Why not just save us both the heartache and never have let it happen? Or let her get pregnant in a year, when the pregnancy would have been healthy? God, I don't understand!"

Searching for some kind of a response, he looked down at the open Book in his lap. The words seemed to stand off the page. "Peace I leave with you; my peace I give you."

"I don't feel peace," Bill admitted weakly. "*She* doesn't feel peace."

The verse went on. "I do not give to you as the world gives. Do not let your hearts be troubled and do not be afraid." Bill shook his head, closing his eyes. It still made no sense, and yet a sense of peace did settle over him, quieting his heart, quieting his mind.

Still hurting, but less angry and chaotic within, he shut the Book carefully and crossed the room back to the bed. He picked up her clothes that still lay on the floor, took them into the bathroom, and put them back in the trash can. Quietly, not wanting to wake her, he crawled around on his hands and knees on the bathroom floor, cleaning up all the traces of blood, not wanting her to see the reminder of what had happened when she woke up. His stomach churned as he cleaned, realizing how close he must have come to losing her. Though she had lost their baby, he could have lost her. The very idea was unthinkable.

Needing the reassurance of holding her, feeling her warmth, and hearing the sound of her breathing, he hurried back to the bed as soon as he finished, wanting to see again with his own eyes that she was okay. Lying down once more, he took his young wife in his arms and held her while she slept, praying throughout the early morning hours. He prayed for himself, for his emotions. He prayed for guidance, understanding, and for the wisdom of God to be revealed, but he mostly prayed for Jari. He prayed for her heart, her mind, her body, and her soul.

He had never seen her like she was the night before. With no other way to describe it, Bill only knew that sometime during the hours yesterday, as she lost their baby, she also lost the life that had always shone from her eyes, bubbled from her every word, and emanated from her very being. Their unborn child had not been the only one who had tasted death.

That knowledge chilled him to the bone. He determined that he would take her to the doctor when she woke up, regardless of any protests she might make. He regretted not doing so the night before. They had lost their baby. He could not, would not, lose her too.

When Jari woke up a couple of hours later, she blinked slowly, seeming confused. Bill watched her quietly, wondering what would happen next, wondering how she would react to everything in the light of day. His heart hurt thinking about the anguish she would be in when the memories came back. As much as he wanted to, he knew there was nothing he could do to help her and that was a terrible feeling. When she focused on his face, he forced himself to smile and hoped it didn't look strained. "Good morning."

Jari's eyes darted to the window, then to the clock, and back to him. Tears pooled. "If it's light out and you're still here, then it wasn't all a bad dream, was it?"

Bill's throat hurt, and he cleared it before shaking his head. "No, honey. It wasn't a bad dream."

Her hands shook as she drug her slender fingertips below her eyes. "So, it really happened? I really . . . lost the baby? I'm not pregnant anymore?" Her voice was as shaky as her hands, and she sounded young and scared. He wished he could tell her that it had indeed been a bad dream, that she was still pregnant. He wanted to see joy and hope spring back into her lovely face. For one bizarre moment, he considered doing just that and dealing with reality at a later time. Knowing that was ridiculous, he forced himself to shake his head in response. Jari bit her lip, more tears pooling in her beautiful blue eyes.

Rolling onto her back, she stared up at the ceiling for a long time. Fighting the urge to be a fixer, Bill didn't say or do anything. He simply laid with her and allowed her to process.

He had been reading a book on women lately, one he had snuck into his office and made time to read a few minutes each day. Since the beginning of summer, he had felt the need to be intentional about knowing and understanding his wife better, and now he was glad he had put in the time and effort. To his dismay, he had learned that sometimes Jari may not want him to fix a problem as much as she wanted him to be at her side through it. Now he would have to fight the natural, assertive part of his nature that wanted to get the situation fixed and Jari better, and put into practice what he had learned. As the silence stretched, he began to consider just how hard that could prove to be.

"Yesterday, I was so confused," Jari finally said, breaking the silence and startling him. Her voice was shaky and unsure. When she didn't go on, he wondered if he should respond, or if she was simply thinking. He was just opening his mouth to do so when she finally continued. "When I went into the bathroom, I didn't know if I believed in God anymore." He tried not to show how much her statement shocked him.

"I thought why, if it was His will, if He had brought us to this place, why in the world would this be happening?" Her voice quivered, and he saw a tear roll down the side of her face and land in her matted blonde hair. "I was so angry and heartbroken. I have never felt so unsure or so utterly hopeless in my entire life. Everything I have put my hope in for the last six and a half years felt so useless and fake. I've not experienced such darkness like that since . . . well, since I used to live a very different life."

Absorbing her words, thankful she was finally talking and verbalizing what had happened, her last sentence distracted Bill from the issue at hand. He wondered what kind of life his wife used to live to cause her words to sound so haunted. He wondered what things she had done that now caused her face to look so pale and full of shame.

They had never really talked much about their pasts. When they first started their affair, it didn't seem important. All that mattered then was being together and how it felt when they were. After they were married, Bill had no desire to pry into what his young, beautiful wife had done or who she had been with. Even suspicions made him jealous, and he had no desire to open a can of worms that could potentially drive a wedge between them. She, as young, beautiful, vibrant, and full of life as she was, wanted to be with him. In his mind, he was the winner. That was all that mattered, and he had thought if she didn't need to tell him about her past, he didn't need to hear it. Likewise, he figured that hearing about his life with Carla would only make her feel awkward and jealous as well, so they had lived as though both of their lives had started at the time they met. It seemed logical at the time, but now he wondered what kind of burdens of the past she had carried by herself all these years.

Jari brought him back to the present when she continued. "But there was one point, Bill, during . . . it . . . that I had lost so much blood, and I felt so weak and dizzy that I wanted to get to my phone so I could call for an ambulance, but I physically couldn't make it.

When I tried, I collapsed on the bathroom floor. I thought I was going to bleed to death right then and there."

Bill could feel the color draining from his face and was thankful her eyes were trained on the ceiling, so she didn't see his reaction. He had seen the blood on the floor, but even at that, he hadn't realized just how bad it had been. His stomach dropped as he began to grasp just how close he had come to losing her.

"And in that moment, Bill, when I wasn't strong enough to stand up, from the very depths of my spirit, I found myself calling out to Jesus. And I knew that no matter how confused I felt, or how much it didn't make sense or how angry, alone, or empty I felt, I knew that at the core of my being, I believed." She paused and wiped at fresh tears. "And so this morning, even if I don't know or understand anything else, I know that He is real, and I believe in Him. At my darkest hour, when I had come to the end of myself and my reasoning and my own strength, still, He was there."

Even without being the one to experience it, Bill felt the weightiness of what she said settle over him. There was a sureness in her voice, a confidence in the existence of God that he had never heard before. She and Jessica were the ones who had led him to the LORD. Jari served as a roadmap and a rock for him to cling to in the early days of his faith, as he learned about the One he had given his heart and life to. He had never doubted or questioned her faith, but now, with this new quality of assurance in her voice, he knew something had changed—something that would change everything about her. "What happened then?" he asked after a full minute of silence had passed.

"I blacked out, and when I woke up, the bleeding had stopped, and my strength was returning. I could feel it. It was like it was being poured back into me. The room had stopped spinning, and I could sit up again. I don't know how to describe it any more than that, but when I called out to Him, Bill, and realized I believed—no matter what was happening—it's like He saved me. Again. I knew that I was physically going to be okay."

"Why didn't you call me then?"

She bit her lip. "My strength was returning, but being able to sit up and walking downstairs to where I had left my phone are two very different things. I guess being physically okay and emotionally okay are very different things too. Even if I would have had my phone, I didn't know how to tell you."

Bill took a deep, shaky breath, unnerved by her harrowing tale, and let the silence stretch. He tried to picture what the day must have been like for her. As a result, he put his arm around her and tucked her in tighter against his side. "How do you feel today?"

"Confused. Sad. Angry. Almost like I don't believe it happened," she said slowly, pausing between each emotion she identified. "I don't understand why it had to happen like this . . . or why it happened at all. I don't understand why He took a baby He had so obviously planned and made a way for." Her voice broke. "I don't know what I did wrong." The tears came again, like a dam that had broken.

"Shhhh. You didn't do anything wrong. This wasn't your fault," he told her, wanting to help. He stroked the hair back out of her face.

"You don't understand. It was my fault," she sobbed.

"No, it wasn't," he assured her, but it didn't seem to do any good.

"After being so unsure, you were so excited about having a baby . . . about being a father again. I could see it. You looked happier than I've seen you look in a long time." Bill didn't know what to say. It was true. "It was my job—mine and mine alone—to take care of it, to grow and develop it, and I couldn't! I couldn't hold it in! I couldn't keep it alive. I couldn't hold on to it. It was my body. I should have been able to hold on to it."

Still, Bill didn't know how to respond. He had no gauge, no safe response for this torrent of guilt his wife seemed to be drowning in. "You did the best you could," he finally offered, hoping it was the right thing to say.

"The best I could? Obviously, my best wasn't good enough. My best didn't give you a baby, did it? My best didn't produce a child for you to hold, love, and find joy in. You'll never have the opportunity to love this little one, be proud of it, or watch it grow up and start a family of its own. You did your part, Bill, but I couldn't do mine, and I'm sorry! I'm so sorry!"

Feeling like he was being thrown against the rocks by an angry sea over and over again, tears filled his own eyes as he tried to make sense of both his grief and hers. "I don't blame you," he told her. "I don't blame you."

She wept; he cried.

When their tears had again been spent and silence had fallen over the room like a blanket, Bill thought about how to move forward. He was trying to appreciate her need to simply be together during this difficult time, but there were logical, physical needs as well, and he needed to address them.

He broke the silence with the most logical first step. "Have you had anything to eat or drink since the miscarriage?" Jari shook her head. "Okay, I'm going to go get us both something to eat, and I'll bring up some water. Does anything sound good?" Again, Jari shook her head. "Will you eat something if I bring it to you?" He didn't wait for her to answer. He wasn't giving her a choice. "You have to eat, honey, to regain your strength. I'll be back." He pushed himself off the bed, but before he could leave, she reached out and grabbed his hand, clinging to it.

"Bill?"

"Yes?"

She pressed his hand to her face. "Thank you for being here today. I . . . I need you to be here, and you are. Fully. Thank you."

Tears pricked his eyes, and he bent down and kissed her firmly, feeling overcome with emotion. "Honey, there is absolutely nowhere else I would be today." She sent him a shaky smile, and he kissed her again before straitening. "Now, I'm going to go get you something to eat and drink to start building your strength back up. I'll be right back."

Downstairs, he found some artisan rolls on the counter and smoked turkey in the fridge. Adding sliced pickles, sliced tomatoes, and finishing with a swipe of mayonnaise, he put both sandwiches on a plate. Cutting an apple in quarters and scooping the seeds out, he added it to the plate as well. He found Jari's empty water bottle in the living room and filled it up, then brewed her a cup of her favorite tea. Arranging it all on a tray and adding a bag of potato chips, he carried it upstairs.

Entering their bedroom, he saw that Jari was no longer in bed. Breathing a sigh of relief that she was once again in motion, he found her in the bathroom, trying to brush through her tangled hair. "How are you feeling now that you're up?"

"A little weak, but mostly okay," she told him. He noticed her arms shaking from the slight effort of brushing her hair and suspected she was sugar-coating the truth. Stilling her movements, he took the brush from her hands and gently started working through the tangles. When he had her long blonde hair brushed out, he put his arm around her for support and helped her back to the bed.

"Are you ready for lunch?" he asked, putting pillows up against the headboard to add cushion to their makeshift picnic spot. She nodded, and he helped her sit down and get comfortable. He drew the blankets up over her legs to keep her warm and handed her the water bottle. Accepting it, she drank deeply before setting it on the nightstand beside her. Taking his sandwich, he handed the plate to her. She looked at her sandwich for a few seconds, and he nudged her with his elbow. "You have to eat."

She glanced at him. "I know. It looks good. I just don't have much of an appetite."

"Well, eat as much as you can." She nodded and lifted the sandwich, dutifully taking a bite. Bill smiled when he looked her way again, his own sandwich half-gone, and found that hers was nowhere in sight.

Jari shrugged. "I guess I was hungrier than I thought."

He chuckled, relieved, and passed her the plate of apples. "I thought you might be. Not eating for twenty-four hours can do that."

As he ate, Bill mentally assembled a list of phone calls he needed to make. He needed to call the doctor and ask if he should bring Jari in, call Jessica and let her know what had happened, and call Ryan to tell him to cancel the trip they were supposed to be leaving on in the morning. Suddenly, another task from another time filled his mind.

He cleared his throat. "Before Jessica was born, Carla had a miscarriage."

Jari's head snapped around, and she stared at him. "Really?"

He nodded. "It's not uncommon for women to miscarry during their first pregnancy." He wondered why that statement caused Jari to drop her eyes and look away. He continued slowly, worried that she felt he was discounting or discrediting what had just happened. "It didn't feel like this, Jari. This feels . . . different. And I think it's because of the journey we've been on to get here, and even because of how we felt like this was so planned and orchestrated by God. When Carla was pregnant, we were young and immature. We weren't sure we were ready for a baby. We treated the whole thing with caution from the beginning, knowing it could end like it did. It wasn't like this, but it was still a painful experience."

Jari was watching him again, and he wished he knew what she was thinking. He plunged ahead, hoping he wasn't driving the knife deeper by reminiscing about a similar experience with his ex-wife. "I know one thing that was helpful in getting through that was the closure we were able to have. When it all started, Carla called Maybelle, and Maybelle suggested that we try to keep the baby if at all possible. We did, and after it was all over, we took it out in our backyard and buried it. In a strange way, having our own little funeral for it helped." He paused. "With or without the baby, we could have a funeral."

Quiet settled over the room. Bill tried to gauge Jari's reaction, but her face was unreadable. Suddenly, she set the potato chip bag aside, unfolded her long, slender legs, and stood. "Come with me," she told him, and he stood too. He followed her out of their room and down the hall, noting that her steps looked a little steadier than they had earlier. Quietly, almost reverently, she opened the closed door to the room that would have been their nursery. He had no idea what she was doing.

He watched as tears welled up in her eyes as she entered the room and looked around, almost as if she were picturing what it might have looked like painted and decorated. Finally, she crossed the room to the dresser and picked up a small box. Turning, she held it out to him. "I think it would be good to bury it."

Surprise filled his face. "It's . . . it's in the box?" She nodded. Holding his hand out for hers, he led her down the stairs and out onto the back patio, going slow, keeping his eyes on her to gauge her strength. On the far side of the pool, he pulled over a chair for her, and then headed for the small garden shed. Jari sat in the chair and held the box while he found a shovel. Looking around their perfectly landscaped yard, he searched for a place to bury it.

"Let's bury it in the sun," Jari said as she wrapped her arms around herself and tilted her face up to the sky.

"That's a good idea," Bill agreed, and he started toward a pretty patch of grass that was in full sun. Jari watched as he dug a small hole and then carefully set the box inside of it. She went down on her knees beside the little grave, and Bill crouched down beside her. Putting his arm around her shoulders, he led them in a prayer. Tears dripped off Jari's chin, and he swiped at his own eyes once or twice. When he finished, he pushed the dirt over the box with his hands and replaced the chunk of sod that he had shaved off with the shovel, patting it back down into place. Standing, he dusted the dirt off his hands, and they both stood there quietly for a long moment.

Jari was the first to turn and head back into the house, her steps shaky again, and Bill fell into step beside her, matching his stride to hers. Once inside, he filled up her water bottle again and handed it to her. "How are you feeling?"

"I'm still cramping, but it's nothing like it was yesterday," she responded after draining half of the water.

"I'd like to call your doctor and see if she can get you in. Is that okay?" Jari nodded. "Good. Why don't you sit down and rest, and I'll get your phone." He could tell she was in pain and even more so now after being up and walking around for a while.

"Thank you, Bill," she told him, a glimmer of a smile showing up for just a moment before disappearing once again. She made her way into the living room and stretched out on the couch while he got her phone. He came back with her cup of tea, and she sipped on it while he called the doctor and made an appointment to bring Jari in that afternoon.

Next, he called Jessica and broke the news. Finding the words to tell her what had happened was difficult, and he began to understand why Jari hadn't wanted to call him the day before. Jessica cried when he told her the news, and he had to put effort into making his own voice stay steady and sure. He wanted to comfort, not require comforting. He deeply appreciated that his daughter felt their grief with them.

"How's Jari? Is she okay?" Jessi asked, sniffing.

"She will be." He didn't know what else to say. His wife was beginning to bounce back, or at least show signs of being able to bounce back in the future, but there was no denying that he had never seen her like this before.

"Should I come? I could be there by tonight."

"I don't know," he admitted. "I'm not sure what she needs right now. I appreciate your offer, and I'm sure she would too, but I have no idea what to tell you."

Jessi was quiet, obviously thinking things through. "I won't come for now. I don't want to overwhelm her or make her feel like she needs to entertain us when she should be resting. But please, tell Jari that I would love to come if she wants me there at any point. All she has to do is send me a text, and I'll be on the next flight out."

"I'll tell her," Bill promised, touched by his daughter's thoughtfulness. She really did love his wife. Knowing that made him smile.

The conversation ended after a few more minutes and a promise to let her know if there was anything she could do. He made his way back downstairs to tell Jari what Jessica had said and to let her know about her appointment.

When he took Jari to her doctor's appointment, they found her hemoglobin level had dropped very low from her loss of blood. She was on the brink of needing a blood transfusion, but since her bleeding had slowed, Dr. Corvich sent her home with vitamins and tea, a follow-up appointment for the following Monday, where they would again check her bloodwork, and strict orders to go to the hospital immediately if her bleeding picked up or she started to feel dizzy again. The doctor instructed her to take her phone with her wherever she went, and to not hesitate to call an ambulance if she even suspected she might need one.

Bill felt shook up on their way home, having seen how concerned Dr. Corvich was, and understanding medically how dangerous the ordeal had been for Jari. He kicked himself for not having known something was wrong. If only he would have called to check on her and gone home when he couldn't reach her. Taking a ragged breath, he reminded himself that what was done was done, and he could only focus on doing better in the future.

He asked how she was feeling, and she told him she was okay. When he glanced over again, he saw she had dozed off in the passenger seat, and he was glad she was getting a little nap. Once home, Bill got her settled on the couch with more hot tea. For the rest of the afternoon, they stayed together on the couch and watched old movies. There wasn't much conversation, but he held her in the crook of his arm, against his side, and felt content simply to be with her. He hoped it was enough for her too.

He would have talked, but there didn't seem to be much left to say. He didn't know what she needed to hear, or if saying anything would help. Even for him, words didn't seem as necessary as simply being together, knowing that they weren't experiencing their loss alone, and that they both understood.

For dinner, he insisted on steak with a spinach salad, hoping to bring her iron levels up through food, and put her to bed early, knowing she needed her rest. For the second night in a row, he fell asleep holding his wife, thanking God that she was still there to hold.

Fourteen

J ari stayed in bed a long time after she woke up the next morning. When Bill had talked to her about the campaign trip the night before and told her he planned to cancel, she had been surprised and touched that he would even offer. Still, she convinced him to go without her. While she had loved having him home with her, and appreciated that he was putting her first, she needed a few days on her own to process all that had happened. He had finally agreed to go but made her promise to always have her phone with her, just as the doctor ordered. He'd told her if he texted or called, and she took more than ten minutes to answer, he would call emergency services and be on his way home. Appreciating his concern, she'd promised she would keep her phone with her.

Reminding her that she needed her rest, he'd insisted she sleep in, rather than getting up to see him off. Tired, she had agreed. He kissed her goodbye before he left at six, and she went back to sleep.

Now, several hours later, Jari was still lying in bed, lacking the motivation and energy necessary to get up and face another day. It was still hard to comprehend what had happened less than forty-eight hours earlier. It was still hard not to think it had simply been a dream. She pressed her hand to her stomach and cried. Then she just lay quietly, feeling empty and lifeless.

Her cell phone went off on the bedside table beside her. Reaching for it, she saw a text message from Bill reminding her to eat. His thoughtfulness drew a smile, and she flipped back the covers and stood. She texted back that she was heading downstairs to eat something. She put a smiley face at the end.

After brushing her teeth, she did what she had told him she would do. She fixed herself a slice of avocado toast and steeped a cup of red raspberry leaf tea, as the doctor had suggested. Adding a little milk and sugar to her tea, she carried her breakfast into the living room. She wanted there to be noise in the house. As it was, it felt very quiet and empty, and the thought that it always would be was too much.

She turned on the television, started one of her favorite movies, dragged a blanket off the back of the chair and sat down with it to eat her breakfast. When her toast was gone, she sipped her tea until it was gone as well. Then she stretched out on the couch, covered up with the blanket, and watched her movie. She was thankful she had already prepared to be out of town for the rest of the week with Bill, so she didn't have to cancel any plans or reschedule any appointments. She was free to rest, process, and grieve, and that was exactly what she planned to do.

Jessi called in the afternoon, and they cried together. Her friend asked how she was feeling and asked if she'd remembered to eat lunch. When she said she wasn't hungry, Jessi made her promise to at least eat dinner, and told her she would be calling to make sure she did.

Jari stayed in her pajamas all day—something she hadn't done in a very long time—and went back and forth between watching movies and lying on her back, staring at the ceiling and thinking. Tired of the thoughts that only seemed to break her heart over and over again, she considered asking Jessi to fly out to be with her. If nothing else, the distraction would be nice. Still, somewhere deep inside, she knew she needed to think the thoughts, process the emotions, and deal with the loss. Distracting herself would only prolong it. The time for moving on would come, but for now, she had to walk through the valley, embrace the suffering, and see for herself what could be on the other side.

So for the next several days, she slept, watched movies, thought, read, and asked questions that seemed to go unanswered. She ate when she remembered, drank tea, and talked to Bill whenever he had a free moment to call. When he called, she put considerable effort into making her voice sound normal. She knew he had been hesitant to go, and she didn't want him worrying about her while he was out on the campaign trail. Elections were just a month away, and the rallies he was attending were important. He couldn't be distracted.

She didn't tell him what her days consisted of, or that she hadn't changed her clothes since he left. She didn't tell him she cried until she fell asleep every night, or that her guilt seemed to fill the empty house. She didn't tell him that she thought about her abortion unceasingly and wondered if losing the baby was a just punishment for what she had done. She had thrown away a baby she didn't want, and so a baby they had both wanted was taken from them. It made sense.

Instead, she asked about how the trip was going. She asked about his speeches and how he felt the deliveries had gone. She asked about who he had met with, and if there were any special moments with his constituents throughout the day. She asked what was next on his agenda, which towns he would be stopping in, and what kind of predictions there were. She asked if the trees were turning yet in the valley, and if he'd run into any rain. She told him she was doing fine and staying busy. She assured him that yes, she remembered to eat, and yes, she had been drinking the tea and taking the vitamins as her doctor instructed.

When they hung up, she would sit and cry, her head in her hands, feeling hopeless and alone once again; knowing despair in the simple fact that she was pretending to be okay when she absolutely wasn't. Eventually, the tears would subside, and she would feel quiet within—just like the big house felt quiet. Then thoughts would begin to bounce around again; thoughts about the baby, thoughts about having children, thoughts all centering around the question 'why.'

In those moments, she vowed to herself that she was done—she no longer wanted children. If this was how it could end, if the heartache could be so great, then she was finished. Perhaps in brighter days, far in the future, she would reconsider, but for now she felt certain that she never wanted to feel this sorrow again and would do whatever she could to avoid it.

After that, thoughts about God would come. Why would He allow something like this, and why didn't it make any sense? Where was the testimony in it all? Was He really not kind and merciful as she had believed? Was He actually cruel? Was He taunting her? Or was it simply that He was a just God? Was she only getting what she deserved? Was He still her Friend, her Savior, and her Father, or was He distant and cold? That question led to the greatest deal of loneliness, the greatest sense of being utterly alone.

Oh, she knew that she knew that she knew that she believed in God—that had been proven in her darkest moment during the miscarriage—but was He who she thought He was? Was He truly merciful and good at the very core of who He was? Did He really love her like His Word said He did? And if so, why did everything feel so awful and wrong? If He was good, then why was her baby, a good gift that He had given to them in a miraculous way in simply miraculous timing, buried under a sunny patch of sod?

Stories from the Bible would come to mind, and she would think about women like Sarah, Hannah, and Elizabeth who had all struggled to conceive. She would think of the tears Hannah had cried and the way Sarah tried to take things into her own hands when they didn't see the children they longed for, and she would realize anew that sometimes bad things happened to good people. She would remember that she was not immune to hardships and that living in a fallen world resulted in fallen circumstances. Eventually, Sarah, Hannah, and Elizabeth had held their child of promise in their own arms, and she felt hope spring to life within her.

But then the memories of the abortion would come, laced with guilt and shame. She relived the actual act and the days that followed it in her memory over and over and over again. Each emotion she had felt, she felt again. She picked up the guilt and shame that she had spent the last six years lying down at the feet of Jesus and added it to the load she carried from her recent miscarriage. She knew she had gotten what she deserved, and yet, still, the score was not settled. Her slate was not wiped clean.

She thought about confessing to Bill what she had done and explaining why she was so sure she was responsible for what had happened. She thought about telling him about her abortion. But every time she considered the possibility, fear of what he would say overtook her. She couldn't tell him. She couldn't tell anyone. Not now, not ever. Then he would understand that it was her fault that she had lost the baby. She didn't know if she could survive the look of judgment and condemnation that she was certain she would see in his eyes every time he looked at her.

Whether he was a hundred percent on board and ready before the baby or not, he had been excited about being a father again. He had been thinking about what life would be like with a little one. He had been looking forward to the future and had already begun to love the baby. Jari was sure of it. How then could she tell him that it was her fault she lost their child—that it was the retribution of a past sin?

She shook her head. She couldn't do it. Not now, not ever.

After coming to that conclusion, a feeling of empty despair would creep over her, and she was more aware than ever that she was alone in her skin. She had never felt the baby move, never heard the heartbeat, but somehow, someway, she had known there was another human being inside of her. She had never been more aware of that than she was now that it was missing. She felt its absence so acutely that it haunted her every thought, every moment, every waking hour. She felt utterly alone from the inside out.

On Saturday evening, she was startled when the doorbell rang. Checking the security camera, she was surprised to see Bill's ex-wife Carla standing on her front porch. For one brief moment, she thought about pretending she wasn't home. After all, she wasn't feeling up to having company. But already Carla was knocking on the door again, and Jari knew the woman wasn't one to be deterred. When she swung open the front door, Carla held up a pizza box with a hopeful smile.

"Want company?"

Jari was puzzled. They had never hung out just the two of them. Then it dawned on her. "Jessi called you," she stated flatly, the pieces falling into place.

Not waiting for an invitation, Carla breezed past her, shutting and locking the front door behind her. "Yes, she did. She's worried you're not eating. So's Bill." Carla paused to give her a pointed look. "So am I. We know how you are."

Jari followed her into the kitchen, guiltily realizing she hadn't had anything but a cup of coffee all day. She had meant to, she really had, but she just hadn't been hungry.

Carla put the pizza on the kitchen counter and pulled two plates out of the cupboard. She put a slice of pizza on each plate, added salad from a takeout container, and handed a plate to Jari. She held onto the plate, even after Jari reached for it, and when Jari looked up, Carla's blue eyes were full of concern. "We're all worried about you. Are you okay?"

"Yes," Jari answered cautiously. Her husband's ex was the last person she expected to spend the evening with, and yet, she felt touched that she had come and comforted that she was there.

"Are you?" Carla pressed, her face gentling. Jari nodded, her eyes brimming with unwelcome tears. Reaching out, Carla gave her a firm hug. "It's been a long time, but I still remember what it was like . . . it's not easy. And now with Bill being gone, and Jessica and the girls, too, I'm sure this house has been feeling pretty empty." Jari nodded again. After patting her back, Carla released her. "I don't know about you, but I'm starving. Let's eat."

They took their pizza to the living room, and Carla found a movie that they had both been wanting to see. They ate their dinner together in comfortable silence. When the movie was over, Carla gathered the dishes and carried them out of the room. As she bustled around the kitchen, washing the dirty dishes that Jari had allowed to collect in the sink, wiping off the counters, cleaning the coffeepot, and putting the leftover pizza in the fridge for Jari to eat later, Jari simply sat at the breakfast bar and watched.

"You know, back in the day, we had a maid that came in to do all this," Carla observed.

Jari cringed. She knew the house was a mess. "We still have someone that comes in once a week, but I told her not to come this week. I know it doesn't make sense because I'm lonely, but I just wanted to be alone. I've been resting like the doctor said, and I knew I'd feel lazy if she was cleaning my house while I laid on the couch. It's only once a week, so since I canceled, things have been piling up. I'll clean up. I really will. I was just waiting until right before Bill gets home."

Carla snorted. "Once a week. This is a big house! There's no way she could get it all finished in a day. You should have her come to clean at least twice a week."

"Yes, well, Bill's been cutting expenses . . . we've been trying to be good stewards of the resources God's given us . . ." Jari explained with a shrug.

"I know, and I admire it, I do. But bless you, because I don't know if I could have done it. I liked having someone here daily to clean the kitchen and sweep the floors. It's a big house."

Jari smiled, realizing her unlikely friend wasn't judging her messy house after all.

"This is weird, right?" Jari finally asked.

Carla laughed. "Weird that we both have lived in this house while being married to the same man?"

Jari nodded.

"Yeah, it's weird." Carla didn't seem at all bothered by the unusualness of the situation. She stopped in front of Jari. "But even though there was a time that I never could have imagined it, I can honestly say I'm happy to have you in the family, Jari. You have been so good for Jessi, for Bill, for the girls . . . for all of us. You make our family better. When Jessi called tonight and told me about what had happened, there wasn't a doubt in my mind I wanted to come spend an evening with you and see with my own eyes that you're okay." She reached out and squeezed Jari's shoulder. "You're going to get through this, Jari. Things are going to be okay. You'll see. You're right in the middle of it now, and it probably feels pretty awful, but someday you'll look back and see it with a clearer perspective. You'll see how God was working in the midst of it, and the beauty on the other side. You know I'm speaking from experience." Jari nodded, knowing she truly was. Jari had been right in the thick of Carla's messy middle.

Carla turned, picking up her purse and keys. "Alright, the sink is empty, so stack all you want. Leave the dishes for Bill when he gets home. Despite what he might say, he does know how to load the dishwasher. There's enough pizza and salad in the fridge for two more meals, and I left two pieces of cheesecake in there in case you need something sweet."

Jari smiled, touched that Carla remembered her favorite dessert. "Thank you."

"I've got to get home to Tim, but if you need anything at all this weekend, you know I'm just a phone call away. We don't have to talk. We can just sit like we did tonight. And whenever you're ready, I know Jess is chomping at the bit to hop on a plane and come be with you."

Jari smiled again. She knew that was true too. Jessi had been texting every few hours. And Jari appreciated her concern more than she could express. She was looking forward to Jessica and the girls visiting soon.

She walked Carla to the door and hugged her, thanking her once more for coming and for bringing dinner. Carla held on for a long time. "You're going to be okay, Jari. So is Bill. You'll get through this." Jari nodded.

Carla stepped back, holding Jari by both shoulders. "Now, I'm going to tell you what I would if you were Jessica. Go take a shower, change your clothes, and brush your hair before you go to bed. You're going to feel so much better if you do. As someone who has spent my fair share of time wallowing, trust me—it helps."

Jari laughed even as she cringed. "I know I probably smell."

Carla laughed too. "I don't smell anything, I promise. It was your bed pillow on the couch that gave you away. I'm guessing you haven't been sleeping upstairs . . . or even going up there, right?"

After a brief hesitation, Jari nodded. "It feels easier to stay downstairs." She didn't mention that walking by the nursery and seeing the bathroom where she miscarried made her feel sad.

"I know. But it's time to join the living again, Jari. Take a shower, brush your hair, change your clothes. As it is, you already may not be able to get that coffee stain out."

Jari glanced down at the dark stain on her sweatshirt that Carla was referring to. "It's tea."

Carla smiled and shrugged. "Whatever. It's not coming out." She gave Jari one last hug. "Call me if you need me."

"I will," Jari said, a full smile filling her face.

Once Carla pulled out of the driveway, Jari set the security alarm, grabbed her pillow, and made her way upstairs. She took Carla's advice. After showering, she brushed her hair and her teeth and then laid down in her own bed for the first time since Bill left. She felt a little less hopeless than she had as she drifted off to sleep, thankful for the unusual family God had put in her life that had shared a bigger perspective.

The next morning, Jari woke up and made the decision to skip church. It wasn't so much that she was angry with God and skipping was her act of rebellion, or even that she didn't want to face the questions that would come as they hadn't told anyone but Joe and Jessi. She simply had so much to process and so many real questions to ask and have answered. She would rather meet with

God in the privacy and safety of her own home rather than going out in public, pasting a fraudulent smile on her face, and taking her questions and emotions to church and back home again, unasked, unanswered, and unacknowledged. Was it the right decision? She didn't know. But it was a decision she felt okay with, given the circumstances.

She smiled as she saw a text message from Joe's mom, Hannah, come in. Jessi or Joe must have told her about the miscarriage too. Jari didn't mind. She appreciated Hannah's text letting her know she was praying for her. They had formed a friendship the year before when Joe and Jessi were getting back together, and it felt nice to know she cared. Just as it did when Carla texted to check on her when she wasn't at church. Jari responded to both women and then put her phone down and focused on her plan for the morning. There was Someone she desperately needed to meet with, and He didn't text.

Grabbing her Bible, she curled up in the sun in her favorite armchair. She opened the beloved Book with a deep sigh. She hadn't opened it since the day of her miscarriage. She didn't know exactly what she was hoping to find, but she knew that if she had questions for God, then a good place to start finding answers was in His Word. She didn't know specifically where to look, but if it was His Word and they were His answers, then surely He could direct her to them. Opening her journal, she added the date to the top of the first clean page, then just sat there for several moments.

She started asking questions she had been asking all week and wrote many of them down. She didn't force her mind to stay focused but let it wander as it would, asking the Holy Spirit to guide her wandering thoughts. She thumbed through her Bible and found herself stopping in the book of Psalms, chapter thirty-four. Skimming the chapter, she whispered pieces of it.

"I sought the LORD and He answered me, He delivered me from all of my fears. Those who look to Him are radiant, their faces are never covered with shame . . . Taste and see that the LORD is good, blessed is the one who takes refuge in Him . . . The eyes of the LORD are on the righteous, and his ears are attentive to their cry . . . The righteous cry out, and the LORD hears them; He delivers them from all their troubles. The LORD is close to the brokenhearted and saves those who are crushed in spirit."

Her head dropped for several long moments, and tears ran quietly down her cheeks. "He is close to the brokenhearted and saves those who are crushed in spirit," she whispered again. Closing her eyes and leaning her head back, she soaked in the sun and contemplated those words.

If she believed in God, if she believed without a shadow of a doubt that He existed and was real—living, breathing, real—then she also had to believe that His Word was real and what it said was true. And if His Word was true, then He wasn't distant even in her current pain. He was close. He was near. He would save her again. Not eternally or physically this time, that had already been done, but emotionally, mentally, and spiritually.

"I sought the LORD, and He answered me. He delivered me from all of my fears," Jari read again, letting those words settle for a long moment. "I'm seeking You, LORD, asking after You . . . asking of You. Will You answer? Are You answering? Your Word says You'll deliver me from all of my fears. What are my fears, God? What are you going to deliver me from?"

Having no energy to be anything but real and honest, Jari listed every fear she had in her journal. The top three items on her list were: 'telling someone about my abortion,' 'going home to Kansas,' and 'never having children.' The list went on from there, but as she looked back at it, she knew those three fears were very real and very big. She had been feeling His encouragement to face the first two for years. In fact, probably for as many years as she had known Him. Yet, every time she felt Him telling her to take action to face those fears, she found a hundred reasons why she couldn't, and had looked the other way.

Now, in the wake of losing a baby, she felt too weak to think of taking on even one of the fears she had listed, and yet she knew that His Word would prove true. There would come a day when He would deliver her from all her fears. The thought of having to face them in the process of being delivered from them seemed overwhelming, but a following verse brought hope.

"Taste and see that the LORD is good, blessed is the one who takes refuge in Him," she read aloud, testing the words on her tongue. It was an invitation to come near and experience the LORD's goodness. To taste and to see was to experience—to feel His goodness firsthand. Amidst the darkness of the past week, that invitation offered hope. When would goodness come? Where would she taste of it? When would she see it?

Again, she had no answers. Nor did she have the strength to take hold of His words and experience them yet; but there was a glimmer of hope, a little flame that burst to life deep within her. It may not be today or tomorrow, but one day she would again taste of His goodness. One day, she would again see it with her own eyes. Because He was good, anyone who drew near to Him and took refuge in Him wouldn't be able to keep from experiencing that goodness. Just as if someone wore a heavy dose of cologne, anyone who was close by would experience the aroma of it. Yes, if He was as close to her as His Word said, then she would experience His goodness.

With each verse, with each realization of what was true and what the days ahead would hold, hope shot down a new root into the worked soil of her broken heart. With each promise from the Word that seemed to speak directly to a question she had hurled at Him, confidence in His character and His proximity to her grew.

She sat in her chair for the rest of the morning and into the afternoon, reading Psalms 34 over and over, journaling each verse and what she took from it. There was no great joy that welled up within her and made her want to dance. There was no quick fix that made her heart, mind, and emotions instantly better. There was no clear path of how to move forward. There were no audible answers to her question of why. There was no explanation for why things had happened as they had, or how it fit into God's plan. But there was peace. Peace with what had happened. Peace with where she was. Peace with what lie ahead.

Sitting in her sunny chair on that Sunday afternoon, Jari knew she had come to a new conclusion in the midst of her pain and suffering; one that would directly affect everything that happened from that point forward in her life. It was a conclusion that she had never before come to so consciously or believed in so wholeheartedly; a conclusion that stemmed from the deepest parts of her being.

There was a God, and regardless of her circumstances, He was good.

Fifteen

T he first few weeks of October were hard, but became easier
with each passing day. Both in a place of peace (peace—not
necessarily joy or understanding) with what had happened, Bill
and Jari woke up each morning and chose to trust the LORD.
They chose to accept what they could not change and move
forward together.

Bill was busy at the office as he juggled his responsibilities in the
Senate and the different committees he served on, along with the
final push for the election. Jari accompanied him on a handful of
short trips as they got out to shake as many hands and meet as
many Virginians as possible before people cast their ballots. She
withdrew from everything she had been committed to and gave
herself the freedom and the space to think, to spend time with the
LORD, and to learn how to move forward at her own pace.

The first time she entered the nursery after the day of their
little funeral was hard. Biting her lip, she summoned her courage
and opened the door, entering the quiet, sunny, cheerful room
cautiously. She looked around the empty space and then closed her
eyes, picturing it painted and decorated as she had when she was
pregnant.

She opened the closet and touched the baby blanket she had
bought. She looked at the tiny outfits that hung next to it.
Suddenly overwhelmed with grief once again, she sat down in the

middle of the room and cried. She cried for the baby that would never sleep with the blanket or wear the outfits. She cried for the joy she had lost and the hopes and dreams that had died along with her tiny son or daughter. When the tears passed, she stood up, looked around again and declared, "I will taste and see that the LORD is good." Then she left the room and went about her day. She made sure to leave the door open.

Having the door to the nursery shut was a constant reminder of what they had lost. It was a constant reminder that the room was waiting for someone who would never come. It was a constant reminder that it was off-limits. It was a description of her heart. If the door was closed, she felt like the miscarriage was something she had not yet dealt with—it was private and closed off. If the door was open, she was reminded that it was an open, accessible part of everyday life and a place from which she could move forward.

Near the end of October, after weeks of the darkly tinted SUV's absence, Bill relaxed his security. Joseph and his team went home, and it was once again only Bill and Jari at their house. Jari felt uneasy the first few days as she readjusted to not having security personnel on the property. She jumped at every noise and found herself glancing out the window frequently. After a week without security, she relaxed, and her anxiety diminished.

As day after day passed, Jari fought the guilt that had overwhelmed her after the miscarriage and now came and went faithfully like the rising and going down of the sun. She felt responsible for what had happened. Deep inside, she believed that it was her just punishment. And she knew she deserved it.

During the days she was actually home, in between unpacking from the previous campaign trip, doing laundry and preparing for the next, she found herself thinking a lot about her past. She thought about things she had done and thought. She remembered the way she had walked out on her family, the men she had been with, the things she had considered fun, her abortion, and her affair with Bill. Not everything she had done was bad, but a lot of it wasn't good. She hadn't used much wisdom or self-control during that time. She didn't show much love, grace, kindness, discernment, or conviction. Anything had been permissible if it made her happy.

One afternoon, she felt restless in her house. They had only been home two days and were set to leave again the next, yet she couldn't seem to concentrate on anything and had very little motivation. Deciding she needed some fresh air, she got in her car and drove to a park near the mall that Jessi had introduced her to several years earlier.

The park was big and spacious, with large trees and nicely manicured grass. A children's play place was situated at one end of the park, with lots of benches where parents could sit and watch. In the middle of the park was a small lake, and a walking path meandered throughout the entire grounds. Climbing out of her car and shrugging into her jacket, she grabbed the bread she had brought for the ducks and headed toward the pond.

Finding an empty bench along the shore, she sat down and crossed her legs. She spent several moments enjoying the feel of the chilly day, the sound of the small waves that lapped against the shore, and the sight of the ducks who were hurrying toward her expectantly. Smiling, she reached into the bag and drew out a piece of bread. Tearing off a small chunk, she threw it to the ducks. As it hit the water, three of them went for it with loud quacks and flapping wings, only one coming out victorious. Their frenzied behavior made her laugh, and she threw another piece.

"Jari?" She turned to see who had spoken her name and was shocked to see who it was. What were the odds, in a city so large, to bump into someone she knew? "I'm Agnes Tundril . . . we waited together for our husbands when they were both in the hospital." The older lady looked unsure.

Jari shook her head, smiling. "You don't have to explain who you are. I remember you perfectly." She stood and embraced the woman. "How are you? How's Rodney?"

Agnes smiled and sat down when Jari gestured for her to do so. "He's fit as a fiddle again! The medication took care of the parasites, and he's steadily regained his strength." Agnes chuckled. "He's already planning our next adventure."

"Where are you going this time?" Jari asked, thrilled at the random opportunity to visit again with her friend from the hospital.

"South America. The country of Peru, I believe. He wants to see Machu Picchu."

"How exciting!" Jari patted the woman's hand. "I'm glad Rodney's better."

"Me too. Thinking of how close I came to losing him . . ." Agnes blinked several times. "It still brings tears to my eyes."

"And understandably so. He sounds like a fine man."

"Ah, yes he is."

"Where is he now?" Jari asked, glancing around at the neighboring benches to see if Rodney was somewhere close by.

"Oh, he wanted to get the tires on our car changed before winter sets in. He's happy to hang out at the tire shop for an hour, shooting the breeze and looking through their merchandise, but I'm not so inclined," Agnes explained.

Jari felt a stab of familiarity at the way Agnes referred to the tire shop. She thought of how many hours she herself had spent in a tire shop, looking at everything they had for sale and shooting the breeze with the mechanics, her dad, and any customers who happened to wander in, while watching tire after tire get repaired or replaced.

"It's not far away, so I had him drop me off here for a walk while he sees to the car," Agnes continued. "I always enjoy this park. It's always so full of life, seeing as how so many children come here to play. I enjoy listening to them laugh and watching them run around. And I enjoy feeding the ducks. I see that's something we have in common. I didn't bring any bread with me today, but I often do."

Jari reached into her own bag of bread and pulled out a piece, which she handed to Agnes. "We can share mine."

"Thank you, dear." A comfortable quiet settled over them as they both set about tearing off small chunks of bread and throwing it to the ducks, who had grown impatient during their conversation.

"Do you believe in Jesus?"

Jari startled at Agnes' question. Recalling praying together in the hospital waiting room and knowing that Agnes already knew the answer to her question, Jari answered cautiously, wondering at the sudden change in conversation. "Yes."

"Do you believe He's your Savior?"

"Yes, I do."

"What do you believe He saved you from?"

"My sins . . . my past," Jari answered slowly, wondering at the older woman's rapid-fire questions. Was she interested in beginning a relationship of her own with Jesus Christ? Jari would have asked if she had been given the chance.

"What about your past?"

Jari considered the woman for a long moment, pondering her intrusive question. Finally, she shrugged. "Things I've done . . . wrong mindsets I've had."

"He saves through forgiveness, right?"

"That's right. Jesus died on the cross to pay the debt for our sins so we don't have to be separated from Him for all eternity or live a life of bondage while on this earth."

"So, you believe He's forgiven you? For your past?"

"Yes, I do."

Agnes met Jari's eyes. "Do you?" the older woman pressed.

Agnes' pointed question caught Jari off guard and rocked her for a moment. *Did she?* And was Agnes making a point rather than being curious about the God Jari served as she had first assumed?

"What do you mean?"

"I'm just asking a question, dear." Jari sat quietly thinking. "How does Jesus forgive?" Agnes asked, moving on, her voice quiet.

"He takes our sin on Himself; He paid the price it demands. His Word says He covers it with His blood, and that separates us from our sin . . . as far as the east is from the west."

"Ah. The truest sense of forgive and forget, eh?"

"Yes, I suppose so."

"Do you believe He forgives you like that?"

Jari turned to look at the woman again and saw the sparkle in her eyes. Turning back to the lake, she let that question sink in. *Did she?*

"To forgive like that, He would have to be merciful, wouldn't He?" Agnes pressed.

"Yes."

"To forgive like that, He would have to want good for you, right?"

"Yes."

"To forgive like that, He wouldn't be the kind to hold things over your head, would He?"

"No, He wouldn't."

"Hmmm." Agnes shifted her attention back to the ducks and threw another chunk of bread. Checking her watch, she stood. "What fun it was to run into you here. I'd love to stay, but Rodney will be back to pick me up soon. We have bingo with the group tonight, and we can't be late."

Jari stood with her, confused by the short conversation and not wanting to miss an opportunity. "Agnes, do you want to know Jesus?"

Agnes' face blossomed into a glowing smile. After handing Jari back the remainder of her piece of bread, Agnes patted her hand. "I've known Him for a very long time. The question, Jari Cordel, is if you believe He's forgiven you?"

Leaving her with that question, Agnes gave a little wave, then turned and headed down the walking path toward the parking lot.

Jari sank down weakly onto the bench, letting her hands rest on her knees.

Agnes' question echoed in her mind. *Did* she believe that He had forgiven her? She believed He had saved her from eternal condemnation. She believed He had saved her from the clutches of hell and given her a hope and a future, both earthly and eternal. She believed He had forgiven her for so many things, but did she believe that He had forgiven her—truly forgiven, as the Bible described—for her abortion? For her promiscuity? For having an affair with Bill?

She rubbed her palms back and forth on her jeans. Forgiven. What did that truly mean? Because Agnes was right. If Jesus forgave like the Bible said He did, He was full of mercy. In fact, the Word described Him as loving mercy to the point that it triumphed over judgment. With a sinking realization of what was true and what wasn't, Jari realized that what she had been accepting as truth was, in actuality, wrong accusations against the heart of God. As Agnes pointed out, if Jesus said her sins were as far from her as the east was from the west, then who was holding her past sins over her head, paralyzing her with guilt and shame, convincing her that she deserved pain and suffering because of what she had done and who she had been? It certainly wasn't Jesus.

Forgiven. The word came like a warm breeze in the dead of winter. She had been forgiven. How many times had she repented, confessed, and asked Jesus to forgive her for the things she had done? How many times had she begged Him to forgive her for taking the life of her baby, only to beg Him once more the next day and the day after that? All along, it wasn't Jesus who was withholding forgiveness and forcing her to pay penance; it was her inability to get past what she had done and actually receive the forgiveness He was offering.

"Jesus, I'm sorry," she whispered toward the heavens. "I'm ready to know what it is to receive Your forgiveness. Please teach me how."

She was reminded of how broken Jessi was when they picked her up from the airport so many years earlier. As a pregnant teen, Jessi had known condemnation. Jari remembered walking her through salvation, assuring her of Jesus' forgiveness, and then helping her walk the path of someone who was forgiven and chose to believe it.

She remembered how broken and grieved Bill was after he had been involved in a car accident that had claimed the life of a young mother. There were still no words to describe those days. He was undone. He felt he shared at least some part of the blame. And yet, through that horrible, traumatic experience, he found Jesus. In such a state of desperation, he learned to work through the guilt to cling to the promise of forgiveness, salvation, and freedom that could only be found in Jesus Christ.

Jari had been there to help him along his journey and to remind him that even though he was guilty of sin in his life, there was very real, very powerful forgiveness waiting for him at the cross. She had been there to tell him that when Jesus took his sin, He took it all. He blotted it out. It no longer defined Bill Cordel, and if he would accept it, Jesus was offering him a cloak of innocence that would make him in right standing in the sight of God.

Almost laughing at the irony, Jari fought the urge to cry. "It's certainly easier to lead everyone else through this and believe they're forgiven than it is to accept it for myself, Jesus," she admitted in a whisper. "I don't feel worthy of Your forgiveness."

Her own words, spoken in response to a similar statement Bill had once made, came back to her mind. "You aren't worthy," she had said. "You can never be worthy. There's nothing you could ever do that would be good enough to earn His forgiveness. It is a gift. You don't have to be good enough, qualified enough, or worthy enough. There's nothing anyone on this earth could ever do to deserve His forgiveness. It's something that's freely given and can only be humbly received."

She sighed. She was clearly better at teaching about forgiveness than receiving it. She threw a piece of bread into the water and watched a nearby duck scoop it up. "I want to learn to receive Your gift. I want to learn how to live out of a place of forgiveness and freedom, not out of a place of self-induced condemnation and constant guilt. Please help me, Jesus."

'Where the Spirit of the LORD is, there is freedom.' The verse from 2 Corinthians blew across her spirit, and she inhaled it deeply. If she could find the courage to invite the forgiveness of Jesus into the dark moments of her past and the secret places of her heart,

which she had, then freedom was within reach. Freedom. True, experiential, life-changing freedom.

She knew what needed to happen first if she was going to begin to experience freedom and live out of a place of receiving the forgiveness of Jesus. She had to tell someone about her abortion. It was in the secrecy of it that she gave the enemy power to stifle her with guilt and shame. By keeping it in the dark, she gave him the ability to beat her over the head with it over and over and over again.

Dreading the conversation she knew she needed to have, Jari threw another chunk of bread to the ducks. They had drifted away when she stopped throwing bread, lost in thought. Now they came back in a flurry of flapping wings and fervent quacking. Their behavior brought a smile to her face, and she continued to throw bread until she ran out.

Standing up, she stretched and disposed of the bread sack in a nearby garbage can. Slipping her hands into her pockets, she started back to her car, thinking as she walked. She had lived a life of promiscuity and sin. She'd had an abortion. She'd had an affair with a married man. And she was forgiven.

Like the sun breaking out from behind a heavy bank of clouds, she understood for the first time that she was no longer defined by what she had done. She didn't have to carry those things around like a sign around her neck, as if they had the right to describe her. Instead, she was defined by the simple fact that she had been covered by the blood of Jesus. She had been made right. She had been made whole. And, if she chose it, that truth could be her definition—her description.

At the jungle gym, she paused and watched a mother pushing her son on the swings. Taking a deep breath, Jari summoned her courage. "Losing the baby was not my fault," she told herself firmly. "It was not my punishment."

She had done everything she could to have a healthy pregnancy. In the short time she knew about the baby, she cut out caffeine, took her vitamins faithfully, went to the doctor, and drank more water than she ever had before in her life. She didn't take any medications or lift anything over the recommended limit. She ate fruits and vegetables and put priority on eating dark, leafy greens, doing everything she could to support and maintain a healthy pregnancy.

God was a good God. He was kind and full of mercy. Whatever the reason had been that the baby within her could not be born, it was not because He was punishing her for what she had done over a decade before. He was not getting even with her. He wasn't paying her back. Her loss had not been motivated by revenge.

He had forgiven her. In His kindness, He had given her a gift she never thought she would have. Whether the baby had lived or not, it was a gift to be able to carry it for nine weeks, and she would be thankful for that.

In her heart of hearts, she knew that miscarriages happened for all sorts of reasons. In many cases, there was nothing a woman could do to prevent it, nor did it happen because of her. Life and death were in the hands of the LORD, and sometimes it simply wasn't His plan for a baby to carry to term. As frustratingly helpless as that simple answer left her, she knew it was true. She might not know the why this side of heaven, but standing at the park that afternoon, she knew what she said was true. Her miscarriage was not her fault. It had simply happened. She could grieve, she could miss the baby, but never again would she agree with and buy into the guilt and shame that told her it was her fault her baby had died. No more would she accept that as the truth.

With her mind made up and her heart set free, she turned from the mother and child on the swings and continued the rest of the way to her car.

~~~~~

Jari was lying in bed reading when Bill finally came home from his office. He had been there since seven that morning, and checking the clock, Jari found that it was a quarter to eleven. Such was life in an election year. And now, with just a few days to go, his schedule was even more demanding as he felt the crunch.

"Hi, honey," he said, bending down to give her a kiss. He looked tired.

"Hi. How was your day?" she asked, placing her bookmark and laying her book aside.

"Long."

"It *was* a long day at the office," she agreed sympathetically.

"And we have to be back by seven a.m.," he reminded her.

Jari nodded. "We're all packed."

"Good. Thank you."

"You're welcome."

"Did you pack my gray suit?"

"Which one?"

"The dark gray one I wear with the gray and purple stripped tie."

"Yes."

"Good. I want to wear that to the rally tomorrow night."

Jari nodded. "I'll wear my gray dress to match you."

Bill sat down on the side of the bed to take his shoes off. Taking a deep breath, Jari sat up and rested her chin on his shoulder. "Bill, there's something I have to tell you."

He stilled, clearly taking a warning from her tone. "Okay."

Jari briefly shut her eyes, not knowing exactly how to start and dreading what she had to tell him. They had never talked of such things. And now, with their marriage improving so much in the past six months and the friendship between them blossoming, she didn't want to take a chance of losing it all. Still, she knew there were things she needed to tell him. She needed to tell him all of it. She needed to come clean. For her sake. For the sake of freedom.

"Before we were married, I lived a very promiscuous lifestyle. I lived with seven different men." She paused to judge his reaction, but there was none. He didn't even flinch. "And I was with a lot more." Her tone was quiet and sad.

"*A lot* more?" he asked with a grunt. She nodded sadly. After a few long moments, Bill cleared his throat. "I guess I always had a suspicion that was how it was."

Jari waited for him to say more, biting her lip. When he didn't, she went on. "Thirteen years ago, I was living in Albany, New York, with a man named Griffin. My modeling career was starting to take off . . . I'd just gotten my first big gig."

"Okay . . ."

"I got pregnant."

"You got pregnant?" he echoed, his surprise both evident and understandable.

"Yes."

"What . . . what happened?"

"I had an abortion," she said, trying to keep her words and tone even. Her throat ached and her eyes stung. "I thought I had the right to choose. I thought it was my only choice. I was young and immature and wanted to model. I wasn't in love with Griffin. I left just a few weeks later. I wasn't ready to have a baby, and at the time, I thought it was the best decision for me. I've since realized how wrong I was," Jari paused, and a short, humorless laugh came out from between her lips. "Every day since then, I've realized how wrong I was. I would have a twelve-year-old child, Bill," she finished softly.

It was quiet for a long time.

"Why are you telling me this? Why now?" Pain saturated his words.

Self-doubt filled her, yet she searched for a way to explain. "Because I've been living with these secrets for a really long time, and it's been eating me up inside," she admitted, tears collecting in her eyes. "All those years ago, I killed my baby, and I never actually believed I'd been forgiven for it. And then, when . . . when we lost our baby . . . I thought God was punishing me for what I'd done. I thought He was giving me what I deserved." Her voice broke, and she stopped.

"Jari," Bill said, turning on the bed and taking her in his arms. "That's not how He is. You know that."

"I know that in my head, but in my heart . . . I was holding onto this secret and blaming myself over and over and over again."

Bill shook his head, his voice heavy. "Don't. Don't do it."

"I just . . . all these years later, I still can't believe I killed my own flesh and blood. I chose to have it ripped from my body."

It was quiet for a long time. Finally, Bill cleared his throat. "While you were having your abortion, I was passing legislation that made it legal. I'm no less guilty than you." His words surprised her, and she looked up to study his face. She didn't see what she had most feared and expected. There was no condemnation in the lines of his handsome face, only deep sorrow. "Jari, I know God has forgiven you, just like He forgave me. And if the LORD can forgive you for the abortion and . . . for the other men, then so can I. Case closed. Now I know, and I still love you. There's nothing to be ashamed of anymore."

His statement was so simple. So blunt. So straight forward. Jari felt both shock and intense relief. Looking up into his blue eyes, she shook her head in disbelief. "Are you sure?"

He shrugged. "I don't know the woman who had an abortion or slept around. You're a different person now, Jari—a new creation. That's not who you are anymore. You're my faithful wife. You've been a good friend to my daughter, a second mother to my granddaughters. You're a godly woman. You serve others with your whole heart, and you love really well. I love you, Jari Cordel. And if Jesus can forgive you for your past, which I'm confident He has, then how can I not?"

She was quiet for a long time, absorbing and processing what he said. She felt unworthy of his response and in awe of her husband. "Thank you. That's exactly what I needed to hear from you," she told him humbly. His reaction, his acceptance, his forgiveness, it was incomprehensible and overwhelming.

The corners of his mouth lifted in a smile. "Good." Bending forward, he kissed her gently and then stood. "I'm going to get ready for bed. I'll be back."

"Okay."

At the closet, he paused and looked back. "If you need to tell me anything else, or if you need to tell me more about the abortion—the details—you can."

She shook her head. She felt fine with what had already been said. "I think I'm okay, but if you ever have questions, please know that you can ask."

"I will," he told her sincerely.

As he went into the bathroom to get ready for bed, she laid back down in shock at how simple and judgment-free their conversation had been. After fiercely guarding her secret for the past thirteen years, after imagining family and friends utterly deserting her after hearing what she had done, it had been neither dramatic nor condemning. In fact, it was liberating. She felt lighter than she had in a very, very long time.

When Bill came to bed a few minutes later, he crawled beneath the covers beside her and turned over to hold her close. "I'm proud of you. That must have been really difficult for you to say."

"It was," she agreed.

He kissed her cheek, laid his head back down and led them in their nightly prayer. Then they both went to sleep. Just like that. There was no fighting, no accusing, no disgust, disgrace, or judgment. Jari went to sleep feeling at peace with life and at peace with herself. There were no more secrets. There was no more hidden shame.

Sixteen

After a crazy sprint to election day, the morning dawned sunny but crisp. Bill was up and on his stationary bike before five a.m. Feeling his excitement and anxiety, Jari woke up and listened to the hum of the bike.

Closing her eyes and rolling over, pulling the covers up to her chin, she stayed in bed and rested, knowing it would be a late night. She wondered, after all of Bill's hard work over the past several years and especially the last few months, if he would win the election. The polls were strongly favorable, but one never knew until the votes were actually counted.

She believed the election would turn out in his favor, but for just a brief moment, she let herself consider what would happen if he were defeated. She had never known her husband in any context other than as a senator. If he didn't win the election, what would he do? What would they do? Would it turn out to be a positive, as he would have more time and attention to devote to a possible presidential campaign? Would a loss crush his spirits and discourage him in his future political aspirations? Was there a chance a lost election would allow them to move to Minnesota? Would they have more time to spend together? For being the worst-case scenario, it didn't sound so terrible. A tiny part of her even hoped for it, though the larger part of her wanted to see her husband succeed in whatever he set out to do.

"Your will be done, LORD," she whispered into her pillow. Her prayer continued as she prayed for Bill, for grace for both of them to accept the public's decision whatever it may be, and for wisdom to move forward strategically.

The bike hummed, and Jari could tell by the fast pace Bill was keeping that he was attempting to work off his nerves. Even after twenty years in politics, an election was still a big event. Though he led in the polls and seemed to have the favor of his constituents, his competition was hungry. They had been giving it their all, determined to take his seat. Today, they would find out if all the trips, all the speeches, all the town halls, all Bill's work on the state of Virginia's behalf in the Senate, his proven track record—would be enough. An hour later, he finally stopped peddling and wiped his face with his towel. Jari propped herself up on her elbows as he climbed off his bike. He winced as he straightened.

"How are you feeling?" she asked, giving him a sleepy smile.

He grunted. "Like biking an hour at that incline and speed was a bad idea. I may not be able to walk later."

She smiled again. "I meant about the election."

He shrugged. "I've done everything I can. We're out of time. Now, it's up to the voters."

"What do you think will happen?"

"If the polls are an accurate portrayal of the voters' loyalties, I'd say we'll pull out a victory."

Jari nodded, even as she noticed that Bill looked grim. "Do you want to win?" she asked suddenly, curious about his subdued tone.

"I always want to win," Bill told her, a grin tugging up one side of his mouth. "Who doesn't?"

"You don't seem happy, even when you acknowledge that the polls are strongly in your favor."

"Oh." He waved away her statement with a gesture of his hand. "Polls aren't official. I'll celebrate a victory when we get the official election results."

Jari nodded, understanding. "So, what does your day look like?"

"Well, I need to stop by the office for an hour or so, and then I have some photo ops and will squeeze in a little last-minute campaigning. Anything to keep busy," he answered, another one-sided smile lifting his mouth. "We'll go vote on our way to pick up Jess and the girls from the airport. By then it will be time to come home, change, and head to the rally in Richmond together."

"That sounds like a really good plan," Jari answered with a happy smile. She had decided she finally felt ready for company, and now she couldn't wait for Jessica and the girls to arrive. She had the whole week planned out. Since Jessi was pulling the girls out of school to come, she had scheduled some educational activities to replace their kindergarten work. They would spend a day at Mount Vernon, a day at their favorite Smithsonian Museum, and a day touring a dairy and visiting a pumpkin patch in the northwest corner of Virginia. They would finish out the week with a day of shopping and a final day hanging out at the house together, watching Joe's game on TV, before taking them back to the airport Sunday evening. Her excitement grew just thinking about it.

"What are you going to do today?" Bill asked as he headed into the bathroom.

"I have those Christmas gifts for the girls I bought last week that I need to wrap before they get here. Other than that, I'm going grocery shopping, having my nails done, and getting ready for tonight," Jari answered, raising her voice to be heard.

"Are you wearing that new dress I saw hanging in your closet?"

Jari smiled. "Yes. Do you like it?"

"I'll like it better when it's on you, but it looks like it has a lot of potential," Bill answered from the bathroom.

Jari chuckled to herself, happy that he approved of her new dress, amused by his choice of wording. The fitted, sleeveless sheath dress in a rich brown had a high neckline and gentle ruching around the midsection that accentuated the waistline and gave a flattering silhouette. It was classic, understated, simple, and tasteful, suitable for an election party, yet the softly clinging fabric and elegant cut made her feel young and beautiful. Even after being a politician's wife for over half a decade, she could still only bring herself to wear shoulder pads and the traditional suit dress so many times a year, and her yearly quota had already been maxed out. She had wondered what he would think of her selection when she bought it and was now glad he approved.

Flipping the covers back, she went to join him at their bathroom vanity.

"You're still planning to wear your navy suit with your brown and navy striped tie, right?"

"I am. Thanks for remembering, honey. I noticed your dress matches," he said, stopping to kiss her on the cheek.

She simply nodded, her mouth full of toothpaste. Finishing, she pulled her hair back in a clip and headed downstairs to start breakfast, while he finished getting ready for the day. When he came down, she was just setting their plates on the table.

"The breakfast of champions," she told him, gesturing to his plate full of fried eggs, turkey bacon, grapes, and a piece of whole wheat toast slathered with blackberry jam.

"Looks good, honey." Bill set his briefcase down and turned toward the front door.

"I'll get your papers," Jari said, stopping him with a hand on his arm. "You can start eating."

Conceding, he sat down and began stirring hazelnut creamer into his coffee. Jari crossed the house to the front door and swung it open, stepping out to collect the papers that were thrown onto the front porch early every morning. A bright ray of sun reflected off something across the street directly into her eyes. She instinctively stepped sideways, trying to get out of the blinding light. Glancing to see what was causing the reflection as she bent to retrieve the papers, her heart jumped. Across the street and down just a little, a black SUV was parked, the morning sun reflecting off the fancy chrome wheels.

Grabbing the papers, she quickly retreated into the house and locked the front door behind her. "Bill!" she called, hurrying back to the dining room. He looked up as she entered, taking a bite of toast. "Bill, the black SUV is back."

"Is it still there?"

"It didn't drive away when I opened the door."

Scooting his chair back, he jogged through the house to the den. Standing beside the window and peering out, his brows drew together. "It's definitely the same one, isn't it?"

"Yes." He spun away from the window, stalking toward the front door. Jari ran after him. "Where are you going?"

"I'm going to go see what this is all about."

"Bill, it could be dangerous," Jari protested, catching at his arm. He easily shook her off.

"I want to know if it's merely a coincidence, or if this person is watching us and is up to no good." His voice was firm, his mind made up.

"There are other ways to find out!" she cried, frightened. "Call the police and let them handle it. Bill!"

"Stay inside," he told her, swinging the front door open and then closing it behind him. Racing back into the den, she stood at the window and watched helplessly as Bill stalked down the front sidewalk and stepped into the street, his destination obvious. Biting her lip, she wished she had her phone with her to call the police. She wanted to go get it, but didn't want to take her eyes off her husband.

As he got closer to the SUV, her stomach felt tied in knots. She didn't know what to expect. Why had the ominous vehicle shown up again the day of the election after being gone for over a month? It seemed likely that it was someone who was not a fan of Bill. Her anxiety continued to rise as she wondered what would happen next. Would the driver pull out a gun and shoot her husband? Would men jump out, grab him, throw him into the backseat, and drive away with him? Would someone get out and beat him up? Would it actually turn out to be a random coincidence—maybe a neighbor's guest in from out of town? Could it simply be someone who wanted to know how the senator lived, maybe snap a few pictures, ask a few questions?

As Bill came within five feet of the SUV, the tires screeched and then squealed as the driver hit the gas, tearing down the street at a high rate of speed. Bill put his hands on his hips and stared after the disappearing vehicle. Even from the back, Jari could sense his frustration and anger. Turning, he stalked back to the house, his expression looking as dark and ominous as the vehicle. She walked to the front door to meet him and waited as he came in, slammed the front door, and locked it.

Turning, he met her eyes, his expression grim. "Well, I don't think it's a coincidence, and I don't think they're friendly."

"You're lucky they didn't shoot you," she scolded, her hands shaking. "You should have waited for the police."

Stepping past her, he went back to the kitchen to get his cell phone. "I saw the driver."

Shocked, she followed him. "You did? Did you know him? Could you identify him? Was it even a him? Were there others in the car?"

"I couldn't see him well . . . not well enough to tell features or anything, but it was a man, and he seemed to be slightly older than I am. Maybe in his late fifties or sixties. As far as I could tell, he was alone."

"Did you recognize him? Did you get a good look at his license plate?"

"No." Bill's lips were pressed into a thin line, his displeasure with the situation evident. "He had temporary tags. We'll check the security cameras, but I can't imagine we have any that will have the right angle to get the tag number. I'm going to call Joseph. Go ahead and eat your breakfast."

Bill went into the den to make his phone call, and Jari quietly took a seat at the table. Eating her fried egg that was now cold, she thought over the past five minutes.

Who was the man? What did he want? Was he dangerous? Did he pose a threat to their well-being? What did he have planned?

Bill joined her again just a couple of minutes later and sat down to finish his breakfast, his countenance grim. "Joseph and his men will be back on the property within the hour," he told her. Jari nodded. "I doubt this joker will be back anytime soon, though. He'll probably tuck tail and run, just like he did last time, waiting a month or more before he shows up again."

"Well, if so, we won't have to keep Joseph here for long," Jari pointed out, trying to add something positive.

Bill shook his head. "I don't feel comfortable with you being here alone anymore. We'll keep Joseph here until we get to the bottom of this."

Jari didn't argue but struggled internally with his decision. She could see his point but didn't like the idea of having security indefinitely. To never be alone on your own property was a difficult pill to swallow. Having security for a few weeks here and there was different than having it full time until someone who had been bothersome and elusive was caught or determined not to be a threat.

Finishing his breakfast, Bill scooted his chair back. "I think I'll skip the office. I'll connect remotely until it's time for the photo ops. Ryan can handle things this morning until we meet up. By then, Joseph will be here."

"You don't have to do that. I'll be fine until Joseph arrives," Jari assured him.

Bill shook his head. "I wouldn't have that much time there, anyway. I might as well just save the commute and leave from here. If you need anything, I'll be in my office."

"Okay." Jari watched him leave the room, taking his newspapers, briefcase, and coffee cup with him. Finishing her breakfast, she took their plates to the kitchen and loaded them into the dishwasher. Then she climbed the stairs to their bedroom and settled down in the sunshine-covered armchair. Running her hand over it, she realized the rich purple fabric was beginning to fade from all the sun. In another year or two, they would have to get it reupholstered.

Pulling her legs up under her, she repositioned until she was comfortable and spent a few moments simply enjoying the opportunity to soak in the November sunshine. Outside it might be cold, but inside the house it was warm. Her sunny spot in the chair always made it feel like spring. Her mind drifted to the little baby that was buried in a sunny patch outside, and she found herself wondering if it was cold. She scolded herself for thinking such a silly thought. She knew it was no longer alive. Still, her heart wondered if it was cruel to leave someone who had been alive and loved so much out in the elements. Sadness began to seep into her. She missed the little life she'd carried, and all the hope it had brought.

Like a soft breeze, the words of Psalm thirty-four came back to her again. "Taste and see that the LORD is good," she said aloud, letting the words soak into her heart and reminding herself that she would experience His goodness.

Like a gentle flutter that disrupts the still surface of a pond, the words, *"I redeem all things,"* whispered over her consciousness.

Quiet, still, waiting to see if there would be more, she remained unmoving for several moments. She heard nothing else, and her mind began to churn over the whispered phrase. He redeemed all things. She knew He did—it was Biblical—and yet this felt personal, like a promise made specifically to her.

He was a God of redemption. He had redeemed her from eternal separation, and she knew He could redeem situations, circumstances, and people, among so many other things. His whispered words brought her peace as she thought through things in her life that needed to be redeemed.

When she had sat in that very chair and read how He would deliver her from all her fears, she felt afraid, weak, and hesitant to see what He meant. To be delivered meant to face her fears. And facing her fears brought up more fear. Now, remembering that He redeemed, she felt a new peace. Redemption was good. Redemption brought joy. Redemption brought reconciliation. Redemption brought peace—true peace. Redemption restored.

How did God redeem promiscuity? She thought of her relationship with Bill and the conversation they had when she confessed the truth to him. He said he didn't know the woman who had slept with countless men before him. She was different, new. Their relationship was growing and flourishing. She felt closer to and more in love with her husband now than she ever had. She believed in her life, in her personal situation, God had redeemed her promiscuity by restoring her innocence and working a miracle to allow her to have a healthy, fulfilling marriage. It had been a long road to walk, but she could see the fruit of His redemption, and it was good.

How did God redeem a godless abortion? As soon as she asked the question, she knew the answer. It was time for her to face what she had done and offer support to others who were in her same situation. Perhaps He would use her story, her experience, her pain, her regret, to keep others from suffering the same heartbreak. If He would use her story to save one baby from the death her own had known—and one mom from the heartache—then maybe that would be redemption.

She made a note at the top of her journal page to check into pregnancy help centers nearby and see if any of them needed volunteers. The thought of sharing her story was unnerving and made her stomach queasy, but the possibility of supporting and helping someone facing the same dilemma made her confident that it was the right path forward. She would pursue volunteering at a pregnancy help center in whatever capacity she could.

How did God redeem the miscarriage of a child that had been planned and orchestrated by Him—a child of promise? A flame of hope began to flicker in the recesses of her heart, and she wondered if someday, at some unknown point down the road, she would get pregnant again. Maybe there would be a time when she would carry a child to term and give birth to a healthy, living, breathing baby boy or girl. As much as her heart still hurt, and even though sadness still overwhelmed her at times, if that happened, maybe she would be ready and feel great joy again.

How did God redeem a family torn apart by affairs, guilt, shame, distance, and time?

"It's time to go home." She saw the sentence in her mind, heard the words in the stillness of the quiet room, and felt them in her heart. Letting her head fall forward, she thought through what it meant. Could she gather the courage it would take to book the plane ticket, face her mother, risk seeing her father, and figure out how to move forward? She felt emotionally depleted from the past few months. Was she strong enough to face going back to Kansas too?

"Father, I'm going to need help," she admitted, closing her eyes and tipping her head back against the chair. "A lot of help."

She didn't feel ready, and yet she knew deep inside that she may never feel ready. It was never going to be an easy thing to do. It was never going to feel like the perfect time. If she waited for it to be easy, to feel excited, and ready to go, she knew she would likely never return home. But it was something she knew—and had known for years—she needed to do. It was something she needed to face, both personally and for her parents. If the LORD was going to redeem her family, then she needed to cooperate with reconciliation and take the first step.

Taking a deep breath, she slowly wrote, 'book a flight to Kansas,' at the top of the page. Blowing that same breath out, she shut her journal and picked up her Bible. Even writing the words felt overwhelming and terrifying. She needed to be in the Word to find some strength and peace.

~~~~~

"Can I have your attention, please?" Jari looked over to where Bill's campaign manager was climbing up to stand on the table next to theirs. Beside her, Bill halted in the casual conversation he'd been having with Ryan. Jessi quieted the girls. Around the room, a hush fell over the crowd as all eyes turned to the man standing on the table.

"The last of the results just came in, and . . . Senator Cordel, you won again! Here's to six more years!" he said jubilantly, lifting his glass. Cheers went up around the room and those gathered—family, friends, donors, staff, and a handful of key supporters—toasted in celebration. The twins were jumping up and down, clapping their hands. Jessica, Carla, Tim, and Maybelle were all applauding. Chris and Hannah, who had driven in for the party and would stay for a few days to join the fun Jari had planned for Jessi and the girls' visit (as would Carla and Maybelle), were cheering.

Her heart full, Jari squeezed Bill's hand, her eyes shining, and leaned close. "You did it, honey! You are still the right man for the job, and this proves it! You've got six more years to make a difference in our state and our country!"

Acknowledging her words with a squeeze of his hand and a broad smile, he stood as the small crowd—led by Carla's husband Tim—started chanting, "Speech, speech, speech."

Loosening his tie as he made his way to the front of the room, Bill's smile was broad as he stood in front of the group and gave a quick speech. He shared his thanks to those who had helped him pull out a victory, made a couple of jokes, and then led them all in another toast before encouraging everyone to eat up the hors d'oeuvres. The crowd applauded, and Jari clapped along with them, prouder of her husband than she could even begin to articulate. From the front of the room, he smiled at her for a long, unhurried moment, his eyes warm and bright. She enjoyed his smile and the moment. She saw his eyes shift to where Jessica and the girls were, then to all the rest of their makeshift family, and Jari could see how much it meant to her husband to have them all there. Happy tears stinging her eyes, she realized anew just how much of a family man he had become. He had truly been transformed. He was no longer only a successful politician; he had become a successful man.

With his speech made, the applause dying down, and most people turning back to their snacks, Bill huddled with Ryan and other staff members around the TV to see who had taken the other open seats in the Senate and the House. Jari knew their conversation would be full of talk about majorities, trends, predictions for the next election, and how it all would affect their great state of Virginia.

Knowing she would hear all the highlights of the conversation on their way home, Jari turned back to mingle with their guests. Kamryn came to sit on her lap awhile later, and Jari snuggled her close, seeing the five-year-old's eyes were growing heavy. Finally, taking his seat again, Bill reached out to hold her hand, his eyes bright. He smiled warmly at her for a long moment before leaning close. "This is going to be a good term, Jari. I can feel it. It's going to be a good season of our lives."

She smiled back. "I believe that too."

Seventeen

After a wonderful visit from Jessica and the girls, Bill delivered on his election promise (to her) and whisked Jari away to the destination of her choosing. They explored old castles in Wales, attended the ballet in Vienna, wandered through Christmas markets in Berlin, and soaked in a Nordic spa in Copenhagen. She enjoyed the vacation, delighted in the sights, was thankful for the distraction, but found the most joy in the uninterrupted time with her husband. After a busy year, she soaked up every minute with him, finding that it became her favorite vacation together to date. They returned home for a few weeks before flying out to Minneapolis to spend Christmas with Joe, Jessi, and the girls.

They rang in the New Year with friends back in D.C., and Jari started back up at the soup kitchen. Knowing she had some difficult tasks ahead if she was going to be obedient to what the LORD had told her to do, Jari reached out to Joe's mom, Hannah, and asked if she would mentor her.

Hannah Colby had quickly become a friend during Kelsi and Kamryn's hospital stay, and Jari appreciated her deep, seasoned faith, solid wisdom, and motherly nature. In the year since, between the wedding, election party, Christmas in Minnesota, and the texts that had started after her miscarriage and grown more frequent since, Hannah had become something between a mother-figure and an older sister to Jari. Knowing she was lacking someone like that in her life, Jari was grateful when Hannah joyfully accepted the invitation. They started meeting together weekly by phone, studying Scripture, and praying together, and planned to grab coffee in person at the twins' birthday party in Minneapolis the first part of March.

Taking the next step of putting action to things she knew the LORD was asking her to do, Jari visited a pregnancy help center and asked how she could serve. She took their required training and started helping in the office, taking some of the strain off those who worked there. She helped organize the donation room, planned two baby showers for expecting moms, and when invited, was able to sit in with the clinic's nurse to share her story with a few women who were considering abortions.

She had come home from each meeting and cried, her heart breaking for the young women who were clearly struggling and afraid. Jari remembered the fear, confusion, and desperation only too well. She wished she could help more.

Even just volunteering, the work was heartbreaking. Jari felt the weight of the crisis and difficulty the women were experiencing, and her heart twisted with compassion.

"A young woman came in today for a pregnancy test . . . she was fourteen, Bill. Fourteen." Jari was sitting beside her husband on the couch, a mug of hot tea in her hand, her legs pulled up underneath her, her cheeks still marked by the tears she had shed before he got home. He looked over at her, and she saw the sadness she had felt for the girl reflected in his eyes.

"Was it positive?"

"Yes, it was. She's pregnant. I've never seen anyone so scared."

"Did anyone come in with her?"

"No. She hasn't told her parents or her boyfriend. She came by herself. She rode the bus." Jari had been invited by the nurse and the teenager to sit in on the meeting for moral support. She had sat in on a few appointments now, but this young one pulled on her heartstrings in a new way. The girl was so afraid. Her behavior and her speech were almost frantic when the nurse gave her the results of her test.

"Will she keep the baby?"

"No. She's in eighth grade. She said she can't take care of a baby. She wants to pass science and make the freshman cheerleading squad next year."

"Will she have an abortion?" Bill asked, rubbing the back of Jari's hand softly with his thumb.

"I don't know," she admitted honestly. "She's thinking about it. She's terrified of telling her parents, terrified of the teachers and kids at school finding out, terrified that her boyfriend will dump her if he knows. She thinks an abortion is the easiest, cleanest option that will keep her life from being disrupted."

"Did you tell her about yours?"

"Yes. The nurse invited me to share my experience. Of course, I couldn't counsel her on what she should do, nor was it my place, but I wanted her to know that I could relate, and that she's not alone." Jari remembered the look on the young girl's face as Jari relayed her own story. She had looked frightened and torn.

Jari felt for her deeply. She could only imagine how hard it would be to think about carrying a baby to term at that age. Jessica had a lot to overcome when she was pregnant at seventeen, and fourteen was a big three-year difference. Jari knew how bleak her options must look and how scary the thought of carrying it must be. Her parents would have to be told, all her classmates would find out, her teachers would know, and she would have to tell her boyfriend. An eighth grader himself, Jari was certain he wasn't any more prepared for parenthood than the girl was.

And yet, Jari knew that the little one inside of the young teenager was a living, growing person who had a soul and a spirit. To abort the pregnancy would mean taking a life. She knew the girl who had sat beside her crying knew that too. The nurse suggested adoption, and the girl was interested, but that left no way around carrying the baby to term and having all those around her find out about her pregnancy.

Jari had stayed quiet, thankful the nurse was the one leading the conversation. She wouldn't have known what to say or how to help. Knowing what she knew about abortion, she knew there was no easy way out for the teenager. As much as she wished for the girl's sake that there was an easy solution, there simply wasn't one. Jari had held the girl's hand while she cried, her own heart full of painful compassion.

A loud ring split the silence that had fallen, drawing her back to the present. Bill snagged her phone off the coffee table and checked the caller ID, obviously ready to silence it should it be an unknown number. With an uncertain look, he handed it to her instead. She glanced at the screen and her eyebrows drew together in a frown. Taking a deep breath, feeling apprehensive, she answered.

"Hello?"

"Jari, it's Mom." Her mom's voice sounded unsure and unsteady.

"Hi, Mom . . . is everything okay?" Jari had called her mother just a few weeks before to let her know she was planning a trip to Kansas and to ask when it would work best for her to come. The conversation had been as awkward as Jari feared, but even in light of that, she could tell her mom was happy she was coming home. Now, her voice sounded entirely different, and Jari instinctively knew something was wrong.

"It's your father . . . he's had a heart attack."

Jari's breath caught, and her mind whirled. Her dad had a heart attack? Now? When she was three weeks away from going home and possibly facing him to see if they could find a way to reconcile? Was she too late? "Is he . . . is he okay?"

Bill, able to hear the entire conversation, shot her a sympathetic look and squeezed her hand. His eyes were trained on her face; she had his full attention. She raised her eyes to meet his, knowing her own must be round and scared.

"He's in the hospital in critical condition. I honestly don't know if he'll make it or not. I only know about the heart attack because the hospital called Tommy, who told Margerie, who called Paula, who called Rhonda, and Rhonda called me." Jari pressed her hand to her forehead. She'd forgotten that's how things worked in a small town. "Anyway, that's all I've heard, but I thought you might want to know."

As angry as she had been with her father, to think of him lying in a hospital fighting for his life made Jari shaky inside. In that moment, she knew she didn't want to avoid him anymore—she wanted reconciliation. She wanted to be at peace with him. And she certainly didn't want him to die before she had a chance to tell him to his face that she forgave him and ask for his forgiveness in return. She glanced at Bill, and he gave her a firm nod, answering the question she didn't have to ask. "I'll be there as soon as I can."

"You'd better hurry, Jari. He may not have much time. Rhonda said it sounded bad."

With that, the phone call ended. Jari sat still for a long moment, processing. She felt panicky. She had told her mom she would come—she wanted to see her dad before anything happened—but she didn't feel ready. She was scared. Planning a trip to Kansas in three weeks had been hard enough, but now, thinking of an immediate trip had her stomach tied in knots.

Bill squeezed her hand. "It's time to go, Jari. Don't let this be something you'll always regret."

"You're right. I know you're right. It's just that I finally found the courage to go . . . in three weeks . . . and then this happens? I'm not ready yet!"

"God's timing is perfect," Bill reminded. He pushed himself to his feet and then reached for her hands, pulling her up off the couch. "I'll change your plane ticket while you pack. Take plenty of clothes. You may end up wanting to stay a while."

"Do you want to come?"

Bill met her eyes for a long moment. "Do you want me to?"

"Yes! But . . . " Jari paused and blew out a breath slowly. "But I think I probably need to go back alone first. I have a lot of things I need to face . . . a lot of things I need to say."

Bill nodded. It was the same conclusion she had come to before, the last time they talked about her going home to Kansas. "I'll fly out for a weekend whenever you think it's time," he told her. "Just keep me posted."

Nodding, she turned to go pack. He grabbed her hand and pulled her back around gently. "It's going to be okay, honey. This is a good thing, you going back. Don't be afraid. I'll be there in just a few hours if you need me, and you know you're supposed to go. Remember that. He redeems all things."

Jari wrapped her arms around Bill's neck and gave him a tight hug. "Thank you." She appreciated her husband reminding her of what the LORD had said. She had needed that reassurance. He patted her back until she stepped away. "I'm going to go pack. Let me know what kind of flights you find."

Upstairs, she pulled her suitcase out and set it on the bed, unzipping it and flipping the top back. Going into her closet, she pulled out jeans, shirts, scarves and sweaters before folding them into the suitcase. She put in a couple of dresses, just in case. As morbid as it was, for the sake of being prepared, she made sure one was black, even while she prayed that the LORD would keep her dad alive. Hustling around the room, she added articles of clothing until she was confident she had everything she would need.

After filling her cosmetics bag and fitting it inside her suitcase, she pushed down on the lid so she could get it zipped. Calling Bill to take her suitcase down the stairs for her, she went into her closet and changed out of her sweats into a pair of good jeans and a black turtleneck sweater. Adding a long necklace and silver hoops, she grabbed her black and ivory plaid, double-breasted wool coat and headed downstairs. Bill was just coming back in from loading her suitcase into the back of his SUV.

"You have a seat on a flight that leaves in an hour. It'll be tight, but I think you can make it. It's either that or wait until morning." She nodded. "You ready?"

Looking around the house, she nodded again, grabbing her purse and cell phone on her way out the door. Bill held her hand all the way to the airport and parked in short-term parking.

"You aren't going to drop me off?" Jari asked, surprised.

Bill shook his head. "Not tonight. I'll walk you in."

She smiled, touched by his thoughtfulness, pleased by the idea of having a few more minutes with him before they went their separate ways. He held her hand as they walked quickly into the airport, pulling her suitcase with his free hand. He checked her bag for her and then gave her a long hug and a sound kiss. "You're going to be fine, honey. Let me know when you want me to come."

"I will. I'll see you soon," she promised.

"I reserved a rental car for you. You can pick it up at the airport in Wichita," Bill told her, walking with her to security. "Call me when you get there."

"Thank you. And I will. I'll call as soon as I get on the road."

"Do. Drive carefully. You look tired already, and it's a long flight and a long drive."

Jari looked at the worried expression on her husband's face and felt her heart warm. It was nice to be reminded that she was loved and cared about. "I love you, Bill."

Having walked as far as they could go together, she gave him another hug and a kiss and waved as she started winding her way through the line. After getting through security, she just barely made it to her flight in time. She brought up the tail-end of the boarding line, but when the plane took off, she was on it. After making it to her seat, she pulled out her phone and texted Hannah about her dad and the last-minute trip. Hannah immediately texted back that she would be praying for her and to keep her posted. She filled Jessi in as well, and Jessica also promised to pray.

Once they were off the ground, she pulled a sleep mask out of her purse and leaned her seat back, getting a blanket from the flight attendant. It had been close to ten p.m. when she received the call from her mom, and she still had a long night in front of her. Once she touched down in Wichita, she had a ninety-minute drive north, and then she would go directly to the hospital. It would be wise to sleep while she could.

As soon as she closed her eyes, though, she was bombarded with thoughts and fears about what awaited her in Kansas. Every reason she had stayed away for the last fifteen years came back to her in a rush. Her hands started to feel clammy, and her heart raced. After so long away, could she really go back? She found herself wanting to catch a return flight to D.C. as soon as she landed. Instead, she pushed the troubling thoughts aside and started to pray. When she ran out of words, she began to repeat Bible verses, focusing on truth until she found some relief from her fears and a peace that calmed both her mind and her heart. Finally, she fell asleep, waking only as they touched down in Wichita.

Jari collected her purse, slipping her sleep mask back inside, and moved to get off the plane when the door opened. Half an hour later, she was leaving the airport in her rented sedan, the heater on full blast. A cold February wind was blowing, and clouds hung low in the sky. She hoped they weren't expecting snow. The streets of Wichita seemed strangely empty in comparison to D.C., and she reflected on the fact that even as late as it was, there likely would have been more traffic in her suburb than there was on the freeways of Kansas' largest city.

Once she was on the interstate and out of the city, she called Bill, keeping her word even though she was certain he was asleep. To his credit, he picked up and sounded semi-awake, asking how her flight was, if the car pick up had gone well, and if she had heard anything else from her mom. After she answered his questions, she told him to get some sleep. It didn't take much convincing, and she smiled tenderly as they said goodnight and hung up.

It was just after three a.m. local time when she parked outside the hospital in her hometown. She was surprised in some ways by how the town had changed and the new businesses that had popped up. At the same time, she was surprised by how much it was the same. Overall, it was almost as if time had stood still.

Taking a deep breath, she sat for a long moment, her hands on the wheel, and prepared herself for what would happen next. When she walked through the front door of the hospital, there would be no turning back. She would be around people she had known, and the news that she was back in town was sure to spread quickly through the grapevine. More importantly, as long as he was still alive, she would find herself face to face with her father.

That felt scariest of all. After avoiding him for so long, she was willingly walking back into his life.

Her mom hadn't called with an update, and Jari wasn't sure if that was a good sign or not. She wondered if her mom would be at the hospital. In a way, she expected her to be, but when she thought realistically about what the past held, she realized that her mom would likely not be making an appearance. In all likelihood, she was probably home sound asleep. While Jari only really knew her parents as a married couple—save the last couple of months before she left town—they'd been divorced for fifteen years. Her mom had only heard through the grapevine, so they clearly weren't still in contact.

As Jari hadn't talked to her dad or even heard an update on him since she left town, she wasn't sure if he was married again or if he had other children. As she took a deep breath and got out of her rental car, she wondered what the situation inside would be like. Who would be there with him? How would they respond to her sudden appearance? Would she be welcome? Was her dad even still alive? If he was, would he be awake? If so, would he be happy to see her? The questions seemed more overwhelming than simply walking in and finding out, so that's what she did.

At the front desk, she was directed to the second floor. Rounding the corner and summoning the elevator, she smoothed her hand down the front of her coat and took deep breaths as she waited for the elevator doors to open. When she inquired about Skip Braxon at the nurses' desk, she was directed to room 209.

The nurse had been two years ahead of her in school, and her surprise at seeing Jari was evident. Making her promise to come back to catch up after checking on her dad, her old classmate had waved away Jari's question about visiting hours and told her to go on in. As Jari made her way to her dad's hospital room, she again recognized how different things were in a small town—even hospitals.

At the closed door, she paused for several moments, composing herself. She had no idea what she was walking into, and her stomach was lurching like a seesaw. Finally, her hand shaking, she reached out and gave a quiet knock on the door. When no sound came from inside the room, she reached for the handle. Her hand was so sweaty that it slipped on the knob. She wiped her palms on her jeans and tried again. This time, the door opened, and she slipped inside.

She was surprised to see the room completely empty, save the man in the hospital bed. His eyes were shut, whether from sleep or unconsciousness, she wasn't sure. Other than the humming and beeping of the machines he was hooked up to, the room was quiet and still. Jari paused to see if he would wake up when she entered. When he didn't, she crossed the room to the side of his bed.

He looked much older than she remembered. There was no red in his hair anymore; he was completely gray. His mustache was gone, and more lines were etched into his face. He seemed smaller than she remembered. Whether it was because he'd always seemed larger than life to her, because of his condition, or because she was all grown up now, she didn't know. She had always remembered him as tall and strong, but now, he seemed very average in build. All that aside, he was unmistakably her father.

Letting her breath out slowly, she contemplated what she should do next. In the surprise of seeing an old classmate, she had forgotten to ask about his condition and wasn't sure whether she should go back out and do so, or simply sit down and wait. She wasn't sure if he was merely sleeping or if they had him in a medically induced coma. Either way, he was alive, and that was the important thing.

She thought about touching his hand to see if he would wake up, trying to decide if she wanted him to know she was there, or if she should let him rest and talk to him in the morning. Finally, she chose the latter. Everything always seemed better in the daylight. That would give her time, too, to adjust to the events of the night and summon her courage.

Setting her purse on the floor by a reclining chair, she sat down and stretched out. She studied her father, letting each emotion, each memory, come and go as it would. She had a deep past with this man, filled with emotions that had never been confronted or dealt with. She wanted to give herself freedom, patience, and grace to let them come to the surface, deal with them, and find freedom. Would it all come during her hours at the hospital, before her dad woke up and the doctor came in? She highly doubted it, but she would let the process begin, and she would stay in Kansas for however long it took to complete it.

Eighteen

J ari woke up abruptly to a loud noise. Opening her eyes, she saw that a different nurse than she had talked to the night before had entered the room with a machine on wheels, which she had carelessly run into the hospital bed. With a quick apology, the nurse began writing information on the chart she held as she checked the machines.

Pushing herself to her feet quickly, smoothing the coat she still wore and running her tongue over her teeth, Jari watched the activity. She glanced at her dad, but he still looked exactly as he had before she went to sleep. She was now sure he was in a coma. She turned her attention back to the nurse, whom she regrettably recognized.

"How's he doing?"

"As good as can be expected."

"What do you mean?"

"Mrs. Cordel, your father underwent triple bypass surgery last night after having a severe heart attack. He's lucky to even be alive. He was fortunate that the cardiologist happened to be in town last night for his monthly check-ups today. Normally, we would have had to transport him to Wichita, and I'm not a gambling woman, but if I were, I wouldn't have bet on him making it."

Jari absorbed the news quietly, her composure in place, despite the nurse's clipped tone. "Will he wake up soon?"

"He should wake up sometime today. The doctor has him sedated to keep him from being too rambunctious after surgery, but he will be weaning down the sedation this morning. After that, we'll just have to see how long it takes him to come around." The nurse, Joanna McGuire, continued doing paperwork, then glanced up at Jari. "Have you been in town long?"

Jari shook her head. "I flew in when I heard what happened. I got in early this morning."

"Have you been over to see your mom yet?"

Jari was tempted to ask the nurse if she'd ever heard of HIPPA. But this was a small town, and she knew things were different here—socially, if not legally. Instead, Jari mustered up a smile. "No. Not yet, but I plan to soon. I wanted to see how he was doing first."

Trying to feel grateful for the woman's decades of nursing experience rather than irritation at her presence, Jari considered the coincidence that one of the biggest busybodies in town would be her father's nurse. News that she was back was bound to be a household fact in less than an hour.

The nurse turned to leave, and Jari rushed to ask her next question, knowing that if anyone would know the answer, it was Joanna. "Is there anyone he would want here when he wakes up? Anyone I should call? A wife, maybe?"

Joanna looked surprised by her question. "Not unless you mean ex-wife, and seeing as how you're here, I'm guessing your mama already knows. No, I think it's just going to be you sitting at his bedside today." There was a hint of condemnation in Joanna's words, and Jari understood it. As his daughter, those were all things she should have known.

Shocked and saddened for the man in the hospital bed, Jari nodded. "Thank you."

Joanna left, wheeling her machine along behind her. Stepping closer, Jari stood by the side of the bed and looked at the man in front of her. After so many years of being angry with him, now all she felt was a deep sadness. Jari wondered what it would be like to be lying in the hospital without anybody to stay with her. Without anyone who cared. She couldn't imagine how lonely he must be.

Her mind running ahead, she thought about what it would be like for him when he went home. He would need help for a while, no doubt, and there would be no one to help him. In her mind, Jari had always assumed he had married Betty. Now she wished he had. Surely Betty would have been better than living his life alone. She reached out and picked up his limp hand, cradling it in both of hers.

Biting her lip, her thoughts drifted to her mom. Was her mother just as lonesome? Was she living a life of solitude, her hours in her flower shop the only time during the day when she had social interaction? Did she go home in the evenings to an empty house without anyone to care about how her day had gone or ask how she was doing?

Guilt began to rise up in her. She felt embarrassed that she didn't know the answers to her questions, ashamed that her selfish lack of courage to face the past had left her parents alone, guilty that she hadn't been a better daughter.

"I redeem all things." The gentle reminder blew across her heart.

Taking a deep breath and standing a little straighter, she broke agreement with the thoughts that were laying siege against her heart. "I'm here now. I can change the present and the future," she told herself firmly.

That's where her mind had to camp. There was no changing the past. Things had happened like they had, and it hadn't been perfect, but it was done. Now, it was time to move forward.

Considering her options for the rest of the morning, Jari gave her dad's hand a squeeze. "I'll be back in a little bit. I'm going to go talk to Mom. I'll try to be here when you wake up."

Grabbing her purse, she left the room, shutting the door softly behind her. Making her way to the nurses' station, she asked how soon they expected the sedation to wear off. Checking his charts, the nurse told her he likely wouldn't wake up before noon. Jari wrote down her cell phone number with directions to call if he woke up sooner than they expected and left the hospital.

Once in her rental car, she gave Bill a call and filled him in on the little she knew so far. She told him she was going to see her mom and get something to eat before heading back to the hospital. He promised to be praying for her and reminded her to keep him updated.

Seeing it was eight o'clock and knowing her mom's store would be opening, she put the car in reverse, backed out of her parking place, and exited onto Main Street. As she passed block after block, she felt like she was seventeen again. It was like going back in time.

It was a strange feeling to be back after being away so long. Something about her still fit here, yet she felt as if time had taken her a million miles away. Her life in Kansas almost seemed like a dream. She was quiet, feeling strangely unsettled and almost reverent in some way.

Finding her mom's flower shop without any problem, she parked outside of it. Seeing that an open sign hung on the front door, she glanced in the rearview mirror and noted that her sleek ponytail still looked fine, but her makeup could definitely use some touching up. Unfortunately, it just wasn't going to happen yet. She popped a piece of gum into her mouth, opened her door, and forced herself to get out of the car.

As she approached the shop door, her heart began to race. She hadn't seen her mom in a really long time. What would she say? How would she react? How would the conversation go?

Swinging the door open, she knew she was about to find out. As Jari stepped into the warm shop, the lovely scent of a giant floral bouquet overtook her, and she breathed deeply, smiling despite her nerves. She hadn't smelled anything so lovely in a long time. She instantly remembered all the reasons why she had wanted to work in a flower shop as a teen.

Her mom glanced up from arranging a bouquet of pink roses as the bell on the door jingled. For just a moment, she froze, her face unreadable.

"Hi, Mom," Jari said, smiling, trying to appear more confident than she felt.

Several tense moments passed while they both stood frozen, looking at one another. Then, like a dam breaking, Mary Braxon left her floral arrangement and ran to her daughter, throwing her arms around her and holding her close as if she were still a little girl. Jari returned her embrace, and they stood like that for a long time. "Thank you for coming home," Mary whispered, tears running down her cheeks. She stepped back, holding Jari at arm's length, beaming at her. "I've waited for this for a long, long time."

"I know. I'm sorry it's been so many years," Jari told her, truly meaning it.

Mary studied her. "Look how beautiful you are!" Her mom's face was wet but bright. "Would you like to go get a doughnut and a cup of coffee? We have a lot of catching up to do. I'm sure we can get that back corner booth. It's nice and private."

"What about your shop?"

"I'll close it for a few hours. The work will wait."

Jari had forgotten you could do that in a small town. "Then I would love to." Mary flipped over the open sign, put on her coat, and held the front door open for Jari.

They walked two doors down to the bakery and went inside. The heavenly scent of baking doughnuts met them at the door, and Jari felt her mouth begin to water. She had missed this place. They used to visit the bakery often to enjoy breakfast as a family before school or on weekends, and she had never found a place quite like it in the city. Everything was fresh and homemade, and they seemed to have a few varieties she had never seen anywhere else.

Approaching the counter, Jari stared into the glass case, considering all of her options before picking the doughnut that had always been her favorite. It was a large square pastry, filled with creme, and glazed with chocolate frosting. A large dollop of cinnamon whipped topping finished it off. It was big, beautiful, and familiar, and Jari's stomach growled. Her mom ordered the same, along with a breakfast bierock and a cup of coffee for each of them. Mary insisted on paying.

Seated at the back corner booth, tucked away from prying eyes and ears, Jari found herself not knowing where to begin or how to start the conversation. Instead, she bowed her head and closed her eyes, thanking the LORD silently for the food before them, for the chance to be with her mom again, for her dad still being alive, and for the reconciliation she prayed was coming. She asked for direction and wisdom to know how to proceed. When she opened her eyes, her mom was watching her curiously. For a moment, they both seemed to be at a loss for words.

"So how are things going at the shop?" Jari finally asked, stirring her coffee.

"Excellent. I'm glad to have Valentine's Day over. Let me tell you, that was a zoo. But really, I can't complain. Business has never been better. It's been so busy lately that I had to hire another lady to come in and work with me in the afternoons, and, of course, Tammy still works with me three days a week. It keeps us all busy, that's for sure."

"That's great, Mom."

Mary dipped her head as she took a drink of coffee. "A couple of years ago, I started offering what we call delectable bouquets and that's gone over real well. I make a lot of them for kids and graduations."

"What's a delectable bouquet?" Jari asked. Though she had an idea, she was desperate to keep the conversation moving.

"We make bouquets out of lollipops, candy bars, and things like that. Kids seem to enjoy getting those more than they enjoy getting flowers. A lot of parents have started ordering them for birthdays and special events. I delivered a bunch of them to the school last week for Valentine's Day, and I expect we'll be getting even more orders next year."

"That's a great idea. What child doesn't like candy?"

Mary smiled, obviously pleased with her daughter's approval. "We've just started offering fruit arrangements too. I take lots of different kinds of fruit, chunk it up, then make beautiful arrangements by putting a chunk of fruit on a long toothpick and arranging it in different ways. It sounds funny, I know, but it looks pretty. We've already taken them to a few baby showers and one wedding, and we have several more booked."

Jari nodded, smiling. "Those sound like great ways to expand your business and open up new markets."

"Yeah, they seem to be working out well." There was a pause. "How was your flight and the drive up here?"

"It was fine. No problems," Jari answered after swallowing her bite of doughnut. "These are so good. I've never found anything else like them."

"I think the filling is what makes them so spectacular. That and the fact that they're so fresh."

"That must be it."

There was a pause in the conversation. "So, tell me about your husband. What does he do? Did he stay home? You know, I realized last night that I don't even know if you have children." There was moisture in her mom's eyes again, and Jari nodded.

"I realized I don't really know much about your life either," Jari said. "I'd like to change that."

Mary nodded, smiling, as she wiped at her eyes. "I'd like to change that too."

"My husband, Bill Cordel—"

"So, your last name is Cordel now? I've wondered," Mary interrupted.

Her mom's simple question made Jari's throat hurt. How, in seven years of marriage, had she never told her mom her new last name? "Yes, it's Cordel now."

"Well, you didn't move too far down in the alphabet, did you? A 'B' to a 'C.'"

Jari laughed. "That's true. I'd never thought of that."

"So what does he do?"

Jari looked up from her coffee in surprise. "You don't know? It's just . . . I always thought you . . . might have heard," she finished with a cringe. With the way she'd seen rumors circulate during her first seventeen years in the small town, she had imagined the gossipers would have had a heyday with a political scandal involving a local. The fear of that was partly what had kept her away.

Her mom swirled her coffee around in her mug, watching it. "I do think there was some talk going around some years ago, but if the busybodies were talking, they didn't talk to me. They learned a long time ago that I won't allow it. I don't want to hear it. I'll only accept information from the source. So no, I don't know anything about you that you haven't told me."

Jari sat quietly for a moment, touched by her mom's quiet strength. She'd forgotten what a remarkable, disciplined woman she really was. Like a wave of clarity hitting the shores of her teenage trauma, she saw the woman across from her as the kind, loving, and steadfast mom she had been; not the woman Jari had spent years feeling awkward, guilty, and fearful of due to her own mistakes. She realized it had been her own anger, guilt, and fear that had separated them, not the actions of the kind woman across the table.

Clearing her throat, Jari started again. "To answer your question, Bill is a senator of the state of Virginia. He just got reelected in November to serve another term. He stayed home in D.C. this time. The Senate is in session and . . . I thought it would be best if I came back alone. At least for now."

"He could have come, you know. I would have loved to meet him."

Jari nodded. "And I want you to. I just wanted to see you and get things sorted out first, before I brought my husband home and added that into the mix too."

"That makes sense."

"We don't have any children of our own yet, but Bill has a daughter, Jessica, who's grown. She lived with us while she was in high school and while she went to college. She has beautiful twin girls. She's one of my very, very dearest friends, and her girls really light up our lives. Last May, she got married, and the four of them moved to Minnesota."

"Do you want children of your own?"

Jari smiled. Her mom had always been perceptive. "Yes, I do."

Sipping her coffee, Jari considered the woman across from her for a long moment. She knew she had a choice to make. She could keep the conversation surface level, or she could face her fears and take it deep. Though the latter felt scary, she had spent fifteen years having a minimal, superficial relationship with her mom and she was longing for more. She was yearning for something real and meaningful. And Jari knew, after running away and shutting her mom out of her life, a relationship like that was only going to be attained by opening up and filling her mom in on her last fifteen years.

Wanting to be close to her mom more than she wanted to keep herself safe within the walls she had erected around her heart and life, Jari took a deep breath and plunged ahead. Laying herself bare, she attempted to explain why she had left, told her mom about her life after leaving town, and about her abortion. She tried to retain her composure but was wiping at tears during parts of her story. To be so vulnerable and forthcoming with her mom was hard enough, but something about telling her mother about her abortion and the pain it had caused her own heart was even more emotional and heartrending than it had been telling Bill.

Tears ran unchecked down Mary's face, and she reached across the table and squeezed Jari's hand, holding it in her own. "We all make mistakes, sweetheart. There's no sense in beating yourself up over something you can't change."

"I know that now. I really do," Jari agreed, but her heart twisted, knowing she wasn't done. She had more to tell. She was sick to her stomach with dread over the things she still needed to confess, but she was done keeping secrets from her mother. No matter how difficult it was, she would tell it all and then see what happened next. Come what may, at least any relationship they might find a way to build would at least be built on the truth. There would be no more shameful secrets she would have to hide.

Over the next hour, she shared how she had met Bill. She had never felt more ashamed of what she had done than when she sat there telling her mom that she was the one who took a man away from his family. She had never felt so dismayed as when she admitted that she was the Cordel family's Betty Wyndsor.

"After all we went through, after you knew how it felt, how could you do that?" Mary asked, her voice broken, her cheeks wet.

"I don't know," Jari admitted, sorrowfully. "I've wondered that myself so many times. But in the moment, I just felt pleased that I was finally enough . . . that I finally was the one who was winning."

Mary shook her head. "Jari, we of all people should know—there is no winner in an affair. Everyone loses. You may have gotten the guy, but at what cost? Even to yourself . . ."

Jari bit her lip, feeling rattled inside. Her mom's words, while valid, were like a punch to the gut. She wiped at fresh tears. "You're right. I know that now, but when I was younger, I didn't. I just felt like I wasn't good enough. I felt like I had to prove that I was worthy of love. But then, Mom, I met a man who didn't ask me to be worthy—He simply loved me with an extravagant, unyielding, unconditional love."

"Bill?"

"No, Mom. I met Jesus." Mary looked confused, and Jari explained how she had met the Son of God and how He had changed her life. She shared about Jessi coming to live with them, and the battle that ensued between Bill and his daughter. She told her about Bill's accident and leading him to the LORD. She walked her through the next several years and shared about her growing desire to have children of her own. Finally, she told her about her recent pregnancy and the miscarriage that had ended it. She explained how she had come to terms with her past through the despair of that experience and how, for the first time, she had truly understood and accepted forgiveness. It was during that time, she told her mom, that she had heard God speak to her heart and had finally found the courage to get serious about returning to Kansas.

As she sat there telling her mom the good and the bad, the beautiful and the ugly about her life, she was struck by the realization of how much she looked and acted like her mother. As a teenager, she hadn't seen the similarities, but as an adult, she certainly did.

Her mom had the same straight blonde hair, the same blue eyes and high cheekbones. She had the same long legs and graceful build. They had the same mouth and the same hands. But even more than that, her mother listened and interacted like she knew she herself did. Mary wasn't just listening, she was deeply feeling and experiencing Jari's story. She wasn't just shedding a tear, she was weeping when Jari expressed pain, laughing out loud when she expressed joy. She was connecting so deeply that it was costing her. She wasn't keeping herself safe behind any walls, either. She was fully entering into Jari's story. Seeing how she was embracing her with real and deep emotion, Jari realized she had inherited her desire to connect with people on a heart-level, feel what they felt, and enter into their story, from her mother.

When Jari was finally finished with her story, Mary sat there quietly for several long moments, biting her lip and watching her. Jari resisted the urge to squirm under her mom's quiet perusal and sat still, waiting for whatever came next. She had no idea if it would be positive or negative. She had revealed a lot and not all of it was good.

Mary cleared her throat. "All these years, I have wondered what kind of a woman my daughter had become. I wondered if you were foolish or responsible, educated or not, sad or happy, dramatic or drama-free, promiscuous or faithful, a party girl or a family woman, angry or at peace, stuck up or humble. I've wondered who you became, what you looked like, what you were into, and what your life was like. Now, I know I have a daughter I can be proud of." Mary paused, her breath catching and her voice breaking. "And a daughter I want to share my life with. I have always loved you, Jari, and have always wanted you to come home, but I've been afraid, too." She stopped to clear her throat again.

"I was afraid that when you did, you would be so different that we wouldn't have anything in common anymore. I was afraid I wouldn't like who you had become, and that you wouldn't be the girl I always dreamt you would be." Mary took a deep breath, wiped her tears, and went on. "But now, I see you have exceeded all my expectations. All the hopes and dreams that built in my heart during the hours I spent rocking you when you were a baby, all the years I watched you grow up . . . I never dreamt that you could be as beautiful and lovely and wise as the woman I see sitting across this table from me." Mary's eyes filled with tears again. "And I am thankful, Jari. Very, very thankful."

"Mom," Jari breathed, not understanding how her mom could say something so nice after all she'd just shared.

Mary held up her hand. "Stop." She reached across the table and squeezed Jari's hand, sniffing as she did. "You made some mistakes, sweetheart. We all have. I've made plenty myself. What's done is done. You're a married woman now who loves her husband, has gone to great lengths for her stepdaughter, and serves her community. You've come home. That's what I care about. What happened in the past is exactly that—it's the past, and I am much, much more interested in the future."

Jari pulled her slender fingertips beneath her eyes and nodded. "Thank you."

"No, thank *you*. You have restored my hope for better days ahead."

They sat in sweet silence for several moments, both wiping at their tears.

"I wish we would have done this years ago. It breaks my heart that I waited so long," Jari said softly. Her regret was deep.

Her mom shrugged slightly. "Maybe this has been so easy, so sweet because of the years that have passed. Maybe we—neither of us—would have been ready years ago. Maybe time has helped us both be ready to forgive."

Jari smiled. She liked that thought. His timing really was perfect. "Would you like another cup of coffee?" she asked, standing.

"Yes, please." Jari took the cup her mom handed her.

Getting them both a refill at the coffee bar, Jari checked the time and found that she still had a couple of hours before noon. Adding a little bit of cream to her own mug, she headed back to the table where her mom sat waiting for her.

"So, Mom, what has your life been like during the past fifteen years?" she asked, setting her mom's coffee down in front of her before taking a drink of her own. "Catch me up."

Mary looked into her coffee cup for a long moment and then took a drink before answering. "It certainly hasn't been like I thought it would be, that's for sure."

"What did you think it would be like?"

"Twenty years ago, I thought that Skip and I would still be happily married today. And that our lives would be full—full of family, full of companionship, full of laughter. Back then, I looked at the years to come, and imagined Skip and I would face them together. I thought our lives would be marked by your big achievements like your high school and college graduations and your wedding. I thought you would be working with me at the flower shop and that maybe we'd have a few grandkids running around by now." Mary shook her head. "None of that happened."

Jari felt her mom's sadness and reached across the table to hold her hand.

"When everything happened . . . with your dad, I was so, so angry. I was angry with the decisions he had made, and I blamed him for our family falling apart. I blamed him for you leaving. I blamed him for the way my life was. I was bitter and alone, and to me, it was entirely his fault. Then, as the weeks and then months went by, and I didn't hear from you, I became angry with you too. I wondered why you were punishing me for something he had done. I didn't understand why we couldn't be together, just because your father messed up. I didn't understand why you weren't on my side . . . why you had deserted me too."

"I'm sorry," Jari whispered, pained by the hurt that saturated her mom's words. Her heart twisted with regret and tears rolled down her cheeks unchecked.

Mary shook her head and her lip trembled. "But being angry with you, my only daughter, my very heart outside my chest, hurt too much, so I took all of that anger and I channeled it toward your dad. I wanted to rip his head off with my bare hands. About six months after you left, his relationship with Betty ended. Looking back, I feel ashamed to say it, but I was glad. I relished his pain. I enjoyed the fact that it didn't work out between them. One evening, a week or so later, he showed up on my doorstep and said he was sorry, that he wanted to work things out between us."

"What did you say?" Jari asked, astonished. She never knew her father came back to apologize.

"I didn't say anything. I was so angry that I spit in his face and slammed the door. I wasn't going to take him back just because it didn't work out with Betty! Not after all he had done . . . all we had lost! Well, you know your father." Jari nodded, already knowing what came next. "He never came back."

"Have you spoken to him since?"

"Oh, I've seen him around. It's a small town. It's hard not to. But we do our best to avoid each other. Then, maybe a year ago, he came into the shop and asked if I'd heard from you. I told him I had, and that you were alive and well, married and living in D.C. That was all I knew, and all I told him. He left."

Jari absorbed that piece of news. "Did he . . . he never remarried?"

"No."

"Did you?" Jari asked hesitantly, not knowing if she should ask or not.

Mary shook her head and wiped her eyes. "Thirty-eight years ago, I vowed to love one man until death parted us. Sometimes, I wish it had. But I'm not going to go back on my word just because he did."

Shocked by what she saw on her mother's face, Jari dared to ask a question she had never even considered. "Mom, do you still love him?"

Mary bit her lip and shook her head, rolling her eyes up to stare at the ceiling. "Jari, we had been together since the fourth grade, and I'd had a crush on him since preschool. I don't know how not to love Skip Braxon." Her mom took a deep, shaky breath and let out a sigh. "Does that mean I want to be married to him again? Absolutely not."

"Are you still angry with him?" Jari asked gently.

"Yes," Mary admitted. "But over the years . . . the anger has faded. When I think about it—about what he did, and what it did to our family, I still feel angry, but most of the time I just feel sad. I feel sad about how things have ended up. I feel sad for the days, months, and years we've all lost with each other. I still mourn for the family we were but aren't anymore. I go home to the home we all shared, and it's empty. I wish it were full again. I see him around town, and I wish that none of it had happened, and that we were still married . . . sometimes I even wish he had waited just another year before showing up on my doorstep. Maybe by then I would have been ready to try to work things out. Maybe I wouldn't have been so angry, and I could have at least listened to what he had to say. I don't know. I guess back then I spent a lot of time wishing things weren't like they were and a lot of time feeling sad, but time has a way of taking the sting out of things."

Mary shrugged and wiped her eyes again. "These days, I'm doing better. I have my friends, extended family, a bridge club, book club, and supper club. I volunteer at the library. I enjoy my work. I have a lot to be thankful for, and my life feels mostly full."

Jari's cell phone rang in her pocket. She checked the caller ID and saw it was a local number. "I think it's the hospital."

"Take it."

Jari answered and was told that Skip was beginning to stir. They expected him to wake up within the hour. Hanging up, she relayed the information to her mom.

Mary took a deep breath and forced a smile. "You should go."

"I don't want to leave you or this conversation," Jari admitted honestly.

Mary smiled again. This time, it looked less forced. "You're not flying home immediately, are you?" Jari shook her head. "Then we'll have more time to talk."

Nodding, Jari knew her mom was right. Taking one last drink of her coffee, she stood. "I should go. I want to be there when he wakes up. I can't imagine waking up alone."

"I'm glad, for his sake, that you'll be there with him."

Jari started to turn. Mary reached out and grabbed her hand. "Sweetheart, if you need a place to stay while you're in town, I'd love to have you stay with me! Your old room hasn't been touched. You can stay in there . . . it would give us more time to spend together."

Her mom's eyes were almost pleading. She couldn't say no, even if she'd wanted to. "I'd love to."

"Good. You'll come for dinner tonight?"

Jari hesitated. "As long as I can leave Dad."

Mary nodded. "I understand. Come if you can," she paused. "And Jari? Let me know how he's doing?"

Jari smiled. "I will." She paused. "I love you, Mom. It has been so good to see you." Mary stood and wrapped her arms around Jari, hugging her tight. Jari returned the long hug and left the bakery, sad to be leaving such a heart-wrenchingly honest conversation, sad to be leaving her mom once again. But she would see her later in the day, she reasoned, and she would stay in Kansas until she chased the shadows out of her mom's pretty blue eyes.

Nineteen

J ari unlatched the door quietly and slipped into the hospital
room. The hum and beep of machines still filled the air, but
when she stepped farther into the room to where she could see the
man in the bed, she found him looking at her. She tried to cover
her surprise with a smile and ignore the misgivings that rose within
her. She hadn't been in the same room as her father when he was
coherent for over fifteen years.

"They said you were here," he said, breaking the silence, his
expression unreadable.

"I'm sorry I wasn't here when you woke up. I stepped out to see
Mom."

"I figured as much," he paused. "How did it go?"

Jari couldn't hold back a smile. Her time with her mom
had gone better than she had ever imagined it could. Their
conversation had brought peace to long-term areas of anxiety,
and to have it over was like a weight lifted off her shoulders.
"Wonderful. It was really good to see her."

Skip Braxon nodded. "I'm glad."

"Me too."

"How is she?"

Jari was caught off guard by the tender way he asked the
question. "She's good. It sounds like things are going well at her
shop."

"I'm glad to hear it." He paused. "You look just like her, you know."

Jari nodded. "I know."

"Lucky girl. Your mom has always been a knockout."

Jari smiled faintly. She wasn't sure if the compliment was meant for her or her mom—probably both, she decided. She took a few steps forward to stand at the end of the bed. "How are you? How do you feel?"

He winced. "Like I got hit by a train."

"That's probably from the surgery."

"I'm sure it is." Skip gestured stiffly to the chair near his bed. "Have a seat. I don't think I'm going anywhere, anytime soon, and unless you're planning to leave in the next five minutes, you might as well sit down."

Crossing the room, Jari did as she was instructed. She tried to think of something to say, but nothing came. Despite her long hours of travel to get to his side and her nighttime vigil in his hospital room, she still had no idea how to address the past or start to move forward.

Skip leaned back in his bed carefully, resting his head against the pillow and closing his eyes. "How's it feel to be back in town?"

"Strange," she answered honestly.

"Guess that's to be expected. How many years has it been? Fifteen? Sixteen? Yeah, strange sounds about right. Did you see the new Italian restaurant we got out by the interstate?"

"I did. Have you tried it?" Jari found the conversation mindboggling. It was as if she had been gone six months instead of fifteen years. While she appreciated the easy chat, it felt surreal to be sitting beside her dad talking about if he'd eaten at the new restaurant in town.

"Oh, a handful of times. Their chicken parmesan can't hold a candle to your mother's, but the alfredo isn't bad. Got ourselves a new Mexican restaurant too. Best enchiladas I've ever had. We got one of those gyms that's open twenty-four hours a day now. I've been trying to get in there a couple times a week. Don't always succeed, but I try. And one of them fancy shmancy coffee shops. I've never set foot in the place. I think my pot of coffee down at my shop suits me better than any four-dollar frappa-whatever-they're-called—but it's real popular with the women in town. Can't imagine all the gossipin' that goes on down there."

"There definitely have been some changes. The town is growing," Jari conceded.

"Yeah, but there are parts that haven't changed a bit. Downtown, for instance. Did you notice how everything's exactly the same?"

"I did."

"All the new stuff's down by the interstate, trying to grab the travelers who are just passing by. Makes decent sense, I guess."

"I guess it does." The silence stretched. "How are things going over at your tire shop?"

"Well, this morning, I'm not real sure. I called Tommy—you remember him? I told him he's in charge till I get back. I guess he'll probably be able to handle things alright. I'll get over there to make sure things are runnin' smoothly once I get out of here."

Jari remembered Tommy well. The loud, rambunctious man was just a few years younger than her dad. He had always been a loyal friend, as well as an employee, and if the reports she'd heard about her dad's lack of a family life that morning were true, it sounded like her dad was in need of good friends. She was thankful Tommy still worked with him at the tire shop.

"With as long as he's been there, I'm sure Tommy will do just fine running the shop until you get back."

Her dad nodded and continued. "Probably so. Other than this little bump in the road, things have been decent. Pretty steady, actually—just like always. Around here, people need cars and trucks, and cars and trucks need tires. I've always run an honest business, and it's paid off. People have been bringing their vehicles to me for years, and my numbers say they're not stopping now."

"Good, Dad. I'm glad to hear business is good," Jari told him sincerely.

"Yeah, I can't complain."

Quiet fell over the room again, and Jari forced herself to relax. She settled into the chair and crossed her legs, instead of continuing to sit on the edge as if she were ready to bolt at any moment. She was here for the long haul. A little bit of stunted, awkward conversation wasn't going to send her running. There were bigger issues to address and peace to seek.

"How are you doing, Jari girl?"

She had forgotten he called her that. It had been ages since anyone had, yet hearing his old nickname for her was strangely comforting. His question was quiet and contemplative, and she knew he was hoping for a real answer. Though it was tempting to take the easy way out and dismiss his concern with a quick answer, she forced herself to take time formulating an honest one. She smiled. "I'm actually really good. It's been a bit of a rough year, but I think I've grown through it, and things are looking a little brighter."

Skip nodded. "I know what you mean."

Jari wasn't sure if he could relate, or if he somehow knew more about her life than she thought he did. She felt unsettled by his answer but couldn't put her finger on why. "You've had a hard year too?"

"In some ways," he answered ambiguously. "But there have been good times, too, and you just got to hold on to those good moments and let the others go. Otherwise, you're never going to make it."

"What were some of your good moments?" she prompted.

For just a moment, his face clouded, and she didn't have a clue as to what he was thinking. Just as suddenly, it passed, and he met her eyes. "Hearing you had been here when I woke up this morning was definitely one of them."

"I'm glad," Jari told him, honestly. "I wasn't sure if you would be happy to see me."

Her statement seemed to surprise him. "I haven't seen you since you were a teenager. Tell me, why wouldn't I be glad to hear you'd come home?"

Jari stammered as she saw he was expecting an answer. "It's been a long time . . . we . . . we didn't part under the best of circumstances . . . I just . . . I wasn't sure."

"When a man thinks he's dying, some things just don't matter anymore." There was a pause. "And some things really do. Family is one of those. Thanks for coming."

Her dad's simple statement settled weightily over Jari. She nodded, understanding. "You're welcome."

There was a comfortable silence that stretched, and Jari noticed her dad's eyes were growing heavy as the sedatives still worked their way out of his system. "Why don't you rest for a little bit? We can talk more when you wake up."

"My darned eyelids won't stay open, will they? You'll still be here when I wake up?" His last question came out sounding as vulnerable as a child's.

Emotion welling up within her, Jari managed a nod. In no time at all, Skip Braxon was asleep.

~~~~~

Jari watched her dad sleep, and her mind raced. What now? She had finally come home to Kansas. Her dad was going to live. She had seen her mom. She had talked to her dad. What now? The question ran through her head over and over again.

Should she address the past? Should she avoid the subject and move on as if it had never happened? What did moving on look like? She knew what would be easiest, but what would be best? And what was she hoping for? Did she want a real, meaningful relationship with him? Or had that day come and gone? Did she simply want peace? Would she be satisfied with being at peace with him, but never trying to rebuild any kind of relationship? Did she want her father in her life? She had gone so many years without having a dad for any practical sense, and now she wondered what it would be like to have one again. Was there room for him in her life?

She sat there contemplating her questions as he slept. One thing was certain. She was thankful, so thankful, she had been given the opportunity to see him alive again. She was thankful the LORD had brought her to Kansas. At least now, now that she was finally home and both of her parents were still alive, there was a chance of reconciliation. She at least had the option to rebuild relationships that had long been in ruins. Yet, there were still a lot of unknowns.

Jari looked at her father lying in the hospital bed in front of her and knew the reality was that he would need someone to take care of him once he was released from the hospital. If he lived alone, there was no other option than for her to stay with him for a time and help him recover. Her mind churning, she contemplated if she could do so. How long could she be away from home? What would

Bill think of a prolonged absence? Though she didn't have a job she needed to take time off from, she had a husband and a life in D.C. Could she step away from all that to stay in Kansas for a while? She had been volunteering consistently. What kind of responsibility did she have as a volunteer? She drummed her fingertips on the arms of the chair. Did she even want to stay in Kansas and take care of her dad?

And if she stayed, would she room at his house until he was able to take care of himself? It made the most sense, but she remembered the look on her mom's face when she asked if Jari would stay with her. She felt torn, and, for the first time, was able to relate to the children of divorce who were forced to choose between their mom and dad.

Avoiding her parents altogether since the divorce had been easier, in a lot of ways, than figuring out life in a broken family. It had alleviated the need to choose between them. Now, coming home and making them a part of her life again, she would have to start making choices and doing what she could to make both of her parents feel loved and valued.

Mulling over questions about what came next as she watched her dad sleep, she realized there was one thing she was suddenly sure about; she didn't just want to make peace with him and then go her separate way. As hard as it might be in the coming hours, days, weeks, and months, she wanted to rebuild her relationship with her dad. She wanted him in her life.

Growing up, she had decidedly been a daddy's girl. Now, being home again, a million memories were flooding her, and nearly all of them of her dad were good. If only she could erase the last few months she was home, she wouldn't have any bad ones. He had never been a warm, fuzzy kind of man, physically affectionate, or even very tender, but he had always been a good dad, strong and stable. He had taken good care of his family, provided well, and made her feel safe and secure. She appreciated that about him. Seeing him, talking to him now, she knew he hadn't changed. Not really. He was still the same dad who had checked under her bed for monsters every night when she was little, bordered on sainthood as he taught her to drive, and made time for her no matter what else he had going on. He had supported her, believed in her, and loved her, and it hadn't been fair of her to let one bad year erase all the good ones.

Sure, he had made mistakes—a myriad of small ones that culminated in a big one which could never be changed or rectified. For a long while, she thought it was a mistake that could never be forgiven. But she had since learned that everyone made mistakes. Everyone did things they shouldn't and wished they hadn't. She now understood that his great mistake did not have to define him. It didn't cancel out the fact that he was a good man and had been a good father. She didn't want to be defined or identified by her past sins, and it wasn't fair to define him by his either.

She contemplated that revelation for the rest of the day. Her dad slept off and on, and they watched television and chatted during the times he was awake. The conversation stayed light, and she found herself enjoying his humorous dialogue. She had forgotten how funny he was.

Around five, his eyes began to look heavy, and she knew he would sleep again soon. Before he could, she collected her coat and purse and stood. He looked over at her warily, a little more alert after her sudden movements.

"You headed out?"

"Mom asked me to come for dinner."

"Do it. This hospital food isn't fit for man or beast. Go get some of your mother's good home cooking."

Jari smiled, appreciating the freedom he was giving her. He could have tried to guilt trip her into staying. "I plan on it. Can I bring you anything?"

"Oh, your mother won't want to feed me too."

"I meant from your house . . . do you need me to pick up anything for you?"

"Oh." He looked embarrassed. "Actually, yes. I'd sure appreciate my toothbrush, toothpaste, and the fishing magazines that are beside my bed. And my Bible."

Jari couldn't hide her surprise.

"Now don't you go judging me before you've even heard what I have to say about it. Just bring it, please. It's in the nightstand drawer on the left side of my bed. I live in a small house on Walnut—408 is the number. I'm not sure if the door is locked or unlocked, but either way, there's a spare key taped under the trim of one of the front porch windows. The one on the right, I think. Call me if you have troubles . . . you know where I'll be."

Absorbing what he said, she nodded. "I will. Get some rest, Dad. I'll be back later . . . I shouldn't be later than nine or ten."

"You mean tonight?" he asked.

"Yes," Jari answered with a smile. He sounded absolutely shocked. "I'm not going to leave you here by yourself overnight. After all, somebody has to be here to make sure you're not giving the nurses a hard time," she teased lightly.

She momentarily saw the emotions her statement stirred up in him before his expression grew guarded again. "Your old bed would surely be more comfortable than that recliner," he answered, his voice gruff.

"Be that as it may, I'll be back."

"Suit yourself." She knew his gruff response was more of a defense than a lack of appreciation, and so she only responded with a smile.

Leaving the hospital, she called Bill on her way to her dad's house. She would swing by and pick up the items he requested before dinner, so she wouldn't have to locate his house and the spare key in the dark. When Bill answered, she felt her heart warm. She hadn't even been gone twenty-four hours, and she was already missing him. She missed his perspective as well as the stability and practicality he always brought to a situation. She missed having him at her side and discussing the details of her day with him.

She filled him in on her afternoon over the phone, staying in the car several minutes after pulling up to 408 Walnut Street, lingering in the conversation. He was gentle and responsive, asking questions and really listening to her answers. He was giving her his full attention, and she appreciated that, as well as the respect he was giving the entire situation. It was clear he knew how monumental returning home was to her, and she was thankful that he felt the weight of it and responded accordingly.

"Bill, my dad lives all alone. It's lucky he was able to call 9-1-1 when the pains first started or else he wouldn't have made it. When he gets out of the hospital . . ."

It was quiet for a long moment. "He's going to need someone to take care of him?"

"I suppose he could hire someone," she said, toying with a piece of her blonde hair, wrapping it around her pointer finger as she waited for her husband's reply.

"But you want to stay and take care of him," Bill said, stating the obvious.

"I don't know. I don't know that I want to as much as I think I need to . . . not just for him, but for me . . . for my mom. I've got to see this through, Bill."

"Then I think you should stay as long as you need to. I'll miss you—I miss you already—but I don't want you to have any regrets, honey. You're there for a reason. Do everything you need to do."

She wished she could throw her arms around her husband in a big hug. "Thank you for your support, Bill. It means a lot."

"I'm really proud of you. I know going back hasn't been easy, but you did it, and I think you're always going to be glad you did."

"I think you're right. I already am." She glanced at the clock. "I've got to go. I told my mom I would come for supper. I probably shouldn't be late."

"I wish I was there to go with you."

"Me too. I love you."

"I love you too, honey. Call me later."

She smiled as she hung up. She was married to a really good man.

Getting out of the car, she started up the sidewalk, glancing around the house. It was definitely small, but it had a tidy appearance. The yard was cut short, and the landscaping was appropriately trimmed back for winter, all of last year's growth having been pruned and hauled away. The house didn't look especially lived in, but she had a feeling it was due mostly to the missing feminine touches. There was no chair on the front porch or welcome sign on the door. There were no drapes in the windows or remnants of flowers in the planters on the porch railings. It was clean and tidy, but didn't look especially homey.

A small driveway led to a carport beside the house, and in the carport sat a vehicle that made Jari's heart stop beating for several moments. Veering off her previous course, she approached the carport cautiously and ran her hand over the back bumper of the vehicle. The black SUV with darkly tinted windows and fancy chrome wheels was all too familiar. Even with Kansas plates instead of temporary tags, she was certain it was the same vehicle that she had seen outside of their Washington, D.C. home and behind her in traffic on a few different occasions. Standing there looking at it, knowing instinctively that it was the very same SUV, she didn't know what to think.

Stunned and almost numb, she finally turned and made her way into the house, where she quickly collected the items her dad had requested. She wanted to stay and look through his house—look for anything that would explain who he was now, what his life was like, and why he had been in D.C., but she felt like she was eavesdropping on a private conversation by being in his house without him. Additionally, she knew her mom was expecting her shortly.

Setting a grocery sack full of the items she had gathered in the passenger seat of her rented car, she drove the short distance to her mom's, her mind humming the whole way. Was the black SUV her father's? If it was, why had he been in D.C.? What did it mean? Had it really been him? If he had been in D.C., why hadn't he come to their door? Why had he hung back like some kind of threatening stalker? Did he realize the worry he had caused them? Had Bill really kept security at their house since the election, all because of her dad?

She forced herself to stop the unrelenting questions. She couldn't be sure it was him. There were thousands of black SUVs just like his in the country—surely even with the fancy rims. She had no license plate number and no other distinguishing markers to go off. Before she jumped to conclusions, before she grew angry with her dad for the distress he had caused them, she had to know if the black SUVs were actually one and the same. And that couldn't be done for several hours. She had dinner to get through first.

Shutting the door on the thoughts that were scattering across her mind like pouring marbles, she pulled up outside her childhood home. For several moments, she just sat still and looked at it. Her mom had obviously had it repainted and reroofed. The Flowering Crabapple tree in the front yard had grown tremendously. A porch swing now hung on the covered front porch. There was a newly landscaped berm by the mailbox. Otherwise, the house that held all of her childhood memories still looked the same.

A strange sense of the past settling over her, she climbed out of the car and opened the back door to pull her suitcase off the seat. Closing the door and locking the car, she wheeled her suitcase up the sidewalk and lugged it up the porch steps. Her mom had the front door open before she got to it, letting a block of light spill out onto the porch as the winter sun had long since set, and twilight was giving way to dark.

Warmth and the aroma of a home-cooked meal spilled over Jari as she got to the door. She inhaled deeply, breathing in countless memories. This is what home smelled like. She had forgotten.

"Come in! Come in!" her mom was saying, stepping back as she held the screen door open for her. Jari tried to concentrate but struggled to stay in the present. The past was like a tidal wave crashing over her. Everything was so familiar, and yet so distant. "Don't mind my messy house," her mom said, following her inside.

Jari smiled. She'd forgotten how her mom always said that whenever someone came over, even if she—and Jari—had spent hours before they arrived, cleaning. "It looks spotless, Mom. Truly. You've really done well keeping up the place."

That drew a happy smile from her mom. "Thanks. I try." She paused and then clasped her hands together. "Well, dinner will be ready in about forty-five minutes. I was thinking you probably haven't had a chance to shower since leaving home, so if you want to get cleaned up, you're welcome to do so."

"A shower would be wonderful," Jari answered, hoping she didn't sound as distracted as she felt. She couldn't stop looking around. Despite little changes—new throw pillows, a new armchair, a couple of new knickknacks on the bookshelves—it was all so familiar.

"I thought you'd say that. Come on. Let's get you settled. I'll take your bag."

"I can carry it," Jari protested, but her mom already had the handle and was pulling it across the living room to the stairs.

"Nonsense. You've had a long day. I'll get it."

Jari conceded, following her mom as she slowly pulled the heavy bag up the stairs. Jari studied the pictures that hung on the stairway wall as she passed them. They were family pictures—pictures of her mom and dad and her—pictures she hadn't seen since she left home. They brought back so many memories. Jari felt the threat of tears in her eyes and blinked them back.

"You know, after the affair, my mom said I should cut your dad out of all our pictures." Mary said, stopping on the stairs to look at the framed photographs, too.

"Why didn't you?"

"Well . . . I thought about it, honestly. When I was angry and lonely, and spending yet another night all by myself, it was most tempting. But I knew this day would come—the day when you would come home, and the anger would fade, and I would wish I hadn't. It wouldn't be fair to you, to him, or to me . . . or to the family we had been. The fact is, Skip was a very big part of our lives. He was my husband and your father, and no matter what has happened since then, that part won't ever change. I thought you might want these someday to remember where you came from . . . and I figured you'd want him in them too."

"Thank you," Jari responded simply. Over the past twelve hours, she had gained a deep respect for her mother—both for the woman that she was and the way she had handled life since the affair. Her mother hadn't denied the reality of how she felt but, even in the thick of things, had stayed rational and mature and thought about the bigger picture. Jari admired that. Now, her mom was bringing up the past and putting it in context for the present and the future. Jari appreciated that it wasn't off-limits, and that her mom was letting her know she could process everything verbally if she needed to. It wasn't like that at first, right after the divorce, but emotions were high and hurt was rampant then. After having years to cool off and come to grips with reality, she appreciated how her mom was now helping guide her through confronting the past.

"How is Grandma?" she asked, going back to her mom's reference to the woman.

"She's doing fine. We celebrated her eightieth birthday last month. It's hard to believe she's at that age already. I'll always think of her in her late twenties, a handkerchief tied over her hair, wearing pedal pushers and teaching me how to ride a bike, with Elvis playing on the record player and floating out the open windows." Mary smiled, but her smile held a hint of sadness. "Time goes by so fast."

"Yes, it does," Jari agreed. She felt sad and guilty over the years she had missed with her grandparents—years she could never get back. "How's Grandpa?"

"He's not in as good of health as he used to be, but he's doing alright. I invited them both to dinner tomorrow night. I hope that's okay. They were anxious to see you when I told them you were back in town. In fact, they would have come over tonight, but I thought it might be nice for us to have dinner just the two of us first. I'm too selfish to share you just yet." Mary finished with a laugh, then climbed the last two stairs and rolled Jari's suitcase into her room.

As Jari walked into her old bedroom, she was startled and yet not surprised to see it looking exactly as she had left it. Her mom had mentioned earlier that it hadn't been touched, but to see it with her own eyes . . . it was like she had stepped into a time capsule. The cream floral bedspread still covered her waterbed, and the matching decorative mauve and country blue bed pillows had ruffles around their edges. The posters on the walls had not been taken down, and pictures she had stuck in the corners of her dresser mirror were still there. When she noticed her mom was watching her, she shrugged. "It's really great to be home. It just feels . . . strange."

"Not much has changed," her mom said, her voice sounding sympathetic. "In some ways, it might have been easier for you if I had moved."

"No, I'm glad you stayed. I needed to come home. I needed to see this."

Mary nodded in response, understanding. "I've been thinking of redoing this room so it was more updated for whenever you came home, but I could never bring myself to do it . . . if nothing else, that waterbed needs to go. It's a miracle it hasn't sprung a leak."

Jari laughed. "I honestly didn't know there were any left in the world." Her mom laughed too.

The silence stretched for several moments before Jari smiled and broke it. "What do you say we re-do it together while I'm here? We can say goodbye to the past together."

Mary's face lit up with a bright smile. "I think that's a really good idea. I've also been wanting to paint a little downstairs. Maybe we could do that at the same time."

"Absolutely. By the way, I like the colors you painted the outside of the house. They go well together."

"Thank you. I had that done two summers ago. It needed to be painted, and I needed some kind of a change."

"The landscaped area by the mailbox is nice too."

Mary bobbed her head. "And did you notice the porch swing? That's become my favorite place to sit on summer evenings. I take my book and sweet tea out there and spend a lot of hours just reading and swinging."

"That sounds nice, Mom." Jari paused. "In D.C., we have a big patio in the back, and when the weather's nice, we like to eat dinner out there. There's nothing like being outside on a summer evening."

"I'd like to see your house sometime if it's okay with you. I'd like to come visit," Mary said, her voice almost hesitant.

Jari's face blossomed into a bright smile. "I would love that! Truly! You are welcome anytime!"

Seeming emotional, Mary turned away and started toward the door. "I'd better get back to the kitchen to check on dinner. You get cleaned up and come down when you're ready. Don't take too long or the food will be cold."

"Yes, ma'am," Jari found herself saying out of habit. "Mom?"

Mary turned back over her shoulder. "Yes?"

"Did I really like their music enough to have their poster hanging on my wall?" Jari asked in disbelief, pointing to one of the faded posters that decorated her room. While fifteen years had felt like it went by in a blink, the hairstyles and fashion of the pop band on the poster made her realize just how long ago it had been.

Mary laughed. "If I remember right, you knew every word to every song."

Jari shook her head, regretfully remembering her mom was right. Perhaps she had blocked out—rather than simply forgotten—that part of her teen years.

When her mom left the room, she crossed to her suitcase and unzipped it, pulling out what she needed and carrying it into the bathroom. Half an hour later, she emerged clean and fresh and made her way down to the dinner table, hoping she hadn't taken too long.

"Feel better?" Mary asked as Jari walked into the kitchen.

"Much."

"Good. Go ahead and sit down. I'm just putting the food on the table."

Jari took her old seat at the kitchen table and took a sip of sweet tea as her mom carried a casserole dish over. A tossed salad already sat between the two place settings. Jari nudged it over to make room for the main dish. Recognizing the food by its aroma before her mom even set it down, Jari breathed in deeply, closing her eyes and smiling. "Chicken parmesan?"

"It used to be your favorite," her mom answered with a happy smile.

"That's something else that hasn't changed." The dish smelled just as heavenly as she remembered. "How funny. Dad was just talking about your chicken parmesan today."

Mary tipped her head as she sat down. "Was he? What did he say?" It was clear that she wasn't expecting it to be anything nice.

"He said the new Italian restaurant down by the interstate doesn't make it as good as you do," Jari answered simply.

"Well, bless him. That was kind." Mary scooped a chicken breast up and motioned for Jari to lift her plate. Setting her plate back down in front of her as Mary dished her own, Jari inhaled deeply again, drawing in the scent of the chicken on her plate. She had requested this very dish for every birthday and special occasion since she could remember up until the time she left, and so had her father. There was no doubt that it was a family favorite and one of her mom's specialties. "How is he?" Mary asked, drawing Jari back from her thoughts.

Jari looked up from putting dressing on her tossed salad. "How's who?"

"Your father."

"Oh. I think he's doing as well as can be expected. He was ready to sleep again when I left. It was like that on and off all day. He was tired and sore, but I think that's all normal, considering what his body has been through."

Mary nodded. "How's your husband?"

Jari filled her mom in on Bill's day and found herself explaining what life was like for a Senator. For several minutes, they talked about last year's campaign, politics, and proposed legislation. Jari wasn't surprised by how easily her mom spoke of political matters. Both of her parents had always been very patriotic and took it upon themselves to be active voters and citizens. Jari wondered now if that's where she picked up her interest in politics that had first caused her to apply for the job in Bill's office all those years ago. She had grown up listening to her parents talk politics at their kitchen table, and now it was part of her daily life.

The discussion moved on to other subjects, and they ate dinner while sharing a lively and comfortable conversation. When Jari put her napkin on the table and stood to clear the dishes, she let out a happy sigh. "That was a wonderful meal, Mom. Thank you."

"It was wonderful to have you here to share it with," Mary answered simply, standing to put the leftovers in the fridge. "I made chocolate chip cookies for dessert, so I hope you're not too full."

Jari smiled, appreciating the thought and effort her mom had put into making her favorite things for dinner. "I'm never too full for cookies."

After helping to clean up the kitchen and spending another hour talking with her mom, Jari found her thoughts turning more and more toward the man in the hospital bed and the questions she needed to ask him. At nine, she stood and shared that she needed to get back. Her mom nodded. "I think it's good that you're going to stay with him tonight, Jari. If I were him, I wouldn't want to be alone."

Jari shook her head. "Me neither."

As she put on her coat and found her purse, shoes, and car keys, Mary disappeared back into the kitchen. She came out carrying a plate covered with tin foil and a clear plastic bag full of half a dozen cookies. "Some of the cookies are for you in case you get hungry." Mary paused and then smiled. "I hope Skip enjoys the chicken."

Jari was stunned by her mom's act of kindness and recovered in time to smile as she accepted the plate and cookies. "I'm sure he will. Thank you."

Changing the subject, Mary stepped around her and made her way toward the front door. "Feel free to come over anytime tomorrow if you want to shower or get something to eat. The fridge is well stocked, I think. Oh, I gave you a key, didn't I? I think I did."

"I have it on my key chain."

"Okay, good. Well, like I said, just let yourself in and make yourself at home. I'll be home just after five again. Grandma and Grandpa will be here for dinner around six. I'll be at my shop if you need me."

"Okay. And you have my cell number, so if you need to call me, you can."

"Right."

At the front door, Jari gave her mom a hug. "Thank you for dinner. It has been really good to see you today, Mom. Really good."

Mary smiled, and Jari saw that tears had gathered in her blue eyes. "Thank you for coming. I hope you get some sleep tonight, sweetheart."

Twenty

J ari entered her dad's hospital room with the covered plate of food and the bag of cookies, her mind racing. She had lots of questions about the black SUV, and she hoped he had lots of answers. When she walked into his room, his eyes darted from the show he was watching on television to rest on her.

"What's that?" he asked curiously as he sniffed. "That's not . . . ?"

"Mom sent it," she answered, handing him the plate.

He took the aluminum foil off and looked at the plate of food like a child looked at a gift on Christmas morning. Closing his eyes, he took in a long sniff, and Jari laughed, his reaction being so close to her own.

"She's a good woman," he said as he reached for the fork setting on his hospital tray. The tray was still half-full, but obviously discarded. "I'm not sure if I should be eating this or not, and I may pay for it later, but I've been dreaming about this chicken for fifteen years. Surgery or no surgery, by George, I'm going to eat it."

"I think I'd do the same," Jari said, laughing as she sat down in the recliner. While he ate, she forced herself to let him enjoy the delicious meal in peace. Her questions could wait. In the meantime, she grew interested in the show he was watching, and when she looked back at the end of it, he had fallen asleep, one bite of chicken remaining on his plate.

Frustrated with herself and frustrated with the disconcerting questions that still bounced around inside of her that would now have to wait until morning, Jari got up and took the plate from his lap. Using her fingers, she popped the last piece of chicken into her own mouth, not having the heart to let any of it go to waste. Almost hoping he would wake up, she lowered his bed until he was in a lying position, and switched off the television. He didn't even stir.

Resigning herself to the fact that she would have to wait until morning to ask if he had been in D.C., she took the pillow and blanket the nurse had left for her and stretched out in the recliner. She spent awhile in prayer and the Word but finally gave in to sleep as it threatened to take her in comfortable wave after comfortable wave of sleepiness.

She awakened in the midnight hours and found a nurse standing beside her dad. Sitting up quickly, Jari tried to make sense of what was going on through the haze of not getting much sleep over the past thirty-six hours.

"I'm fine," her dad told her, waving her back down, his voice gruff again. "No sense in you waking up."

"Your dad was having some painful gas due to eating food that was *not* on the diet regimen we have him on," the nurse explained, her voice testy. Jari wasn't sure if the nurse was mad at her dad for eating the food or mad at Jari for bringing it to him.

"Thanks for broadcasting that, Barb," Skip responded, his tone dry. He winced in pain. "I'm the one with the abdominal pain, so I don't know what you're so grumpy about."

"I'm grumpy because I had to stop reading to come in here and fix you up. You caught me right in the climax of the book. And all because you didn't follow instructions," the nurse answered with a decided harrumph at the end. Jari smiled. She knew as well as her dad did that Barb Studee was all bark and no bite. Barb turned to Jari and sent her a friendly wink. "I gave him something to help with the gas. It should start to kick in and give him some relief before long."

"Thank you," Jari answered.

"Now get on back to your book," Skip added. "I'll buzz you back in here in five minutes, and I expect that your disposition will have improved by then."

Barb gave Skip a testy look. "You'd better not. It'll be more than gas relief that I'll be putting in your IV."

Skip chuckled as Barb left the room, then winced in pain. "Shouldn't have done that," he said, freezing. Jari watched as his expression clouded and then finally cleared. As it did, he directed his attention back to Jari. "Sorry to wake you. Seems like you were pretty tired."

"It's fine. You should have woken me up in the first place. I could have gotten the nurse for you."

"No need. I have a handy little button that goes off at the nurses' desk if I push it . . . see, watch." He grinned as he summoned Barb again.

Jari chuckled but gave her dad a warning look. "You're going to get it."

Barb stomped into the room, took one look at Skip, turned, and stomped back out. Skip grinned at Jari, and she grinned back. As she stretched out in her recliner again and tried to cover a yawn, she grew serious. "All joking aside, if you need anything else, wake me up, okay? That's why I'm here."

Skip was quiet for a moment. "It's just nice to wake up and see that there's somebody in the chair . . . that I'm not here alone."

Jari considered him, her head on her pillow, and contemplated his suddenly serious mood. "Dad, were you in D.C.?" The question came out before she could stop it.

He froze. His expression was unreadable in the dim light, but his silence compelled her to press on.

"When I went to your house, I saw your vehicle." Still, he didn't speak, but he no longer needed to. She already knew. "Why did you come?"

He let out a deep sigh that seemed to come from the pit of his belly. "I just wanted to see you."

Jari felt angry and struggled to hold the lid on her roiling emotions. "Why didn't you come to the door? Why did you just sit outside our house and follow me in traffic?"

"I know what it looked like, and I'm sorry to give that impression," Skip said, holding his hands up; whether in defense or surrender, she wasn't sure. "I was going to knock on your front door, I really was . . . I planned on it. But every time I almost did, well . . . I guess I just chickened out. I didn't have the nerve," he admitted, sounding deflated. "It had been a long, long time, and I knew you were mad at me when you left. I honestly wasn't sure how you would react."

With a twinge of guilt, Jari had to admit that she wasn't even sure how she would have responded if she had opened the front door to find her father on her doorstep. Still, his admission only dampened her anger a little. She was quiet for a while, trying to collect her thoughts, trying to formulate some kind of words to articulate the emotions and questions stirring inside of her. He spoke again before she did.

"I know I'm not real in-tune to feelings and all, but I know you left town because of what I did, and I know your mom blames me for that, and so do I. I blame myself. I know I made a mess of things. I came to D.C. because I wanted to tell you I was wrong, and that I'm sorry. I wanted to ask if you could find it in your heart to forgive me . . . and ask if you would . . . come home. Not to live, of course. I know you're married and settled, but to visit. I was hoping you could find a way to forgive me and to let your mom and I back into your life, Jari girl. If not me, at least your mom. She needs you. She didn't deserve to lose us both."

Jari sat stunned. Finally, she asked him the questions she had been asking since she was seventeen. "Why? Why did you do it? Why Betty? Why weren't Mom and I enough?"

Even in the dim lighting, she could see the pain on her dad's face. "I don't know. I've asked myself the same thing a hundred times. As pitiful as it is, Jari, I just don't know. I have no explanation for you, other than I got confused. I made a mistake. I wasn't thinking straight, and I made some really dumb decisions. I guess she made me feel young again. I think I liked feeling spontaneous and adventurous after years of being at the same job, in the same house, same town, same state, with the same woman." It was quiet for a long moment before he continued.

"I never imagined that the very thing that led me to seek excitement elsewhere would be the one thing I would miss the most. There hasn't been a day that's gone by that I don't regret losing you, your mom, our home, our life, and our family. Regret has been my constant companion these last fifteen years, and there's nothing I can do to take it all back. I can't undo what I did. I can't rewrite the past. But Jari, I can't help hoping there's some way I can still make this right. I guess I just needed to see if you could ever forgive me. I needed to see if there was any way we could pick up something from the ashes and try again. I'm tired of being alone, Jari girl. I can't live like this anymore. I want to be your dad again, and I want to have my daughter back."

"Why now?" she asked, tears stinging her eyes, her throat aching. "I waited so many years, hoping you would come after me, hoping you would still want some kind of a relationship with your only daughter. I'm not blaming you, I made my own decisions, but I did things I never thought I would do, just hoping if things got bad enough, somehow you would know and care enough to come get me and bring me back home, so we could be a family again. Why didn't you come to New York City? Why didn't you come years ago? Why now?"

He sighed another deep sigh and was quiet for several long moments until Jari didn't think he would answer. Finally, he did. "I'm ashamed to say it, but I'm a coward. I thought about it. I really did. I wanted to come after you. I wanted to make things right. But I didn't have the nerve. I was scared of failing . . . scared of being rejected . . . scared of what you would say. I was ashamed of what I had done. I was too proud to get down on my knees and beg for your forgiveness. And I was worried that if I took a giant risk and came and did just that, you would slam the door in my face."

"Like mom did."

"She had every right to be mad, Jari girl. And so did you. Knowing that, knowing the fault was mine, I didn't know how to make it better, and I wasn't brave enough to try. As pathetic as it is, it's as simple as that."

She fought frustration that he didn't have a better answer. She didn't know what she had expected, but it wasn't that. It left her wanting to shake him, wanting something she could understand. She wanted an answer that helped the last fifteen years make sense. Yet, hearing his deflated, flat tone, she knew that was all there was, and that he wished there was something else he could say too. They both sat quietly for a long time.

"Well, about a year ago, I started learning a lot about forgiveness and about repentance too. I started feeling real uncomfortable with how things had been left. I guess through that book there," he gestured to his worn leather Bible, "I found the courage to try to make things right. When I came to D.C., I came hoping to find you. I was planning to show up on your doorstep and ask for your forgiveness the first day I got to town, but then your husband came out to get the papers, and I panicked. It's as simple as that. I was prepared to face you, but I hadn't counted on him being home too. I can't explain it, but it made it harder. So I left. After that, I kept thinking every day was the day. I even followed you a couple of times, imagining I would get my courage up and face you in public, where I thought you might be more likely to hear me out, rather than shutting the door in my face. I learned that I'm not cut out for tailing people, though—I lost you both times. That city traffic is a different beast than what we've got around here. I had asked Tommy to watch the shop for me for a week, and I only had so long I could stay. I had to come back home without ever getting to talk to you."

He stopped for a breath, and Jari sat quietly, waiting for him to continue, the pieces of the puzzle finally fitting into place. "After I got home, I started feeling like a real loser. Even more than I already did. I'd spent all that money on gas and a hotel, left my shop for the first time in years, and drove halfway across the country, all for the purpose of reconnecting with you. And I'd come back home without so much as you even knowing I was in town. So I decided to try again. I made up my mind I would be successful the next time around. The first morning I pulled up in front of your house again, I saw you come out for the papers and was ready to get out of the car and approach you, but then your husband came storming out of the house, looking like he was ready to yank my head off. In hindsight, I can't blame him . . . I probably would have done the same in his shoes. He had security showing up within the hour, and I panicked and left again. Turns out I had no more courage than I'd had the trip before. All I was doing was making life more complicated for you. That day your husband came after me and then security showed up was the first time it occurred to me that you thought I was a threat. It makes sense, it does, it just hadn't crossed my mind before. I don't make many enemies working at a tire shop, so I guess my mind just isn't wired that way. Well, once I realized the trouble I was causing, I came home and vowed not to return. I had gone seeking forgiveness—not to cause more harm."

"We jumped to a lot of conclusions," Jari said slowly, still processing everything he had said.

"Like I said, looking back, I see why you did. It could have been someone who was a threat to you, and I'm glad to know your husband took action."

Quiet settled over the room again.

"Dad, I didn't just come here because you had a heart attack. This trip was already planned, although it got moved up." She could see his surprise. "I learned a lot last fall about facing my fears and living in freedom. I've been afraid too. I've been afraid to come home."

"Afraid to come home?" he echoed, seeming bewildered.

Jari nodded. "I didn't know how you and mom would receive me. I didn't know if you would be angry or have moved on. I didn't know if either of you had remarried and started a new family. But mostly, I made a lot of mistakes in the last fifteen years and did a lot of things I'm not proud of. I was afraid of coming home and facing you, being guilty of the very thing I used to condemn you for all those years."

"Whatever you've done, don't hang on to it. That's one thing I've learned. Let yourself be forgiven," Skip said, each word measured and purposeful. "Obviously, I haven't been a good example of that. I didn't even have the courage to give you the chance to forgive me, but I do know it's what's right. And I know that where it counts most I have been forgiven, and I know you have been too." He paused. "I saw you reading your Bible earlier."

Skip's words brought tears to Jari's eyes. They had taken the same road to sin and now, separately, they had been taken down the same road to redemption and forgiveness. His words echoed what had been going on in her own heart all fall. In that moment, she recognized another bit of beauty that had emerged from the ashes of her lost pregnancy—her miscarriage had opened her up to the working of God. It had been time for her to face her past and her fears and to truly begin to grasp the meaning of forgiveness. Though she didn't believe He had caused it, God had used her loss to work the soil of her heart. Once again, He had taken something naturally bad and transformed it for her benefit. It had led her to this moment, sitting in her father's hospital room, hearing that he had sought reconciliation with her, hearing that he wanted her forgiveness and a relationship with her, hearing that he had gone down a very similar path to get to where he now was.

For the first time, something that had been so painful and felt so bad made sense in a complete, whole, good picture. It was not that she would have chosen to lose her baby, or that she thought it was a divine act of discipline, but after having months to heal, she could see that her loving Father had brought good even from so much pain. With the freedom and forgiveness she had embraced, her relationship with Bill that had grown with her new vulnerability and honesty, and this new, fresh commonality she shared with her father, He had brought beauty from her ashes.

She drug her fingertips lightly under her eyes and stood, stepping to the side of his bed and reaching for his hand. "Dad, I have done some really bad things. I made really stupid choices that I didn't even agree with simply to get back at you for what you did to me and mom. I was angry, and I retaliated, and I'm so sorry. What I thought I wanted was to hurt you, when I actually just wanted your love. In the process, I wound up hurting us both—I wound up hurting us all. I'm sorry for everything I've done and the years I've been away. Will you forgive me?"

Her dad's face was a confusing mix of emotions—pain, guilt, shame, regret—but then peace smoothed them out, and he squeezed her hand. "I forgive you, Jari girl."

She took in a full, free breath for the first time in years. At last, she was right with God, with herself, and with both of her parents. Freedom felt good.

Before she could step away, Skip clasped her hand tighter, keeping her there. "I let you and your mother down. I broke apart our family. I ripped your sense of security and stability away from you. I betrayed you both. I was selfish. And I'm so sorry." His words were simple, yet heartfelt. She felt sincerity in every word he spoke. "Will you forgive me?"

Jari waited until her heart caught up with her brain. She waited until she was completely sure she meant what she was saying, and wasn't answering flippantly. In the midst of her pause, his expression wavered between fear and hope. She could see how much her answer meant to him. After taking the time she needed, she answered with absolute honesty, releasing her dad from fifteen years of guilt, condemnation, and accusation. "I forgive you, Dad."

Twenty-One

After two nights in the ICU and four more nights in a regular room, Skip had healed enough to be released from the hospital. Though she was glad he was doing well enough to go home, Jari found herself with a difficult decision to make. Should she continue to stay with her mom as she had said she would or move in with her dad for the time being to help him as he recovered? To her amazement and deep gratitude, Mary made Skip and Jari an offer that made Jari's heart sing. Her mom invited Skip to stay in her guest room while he recuperated. With her mom's offer on the table, Jari no longer had to choose between her parents.

Jari knew the invitation had been difficult for her mom to make, and she appreciated it immensely. Whether or not Mary had extended the invitation for Skip or simply to ensure that Jari would continue to be around daily, Jari didn't care. Even though her mom still loved him in some way, Jari knew it took a lot of humility and courage for Mary to allow her ex-husband back under her roof after all that had happened. Jari made sure her mom knew how proud of her and grateful she was. Skip graciously and humbly accepted the invitation, and Jari made him comfortable in the spare room.

They spent the next week being the closest thing to a family any of them had known in fifteen years. And as odd of a situation as it was, and as trying as Jari knew it was for both her mom and her dad at times, it felt good—to all of them.

Though Jari missed Bill, and he assured her he missed her more, he continued to encourage her to complete what she had gone there to do. He tenderly assured her that they had the rest of their lives together—he could share her with her parents until she felt ready to come home. Every day, he reminded her that he would be happy to fly to Kansas as soon as she wanted him to come. And every day she thanked him and told him soon.

Jari knew for her life to feel whole and complete, she needed to figure out how to connect her past with her present; and it was simply going to take time. Once she felt like she'd gotten her bearings in Kansas, she would welcome Bill with open arms.

She continued talking to Jessi every other day and texted with Hannah frequently. She was thankful to have the woman's wisdom and deep faith to draw on as she sorted through the messy process of reconnecting, rebuilding, and reestablishing a relationship with her parents and extended family. She was grateful to have Jessi to process it all with and for the way her stepdaughter lightened her days. Jessi's phone calls also helped her connect her past and present as Jari relayed news about the girls to her mom and dad and showed them pictures Jessi had texted. Her mom and dad listened and laughed, eager to see the pictures and learn about the people that filled Jari's life.

The first Saturday after Skip was released from the hospital, he sat on the couch and watched Mary and Jari paint the living room. The next day, the women drained the waterbed in Jari's room and hauled it and the boxes of her old belongings down to the shed in the backyard to be dealt with after the remodeling was complete. Skip gave suggestions from the couch where he was ordered to stay, as Jari and Mary shoved a king mattress and box springs up the stairs and around the tight corner on the stairway landing. They painted the bedroom, hung new curtains, put new coverings on the bed, and added trendy décor, giving Jari's old room a completely new look. Together, they were saying goodbye to the past and embracing the present.

In what seemed nothing short of miraculous, the three of them enjoyed meals together and played board games in the evenings. Skip and Mary were polite to one another, and after having so many years to get past the hurt and anger, even found themselves relating to each other in a friendly way.

When Jari flew to Minneapolis to meet Bill and celebrate Kelsi and Kamryn's birthday with the family, Mary offered to take care of Skip in her absence. Jari thoroughly enjoyed the weekend, happy to get to hug her husband, talk through all that was going on with her best friend, have coffee with Hannah, catch up with Carla, and celebrate the girls. And she was happy to fly back to Wichita when the weekend was over to continue participating in the beautiful work of healing God was doing in her family.

To Bill's apparent relief, she decided on the plane ride back to Wichita that she was ready for him to come to Kansas, and once she relayed that news after landing, he had his ticket booked within minutes.

She wanted to stay until her dad was able to return home and had suggested Bill come the weekend that was scheduled to happen to meet everyone. Then they could fly home together. Though they had a few more weeks to wait, Bill would be landing in Wichita at the end of the month, and Jari was so excited. She couldn't wait to introduce him to her family.

On the first day of spring, Jari carried the box of spring decorations up from her mom's basement. When Mary came home from the flower shop that evening, they put up the spring wreath on the front door, filled the porch swing with pastel pillows, wove florals through the decorations on the fireplace mantel, and set out the ceramic songbirds Jari and her mom had made when she was a preteen. Setting out all the familiar seasonal knickknacks Jari had grown up with brought a smile to her face, and when her mom served carrot cake for dessert that night, the nostalgia nearly brought Jari to tears. Together, they watched the tulips and daffodils come up and bloom, the grass turn green, and the trees start to flower. They took walks in the evenings, and Jari helped her mom at the flower shop in the mornings.

The morning Bill was set to arrive, Jari stood in the upstairs bathroom in a state of total shock. She wanted to jump up and down and shout for joy, but instead she just stood there, thankfulness swelling inside of her until she felt she would burst. Last fall, she had lost the life that had been growing within her, yes. The summer, fall, and winter had been a dark time for her. But now, as spring bloomed across Kansas, she stood in the bathroom of her mom's house after six weeks of being home, her heart singing, tears of joy falling.

She was at peace with both her mom and her dad, and her relationship with each of them grew stronger every day. Her dad was not only still alive, but he was also home from the hospital, and nearly recovered. Bill was flying in later that day to meet her family for the very first time and spend a weekend in her hometown. And now, she was holding a test that felt like the final puzzle piece to God's redemption and perfect timing demonstrated in her life.

Flinging open the door and running down the stairs, not caring if she sounded like a thundering teenager, she ran into the kitchen. Her mom was sitting at the table, a cup of hot tea and a bowl of cereal in front of her as she read her small-town morning paper. Skip was nowhere in sight, likely already at his tire shop, sharing a cup of coffee with his employees as he checked in on things. Mary looked up in surprise.

Jari held out the positive test, grinning. "Mom, I'm pregnant! I'm going to have a baby!"

It was the moment and reaction she had dreamt of—longed for—back in September. Her mom sat still for just a moment, in shock, then she bounced out of her seat and ran across the kitchen to take the test from Jari. Holding it in her shaking hands, Mary Braxon stared down at the plus sign in the results window silently. And then, all of a sudden, she exploded into a jumping, dancing, laughing, jubilant woman, holding Jari as she jumped up and down, tears flowing down her cheeks unchecked. She blubbered words Jari couldn't make out, and yet Jari understood her perfectly.

Jari hugged her mom tight, her own happy tears falling, her heart overflowing with the joy of getting to share such a monumental moment with her mom. It felt right and oh, so sweet.

Mary took Jari's face between her hands, her own eyes teary, her smile bright. "Oh, sweetheart, you're going to be a mommy!"

"And you're going to be a grandma," Jari responded, her cheeks hurting from smiling so much.

There was more dancing, more crying, more celebrating. Mary insisted that Jari sit down, and she made her breakfast—a happy face pancake with a bacon mouth, blueberry eyes, a strawberry nose, and scrambled egg hair. She said she was practicing up for her new grandchild. She gave Jari a glass of orange juice and a tall glass of water, telling her to drink both—for the baby. While Jari ate, her mom pulled out the calendar, and they calculated Jari's due date. The best they could figure, she was due in November and was just over ten weeks pregnant. With all that had been going on, Jari hadn't been paying attention to her cycle or thinking about such things. Now, she sat in wonder, realizing she had already been pregnant before she ever left for Kansas. Before she had ever found the courage to board a plane, the LORD had already set this very moment into action—knowing what forgiveness, reconciliation, and redemption would transpire before she found out about the gift He had given her. She was overwhelmed by His kindness.

As she finished her orange juice, Jari asked her mom for advice about how to tell Bill, and together they hatched a plan for that night. Jari was excited just thinking about it. She couldn't wait to tell him.

After the introductions, she would steal Bill away to the front porch for a few minutes to themselves. There, on the porch swing, she would share the news with him privately, giving them a chance to celebrate just the two of them. She could barely wait to see the look on his face, and the joy in his eyes! When they were ready, together, they could sit down to dinner and with her mom, dad, and grandparents all gathered around the table, they would share their happy news. Just the thought of it felt so complete and full of joy!

After sending her mom off to the flower shop with a promise to be down to help in a couple of hours, Jari settled down into the pillows on the porch swing. Sweet spring sunshine spilled over her, and she let out a happy sigh as she opened her Bible.

As happy as she felt, as thrilled as she was with the second chance she had been given to carry Bill's baby, as much joy as there was bubbling up to overflow her heart, she knew something that she hadn't known before. As wonderful as a baby would be, as much as she treasured her husband, as good as it felt to be at peace with her parents, she knew the only thing that would ever make her truly happy—the kind of happiness that is found deep within that weathers all seasons, circumstances, and days—was to know Jesus Christ.

To know and accept His forgiveness, reside in His presence, be where He was, do what He was doing, care about what He cared about, and live in the freedom He offered—that was where true joy was found. After being on the journey He had taken her on over the past year to get to where she was, she knew one thing for certain—*that was her one desire.*

Everything else was just an extra bonus, a good gift. Even having a baby—the very thing she spent years thinking was the one thing she wanted most in life—was not an end in itself. Now she knew, come what may, however her pregnancy ended, whether or not her parents got back together as she hoped they might, regardless of what state Jessi and the girls lived in, no matter what tomorrow held, she had one desire, and one desire alone.

"The LORD is my light and my salvation; whom shall I fear? The LORD is the strength of my life; of whom shall I be afraid? ...One thing I have desired of the LORD, that will I seek: that I may dwell in the house of the LORD all the days of my life, to behold the beauty of the LORD, and to inquire in His temple." Psalm 27:1,4

A NOTE FROM ANN

Dear Reader,

I hope you enjoyed *One Desire*. It's been so fun kicking off this new series, and I look forward to watching the stories of the next two books unfold. It was fun for me, as a writer, to check in on Joe and Jessi from time to time to see how they're doing and what's going on in their lives, while still getting to concentrate on the story at hand. I look forward to publishing the rest of the *Mothers of Glendale* series and telling the stories of these characters who have become like friends!

Jari's story was a challenging one for me to write. I don't know if I ever feel more vulnerable than when I publish a book, and it's made available to the masses. Suddenly, your story, your thoughts, your characters and the experiences they have are no longer private. Additionally, Jari's story was very personal to me, and it felt a little like laying my own heart bare and exposing the pain of one of the darkest moments of my life for all the world to see. Jari's story is not my own; hers is absolutely fiction. While my own story is different in a lot of ways, the emotions and understanding that came as a result of a similar experience I had did play a role as I wrote certain parts of this story.

In June 2010, I had a miscarriage. It was our first pregnancy, and one that seemed so perfectly orchestrated by the LORD. To explain the significance of the pregnancy, the words that we were given about the baby I carried, and even the way we found out we were expecting would be far too long to include here, but it all resulted in the fact that we had never even considered the possibility of the pregnancy not ending in the birth of our first child. When I miscarried in June, just two days before I hit the twelve-week mark and the relative safe-zone, it took us by complete surprise. What else took me by surprise were the feelings of guilt that came with it. I never had an abortion like Jari did or lived a life of promiscuity—my husband is the only man I've ever even kissed—but still, the guilt came.

In those dark days, I found myself feeling guilty that I could not do something that came naturally to womankind—something that millions of women before me had successfully done. I felt guilty that I had let my husband down. I felt like I had done something wrong or hadn't done something right. And I found myself questioning God's plan and His power. I found myself staring faith in the face and asking myself the honest question of if I believed. In those days, there was so much pain, guilt, confusion, and emptiness that I struggled to put words to those emotions, both at the time and in this book. I was surprised by how deeply you could grieve someone you had never even met or felt, and compassion began to grow in my heart for other women who had gone through a similar heartbreak. I went through a time when just walking into the room that would have been the nursery brought tears to my eyes, and I was convinced that I didn't want to have children after all. As the weeks wore on, though, and then months passed, I began to hear God whisper that He redeems all things. And He did.

Looking back just a couple of years later, as strange as it sounds, I became thankful for that miscarriage. In all honesty, we were not at a place in our lives where we would have been ready for a baby. If it would have happened, I'm sure the LORD would have made a way and it would have been good, but looking back, I'm so thankful for that extra year and a half that I got to spend with just my husband. Just eighteen months later, we were in a completely different place in life and ready to welcome a child to the family. (And—ta da!—we were expecting again! His timing is perfect!) Putting the physical realm aside, I gained so much confidence in the sovereignty of God, His plan that is good and perfect, His big picture, and the kindness of His redemption—through that painful situation. Since my miscarriage, I have had the opportunity to walk with other women as they go through similar situations, with an understanding and compassion I never would have had if I hadn't miscarried myself. As painful as it was, I see that much good has come out of it, and I am thankful.

If you aren't quite to that point yet, and you're still hurting from a miscarriage of your own, whether recent or in the past, please hear these two things—the guilt is not yours and God is good. He redeems all things. Give yourself the time, space, and permission to heal from your loss, then be expectant. Somehow, someway, good will come. He does not waste a tear. I'm convinced He hurts so greatly when we hurt, that He would not be able to bear it if He did not know the good that it would produce in the end. We see in part, but He sees the big picture—and He chooses the best over the good.

On another note, I've known so many women—and have lived like this myself—that go through life always looking for a circumstance to make them happy. In my own lifetime I've thought, 'If I could just get a cupcake doll, then I'll be happy (Don't judge. They were the coolest!).' 'When I graduate and go off to college, I'll be happy.' 'When I get skinny, I'll finally be happy.' 'When I fall in love, I'll be happy.' 'When I get married,

I'll be happy.' 'When we have a baby, I'll be happy.' 'When we get a new house, I'll be happy.' 'When we have more money, I'll be happy.' 'When I get that job, I'll be happy.' The list goes on and on. The thing is, is that even when I achieved one of those things, as wonderful as it may have been, there was always something that was next—something else I immediately set my eyes on that I thought would make me happy. It turns out, while a wonderful by-product, happiness is a terrible destination—because it's a destination that just keeps moving.

Sweet friend, let me bear witness to this—the only thing that can make us truly happy, truly joyful in a way that won't end tomorrow or the next day or the next, that doesn't depend on circumstances that can change, money that can be lost, a spouse that can let you down, a beloved child that rebels, or a perfect figure that disappears as the years go by, is knowing Jesus Christ. Being with Him, knowing Him, spending time with Him, hiding our identity in Him, finding our worth in Him—that is the only thing that is worthy of being the one thing we desire most and, coincidentally, is the one thing that will sustain and fulfill us for the rest of time.

Additionally, I want you to know that there's no condemnation here. We all find ourselves at the foot of the cross together, needing covered by the same blood of Jesus. We *all* (me included) need forgiveness in order to be reconciled to the Father. If you're someone who lives under the weight of past sins, even if you've been to the cross and have been forgiven, I hope that Jari's story has spoken to you. Forgiveness is such a marvelous thing—it cannot be earned or attained; it is *freely* given. But it is also something that has to be personally accepted if you're going to live in freedom today. When Jesus forgives, our slate is wiped clean in the context of eternity, but we have to choose whether we'll continue to live in guilt or whether we'll accept forgiveness and walk in freedom while on this earth. Remember this: If you've confessed your sin and asked Jesus to forgive you, and that dark cloud is still hanging over your head and you still feel defined by what you've done—remember that it's not Him who's keeping it there. In Him, there is no condemnation. You have every right to step out from underneath all of that, tell the master of deception not to walk one more step with you, and choose to operate out of the place of forgiveness and freedom you've been given.

If, through this book, you've realized that in keeping your past a secret, the enemy has kept you trapped in shame, have the courage to tell someone safe the truth. Step out of the enemy's control that he wields through isolation. If you need someone to tell as a first step, tell me. Send me an email. Again, there's no condemnation here. I'm not a counselor, so I can't offer that, but I will write your name on my (private) prayer board and pray for you—for the healing and the redemption that I know God wants to work in your life. Don't stay in the trap of isolation, shame, and secrecy. It's time to step into the light, into freedom, into forgiveness—and to live like you're forgiven.

Stepping back down off my soapbox, I loved writing this story of growth, redemption, and reconciliation. Unintentionally, I ended up writing this book while pregnant with our first child. It was both challenging and sweet to write a story of such an intense desire to have a baby while I was pregnant myself. Something about it felt beautiful as I wrote about so many emotions and thoughts that I myself had experienced after a miscarriage, while I felt little kicks and movements inside of me. The timing seemed so purposeful and made me smile at the kindness of the LORD, as the storyline for this book had been planned for about a year and yet I started on it, unknowingly, the month I got pregnant. I think He's wise, and I think He's good. He truly redeems all things.

Again, I so hope you enjoyed reading this book and that you're looking forward to the next two in the series. Next, we'll be staying in D.C. to follow Carla on an important journey of her own, and then we'll go back to Glendale to sit in on a battle in which Hannah Colby will need the love and support of her husband, Chris, and every other Glendale character we've grown to love, in order to make it through.

Although I love to write, I write for my readers. With that constantly in mind, I would love to hear from you. I enjoy connecting via my website, getting emails, hearing from you on Facebook and Instagram and getting to know you. So please, always feel free to drop me a note!

Until next time, may the Redeemer of the world show you His redemptive power in a very real and personal way,

W A N T   M O R E ?

WE HAVE TWO WAYS YOU CAN EXPERIENCE MORE OF *THE GLENDALE SERIES* TODAY!

1. FREE DISCUSSION GUIDE

There's a lot going on in these books, and we know how helpful it is to dig in a bit deeper and process them with someone.

If you're in a book club (or want to start one), the discussion guide can be used to facilitate conversation about the books.

OR--if you just want to go a bit deeper on your own, the discussion guide can help you process through what you're reading, what you can take from it, and how it applies to your own life.

Designed to feel like you're reading with a friend, the discussion guide utilizes questions, commentary, and Scripture to provide company and prompts to help you experience these stories in a deeper way. To get your free guide, visit:

https://anngoering.com/discussion_guide_glendale_series

2. Q&A WITH THE AUTHOR

Go behind the scenes with Ann Goering as she discusses the inspiration behind and the undercurrents of *The Glendale Series*. Hear her expand on the Biblical themes woven throughout the books, the purpose behind her storytelling, and how it applies to you (her beloved reader!).

If you enjoyed the books, you won't want to miss this video Q&A with the author! To watch it visit:

https://anngoering.com/Q&A_Glendale_Series

AUTHOR BIO

Ann Goering is an award-winning journalist and author of Christian fiction.

Goering is passionate about helping women encounter Jesus, experience transformative hope, and live a life deeply rooted in the Word of God. She's worked alongside an international Christian ministry for the past 15 years, as well as serving at her local church, and leading groups of women into encounters with Jesus through small groups and Bible studies.

She believes so much in the power of stories to illustrate spiritual principles, grow faith, and increase empathy, so wherever she is, you'll find her sharing stories that reveal the beauty of Jesus amidst everyday life.

Goering loves entrepreneurship, travel, rodeos, interior design, deep friendships, and good hair days, but her absolute favorites are the people in her life.

She's a Midwest girl soaking up the sunshine in the American Southwest, living on chicken molé and sweet tea, homeschooling her three best friends (aka daughters) with the only guy she's ever kissed.

CONNECT WITH ANN!

Website: www.anngoering.com
Facebook: www.facebook.com/AuthorAnnGoering
Instagram: www.instagram.com/ann.goering
Email: ann@anngoering.com

Love *One Desire*?
Please consider taking a moment to leave a review!
It truly means so much to the author – and your words mean
more to future readers than ours ever could. From the bottom
of our hearts, we truly hope reading *One Desire* has been a 5-star
experience!

www.ingramcontent.com/pod-product-compliance
Lightning Source LLC
Chambersburg PA
CBHW032021240626
47153CB00013B/1796